Unspeakable Acts

The Clearwater Mysteries

Book three

Proofread by Ann Attwood
Cover Design by Andjela K

Printed by CreateSpace, an Amazon.com company.

ISBN- 9781071152768

Available from Amazon.com, CreateSpace.com, and other retail outlets.
Available on Kindle and other devices.

Unspeakable Acts

Jackson Marsh

One

The Times, Thursday, December 1st, 1888

Opera House Gala

*F*amed countertenor, Mr Cadwell Roxton is to make his debut appearance at the Opera House in "Aeneas and Dido", an acclaimed if unusual work by Austro-German composer, Johann Bruch.

Mr Roxton was the sensation of the 1887 Paris season, following that triumph with another in Leipzig the subsequent spring. His debut at our opera house this month will herald the beginning of what this publication hopes will be an illustrious career on the opera stage for a countryman returning home from his studies after training in the conservatoires of Europe.

Mr Roxton's performance, however, is not for the purpose of his own self-progression. The presentation is a gala event in aid of The Clearwater Foundation, a benevolent trust recently inaugurated to benefit the destitute men of the City's East End.

Readers will be aware, no doubt, of the good works undertaken by the late Viscount Clearwater (1838 to 1888) in the assistance of destitute women. His son, previously the Honourable Archer Riddington, was elevated to the title in the summer and has already taken up the reins of philanthropic leadership.

Charles Tripp closed the newspaper. He'd read enough about the good works of the sodomite, Clearwater, and instead turned his attention to the sodomites of the Central Telegraph Office, a group of young men occupying the adjacent table.

It wasn't that Tripp had any desire to be among their company, he was well into his sixties and far above their juvenile banter, and his intent — which was no-one but himself — the true reason for his passionate hatred of the man had nothing to do with his perversion. That was only its focus. The man had fired Tripp and disrespected the good name of the late and noble viscount. Tripp wanted his revenge. It was that simple.

What was not so simple was finding the way to knock the man from his perch of respectability, to serve him the retribution he deserved, to crush him beneath his foot in the way the viscount had crushed Tripp, and to shame and expose him for the upstart and cad he was. Clearwater wore the strongest of social armour, but there was one chink. He was queer, and that was the easiest point of attack.

An idea forming, he opened the newspaper again, returning to where he had left off.

'Hello.'

He looked up and into the cratered face of a tall, wiry man in his mid-twenties. Casually but smartly dressed, the youth was in the process of greeting his fellow messengers, and yet was addressing Tripp.

'Ah, good evening,' Tripp replied, folding his paper once more and offering the opposite seat. 'A word?'

'In return for a drink.'

It was a straightforward barter and one which would award Tripp a few moments of the lad's time. He attracted the landlord's attention, and when his companion was delivered a beer, paid for it and pushed out the chair with his foot.

The lad sat.

'How are you tonight, Mr Tripp?' he asked, turning his beer glass so the handle faced him, an unnecessary ritual Tripp had noticed on several occasions.

'I need information,' Tripp replied.

He kept his voice low. Although the messengers were speaking loudly tonight, and the volume increased parallel to their consumption of alcohol, if he could hear them in quieter moments, so they could also hear him. His companion gave a silent nod of the head, showing he understood, and moved his glass to position the handle at right angles to the table edge. It was another pointless exercise, because he drank with his left hand and by holding the glass not its handle. When the boy had completed his manoeuvres and told his friends he would join them presently, Tripp had his attention.

'Have you been busy of late, Mr Lovemount?' he asked. He had known the man only a few weeks and only superficially, but he was convinced he used a pseudonym.

'Busy as always at this time of year, Sir,' Lovemount said. 'Sending cards at Christmas is a growing trend, and each year they send them earlier. We're weeks away, and already they've started.'

'It's a fashion that has been growing in popularity since I was your age, Lovemount. I would have thought the post office was prepared. It was, after all, an invention by the office itself.'

'Yeah, one of those things you wish you could uninvent,' the messenger grumbled. 'What can I do for you?'

He was a skeleton of a youth, but under the ravaged skin of his head, he housed a brain that thought quickly and well when it was to his advantage. He and Tripp had other things in common and were more akin than the casual observer might think.

'Did you know a messenger called Wright?' Tripp asked. If Lovemount could come directly to the point, so could he. 'James Wright?'

Lovemount lit a cigarette, and it wasn't a cheap brand. 'Depends,' he said.

'Half a crown.'

'Then, yes, I did.'

'But I will need more than that.'

The messenger inhaled and held the smoke, waiting for Tripp to add to the reward. When he didn't, he exhaled and sent a cloud billowing directly into his face.

'So will I,' he said.

Tripp waved away the pollution. 'A crown if I am satisfied.'

Lovemount nodded and rested one arm on the table, turning his back to his colleagues. 'Go on,' he said.

'I understand you are the senior messenger at the Riverside office. Tell me what you know of Mr Wright.'

Lovemount's hooded eyes narrowed, and his lips pursed. He studied Tripp's face (an unnerving trauma for anyone to endure), but Tripp allowed it until a dubious thought occurred to Lovemount, and his expression warped into a leer.

'He's a clean enough lad,' he said. 'A pretty boy, got stamina, average cock, I'd say.'

When Tripp swallowed, the folds of his chin vibrated as his Adam's apple rose and fell like a fairground sideshow.

'I didn't mean "know" in that respect,' he said, disgusted.

'Oh, as a post worker? Always on time, always neat, fast, accurate with his money. Why?'

'Discreet?'

'Very, I should say. We see a lot of stuff on our deliveries, Sir, but none of us talks about them.'

'Well, I know that's a lie, Lovemount. Tell me some truths.'

'About what?' Lovemount continued smoking, but he blew it from the corner of his mouth, for which Tripp was grateful.

'About Mr Wright.'

'Such as?'

'Don't play games.' Tripp lowered his voice further, but aimed his words forcefully at Lovemount's impertinence. 'I have recently come into substantial resources, and I need information. I will pay well for discretion, and if you are my man, you will speak with honesty, and benefit in silence.'

'You can trust me,' Lovemount said.

'If that is true, you will ask me no questions, but answer all of mine.'

Lovemount nodded, and Tripp moved closer.

'I have heard of a place in Cleaver Street,' he said. His companion registered no surprise. 'Did Wright ever visit there?' His meaning was obvious, and Lovemount, to his credit, had fallen serious and did not continue his game.

'No, Sir. I can tell you that with my hand on my heart, 'cos it's a place I have a special association with.'

'You procure young messengers to work as boy-whores,' Tripp said. 'Yes, I know.'

Lovemount was taken aback, and the sight awarded Tripp an unfamiliar shiver of joy. 'Your voices carry,' he said, jerking his head towards the next table. 'But you are certain Wright has had nothing to do with the place?'

'He's too much of a goody-goody,' Lovemount whined. 'Tried to get him once 'cos of his looks and his body, see? Some men like them tough and rough, others like them tough and pretty, like him.'

'Yes, alright. Enough detail. Did he use any other such places, do you know?'

'Not that I'm aware of. Why?'

'I said to ask no questions.' Tripp growled.

'Quite right, you did.'

'Going back to Cleaver Street,' he continued. 'I was thinking of taking apartments there. Number twenty, to be exact. Number nineteen is opposite, and I wondered, do any noblemen use the establishment?'

Lovemount glanced about to make sure he wasn't being watched, and nodded.

'Any local to here?'

The messenger didn't understand.

'Clearwater?' Tripp hissed, leaving the boy to read his lips rather than hear his words.

'Oh, I get it.' Lovemount's face erupted into a grin that created peaks and troughs among the craters. 'No, Sir. Again, I can honestly say that in the five years I been having dealings with Cleaver Street, Viscount Clearwater has never stepped foot in the place – that I know of. Probably never in any other kind of molly house neither. Clean as a whistle. Sorry.'

Tripp growled. Had Lovemount said the opposite, he would have all the ammunition he needed to ruin the viscount. As it was, he was back to square one.

'Is that today's Times, Sir?' Lovemount asked, changing the subject

'It is. Why?'

'May I?' The messenger took it and thumbed through to a particular page. 'Clearwater has never been to Cleaver Street,' he said. 'But I can tell you someone who has.'

Tripp waited, but the boy didn't move. Realising, he sighed and drew a crown from his purse, placing it pointedly on the table.

Satisfied, Lovemount opened the paper, turned it and showed Tripp a name.

Until that moment, Tripp's mind had been fogged by a frustrating cloud of impotence. Other than bribe James Wright, he had no planned course of action. However, as he read the name on the not unfamiliar page, the doubt cleared as an idea came crashing through. It was bold and gave no thought for his safety. It took no prisoners, charging onto the battlefield of his mind in shining armour, its pennant held proudly aloft on a spear of justice.

It was the way forward, but for the battle to be won, he would need to form an alliance with the enemy; the queer sitting opposite grinning like a gargoyle.

'I see,' Tripp said, closing the paper. 'Tell me, Mr Lovemount, how would it please you never to have to deliver Christmas cards again?'

What Tripp didn't know was that Lovemount, the name in the newspaper and Clearwater were already connected. Not by himself, not yet, but by others plotting against the viscount for their own reasons at that very moment and only a few miles away. Nor was Tripp able to know, as Lovemount's ravaged face contorted into a grin of comradeship, that he had just put in place a chain of events that would ultimately lead him to the most notorious boy brothel in the city.

Two

Silas Hawkins had known Archer for less than two months, but in that time his life had changed beyond measure. One day he was an Irish immigrant rent boy searching for dropped coins in an East End gutter, and the next he had a suite of rooms at Clearwater House. Behind closed doors, he had a man he loved without question and who wanted him because he was Silas. In public, he was the viscount's private secretary, and it was in that capacity he found himself approaching the stage door of the City Opera House under a cloudless but unforgiving sky. Dressed in a fine suit and checking the time on a new pocket watch, he grinned, half-impressed with what he had achieved and half-bemused by his change in fortune.

Whatever he felt, however, was nothing compared to the feelings he had for Archer.

By arriving early, he hoped to have time to admire his lover at work. Archer had delegated most of the gala arrangements to others on his committee, and Silas' job was to be on hand for anything the viscount might need. That could vary from sending telegrams and letters, to voicing his opinion, from sharing his insight, to sharing his bed, and no matter the request, Silas was there and more than willing. He had half an hour to spare, but Archer appreciated punctuality, and Silas was keen to be in the building and out of the biting, December breeze.

He had never visited a theatre, let alone an opera house and was surprised that the entrance was so bland. It was if he cared to think back, not dissimilar to many doorways he had used in his previous life, at night and in secret. His initiation into the world of theatre came in the form of an open, wooden door not much bigger than himself. Not the grand staircase and pillared portico of the front, but the back, tradesman's entrance, as Thomas would have called it, an almost secret way into a world as yet unexplored. He crossed the threshold, his excitement as keen as his intrigue.

What he saw was unimpressive. An elderly man sat reading a newspaper at a counter in front of a row of keys and pigeonholes. A ledger lay open on the table beside a steaming mug which the man held to warm his fingers. He looked up as Silas entered, stepping down into a small waiting room off which led a passage and two doors.

'Good morning, Sir,' the man said, folding his paper. He was well spoken and smartly dressed, his white whiskers neatly trimmed, and his wrinkled face creased more as he offered a welcoming smile.

'Morning,' Silas returned the affable greeting. 'I'm here to meet with Lord Clearwater. The name's Silas Hawkins.'

The doorkeeper put yesterday's news to one side and ran his finger down a page in the ledger.

'Ah yes,' he said, finding the name. 'Will you sign in, please, Sir?'

Silas wrote his name as legibly as he could. His schooling had been brief, and he was still struggling with the use of an ink pen, but his handwriting like much else, had improved since meeting Archer.

'His Lordship is meeting with the Director of Productions,' the doorkeeper said. 'But he left instructions for you to wait for him in the house if you would like.'

'The house?' Silas imagined having to turn around and find a cab to drive him home.

'The theatre,' the man clarified. 'The house is closed just now. They've just struck Don Giovani, and we're dark until the gala, but you're welcome to take a stall or wait prompt side.'

None of what he said made sense and Silas was buzzing with questions. Why call a theatre a house? What had Mr Giovani done to deserve being struck? Why were there no lights, and what was prompt side? Silas was early, so definitely prompt, but why did he have to wait in a stall? Surely they had seats.

The doorkeeper noticed his confusion. 'Shall I get Tricky to show you around, Sir?' He asked. 'His Lordship did say you'd likely be early. You've got time to see the boards.'

'Yes, please,' Silas said, wondering what was so special about planks, but thinking it best not to show his ignorance.

The man slapped the counter bell and pointed to a seat.

Silas was about to sit when one of the doors opened, and a young man appeared. He was smartly dressed, but wore no jacket and, by his features, Silas put him at no more than sixteen.

'Yes, Mr Keys?' the lad said, hurrying to the counter and tucking in his shirt.

'This gentleman is with Lord Clearwater,' the doorkeeper told him. 'You're not busy are you?'

'Always busy, Mr Keys.'

'Yes, well I know that's not factually correct. Take some time away from the stress of playing cards and show Mr Hawkins the boards would you? He has time for a tour.'

'Certainly.' The youth turned to Silas, touched his forelock, and chirped, 'Morning, Sir. You want to come with me?'

The lad was marching towards the corridor before Silas had a chance to thank him and, with a wave to the doorkeeper, he set off to follow.

'You here about the gala?' The lad asked, turning a corner and mounting a set of brick stairs two at a time.

'I'm His Lordship's secretary,' Silas replied. 'What's your job?'

'Runner, Sir. Sometimes I help with dressing as that's what I want to be next. A dresser.'

A dresser was where Mrs Flintwich kept her pans, and where Thomas kept the servants' crockery. Silas questioned the lad in more detail.

'Oh, I do the calls,' he said, taking a turn and running up another flight. 'Half-hour before curtain rise, fifteen, ten and five. Running from one dressing room to another. I'm in charge of principals now.'

'Do I call you Tricky?' Silas asked, already out of breath.

'If you like, Sir. The real name's Jake. Just along here.'

'Thank you,' Silas panted. 'Can you slow down?'

Silas wasn't unfit. His body, weak and thin when he first came to Clearwater, had filled out over the weeks, but he spent most of his time sitting or riding in carriages. He was still learning to ride a horse, but Fecker had only taken him to the trotting stage, and it was hardly exercise.

'As you wish,' the boy said, waiting by a door marked "To The Stage. Silence".

Silas joined him, looking where the brick staircase ascended further.

'Dressing rooms up,' Jake said, following his gaze. 'Offices, costume department, fine carpenters near the roof, entrance to gallery, second-level flies. Next floor up one and down to the scenery dock, heavy carpentry, sub-stage, props, gas room and generators. Above that, crossing to OP and principal working gallery, up to windlass and gridiron.'

Silas wanted to ask for a translation, but he remained silent.

'We're going through here.' Jake had his hand on the door and a grin among his acne. 'The house is dark right now, Sir,' he said, 'but the workers are on.'

'Will we be disturbing them?'

'Who?'

'The workers.'

Jake laughed and gave Silas a cheeky smirk. It was exactly the kind of expression Silas employed when being knowingly mischievous, and although some would find it impertinent, it endeared him to the lad.

'The workers are lights,' Jake said. 'You don't want to be on stage under the limes, nor the follows, it gets real hot out there. This way, Sir.'

He pushed the door, and from the familiar, stark reality of the brick stairwell, Silas entered a world he could never have imagined. He had no idea what to expect from a theatre, except what the papers and Archer had told him; that it was a magical world where anything could happen and where dreams and nightmares alike came true. There was nothing magical about the backstage area, it was more like a construction site. To the left stood a scaffold of planks and iron bars, spiral staircases and platforms, and behind, or rather through the framework, a wall lined with ropes and levers. Everything was draped in the smell of paint and wood.

To their right stood a barrier of canvas scenery, the backs of flats on which were written numbers and words. "A & D, PS, A2, Up 4."

'What's all that mean?' Silas asked, pointing.

'Tells the hands where to put the scenery,' Jake explained, pausing in his trot so he could point out each word as he translated. 'Aeneas and Dido, the gala piece; prompt side, that's where we are; act two; upstage, flat number four. All goes with the stage manager's master layout. This way.'

The false wall continued, and they passed a curtained entrance.

Jake tapped the list pinned beside it. 'Props check,' he said as if it meant anything. 'And here's the main props table.'

There was nothing on the trestle except trays marked with handwritten labels.

'Aeneas' sword,' Jake said, pointing at the empty spaces. 'Messenger's scroll, cup of poison, oh, that's a beauty. We're using real gold.'

'Where are they now?' Silas asked. 'Come to that, where are all these carpenters and hands you mentioned?'

'Like I said,' Jake replied. 'We're dark right now, so props are locked away and most of the men ain't at work. Least, the craftsmen and seamstresses are upstairs and down, but the stagehands have set act two ahead of a chorus rehearsal, so they're on a tea break. Just us. Oh, and Mr Hampshire up there. Alright, John?'

Silas craned his neck to look above as Jake was doing. The wall of scaffolding and iron seemed to climb forever until it became one jumbled mess of bars and beams. Someone was waving down, but from that distance, he was a mere blur. It made Silas dizzy just looking, and he dropped his head.

'Bloody hell.'

Jake sniggered. 'Sorry, Sir,' he said. 'Don't hear language from gentlemen, mainly just the crew.'

'Yeah, well, I'm kind of both.'

Silas was comfortable with the lad. Jake reminded Silas of himself at that age, keen, positive and eager to please. He pulled himself up short when he realised he was only a few years older.

'My apologies,' he said.

'No need for that. Down here.'

Jake was off again, trotting along the passage which now sloped gradually towards the front of the stage. They came to the end where a large desk stood beneath shaded lamps. Above was a bank of switches, each one labelled, and near it, comfortable chairs waited in a neat line.

'Principals resting, and prompt corner,' Jake explained. 'Just beyond, that's the door to the Grand Tier.'

'The audience is only a few feet away?' Silas was having trouble placing himself. They had come up and forward from the stage door, but it was difficult to tell how far. His sense of time and direction were distorted.

'That's right, Sir,' Jake said. 'The door's always unlocked in case of fire, but luckily we haven't had one here since fifty-six, not that I was born then. Only known the old girl as you see her now.'

'The old girl?' Silas chuckled. 'You like your job, I take it?'

'Best job in the world, Sir,' Jake beamed back. 'Apart from dressing.'

'You mean dressing the actors? Like a valet?'

'That's it. I ain't got the talent to be on the stage, but love being behind it.'

'How old are you? If I may ask.'

'Seventeen last week, Sir. Been at the House since I was eight.'

'Eight? What about school?'

'Life's a school, Mr Hawkins,' the lad said. 'If I can call you that?'

'You can call me Silas if you want.' Silas liked the lad's directness. 'I am only an assistant like you.'

'Very kind, Sir, thank you. So, you want to see the stage?'

'This isn't it?'

Jake roared a laugh which vanished into the fly tower. 'No, Sir,' he said. 'Oh, this side of backstage is half as wide as the main stage of course, as is OP, but you ain't seen nothing yet.'

Silas judged the distance from where they stood to the side wall and ropes. It was at least twenty feet.

'If you want the details,' Jake said, 'the stage is fifty feet wide, wings half of that each again, fly tower tops out at one-hundred-and-twenty feet, and there's sixty feet below us.'

Silas couldn't imagine it. He looked up again, but his head spun.

'And if you want more, the curtain weighs nearly three tons.'

'Blimey.'

'Through here.' Jake held back a black drape hung between two flats. 'After you.'

Silas had seen many new sights since leaving the East End, but nothing prepared him for what he saw. He experienced the

20

opulence of Clearwater House daily and had adjusted to having a bed too large for his needs, his own sitting room, and enough space to bring up an extended family on one floor with rooms to spare, but he had never been lost inside a building as he was now. He had never felt so small or inconsequential either and was disorientated as soon as he stepped onto the stage.

Facing the front, he was met by row after row of plush, red seats in three regimental blocks. More stood behind them, empty beneath the golden sweep of a balcony adorned with crystal lamps. Two more semi-circular balconies tiered above to where the seats were almost vertical, perched beneath a distant arch. The ceiling was blue, the floors and seats red, and the trimming gold. Central to the spectacle was a chandelier, high and bowled, one mass of glass covering much of the ceiling. The chamber was a cave of unimagined splendour, and even under the dull working lights, crystal glittered, and mouldings shimmered. The whole thing was blanketed in a reverent hush and smelt of dusty grandeur.

'That's room enough for two-thousand people,' Jake said, lowering his voice as if he was in church.

'Fuck me.' The words escaped his lips before Silas could stop them, but they made his companion snort a laugh. 'Sorry, Jake,' he said, unable to tear his eyes away from the auditorium. 'Never seen anything like this.'

'Ah, it's alright', Jake said. 'But you should see her when the house is full, and the lamps are lit. I tell you, Mr Silas, you'd think you were in heaven.'

Silas couldn't even picture it. Until now, the most glittering thing he had seen was Archer's dining room, but that was just a star in comparison to this firmament. He imagined two thousand people looking back at him, and his knees weakened. He wouldn't be able to speak, let alone sing.

'We're set for Dido,' Jake said, and the cryptic statement brought Silas back to the real world.

'What?' He managed to turn his back to the looming magnificence and found himself standing on the deck of a ship.

'The opera?' Jake was grinning.

Maybe it was the sudden change in view from the auditorium to the set, or the change in scale of the house compared to Jake, shorter than Silas by a couple of inches, but until then he hadn't taken much notice of the boy's face, only to register that he had acne and not the pox. Suddenly he saw it clearly. Jake had blue eyes and dark hair. His eyebrows rose towards his temples, and his nose was snubbed. Silas was unnerved at the lad's similarity to himself and his sisters.

'Sorry,' he said, realising he had been staring. 'What's this ship all about?'

'That's act two,' Jake explained. 'The back's been brought down and the drop flown in, so you're only seeing about half the depth.'

As before, his words were dumbfounding. 'Can you say that in English, or Irish, if you have any Green-Isle blood in you.'

'I don't, Mr Silas, as it happens,' Jake replied. 'West End born and bred, me. I was saying, they've moved the back of the scenery forwards and dropped in the sky, so this is only half the stage.'

'Dropped the…?'

The height of the tower skewed his perspective. It was crossed by parallel catwalks at increasing heights, with beams and bars, cloths and weights ascending above. Through them, he could just make out a grid at the very top, threaded with ropes that led through pulleys to the walls below.

Nausea accompanied his dizziness this time, and he instinctively reached for Jake's shoulder. He looked down and shook his head to clear it.

'Yeah, gets you like that a few times at first,' Jake said. 'You should see what us down here look like to them up there.'

'I'd rather not,' Silas grimaced. The last time he had been at that height he had been escaping the Ripper and dangling from a rope over the river. He let the lad go as his balance returned.

'It's called the fly tower,' Jake explained. 'Where the scenery flies off to, and sometimes people. You see that?'

Silas glanced briefly, but enough to show him a contraption of four weights, ropes and wires sixty feet above his head.

'What is it?'

'Technology, Sir.' Jake glowed with pride. 'Counterbalanced clouds that come down carrying two lads dressed as cherubs. It's for the end of the show. Spectacular, it is, what with Herr Director calling for flames and smoke from below, and the boys dropping

22

rose petals while the tomb rises. Them barrels up there, they're the balance weights, about two hundred pounds each and attached by the latest in steel cabling. Amazing trick it is. Apart from that, though, there's not so much going on up there in this production, but there's enough, and they ain't finished rigging yet what with the gala still a couple of nights off. You involved in that and all, Mr Silas?'

'Yes, in a way,' Silas said. He looked at the time. 'Do you know where Lord Clearwater will be?'

'Forty-four A on the balcony.'

It was a shout, but barely audible. Silas, however, would have recognised the voice from any distance. He sheltered his eyes from the working lights and peered out front.

'Balcony's the second one down,' Jake said. 'Front middle.'

Silas picked out a shape darker than the deep red around it, and waved.

'I can hear your every word clear as a bell,' Archer yelled. 'I'll be down immediately.'

Silas waved again, and the figure was soaked up by the darkness.

'Well, thanks, Jake,' he said, returning his attention to the runner. 'You've been very helpful.'

'That's alright, Mister.' Apparently, Jake was never without a smile. 'I like showing her off, but I'd best wait with you until His Lordship gets here. Safety reasons.'

'Safety?'

Jake laughed and looked at the tower. 'Mr Hampshire?' he called.

'Aye?' A distant echo.

'Can you show Mr Silas a drop? Downstage right's safe enough.'

'Aye.'

Silas was about to remind Jake that his name was Hawkins when someone shouted 'Below!' A second later, a bag of sand landed a few feet in front of him with a loud thud. The boards shuddered, and Silas leapt back, swearing.

'And that's only a lightweight,' Jake said. 'Thanks, John,' he yelled up, and the sandbag was hoisted away. 'You can imagine the damage one of them lead weights would do. In fact, they had one fall on an alto in a Handel. Killed her in a downbeat, hence the new steel cables. Before my time, of course. Since then, anyone using the stage has to have a demonstration of the dangers. There's traps, flies, and don't get me started on this new electric lighting. We still use some oil and gas, but if one of them incandescent thousand-watters gets anywhere near you, you burn. Anyway. I'll hang on here while you wait. I like talking to you.'

'I haven't had much chance to say anything,' Silas muttered, alarmed at the falling weight but amused by Jake's enthusiasm.

'Yeah, sorry about that,' the lad replied. 'Most of the time, I'm only allowed to say yes and shout the calls.'

He and Silas had more in common than similar features. Jake was also openly direct and cheery. Every time he spoke Silas warmed to him more.

'Did your mam and dad mind you not going to school?' he asked.

'Don't know,' Jake replied. 'I've been brought up by my granddad. You met him at the door.'

'Mr Keys?'

'Good memory, Mr Silas.' Jake winked. 'It's a nickname 'cos he keeps the keys, see. Everyone's got a nickname. I'm Tricky, Mr Hampshire is Dropper, and we got four Georges back here; Hell one and two, Stage and Gods on account two work under-stage, one where we are, and George Gods is master flyman up there. Granddad got me work here when I was eight, not official, mind, but when the old call boy gave it up, I stepped in. I was twelve by then. Not a bad place to live, eh?'

'You live here as well?'

'That I do. We both do now Nanna's dead. Just me and him in the room off the stage door, and he's getting on, as you saw.'

'Is that why you want to be a dresser? So you can support yourselves when he retires? I imagine it pays better.'

'Retires? He ain't going to do that. You don't retire from the House, Mr Silas. No. Granddad'll battle on until he drops at his desk, but yeah, I'd like to earn a bit more.' He tugged at Silas' sleeve and jerked his head upstage.

At Jake's prompting, Silas sat on a powder keg.

'I have my life planned out, see?' Jake said, dropping his voice. 'Work my way up by being a dresser starting off with Madame LaRache in costume, learn about styles. I can already sew good, and then go into making my own. I mean, clothes for other people, but I'd make them. I help the seamstresses upstairs, even drawn my own designs. I'll open a shop one day.'

'You're good with a needle?'

'Bloomin' best,' he said with pride. 'Least, for a man of my age. They're always calling on me to stitch something at the last minute. I love it.'

'You seem to love everything,' Silas said, smiling.

'Hey, life's not a rehearsal, Mr Silas, you got to make the most of it. Find something you love, work hard, enjoy it, don't hurt no-one else and you'll sail through. Go the other way, you know, grumpy and that, and your life might feel like it lasts longer, but it'll be over before you know it.'

The smile on Silas' face remained as he regarded the young man with awe. 'How do you get to be so wise?' he asked, impressed with the boy's attitude.

'How did you get where you are?' was the instant reply.

'Same as you,' Silas admitted. 'At sixteen, I was on a coach from Westerpool to the city. No money, no possessions but, like you, I have someone to support. Two sisters. And now, four years later, I'm assistant to Viscount Clearwater. Hard graft all the way.' He was not going to tell the boy the exact nature of his previous work.

'Nice one.' Jake dropped to the floor unexpectedly and sat with his legs crossed drawing them in and clutching his arms around his knees. 'What do you think about the gala then?' he asked out of the blue. 'I mean, what's it all for?'

'You mean the Foundation?'

Jake nodded, keen to chat, but Silas wasn't too sure how much he should say.

'What do you know about it?' he asked.

'It's raising money to help renters in the East End,' Jake said, as if it was an everyday subject.

'You know about that?'

'Course I do, mate.' He laughed. 'What the thing's for makes no difference to me. Getting to work with Cadwell Roxton and Signora Campanelli is what it's all about. They're a far cry from what goes on over east, but folk'll pay a lot of money to see them. Does that kind of stuff really go on?'

Silas was having trouble keeping up. 'You mean, in the East End?'

'Yeah. I know girls do it, plenty of them 'round Five Dials and Soho where the arty set lives. Sometimes they try and get up to it in the stage door porch as I know some lads do, but with toffs. I didn't know poor people paid for it.'

The naivety was alluring. 'You're not poor yourself then?' Silas ventured as a way to change the subject. If he told Jake everything he knew about renting in the East End, they would still be on stage when the gala began.

'We don't have much money if that's what you mean,' Jake shrugged. 'But I reckon I'm rich in this.' He threw up his hand and circled it above his head. 'I mean, if anyone asks, I can say my home's got seventy-one toilets, a staff of four hundred, three bars and a cafe. I live in the heart of the city too. Prime location, free music from the best in the world, and I get paid a bit. Signor Broccolini gave me a good tip after doing only one Sullivan aria in a concert, he's usually over at the Savoy. Mr Bentham's another tipper, but it ain't the money so much. If you're talking poor in life, or quality of life, then me and Granddad are the wealthiest buggers in the metropolis.'

Silas was winded by the lad's fluency, despite his rough accent. His outlook was delivered with such confidence, Silas thought he had met his equal on all levels. Except one; experience. He wouldn't wish his East End past on anyone.

He was about to compliment Jake for his attitude when he was distracted by a dull thud beneath the stage. He felt it rather than heard it, but it brought Jake to his feet. In one deft move, he had turned and was sitting shoulder to shoulder with Silas on the fake keg looking towards the cavernous auditorium.

'Watch this,' he said and stamped his foot in reply to the thump from below.

Silas watched, wondering what to expect, but he didn't have to consider for long. Part of the stage vanished before his eyes, lowering itself to leave a gaping hole three feet square. He looked at Jake for an explanation, but the lad nudged his elbow and nodded towards the opening.

A top hat appeared followed by a pair of broad shoulders from which were draped a perfectly cut tailcoat of ocean blue. A jaunty arm pressed a silver-topped cane to the ground beside long legs, one bent behind the other, resting on its toes. The gradual appearance was accompanied by the grinding of ropes on wood somewhere beneath the pit which, when the apparition was complete, became once again part of the stage.

'Basic trap lift,' Jake whispered as the figure turned.

'Afternoon, boys.' Archer raised his topper and bowed. He was as animated as a child with a new toy. 'This is going to be fun.'

Three

His juvenile sense of enjoyment was just one of the things about Archer that Silas loved more each day. Since the gala performance had been announced two weeks ago and Cadwell Roxton booked to appear, his enthusiasm for life had hit a peak so far unseen. He was, as Silas' mam used to say, as giddy as a schoolboy, which is how he was behaving now, shuffling his feet in a quick dance and offering his hat for a tip.

'Your meeting's over, I take it?' Silas said, standing.

'It is, and very positive it was too, and mercifully short. Did Fecker bring you?'

'He did, but I sent him home. Wasn't sure how long we'd be.'

'Another minute. Hello, Jake.' Archer shook the lad's hand.

'Hello again, My Lord.' It was a mischievous, Cockney-sounding greeting gilded with a title and accompanied by a sharp nod of the head.

'Jake's been telling me about the theatre,' Silas explained.

'You've had the tour then?'

'Part of it,' Jake said. 'You want to go into the flies? See the windlass? I ain't shown you the sloats yet.'

'But he keeps speaking this weird language.'

Archer laughed. 'We're in a different world, Silas. Unfortunately, we must return to the real one. We have guests for dinner tonight, and before that, lunch. Will you come, Jake?'

There was another thing. The way Archer latched on to people and accepted them as equals no matter their station.

'Kind of you, Sir, but I've had me sandwich, and we've got the chorus in shortly. I've got to work.'

'That's a shame. Next time. Shall we go?'

Jake led them from the stage, back through the wings and down to the stage door. There, they signed out and thanked the lad, Silas giving him a sovereign as a tip, because he liked him so much.

'Very kind of you, Mr Silas,' Jake said, wide-eyed. 'If you want to see the rest of the house, just call by. We're always here.'

They left the theatre and turned towards Five Dials, picking their way through the vegetable market where the well-to-do placed orders and the working class haggled over prices. The stallholders were not dissimilar to those Silas knew in Cheap Street, but their language was polished and their aprons cleaner. Passing baskets of flowers, bouquets and arrangements, Archer ignored the calls of, 'Penny a bunch,' but bought two carnations from a child selling the flowers on the corner of Mercy Street. He broke the stems and placed one in Silas' buttonhole before fixing the other to his overcoat.

'How was it?' Silas asked.

'Everything is going perfectly,' Archer replied. 'Apart from Signora Campanelli.'

'That's the other singer, right?'

'One of them. She's booked to sing opposite Cadwell, but insists she doesn't need a rehearsal. Cadwell, being less of a diva, expects at least one with her, but she's not having it.'

'Just one? Thought they'd need more than that.'

'Quite. Anyway, Mr Bursnall is dealing with her manager as they know each other well. She'll come around in time, I'm sure of it. The gala is the talk of the town, and nothing must go wrong. Did you enjoy your tour?'

'Yeah, he's a nice lad.'

'Agreed, though he's not on our crew.'

He meant that Jake wasn't queer, and Silas wondered how he knew. 'Did you ask him?'

'Certainly not. I'd have embarrassed the boy. No, I can just tell. Shall we go to the Grape Vine?'

'Is it costly?'

'Does it matter? It's my treat.'

'Well, it's never going to be mine. I'm happy with a sausage from a stall, but you're the boss.'

Archer stopped and tugged at Silas' arm, pulling him into a recess.

'You often call me that. You don't think of me as merely your employer, do you?' he asked, concerned. 'You must never think that.'

There was another thing to love; the way Archer was confident one moment and vulnerable the next. His vulnerability only showed when the subject was love or friendship, and it was adorable.

'Course I don't, Archie,' Silas said, resisting the urge to kiss him. 'In fact, I never feel like I work for you.'

'But, you don't feel like I'm keeping you?'

'If I didn't want to be here, I'd be off. You know that.'

He meant it teasingly. He couldn't envisage any reason to leave Archer.

'Yes, well, that's true enough,' Archer smiled. 'I'm lucky to have you.'

'Ha! If anyone's lucky around here, it's me.'

'I want to kiss you.' Archer leant in as if about to whisper something in Silas' ear.

'Want to sneak into an alley and get your dick sucked?' Silas whispered back.

'You are such a slattern.'

'Be anything you want, mate.' Silas used his renter voice knowing it aroused Archer. 'But you'll have to stop using fancy words.'

A soft brush of lips on his ear, Archer's arm through his and they turned back to the street.

'Best leave that for later,' the viscount said.

He let go of Silas just in time to greet an acquaintance with a doff of his hat, stopping a few yards later to examine a costumier's window display.

'That's what your new friend Jake wants to do,' Archer said, pointing to the fancy designs.

'Yeah, he told me. And you say he's not queer.'

'You don't have to be on-board to be a tailor.'

On-board, part of the crew, a captain's mate, they were all euphemisms Archer employed to keep his meaning away from prying ears.

'You like him, don't you?' Silas enquired, examining a dress covered with glass beads.

'I like his outlook on life,' Archer replied. 'I don't go for his looks, if that's what you mean.'

30

'Didn't mean anything apart from what I said. I like him too. Very personable.'

'Yes.' Archer sighed and stood back. 'I wish there was some way to help them. I'll have a word with Lady Marshall. I believe the lad is interested in clothing design, and she knows everyone.'

They continued their walk.

'You can't help them all,' Silas said. 'On which note, how much have you shelled out for this play?'

'It's an opera, and nothing.'

'Eh?'

They crossed a narrow but busy street and entered Five Dials, so called because five thoroughfares met at one junction in the centre of five blocks. The area was known for its theatres, warehouses and drinking establishments, but it was also the home of one of the city's fancier restaurants much beloved by actors and artists.

'I've spent nothing,' Archer continued, once they were away from the clattering carts, 'because of Marks' tactical planning.'

'What's he got to do with it?'

Marks was Archer's solicitor and member of the Clearwater Foundation.

'He's a slippery old devil,' Archer said, paying a compliment. 'I was expecting to pay for renting the opera house, and that's a pretty penny on a Saturday night, but Marks found a way of closing one trust and opening another.'

'You'll have to explain.'

Although he was officially Archer's private secretary, his involvement in his charitable work was more hands-on than business related. It had been Silas' job to find a building in Greychurch for the Foundation to use as a hostel. He had done that with Fecker's help, and now he had few duties other than to advise from a renter's point of view and liaise with the would-be clientele, the fellow rent boys from his previous life. He did this privately with Archer who then translated the information into acceptable language and presented it to the committee.

'In a nutshell,' Archer said. 'Marks closed down my father's old trust and transferred its finances to mine. Some ancient law of charitable inheritance that, frankly, I didn't quite grasp, but it's legal. We were able to use what was left in the trust for the theatre hire and house payments, though I am paying the admission for half the audience.'

'You're too bloody generous, you are,' Silas mumbled.

'One must lead by example,' Archer said. 'We are asking patrons to pay through their pince-nez for their tickets and make a donation on top.'

'Yeah, alright. This it?'

They had arrived at The Grapevine, a three-storey brick building on the corner of two streets. Its windows were leaded, its awning green and, from the outside, it looked like any other West End bistro.

Inside, however, was a different matter, and Silas understood why Archer had insisted he wear his best suit.

Central to the restaurant was 'the island,' a circular bar with row after row of liqueurs and spirits, every bottle neatly arranged and backed by a perfectly polished mirror. The bar was mahogany, as were the stools against it and the wood panelling. The lighting was subtle, catching glass and silver, giving enough for the diners to see by, but also lending an evening atmosphere even in the middle of the day.

No sooner had they walked into the heated foyer than a liveried attendant was at Silas' side, helping him out of his coat and greeting Archer like a long-lost relative.

'We have your banquette as requested, Your Lordship.' The man bowed. 'We trust you are well.'

'I am, thank you, Daniels,' Archer replied. 'My assistant, Mr Hawkins.'

'Welcome, Sir.' The attendant bowed again.

Silas wondered if he would ever adapt to being treated this way. He hoped not. He enjoyed the pretence of being a gentleman more than the respect the façade gave him, but even more, he enjoyed wondering what people would think of him if they knew his real background. The way Daniels was behaving, he doubted the man would bat an eyelid, and although his manners were impeccable, he probably used them on every customer no matter if they were aristocrat or actor.

They were shown to their table as if they were processing to an altar, Archer tipping his head to a few people he knew, and Silas watching their reactions carefully. He wasn't introduced to anyone, and held his head high, expertly playing his role until he was seated in the private banquette. It was a few minutes later, once a waiter had fussed and Archer had ordered wine, that they were able to continue their conversation.

'So,' Silas began. 'Is there anything else that needs to be done before the show?'

'Lots,' Archer replied. 'But nothing I have to worry about. Bursnall is directing the production and dealing with everything at the theatre, and Marks has everything in place on our side. All we have to do is entertain Mr Roxton and look after him while he's in town.'

'Staying with Lady Marshall, right?'

'Yes.' Archer suddenly clutched Silas' hand across the table, disturbing his row of forks. 'Silas, you're going to love him,' he enthused. 'Apart from his voice, he is so witty, so charming.' His eyes misted. 'I do hope you get on.'

'We will, Archie.' Silas slid his hand free as the waiter returned. 'You've known him a long time and any friend of yours…'

'Ah, the wine.'

Silas remained silent while the waiter put on a song and dance, showing Archer the label, flicking a white cloth over his arm before delicately popping the cork, twisting the bottle as he poured a drop and standing back to await the verdict. Archer lifted the glass, examined the spit of wine against the light, rolled it around several times, lifted it to his nose, sniffed, made approving noises and finally took a tiny sip. Even that was a process, and Silas rolled his eyes.

'Perfect as always.' Archer spoke to Silas and winked. Daring.

The waiter poured them each a disappointing measure, and a rigmarole with the cloth and an ice bucket took place. It was a good minute later before Archer was able to top up their glasses to a decent level, and Silas said, 'Bloody hell, that was a palaver.'

'I know,' Archer agreed. 'But what must be, must be. Yes,' he went on without a breath. 'Cadwell and I go back a long way. Prep school.'

'Which was when you were little, right?'

'I was eight, so was he. But where I left at thirteen to attend the academy, he was a student of the classics and the arts, lucky bugger, and stayed on. We kept in touch and would visit each other when we could, the best of friends. But then I was sent to sea and meeting became more difficult.'

'Not part of your crew then?'

'Not literally, no.' Archer knew what Silas meant. 'And not figuratively, as far as I know. He's married, not that that means anything. Either way, no jealousy needed.'

Silas never suffered from jealousy, but Archer's enthusiasm was not as contagious as usual. Somehow, Silas felt it was misplaced, which was wrong of him. He'd never met Cadwell Roxton. He'd met few of Archer's friends, but those who had visited, he had liked. There was no reason why he should be uneasy about a man he'd never met. Unable to explain it, he opened his menu.

'Oh,' he said. 'What's this?'

'French, sadly,' Archer sighed, opening his own. 'One of the establishment's less popular affectations. Shall I translate?'

'Do they do bacon and cabbage?' The menu meant nothing to Silas, and the script was so fancy he would have had trouble reading it in English.

'They have loin of pork with fennel and haricot beans.'

'Yuk. A sandwich?'

Archer put down his menu, his face clouding.

'Sorry,' Silas said. 'I'll have whatever you have.'

'No, it's not that.' Archer was worried. Silas could tell from the way his mouth turned down, and he blinked several times.

'What's up?'

'I just remembered.' The viscount glanced around the room before focusing on Silas. 'The last time I was here was with Benji Quill.'

Silas shuddered. 'Instant indigestion?'

'Not at the time. I had no idea he was…' He mouthed the words. 'The Ripper.'

'No-one did, and no-one does,' Silas reminded him to put him at his ease.

There had been no news of Quill since they saw him falling into a train crash, and both assumed he was at the bottom of a river. He'd not, as Archer first feared, shown up at the sanitorium in Holland where Archer's brother was held, and no more murders had been reported. Still, the memories were fresh. Any more of them and Silas would lose his appetite.

'Done and dealt with,' he said, keen to change the subject. 'So, no boiled bacon, no sandwiches. What is this place?'

Archer's mood was lifted, and he raised his eyebrows. 'Coq au vin?' he suggested.

'If it's got the word cock in it, I'm up for it.'

'Shush!' The viscount hid his laughter behind the menu. 'You behave yourself, Mr 'awkins,' he chided in a faux East End accent. 'Or you'll be on bread and water.'

'Sounds highly preferable, My Lord,' Silas grinned back in his more polished upper-class impersonation.

The waiter arrived as if he had telepathically known Archer was ready to order and, that done, they returned to the subject of Cadwell Roxton.

Archer spoke at length, singing his virtues and loading praise on the man. It was rewarding to see him so excited. He had worked hard over the past few weeks and all for the good of other people. Yet another admirable trait that Silas couldn't resist. Despite his unfounded misgivings about the opera singer, he listened silently as Archer told him about their shared past. By the time their meal was delivered and devoured, he knew all there was to know about Cadwell Roxton.

At least, that was what he thought at the time.

Three miles away, the winter sun filtered through the grime of a cracked window, throwing jaundiced light across a sheet of paper. Below, in the streets of Greychurch, people went about their daily lives unaware of and not caring for the man and woman who lived in the room above the Cheap Street coffin shop. Had anyone called to the room to enquire after the young lady, they might have been greeted by the man. Had they called to visit him, they might have been met by the woman. It depended entirely on what purpose each character was serving, for they were one and the same person.

He admired his arm beneath the faint yellow sun, turning it from the smooth underside to the equally as smooth upper skin, extending his fingers and admiring the Chinese lacquer recently applied to his long nails. He curled his fingers into his palm, comparing the nails to his delicate skin, and flexed his powerful biceps. Having smiled at the strength behind his demure outward appearance, he unwound his fingers, curling his hand like the unfurling of wings and brought it to land on the tabletop. There, he selected a reservoir pen, recently loaded with black ink and with the nib prepared, and unscrewed the lid. Every movement was precise and delicate, as fitted his female character, while behind his shadowed eyelids, he considered the words he was to write with the cunning of a man accustomed to deception.

Nothing must be too obvious, but nor could it be too much of a conundrum. Time was limited, and it was imperative the message be understood clearly by its recipient. The terminology would ensure only a musical mind, or one as devious as his own, would fathom the threat, yet the statement accompanying it should leave no doubt.

He took a deep breath to calm his excited heart, his diaphragm fighting his corseted bodice, and when the breath was released, produced a sigh of feminine satisfaction.

The nib touched the virgin paper, and he began to write.

Cadwell Roxton…

Four

Later that evening, Silas stood before the bedroom mirror and tugged his waistcoat to straighten it before adjusting his collar. The high, starched band was designed to keep him straight-necked. If he lowered his chin even slightly, the collar rubbed uncomfortably, and its confines irritated more than just his skin.

'I don't think I'll ever get used to this, Jimmy,' he said to the footman waiting behind him, a tailcoat held open ready to receive his arms.

'The collar, Sir?'

'The whole lot. The narrow trousers, waistcoat, this trap at my neck, and the jacket. Looking straight ahead, flicking tails when I sit. Blimey. How does anyone dress like this every day?'

'You get used to it, I suppose.'

Silas regarded the footman's reflection thoughtfully as he centred his cravat. 'Not so long ago you were running messages in a blue uniform,' he said. 'Now you're in completely different garb. How does that feel?'

'Speaking honestly, Sir, it makes me proud. The uniform reminds me of who and where I am.'

'A servant to a man with money?'

'It's more than that, Sir. Your dinner jacket?'

Silas sighed. 'Yeah, I suppose I must.' He threaded his arms into the sleeves and James dropped the tailcoat onto his shoulders.

'We must all look our best for the evening,' the footman said. 'And you do look elegant.'

'Thanks, Jimmy.' Silas had to agree. 'I'm not complaining,' he said as James reached for the clothes brush.

'Of course.'

'How are you getting on?'

'Mr Payne seems happy with my work, Sir,' James replied, skimming Silas' shoulders with the soft bristles.

'You've picked it up quick.'

'Mr Payne is a good teacher.'

Silas didn't doubt it, and he knew for a fact that Thomas was teaching James more than just the duties of a footman and the etiquette expected in a noble house. The sounds he heard through his bedroom ceiling at night suggested the couple were learning something more intimate than dinner service and answering bell-pulls.

'How's it going?' he asked. 'You and Tommy?'

The footman's brush paused in its work, and the mirror reflected his embarrassment.

'Asking as a mate,' Silas said. 'Tell me to mind my own if you want, but after what we've been through, I reckon we're mates. Are we?'

'At the appropriate time, Sir.'

'And this ain't one of them?' Silas questioned. 'Come on, Jimmy. We're alone in my room like we are just about every day, and you're the only one I've got to talk to.'

'His Lordship?'

'Yeah, sure. I talk to him about all sorts, but I mean, friends talk differently to each other than they do with lovers. Who do you speak to about you and Tommy?'

James blushed further. His round cheeks glowed, and he lowered his eyes to study the fall of the tailcoat.

'My Payne would say that this is an inappropriate conversation, Sir.'

'Yeah, maybe, but Lord Clearwater wouldn't, and he's the boss. We're on our own, Jimmy. I trust you as much as I reckon you trust me, and besides, I can always pull rank and demand you tell me.'

'You don't need to do that,' James said, standing back. 'May I see the front?'

Silas turned to him. James was five years older and several inches taller, but had more flesh on his bones. He wasn't fat, but he was solid, and his stocky body contained by his smart evening livery strengthened his presence. He radiated reliability.

'It's going alright, though. Isn't it?' Silas pressed.

James tipped his head as a yes, and his naturally smiling lips curled further. 'I have only been at Clearwater a few weeks, Sir,' he said. 'But they have been the most exciting of my life, and in more ways than one.'

'Yeah, well, I know what you mean there.' Silas took the brush. 'Here.'

'What are you doing?'

He brushed James' lapels and his collar. 'We're pretty much the same you and me,' he said, ignoring the footman's protestations. 'Except you're not as rough.'

'Rough?'

'Background and that.' He turned James and attended to his back. 'Happily mooching along in life and then comes Archer bringing murder, mystery and mayhem. You know.' He laughed. 'Me mam wouldn't have believed it.'

'Mine still doesn't.'

'Of course, he also brought Thomas.' Silas winked knowingly into the mirror. 'Which is something that's changed you as much as Archer has changed me. You'll do.'

When James turned to face him, his smile had gone and was replaced by uncertainty.

'Do you feel different?' he asked. 'If that's not an inappropriate question.'

'Jimmy, I know as much as you do about what's appropriate in this house. In fact, you probably know more. But I don't mean changed in a bad way. I love it here, I love Archer, and I see you every day mad in love with Tommy. There's no point hiding it between ourselves when we're alone. I like talking to you. I ain't got no-one else.'

'Mr Andrej?'

'Well, yeah, of course.' Silas replaced the brush on the dressing table. 'There's always Fecks, but he's Fecks.'

'We all need friends, Sir.' James set about tidying Silas' other clothes. He shook a jacket and hung it before collecting a shirt for the laundry.

Silas voiced his thoughts as he combed his hair.

'I mean someone who understands this change like you do,' he said. 'We were both on the streets, obviously doing different things, and your old job was respectable, but we were both street-runners one day and here the next. How do you cope with that?'

'It's an act that comes with the position. That's all. And, speaking of acts, the guests will be arriving in a few minutes. Is there anything else?'

Silas gave himself one last look in the glass. 'Yes,' he said. 'Can you come here a minute?'

James dutifully stood at his side, and they regarded their reflections. Two young men, one dark, one blond, one slim, one fuller-figured, and both a hundred miles away from how they were a few weeks ago. A servant and a gentleman, both inexperienced in their new roles, both in love with other men in the house, and both born to a class below their current station — several classes in Silas' case.

'We look nifty,' he said.

'An unlikely pair.'

'But a pair of mates, Jimmy? Brothers in arms?'

'Against a sea of battles?'

'Whatever that means.'

'Mr Hawkins, I'm not sure what you're thinking.'

'What I'm trying to say…' Silas put his thoughts in order. 'We play our roles as we have to, but neither of us has anyone in the house we can talk to about real stuff. You know, where we are, how we got here and the men who make us what we are.'

'We make ourselves what we are.'

'Yeah, don't get all deep on me, Jimmy.' The corner of Silas' mouth twitched in a faint grin. 'If you need to talk to someone about you and Thomas, or anything, you can come to me, yeah?'

'Thank you.'

Silas waited, expecting the offer to be reciprocated.

Beside him, the blond lad drew in a breath and cleared his throat quietly. 'Is everything alright with you and His Lordship?'

'Oh yeah, perfect.' It was. That was not what Silas was trying to communicate. 'Just, sometimes, I want to talk as meself, you know? I do with Archer when we're alone, but I've got no-one else to let off steam with. There's Fecks, yeah, and he is me best mate, but he don't do conversations, just two-word advice, and one of them's usually in Russian. You, though… You and I have things in common, I want us to be frank with each other.'

'Confidants?'

'Yeah, I think that's what I mean. See? You know what I'm thinking, and you know how to reply.'

James shrugged.

'Alright, mate,' Silas said. 'Sorry. Didn't want to mortify you, but one last promise, yeah?'

James tipped his head again.

'You got any problems, you tell me. Anything. You trust me enough, Jimmy?'

'I do.'

It was hard to know if James responded with what Silas wanted to hear, or if it was what he truly wanted to say.

'Then we'll do what Archer would expect us to do,' Silas said, and turned to him. 'Shake on it.' He offered his hand. 'We're both new to this, so we're in the same boat. On the same crew.'

James considered his hand with thoughtful, hazel eyes before fixing Silas with them seriously.

'It would be an honour, Sir,' he said, and took it.

'Then would you sound like you mean it?'

'I do!' James protested. He glanced around the room as if to find a way to prove it. He squeezed Silas' hand harder. 'I mean it, mate,' he said. 'And cheers. I've got no-one else either, Thomas aside. So it's reassuring to hear what you say.'

'You'll get to like me, Jimmy,' Silas winked and let go of his hand.

'I already do.'

'That's good, 'cos we're newcomers to a strange world, and we need all the friends we can get. I mean it,' he repeated. 'Anything you want, you can talk in here when we're alone.'

'Same goes for you,' James said, and added, 'Silas.'

The use of his name was reassuring. James had broken through the etiquette, and that was enough to put Silas' mind at rest.

'Right,' he said. 'Thanks for that, but now I better get into character and put on me act.'

'*My* act, Sir.'

'Cheers, Jimmy.'

'*Thank you*, James.'

Silas smirked. 'Let me enjoy being meself a bit longer.'

'Right-oh, Silas,' James returned the grin. 'It feels good to drop the façade.'

'Which was the point I was trying to make.'

A dull clang trembled through the house, and James immediately squared his shoulders.

'The first guests are arriving, Sir,' he said, smoothing the rough edges of his accent as he smoothed Silas' dinner jacket. 'I shall leave you.'

'Thanks, James. I mean it.'

James bowed. 'Will there be anything else, Sir?'

'Not right now, but this is my first posh dinner party, so you might need to keep an eye on me. Make sure I get things right.'

'I am sure that between them, His Lordship and Mr Payne will manage, but I will be right behind you.'

With that reassurance, James left, and Silas took one last look in the mirror.

He shook his head in disbelief. Less than two months ago he would have been scrambling for a bench in the rope-room. He might have had sixpence in his pocket if he was lucky and he might have eaten a bread roll all day. He would certainly have been cold. Tonight, he wore tailored tails, his hair was neatly cut and clean, the acne of his youth had gone, and he was starting to put some muscle back on his bones. He was still full from lunch. A fire crackled in a grate, he had the most generous, loving man waiting for him a floor below, and he was safe. Now, having had a conversation that had been on his mind for days, he had someone in whom he could confide. Not that he had anything to confess other than his love for Archer which, to James and Thomas, was ever-apparent, and something he spoke to Fecker about whenever he could. With Fecks on one side offering an ear, but two-word replies, and Archer on the other offering long, deep discussions about love and society, he needed someone in the middle, and James was the only person he had.

'Right,' he said, with an air of finality in just the same way Archer did when changing the subject. 'Time to make your man proud.'

He approached the bedroom door. On the other side, he would be a different character entirely. Tonight, he was to be the quiet, polite, well-mannered assistant to Lord Clearwater, a role he assumed with ease. He was used to acting. From playing the bewildered street urchin to the confident whore, the cheeky Paddy to the tough little street-rat, and now the lover to the secretary, he slipped into whatever was called for with the talent of a trained actor. He had been born with the chameleon-like ability, but his skills had been honed out of necessity on the East End streets, and it was just as well. He was about to dine with one of the leading lights of the theatrical world, and he had to play his part faultlessly.

Archer depended on him to say and do the right thing, and for a reason he couldn't place, Silas knew it was not going to be easy.

Five

The hall was alive with a flickering light that welcomed the guests as they hurried in from the rain. Thomas was at the door, and somehow, in a few short minutes, James had delivered Silas' laundry to the basement and made it to the hall to assist. Doctor Markland had arrived and was entering the drawing room with a finely dressed young lady on his arm, while another couple were being helped out of their hats.

Silas didn't know them, but he knew the guest list. She was not Lady Marshall, so he could not be Cadwell Roxton. The couple could only be Archer's solicitor, Marks and his wife, a woman who was as round as she was tall. They were well matched, and neither of them looked desperately in need of a meal. In fact, it wouldn't hurt them to miss a few.

Silas paused at the turn in the stairs to straighten his tails. The costume prepared, he took a deep breath to ready his mind, and, without the slightest hint of stage fright, continued down to greet the couple.

'You must be Marks,' he said, approaching the man with an interested smile and a confident hand.

Thomas closed the door against the blustery drizzle and saw to the solicitor's cloak.

'That I am,' Marks said. His ample jowls were as smooth as his barren forehead which swept up and over a mainly unfertile head. He wore a thick moustache waxed at the tips. 'And do I have the pleasure of addressing Mr Hawkins at long last?'

'You do, Sir,' Silas said, shaking his hand and wondering whether it was appropriate to congratulate the man on his ambitious whiskers.

'And your good lady wife, I assume.'

'Aye, that's her.' Marks was unimpressed by the reminder.

'Mrs Marks,' Silas bowed and kissed her glove.

'Mr Hawkins.'

Her greeting could not have sounded more sombre had Silas been in the dock at the Central Criminal Court. He imagined he was about to be sent down for life.

'His Lordship should have warned me of your elegance,' he said, taking in the woman's look of distrust. She narrowed her eyes, and he nearly lost sight of them behind her bulging cheeks. 'How kind.'

It was extremely kind. Her hair, parted widely in the middle, fell limply on either side of her face as if it had given up on life, and her dress bowled out from somewhere around her bust, over a wide crinoline to root her to the floor under its own weight. She reminded Silas of one of the lids James whipped off his dinner dishes; a cloche, he called it. The footman was standing directly behind the woman, and Silas didn't dare catch his eye.

'You are Lord Clearwater's… what, exactly?' Mrs Marks demanded, hardly disturbing the narrow slit which was her mouth.

'Assistant,' Silas replied.

'And what, pray, is one of them when it's 'ome?'

'It's whatever His Lordship needs. I assist here at the house and at the refuge in Greychurch. I am a go-between if you like.'

Mrs Marks wasn't impressed, but then she looked like the kind of woman who never was. 'Have you a title?' she asked.

'Yes. Assistant.'

She rolled her eyes and tutted impatiently.

'Ah, I see.' Silas hated her already. 'No, not that kind of title.'

'From the East End aren't you, lad?' Mr Marks was from the north.

'No, Sir.' He struggled to keep his tone civil. 'I was conceived in Ireland and born in the Canter Wharf area of Westerpool. I have been in this city four years. I can tell you come from somewhere like the Peak District, but you've lived in the south for some time. Your lady wife, on the other hand, is from the borough of Riverside.'

The couple exchanged glances, unnerved.

'Aye,' Marks said. 'You have read us, Mr Hawkins.'

'North Riverside,' Mrs Marks emphasised. 'No-one of importance is from south of the borough.'

Behind her, James stiffened.

'This way, Sir, Madam.' Thomas brushed past taking the tension with him, and the couple followed.

Silas paused at the footman's shoulder, leant in and mimicked Mrs Marks. '"No-one of importance is from south of the borough."' James was doing his best not to laugh. 'No-one apart from you, Jimmy. Ignore her. She's a fecking snob.'

He left James sniggering, and the dazzle of the hall gave way to the glamour of the drawing room. The pear drop chandelier, the mantle candles, table lamps and fire warmly lit the lavish room. The furniture had been brushed, fresh flowers arranged, and the decanters on the sideboard gleamed. Thomas offered a tray of delicate glasses to the Marks couple who fell on them while Markland accepted more politely.

'Ah, Hawkins,' Archer said as Silas entered. 'You've not met Miss Arnold.'

Silas was introduced to Markland's companion, a striking beauty whose face did justice to the layered skirt and narrow-waisted bodice. She offered a slender, gloved hand to be kissed and Silas did his duty.

'Hawkins has been working with me to prepare the Cheap Street building,' Markland explained. To Silas, he said, 'Miss Arnold is the actress I was talking about.'

He had, in his eyes, all the adoration Silas displayed whenever he looked at Archer. The doctor was smitten with the woman. He had spoken about her so relentlessly during Silas' visits that Silas resorted to asking what she was like in bed, hoping to embarrass the man into silence. It was not one of his better ploys. Markland hadn't been intimate with the woman, he insisted, their love was too pure for that, and it wouldn't happen until after marriage. Silas wished he'd never asked.

'At last I meet the radiant beauty,' he gushed, cringing inwardly. 'You must have Irish blood in you. I have only seen such loveliness there.'

He caught a brief glare from Archer. Silas had never been to Ireland, and he wondered if he wasn't overdoing the charm.

Miss Arnold soaked up the adoration and chuckled coyly while Mrs Marks paid Silas no attention. She monopolised the viscount and drew him into a discussion about what she saw as the distressingly shameful state of the Riverside streets.

'Choked with unhealthy men too lazy to find work. What can you do about it?' she complained as if unemployment was Archer's fault.

'Leave the man alone,' her husband protested. 'We're here to talk about the gala.'

'Well, if we can't clean our own streets, what hope do we have for the lower classes?'

Mrs Marks laughed at what she thought was a joke, and Silas helped himself to a glass of sherry.

'We are also here to discuss Mr Roxton's performance and, most importantly, his speech,' Archer said. 'Have you met him before, Mrs Marks?'

The woman shifted uncomfortably on the settee, and it creaked. 'No,' she said, unable to hide a grimace. 'My husband refuses to represent people in that… profession.'

'Oh?' Miss Arnold, beside her, maintained her charming smile despite the way the statement had been made. 'Why is that?'

'It's their reputation, isn't it?'

'And what reputation would that be?'

Silas immediately liked the younger woman. Not only was she glamorous and poised, but she also was not afraid to challenge, and she was a good actress. He could feel the heat of her anger from across the room, yet her face displayed none of it.

'You know,' Mrs Marks said. 'Their reputation.'

'For?'

The larger lady showed no signs of floundering.

'It's not savoury,' she said. 'And best not discussed in His Lordship's presence.'

'Oh, I am more than happy to discuss the reputation of the acting profession.' Archer swept onto the opposite settee. 'Only last week I was in conversation with the Marquess of Salisbury on the very subject.'

Not even the mention of the Prime Minister could dissuade Mrs Marks from making her point.

'And I am sure he agreed with me,' she said. 'That ladies should not be on the stage, and some subjects not laid bare for us all to see.'

'Quite the contrary,' Archer persisted. 'Robert, like myself, had much praise for those who tread the boards. It is hard work.'

Whether Archer was dropping names on purpose or whether he really did call the Prime Minister by his Christian name made no odds to the woman. She might have dug herself into a hole, but she showed no signs of putting down the shovel. Entertained, Silas moved closer.

'Of course,' Mrs Marks said. 'Men on stage is another matter, but honestly, Archer, are you telling me Salisbury approves of young ladies baring their souls in public, let alone their legs? Is that something of which our country should be proud?'

'I don't think we need to talk about rough subjects with His Lordship,' her husband chided, emphasising Archer's title to remind his wife of her place.

'Archer doesn't mind, he said so.' The woman didn't take the hint, but she did take a second glass of sherry which Thomas was offering to Miss Arnold.

'I find the mysteries of the theatre quite compelling,' Archer said. 'The spectacle, the lights, the way one is drawn from the real world and enters another. Don't you agree, Hawkins?'

'I do, My Lord,' Silas said. 'When you think about it, life is a theatre. The spectacle of what we see around us day by day is merely reflected on the boards, albeit in a higher, more cerebral way.' Archer had said it recently, and he had memorised the speech word for word.

Silas was pleased with himself, and Archer was also satisfied. Despite his serious expression, there were tiny signs of his amusement which only Silas caught. A brief twitch of an eyebrow, his lips creasing into a smile which he controlled as he opened his mouth to speak.

'I am looking forward to seeing Miss Arnold's Cressida next season.'

'And there's my point,' Mrs Marks exclaimed. 'Miss Arnold, is it right that you show such things to all and sundry in a public place?'

'Such things?'

Miss Arnold looked to Archer for help, but he was too busy disguising a laugh with a cough. Silas was unable to assist, he had no idea what a Cressida was. Doctor Markland, however, came to Archer's rescue.

'I think you are confusing a tragic heroine with the *cressida vertamulis*,' he said, foxing everyone including himself.

'Am I? What's that?'

'Nothing to concern yourself with,' the doctor said. 'I think the point here is that some of us see no issue with ladies appearing on the stage. It has happened for many years. Why, Shakespeare was at it all the time. I admit, the bawdiness of the music hall may be considered low entertainment, but when one is patronising the arts, then surely the art is what matters.'

'Oh!' Mrs Marks clutched for a string of pearls she wasn't wearing. 'Doctor, are you one of those athletics?'

Markland sniggered but made it sound like a hum of consideration. 'I think you mean aesthete, madam. The words are of a similar derivation, from the Greek.'

'And we'd better not bring *them* into the discussion,' Mrs Marks declared to the room, seeking wide-eyed approval but finding none, particularly not from the doctor.

'The Greek is *aisthetes*,' he continued. 'A person who perceives, while the word, athletic derives from *athletes,* one who competes for a prize.'

He had foxed Mrs Marks, and Silas was having trouble keeping up.

Archer wasn't. 'A most noble statement, Doctor,' he said. 'I might also consider myself aesthetic as I am concerned with beauty. In the arts…' He turned to Silas and twitched his eyebrows. 'In people…' Then, to Miss Arnold, 'and within ourselves.' To Markland, he said, 'But please, Philip, elucidate further with your knowledge of ancient languages, what exactly is one's cressida vertamulis?'

The doctor glared at him, but not in anger. It read as panic beneath barely suppressed laughter as if to ask, 'Did you have to?'

'It's…' He stumbled. 'Actually, it's a…'

'A subject we really shouldn't discuss in front of the ladies,' Silas said, rescuing the doctor and Mrs Marks at the same time. They both appeared grateful, although the relief on the doctor's face turned instantly to a snigger.

'No, quite,' Archer said, having had his sport. 'Each to his own, Mrs Marks. Not everyone approves of the theatre, because of the way the audience attends merely to be seen. There are other reasons for disapproval, of course, but disapproval is a right that should be protected.'

Mrs Marks grumbled, but seeing she was outnumbered, remained silent.

'And on the subject of talents,' Markland said. 'Will Mr Roxton be singing for us this evening?'

'Oh, I hope so.' Miss Arnold clasped her hands, entreating Archer with dewy, hopeful eyes.

Silas could see what Markland saw in her. She was a rare specimen of a woman. Her well-defined features were smooth and handsome, almost boyish, and her blonde hair daringly short, but behind the intriguing appearance was a contagious, juvenile enthusiasm for those around her. Knowing Markland as Silas did, he wasn't just charmed by those qualities. Her breasts were barely detectable, and her voice was deep and rich.

'Won't we, Hawkins?'

'What?' Silas was caught off guard. He tore his admiration away from Miss Arnold and planted it firmly on Archer's face. 'I beg your pardon, Sir?'

'I said we shall have to gently persuade Mr Roxton to sing.'

'Oh, yes. Of course. Gently.'

'And on that note,' Archer continued, giving Silas a puzzled stare. 'Before he arrives, we should just remind ourselves of the importance of his role in our endeavour.'

Miss Arnold sat attentively while Mrs Marks twiddled her sherry glass and frowned at the paintings. Markland, as tall as Archer but not quite as elegant, stood on one side of the fireplace, and Marks on the other, framing the stonework like a pair of mismatched bookends. All eyes were on the viscount, and Silas looked on proudly.

Tonight, as always, Archer was assured, eloquent and charming. He was more dashing than usual because of his tailored dinner-tails and white bow tie. His waistcoat shimmered like flames when the light caught the silk, and its cut drew the eye downwards where it ended in two points; arrows directing attention to his crotch. Silas drew in a deep breath and focused elsewhere.

'As you know, Mr Roxton is the highlight of the opera season this year and will be what the newspapers call a star attraction at the gala night.' Archer said. 'He has agreed to make a speech before the performance, a most unusual break in theatrical tradition, I am told. That speech will further break tradition because of its subject matter; our mission in Greychurch. I can hear your horror, Mrs Marks.' He bowed deferentially to the flustered woman. 'Before the doctor leaps on you with smelling salts, let me reassure you that his speech will not shock. He will refer to our cause as a mission to assist men of the East End and do it in such a way that everyone understands the nature of those we seek to help without being offended.'

'I should think not,' Mrs Marks tutted, shivering with disdain.

'Aye,' her husband said. 'Well you're not on the committee, woman, so kindly keep your tongue in your head and be grateful His Lordship saw fit to include you in his party.'

He received a glare that, had it been directed at the flower arrangements, would have caused them to shrivel.

'My point is,' Archer went on. 'Mr Roxton is firmly on our side. He, like us trustees, is compassionate, but unlike most of us, is in a more public position to drive the message home. I do what I can at the Lords, and I hold my personal political views which, although the majority oppose, I air in the chamber when appropriate. Mr Roxton can do it on stage in front of the public. It will be reported in the newspapers, it will no doubt ruffle some feathers, but we are prepared for that. Although Cadwell is our most public and powerful mouthpiece, we do not need to tread gingerly around him. He and I go back years, we knew each other well, and he is both charming and enlightened. Therefore, we may relax and enjoy the company. Later, if I feel it appropriate, I will ask him if he will sing.'

James crossed the hall, distracting Silas briefly.

'I've read the speech, Sir,' Marks said. 'It's near enough settled. When it is, there will be nothing in it that can come back on the theatre nor us. No words, suggestions or incitements for the Lord Chamberlain to complain about neither, all above board, Mrs Marks, Miss Arnold.'

It was strange that a man should call his wife missus, Silas thought. He imagined being called Mrs Archer Riddington. Or would it be Lady Clearwater? He smirked at the idea, but baulked when he imagined himself in a dress and bustle. His eyes drifted back to Miss Arnold as the conversation continued in the background. He was contemplating the high neck of her dress and soft collar that covered her throat when James appeared in the doorway, a coat draped over his arm.

'The Viscountess Delamere and Mr Roxton,' he announced.

A display of silver chiffon and diamonds arrived in the shape of Archer's godmother, a suited gentleman hanging from her arm. Silas took no notice. His eyes were on the coat.

The distinctive, red velvet collar took him back to a dark recess of his previous existence. He had seen it before, somewhere… Somewhere unsavoury.

Lady Marshall glided confidently across his path.

'I do hope I am only fashionably late,' she announced. 'I come bearing gifts. Clearwater, you remember my nephew, Cadwell?'

As soon as the man entered the room, Archer's face lit up like the chandelier. He put down his glass, nearly missing the table, and strode towards Roxton with open arms. Thomas, watching silently from the sideboard, raised his eyebrows at the greeting, and even Silas found it unusual that the two fell into an embrace. It wasn't the hug of old comrades either, but the kind usually given by parents reunited with a child they thought lost. Silas was surprised, but relieved, that they didn't kiss.

'Caddy! You old cad,' Archer boomed.

They admired each other at arm's length, eyes dancing, smiles fixed. They were of similar age, but Roxton was taller, and whereas Archer had a thick mane of hair, Roxton's was already receding. Not quite as dramatically as Marks, but it wouldn't be long.

'Six years is it?' Roxton said.

'I can tell you exactly,' Archer replied. 'November the twenty-fifth, eighty-two. Savoy Theatre, opening night of Iolanthe. You were superb.'

'Oh, my God! That dinner afterwards.'

'Simpsons in the Strand.'

'Did you enjoy the trout?'

'That's no way to talk about the contralto.'

They roared with laughter at the shared memory, shaking their heads in wonder.

'It's been too long,' Archer said.

'And it has been too long since you gave us your performance, Clearwater,' Lady Marshall tutted.

Archer was still smiling at Roxton as if he couldn't believe he was there. 'Performance of what?'

'A man with manners.' Her Ladyship clipped his ear.

'My fault,' Roxton declared, and threw himself on his audience. 'Hello.' He greeted Mrs Marks with deep interest edged with concern, and gasped when he moved on quickly to Miss Arnold.

The actress, until then a model of calm, became nervous at meeting such an esteemed and not unattractive, star of the stage. She fumbled her curtsy.

'I hear you are to debut as an actress,' Roxton enthused. 'What is to be the play?'

'Toyless and Watercress,' Lady Marshall quipped, glaring at Mrs Marks who occupied her preferred seat.

'Troilus and Cressida,' Miss Arnold said, with a coquettish lowering of her head.

'Gosh. I can see you as more of a Rosalind. You have the beauty, but also that rare, manly poise needed for Ganymede. Honoured to meet you, Miss Arnold, but I can't help thinking we have met before.'

'I don't think so, Mr Roxton,' she replied, blinking fiercely. 'I have not yet had my debut, but the honour is mine.' She offered her delicate fingers for his attention, and he kissed her glove.

'A pleasure, Madam.'

'The pleasure is all mine, Mr Roxton.' She turned away demurely and sat.

Roxton greeted the men more formally. 'Doctor Markland,' he said, bowing. 'Your reputation precedes you.'

'As does yours, Sir.'

'And Marks.'

They shook hands while Lady Marshall greeted the other guests, and Thomas offered his tray. Silas hung back at the sideboard, intrigued by the opera singer. He must have seen his face in a brochure, or on a poster as they had never met, and yet, there was something about him he recognised, as there was with Miss Arnold. Perhaps it was a talent every actor had, he thought — an ability to be familiar with strangers as a way of putting them at their ease.

Silas, however, was far from easy, and it wasn't until Archer brought Roxton to meet him that he understood why.

'May I present my assistant,' he said. 'Silas Hawkins.'

Silas' hand was grabbed, pumped and held as Roxton stared deeply into his eyes. 'Have you been with His Lordship long?'

'Not long, Sir, no.'

The man's hand was warm, and his grip was powerful. He stood several inches taller than Silas, broad in the chest, but not overweight, and had he not known otherwise, Silas would have thought him an athlete, a swimmer perhaps.

'Her Ladyship speaks very highly of you,' Roxton said, indicating Lady Marshall. 'What were you doing before?'

Silas' blood ran cold, but his skin glowed hot. He looked at Archer for help, not because he wasn't allowed to tell Roxton the truth, but because he was confused. He was sure he knew this man, but couldn't place how, and trying to remember was sapping his concentration.

'We can go into all that after dinner,' Archer said, saving him. 'Now, Caddy, come and chat to Marks, he has questions regarding the speech and we should get the boring things dealt with first. Excuse us, Hawkins.' He gave Silas another quizzical look as he led the singer away, glancing back over his shoulder and mouthing 'What?'

Silas adjusted his expression from shock to interest as Markland approached.

'Is everything alright, Silas?' he whispered, leaning close to his ear as he put down his glass. 'You are pale.'

Silas swallowed. No, everything was not alright, but he couldn't explain it to the doctor.

'Just a bit hungry,' he replied, his eyes fixed on Roxton.

'You seem concerned.'

'Ah well.' Silas' gaze returned to Miss Arnold. 'Things aren't always what they seem, are they?'

Markland stood back questioningly.

'Ignore me,' Silas apologised. 'I'm thinking aloud.'

Reassured, the doctor managed a sympathetic nod and returned to Roxton. The doctor must have said something funny, because the singer let loose a piercing, high guffaw. It rang through the room, darted among the chandeliers and crashed into Silas' ears. To everyone else, it was an eccentric, affected laugh, but to Silas it resounded like the clang of a bell, shattering his intrigue in Miss Arnold and leaving his mind clear to remember where he had seen Roxton.

Where he *thought* he had seen him.

He was dredging his memory when the dinner gong sounded, and James reappeared.

'Ladies…' Archer spread his arms to the assembled company. 'Gentlemen. As you know, we do things differently at Clearwater. Thus, Lady Marshall, would you and Cadwell lead us in? Mrs Marks, Miss Arnold?' He herded his guests towards the hall. 'Mr Hawkins?'

Silas joined him as James processed the others to the dining room.

'Having fun?' Archer whispered.

'Interesting.'

'Don't be concerned at the way Cadwell and I are together,' Archer said. 'We are old friends, and we haven't seen each other for a long time.'

'That's alright,' Silas smiled. 'But is it right that you and I go in to dinner together? I mean, like a couple?'

'We are a couple.' Archer nudged him. 'A couple of friends sharing my house, outwardly respectable and nothing out of the ordinary.'

Archer was right. They had nothing to be ashamed of.

When it came to Cadwell Roxton, however, he was not so sure.

Six

Crossing the hall, Silas' gaze fell on the cloak hooks in the vestibule. Roxton's black coat was there, hanging neatly and displaying its unusual, red velvet collar. The sight continued to pull a loose thread at the back of his mind as he skirted the round table a step behind Archer until he was once again distracted by Lady Marshall.

'It appears I am to be everyone's mistress,' she laughed, as they entered the dining room.

Although it was not her house, Lady Marshall played the role of hostess while Archer played host, taking the head of the table with his godmother opposite. He seated Roxton to his right as the guest of honour, with Silas to his left. Silas was grateful. Since living with the viscount, he had only attended informal dinners, and being close to Archer brought security. Thomas and James had done their master proud. The table was as dazzling as the rest of the house, and there were more knives and forks than Silas knew what to do with. If in doubt, Archer would silently help him do the right thing.

Mrs Marks was planted between Markland and Roxton, but as Archer and his old friend had much catching up to do, it fell to the doctor to quell the large lady's enthusiasm for snobbery, and she was politely reminded of its unattractiveness several times during the four courses.

The talk was mainly of the upcoming gala and how Archer's party were to take a backstage tour during the interval. The viscount had made the arrangements that day, and once enough delighted surprise had circled the table, the conversation turned to Roxton's part in promoting the charitable mission.

Although Silas was as keen as anyone to see the project succeed, he quickly tired of the chat, having heard most of it before. Beside him, Miss Arnold said little, for which he was grateful. She was more intent on watching the opera singer with dewy eyes and a deep inquisitiveness which Silas found unsettling. Her intrigue allowed him to enjoy his meal alone and watch Thomas and James expertly serve and clear, but the black and red coat nagged at him. During one of the quieter moments among the praise for Mrs Flintwich's cooking, his mind wandered back to the summer.

It had been a hot August with long, dry days. The puddles, usually traps for the unwary, because they disguised potholes and blocked drains, had soaked away, and there was little to disguise the stench of the sewers. Shorter nights meant less time for renting, but Silas had seen fair trade, and he and Fecks took up a more nocturnal routine.

The rope-house was always their last resort, but with warmer evenings, people took to sleeping in the yards, and the rope-rooms were quieter, the communal pumps and taps less busy, and the East End population generally more at ease. As the temperatures rose, however, the smell of sewage and rotting rubbish became unbearable. When the yellow, acrid peasouper descended to blanket the East End with its choking smog, people took to wearing scarves across their faces, but when the days were stifling, they were worn to mask the stink of the fleets and effluent which trickled and slopped rather than flowed and sloshed in open channels.

The smell more than the lack of dark hours deterred potential punters from a few minutes of fumbled release in the alleys and ginnels, and instead, those who could afford it took their business to the molly houses. Here, they were not only away from the fumes, but also safer from detection, although should a house be raided as they frequently were, the chances of escape were fewer. For renters like Silas, the choice was between the quieter, familiar streets, or finding a house that offered reasonable security. That was no easy matter without an introduction via a renter already employed there, or an invitation from a molly-owner to join the 'parties', as nightly gatherings were euphemistically called. He knew of several and had drunk with a few of the boys who used one, but had never followed them up on their offer to attend. He had always found the idea of working at a brothel too organised and false, preferring the anonymity of the alleys, and if he was to be honest, the danger.

He was, however, tempted to consider brothel life one sweltering night in August.

Fecker had found work at the docks and good work at that. It was only temporary, but his strength and stamina put him in demand, and he was one of the few chosen daily from the line of hopefuls who gathered at the wharves. This meant that he and Silas were able to rent a room rather than hang off the rope at nights, but the long hours also meant that Silas was left on his own, Fecker being either at work or sleeping off a day's labouring.

It was on one such evening when he had a few shillings in his pocket and no need to look for trade, that he treated himself to a social night at The Ten Bells and fell into the company of a lad a few years older than himself.

His companion that evening was an affable man in his mid-twenties, reasonably well-spoken and well dressed. He wasn't out of place in the Greychurch pub, and his was a face Silas recognised, although they hadn't spoken until that night. He wore a smart jacket over a waistcoat and bow tie, his hair was neatly cut, and although he was slim, he didn't look undernourished, despite his pockmarked face.

'Mind if I sit with you?' he said, opening the conversation.

'Help yourself.' Silas offered the opposite chair.

The pub wasn't busy, it was early evening, and the last of the daylight was visible through the etched windows. Without Fecks, he had no-one to talk to, and if the man wasn't a potential punter — he never said no to easy money — at least there might be conversation.

Around them the bar hummed with dull chatter. The working girls had not yet arrived. Although many of them inhabited the pub from opening time to closing, filling the smoky air with cackles and swearing, bawdy talk and competition, they like many others were making the most of the fair weather and plying their trade down by the river.

'The name's Billy,' Silas said, using his false name as he always did when meeting someone new.

'Eddie.' His companion lowered his lanky frame into the chair and put down his beer. 'I've seen you in here before.'

'Yeah,' Silas nodded. 'It's my office, same as many.'

Eddie grinned, understanding his meaning. 'One way of putting it,' he said. 'Been working long?'

It was not unusual for renters to discuss their work as though it was something commendable that offered a career path.

'Nearly four years. You?'

'Oh, I've been working since I was nine.'

'Nine?' Silas was stunned, and it took a fair amount to shock him. 'Get away with you, man.'

'Not like that.' Eddie laughed. His grey eyes wrinkled, and his cheeks filled. 'I'm not a renter.'

'Looking for one?'

'Not exactly.'

'What does that mean?'

'I work as a messenger.' Eddie brushed his hands up and down his jacket as if showing off a uniform. 'Been doing it since I was nine, see.'

The lad's clean-cut appearance suggested he would have been more at home in one of the middle-class boroughs, but the more comfortable he became with Silas, the more his accent slipped to reveal a harder, less educated voice.

'So why are you in Greychurch?' Silas queried.

'Having a drink, meeting new mates.'

Eddie winked to convey a meaning Silas couldn't read. He raised his eyebrows by way of a reply.

'I turn a few bob scouting,' Eddie said, lowering his voice unnecessarily. 'You must get fed up with tramping the streets. Can't be any fun.'

That was true enough. Silas had warmed to him, but without knowing his purpose, remained guarded.

'You have no idea,' he said.

'Actually, I do.' Eddie took a sip of beer. 'It's what I do most days from morning until night, but at least I'm guaranteed a pay packet. What's your real name?'

The question caught Silas off guard, and he almost gave himself away with a chuckle. 'Billy,' he said. He didn't know this man well enough to come clean. 'What's yours?'

'Oh, mine's Eddie. I've got nothing to hide. 'Eddie Lovemount.' He stuck out his hand.

'You're making that up.'

'No, mate, honest. Edward Lovemount at your service.'

'And what service would that be?'

'Making you money.' Eddie's hand was still waiting.

Silas took it briefly before picking up his glass of gin.

'I'll get you another,' Eddie said, rising to his feet.

'Why?'

'So you'll feel obliged to listen to my proposition.'

Silas liked his honesty, and when a fresh glass was delivered, heard what Lovemount had to say.

The proposal was a simple one. Silas could earn money from working in a molly house. He would have protection, he could earn more than on the streets, be more comfortable and safer. He would, though, have to give most of his earnings to the house, but even then, Eddie said, he would be walking away with more than he could make during a night on the streets.

'You don't know what I earn,' Silas countered warily. The word 'protection' had set his ears pricking. It was usually a precursor to a threat. 'I ain't paying for protection. I don't need it.'

'Oh, I don't mean like that,' Eddie sounded genuine enough. 'I mean from snoops and busybodies, the rozzers and the beak.'

'I don't need no insurance against the law neither.' Silas remained firm. 'I've been in and out of City Street station loads of times, and although they bring me in, they never let me out. I do that on me own.'

'You look like a slippery customer.'

'Yeah, well I'm good with slippery customers and all. Thanks mate, but I'm not interested in joining a molly. I work alone.'

'Fair enough,' Eddie said. 'But let me ask you this. Do you enjoy what you do?'

He came to sit beside Silas on the bench, facing the bar as if he wanted to see who might be listening.

'How do you mean?' Silas shifted to give him room. The man wasn't unattractive, but his dark features suggested he could easily turn from friendly to fierce. He was, however, wearing skin-tight breeches that left no doubt as to his manliness.

'I can see from where you're looking that you're interested,' Eddie said, as he slipped into the seat. 'I don't mind you looking, mate, but if you want to play, you have to pay.'

'Seen it before,' Silas said, doing his best to be unimpressed. 'Me best mate's got more than that to show for himself, and I get to see it regular.'

'Your man, is he?'

'Aye, but not like that. Just mates. Unless we're working together.'

'You've got the right attitude,' Eddie said. 'You got a good prick?'

'Works for me.'

'How big?'

'Why's that important?'

'Some gentlemen pay loads for big dicks.'

'Then they'd be paying me an average amount.'

'Definitely got the right attitude.'

Eddie was impressed, but Silas was giving away too much. He found the man so easy to talk to, he had to hold himself back from displaying trust.

'I do whatever needs to be done,' he said. 'Like this.' He put down his drink and turned sideways to face the man. 'What are you after? You want to fuck me? If you do, I charge. You want me to sign-up to a molly house? You can forget it. You want to be mates? Then stop fucking around and talk about something else. Over to you, lanky-boy.'

There was no flash of anger, if anything, Eddie was impressed.

'Your black hair,' he said. 'Irish I guess from your accent. Blue eyes... Men like blue eyes. Not to mention your age. Twenty-four?'

Silas shook his head. Everyone thought he was older than his years. It was something to do with living on the streets.

'Twenty-five?'

'Leave it out. Nineteen.'

Eddie's expansive jaw dropped, and he wrapped long fingers around his glass before lifting it to his lips. He studied Silas over the rim as he took a gulp.

'It's extra shillings if you make them think they're your first, keep it tight and squeal a lot,' he said.

'Get away with you.'

'No, honest.'

'How many shillings?'

'Maybe a sovereign if you're lucky. Some goes to the house, of course, but if you're up for turning four in one night…'

Tempting. Silas could turn four tricks in a night and pretend that each one was his first time. He'd been renting since he was sixteen, and faking innocence came with the job.

'Yeah,' he said. 'But how much goes to the madam, and how much to me? I still say no thanks, mate. Good luck with your search.'

'At least come and have a look. I'll get the cab, and I'll get you one back after if you don't like what you see. Danvers is having a party tonight, and if we hurry, we'll be early there and you'll get the best punters.'

Silas said no for what he thought would be the final time, but all the same, an hour later, found himself in the hallway of a stranger's house in the West End.

'Oh, what treasure is this?' the molly owner said, as he emerged from behind a beaded curtain. His face was powdered, and he smelt of women's perfume; an immediate turn-off for Silas. If that wasn't bad enough, he fawned and touched him as if he was already owned goods, feeling his soft cock through his grubby trousers and fingering his hair.

'This is Billy,' Lovemount said, standing back. He watched in silence, only raising a smile of encouragement when Silas glared.

Mrs Danvers, as the effeminate host liked to be called, was good enough to offer Silas a bath and find him some alternative clothing on the understanding that Silas would stay and consider the offer of being a kept boy. The bath was memorable, but he was only allowed a few minutes in it, and he left it black and scum-covered before dressing in second-hand underwear, trousers and a shirt far too flouncy for his liking. More intrigued than excited, he joined Eddie in the 'salon', a pokey back room draped in exotic fabrics where lamps burned dimly under red shades, and the smell of stale tobacco clung to the furniture. At least he was given a warming glass of gin while he waited.

After a short while, another boy joined them. From what Silas could see beneath his long, straggly hair, he was no older than sixteen. He was sallow and withdrawn and turned his face away using his fringe as a pair of curtains. With his legs curled beneath him in an armchair, he fiddled nervously with his nails, his head down. The fact that he was naked went unmentioned by the other boys who arrived one by one. They ignored him, and that, Silas assumed, was what the gaunt lad was hoping for.

Danvers swished into the room. He had applied more makeup and added a floral hat. Silas' stomach turned over.

'Our gentlemen are upon us,' the madam announced, with a clap of his hands. 'Thank you, Edward, I need you on the door.'

Eddie gave Silas a thumbs-up and left. The other boys, who had ignored him, tidied their appearance, draped themselves together in pairs and began playing with each other. One boy lit a pipe, sending acrid smoke drifting through the hushed atmosphere. Within a few minutes he was glassy-eyed and swaying with the effects of opium.

Silas stood to leave.

'Where are you going?' Danvers blocked the doorway.

'This ain't for me, man,' Silas said, trying to pass.

'Stay, my boy.' The man clutched his chin and dragged his face close. 'You don't know the pleasures you will miss.'

'Reckon I do.' Silas pushed his arm away with enough force to show he wasn't scared. 'I know what I'm doing, and I know what you're doing too. Excuse me.'

The man was floored, and Silas guessed he'd never had anyone refuse his offers. The owner's stunned silence gave him time enough to leave the room, but as he passed, he was halted by the sight of the plaintive, naked boy in the armchair.

'You alright, mate?' he asked, one eye on Danvers in case he turned nasty.

'He's fine,' the man said. 'Young Stella has her favourite gentlemen calling shortly.' The voice was patronising.

The boy woke up, and through the drape of hair, Silas thought he saw the edge of a smile. The lad nearest him offered the opium pipe, and he took it to suck gratefully. As he did so, he stood to rearrange his hairless legs, turning and revealing his back. It was striped with red welts, some raw, some healing. They ran from the base of his spine to his shoulders in unbroken lines of torn skin, some recent, others older and faded.

Sickened, Silas looked away. 'I'll bring your clothes back when I find others,' he said, and leaving Danvers no time to protest, walked confidently from the salon.

His self-assurance came from anger, but turned to intrigue when he entered the hallway. Eddie was just closing the door behind a cloaked man who was in the process of removing his hat.

The man was tall, well-built and athletic. His receding hair was dark and fashionably cut, his clothes suggested wealth, and he carried himself with the poise of a gentleman. Silas couldn't see his face for a scarf he wore covering his mouth and nose, but he heard his voice. Deep and croaky, it somehow didn't match his appearance, and he wondered if it was put on.

'Good evening, Edward,' he said, coughing. 'Bring me Stella. A room away from the others. Don't want to disturb the neighbours.'

'Of course, Sir.' As Eddie took his cloak, he noticed Silas waiting for them to clear the exit. 'Unless you would like someone new?'

He thumbed towards Silas who dropped his head as the man turned. He didn't even want to be seen in the place. The house had left him with an unease that he would only shed once he was back on familiar streets with Fecker.

'No,' the gentleman said, and headed for the stairs. 'Tell Stella to bring me a pipe and Champagne along with my belts. She knows the role.'

The last Silas remembered was a shrill, piercing laugh filling the house as he closed the door. The gentleman, no doubt, ecstatic at the pleasure he was about to receive when inflicting pain on the silent boy.

Silas had only caught a fleeting glimpse of the punter, but, as James cleared his plate, he raised his eyes to the opera singer. He couldn't be certain Cadwell Roxton was the same man. The past was out of tune and muffled through the memory of too many punters. What he was sure of, however, were the scars on the boy's back. No wonder he used opium. It must have taken a lot of it to numb the sting of the lash.

He was also certain that beneath the man's cloak, he had been wearing a black overcoat with a red velvet collar.

Archer was deep in a passionate conversation with his old friend, and Silas watched from the corner of his eye.

'Of course! That's exactly what we feel,' the viscount was saying. 'I am so glad you are of the same opinion, Caddy.'

Roxton gripped Archer's hand, and the viscount didn't pull away.

'Anything, Clearwater, you know that. I may not be of the same persuasion as you, but I, as everyone else, am abhorred by the advantage those men take over those poor boys.'

Silas' eyes narrowed.

'And what does Mrs Roxton think of your involvement?'

'Oh, she doesn't mind what I do,' Roxton dismissed his absent wife. 'She was sorry not to be here this evening, but her condition keeps her confined.'

'She is with child?' Archer added his other hand, clutching Roxton delightedly with both.

'Sadly, no.' Roxton leant, and whispered privately.

'Ah. I see.' Archer nodded sadly, patted Roxton's hand, and let go. 'Right. Well, while you are in town, we must dine at the club. There's so much to catch up on.'

'I'll take you up on that, Archie.' Roxton sat back to allow Thomas to place his next course. 'When rehearsals permit. If, of course, Signora Campanelli will lower herself to attend.'

Miss Arnold distracted Silas by asking him about the location of the charity's mission, but he kept his eye on Roxton while he answered. Archer and the singer might only be reminiscing, but they were over-familiar. Silas could see past that, he trusted Archer. On the other hand, he hadn't known him long, and Roxton's marriage might be a convenient cover for a darker, hidden life.

Miss Arnold was served and left Silas in peace just in time to hear Roxton's reply to a question.

'Yes, Archie. Definitely. As I said, we must do all we can to keep those molly boys in good shape.'

It was the tone which made Silas' blood curdle. Roxton considered molly boys things to be kept up to scratch, and he said so with a flippancy that came from familiarity, as if the boys he referred to were his personal staff. *Not be of the same persuasion*; Silas' 'kind' were patronisingly dismissed. The advantage *those men* take, spoken as if Roxton wasn't himself one of the kind he sneered at. Those boys, not men, not even youths, but boys. Naked, drugged and damaged.

Silas was more convinced. The mouthpiece of Archer's good works, the friend once again holding his hand, was the same punter who called for his opium, his whipping boy and his belts.

'Everything alright, Sir?' James whispered as he placed Silas' plate.

'Why?' Silas replied through gritted teeth, glaring at the opera singer.

'You're about to crush your wine glass.' James covertly touched his wrist. 'Whatever it is, let it go before you hurt yourself.'

Seven

James carried the last of the dishes to the butler's pantry and set them on the table with the others. Lady Marshall had sent one of her footmen to help below stairs, and Oleg was currently washing the crockery. A giant of a man, even the serving dishes were small in his hands, but he was careful, almost prissy about the way he washed and rinsed.

'Last ones,' James said, picking up a towel.

'You go up.' The Russian threw his head skywards where it almost brushed the ceiling. 'I do this.'

'Are you sure?'

'Tell Mr Payne I go afterwards.'

James was more than happy to let him finish the task, it shaved half an hour off his work time and left him free to help Thomas.

The ladies and Roxton had moved to the drawing room, the gentlemen to the study to smoke, and having served coffee, Thomas joined James at the dining table where he was brushing the cloth.

'Good job,' Thomas said. 'Nothing went wrong.'

'I enjoyed myself.' James dusted off his hands at the fire. 'Did I do alright?'

'You always do alright,' Thomas said, straightening the already neatened chairs. 'What were you whispering to Mr Hawkins?'

'Blimey, you don't miss much.'

'Was there a problem?'

'No. I was asking him if he wanted more wine.'

Thomas fixed him with his piercing green stare. He didn't believe it, and James knew better than to lie. Besides, the wine was the butler's domain.

'No, actually,' he said. He was unable to keep anything from Thomas. 'He was angry about something and looked like he was going to break his glass.'

'Whatever you said, it worked.' The table done, Thomas closed the window shutters. 'But it's really not our business.'

'You asked.'

'We'll talk about it upstairs.' Thomas looked across the hall to the open drawing room. Lady Marshall was centre stage telling a story, and laughter rippled across the rugs. Seeing the coast was clear, he took a long way around to the next window, passing James and whispering, 'Later, in my room, if you'd like.'

A familiar tingle ran through the footman, flicking his heart into a faster beat and weakening his knees. He knelt to see to the fire, but watched Thomas' fine figure as he crossed the room. Everything about him was handsome. His sculptured, auburn hair was never out of place, and his perfectly fitting tails drew the eye down from his strong shoulders to his slim waist. His frame was alluring enough from behind, even though his uniform tails covered what James now knew to be a toned and smooth backside, but the sight from the front always set his pulse racing. Thomas' lean face, serious expression and those jewels for eyes were dreamy enough, but his regal bearing and trim figure simply added to the spectacle. The room was warm, and the servants had been up and down stairs all evening, Thomas' cheeks were flushed, highlighting his freckles. James loved every single one of them, and the ones he had on his shoulders. He loved Thomas' mild lisp too, but the crowning glory lay between his flat stomach and his powerful thighs. James only needed to see the bulge of Thomas' trousers for his own cock to start nagging. It had been like that since they'd first met, but now he knew what lay behind the stretched material, his excitement was no longer tempered with erotic curiosity, it was hardened with lust.

'What time do you think we'll be finished?' he asked, knocking the embers through the grate with the poker.

'One of us will have to stay and lock up,' Thomas said. 'And it depends if His Lordship needs valeting. Has Mr Hawkins asked for you to attend him later?'

'He hasn't said, but I expect so.'

Thomas dropped the bar across the shutters and pulled the curtains. 'Finish in here,' he said, throwing his critical eyes around the room. 'Then come downstairs for a cup of tea. No need to make up the fire. Is it out?'

'Yes, Mr Payne.'

James stood and collected the gloves he had used for serving, threw his towel across his arm and was about to close the doors when Silas hurried from the drawing room. He stopped and furtively thumbed towards the stairs.

'Coming?' Thomas was at the servant's door in the far corner.

'I'm needed,' James said. 'Mr Hawkins.'

Thomas bowed his head, giving permission, and James followed Silas to the staircase.

'Yes, Sir?'

Mr Hawkins was on edge, shifting his weight from one foot to the other. 'I need to speak to you,' he said, standing so close that James could smell the wine on his breath.

'Of course. Is everything alright?'

'I don't know. Can you spare a minute?'

'I am your footman, Sir, it's up to you.'

Their conversation was interrupted by a high-pitched, shrill laugh that rattled around the hall. James winced, but Mr Hawkins gasped and said, 'Fuck.'

He grabbed James' arm, tugged him onto the stairs and didn't let go until they were at the turn.

'I need your advice, Jimmy,' he said.

'Really?' James was both surprised and flattered. He'd never been asked for advice. 'About what?'

The secretary was having trouble finding the right words. He kept looking down to the hall and then at James, opening his mouth to speak and then not saying anything.

'Sir?'

'It's not easy.'

James could only see one way to break his deadlock. He passed Mr Hawkins and climbed to the landing, giving him no option but to follow. When they approached the bedroom, James stepped back to let the other man enter first. Once inside, Mr Hawkins was no less ill at ease, but at least their pretence could be dropped.

'I'll light the fire,' James said. 'It'll give me a reason to be in the room should anyone ask.'

Silas followed him to the grate as if he was a stray dog given the promise of a good home. When James knelt to attend the kindling, he drew up a footstool and rested forward with his forearms on his knees. It was time to switch roles.

'So, mate.' James spoke quietly even though the door was closed. 'What's up.'

'Thanks, Jimmy.' Silas' words came with a sigh of relief. 'I don't know what to do.'

'About what?'

'It's stupid. I always know what to do, and if I don't, I do it anyway.'

'And what is it you don't know what to do?'

'Next.'

'What?'

'I don't know what I should do next.'

James put down the log basket. 'Look,' he said. 'How about you start by telling me what's worrying you. I saw it at dinner. You don't like His Lordship's friend, do you?'

Silas regarded him from beneath his dark brows and shook his head. 'I don't know yet.'

'But something got you wound up. I could see it in your knuckles. Another second and you'd have shattered that burgundy glass. Thomas would have been outraged. Can you imagine the drama?' Making light of Silas' earlier mood didn't lift his current one.

'Yeah, thanks for that, mate,' he said, but ran straight into, 'Now I'm away from it, I feel better. I just had to get out of there.'

'Why?' James' interest turned to concern. 'What's up?'

'Nothing.' Silas sat. 'Sorry, I'm thinking aloud. I shouldn't have dragged you away.'

'No, come on,' James nudged his knee with an elbow. 'Won't go any further.'

Silas was looking off into the distance, and clamped his bottom lip under his top teeth, sucking in air and thinking. James returned to the fire. It was best to stay quiet; Silas would talk when he wanted to.

'Yeah,' the Irishman said at length. 'Sorry again.'

'Makes no matter to me,' James shrugged. 'I'm just worried about you.'

'Ah, don't be worried,' Silas smiled, falsely James thought. 'There's something I want to talk about, but I ain't sure. Can I ask you something, though?'

'You can ask me whatever you want.' James took the matches from the mantlepiece and shook the box. He would need to refill it in the morning.

'You and Thomas,' Silas said. 'You said you talk to each other, but do you talk much?'

'All the time. Below and above stairs.'

'It's the below stairs stuff, I suppose,' Silas mumbled. 'I mean when you're alone. You talk about what?'

'Everything from where we grew up to cleaning silver,' James admitted. 'We sometimes sit up until well after two in the morning just chatting about all sorts of things. His dad's farm, the problems I had at school. All and nothing I suppose. Don't you?'

'Yeah,' Silas said. 'But what if it's something… tricky?'

'We haven't come across any difficulties yet,' James said, assuming he meant an emotion like jealousy, the topic of being queer, or similar. He and Thomas never used the word, they swapped it out in sentences such as, "When did you know you were like this?" Or, "Can you imagine not being how we are?" Polite euphemisms which eased the built-in guilt of being different.

Silas was thinking again, gazing wearily at the bed. 'Once you've been physical it's hard to admit things you should have said before.'

James didn't understand. 'It shouldn't be,' he said. 'Actually, with me and Thomas, it's the other way around. It was awkward at first, seeing as how we didn't know each other and how he's my butler, but we've found a way, and now we share a lot.'

'You feel you could tell him anything?'

'I do, but it would depend on the place. If we're in the pantry, say, then I'd ask him if that coffee pot was clean enough for his liking even if I knew he had been the one who last cleaned it. I wouldn't directly criticise him for bad work, not that I've seen any. But when we're alone in our rooms, I have no trouble telling him to…' He wondered how graphic he could be and how much Thomas wouldn't want him to say.

'Yes?' Silas was waiting for an answer.

James welcomed the chance to share his excitement, wonder, call it what you will, but it might be betraying Thomas' trust to be too detailed.

'Was going to say, I have no trouble telling him what I want to try, pleasure-wise, but he might not like you knowing that.' That seemed to cover the point while also stressing the need for discretion. James thought he'd done rather well.

So did Silas. He grinned broadly and even managed a chuckle. 'Really?' he said. 'And how far has that gone? Is Tommy the bottom boy?'

'Please, you mustn't say a word,' James insisted through an embarrassed laugh. 'I'm not putting Tom down. He knows how to get me going, and we've only been doing it a few weeks, but I've got to tell someone. I'm that in awe of him.'

'What? For letting you fuck him?'

James instinctively slapped Silas' leg. 'Don't be filthy,' he gasped. 'We haven't tried that. He's worried about them new laws. I meant I'm in awe because… well, it's got to hurt, hasn't it? And yet he says he'll put up with it for me.'

'He's gone topper-over-toes for you, mate,' Silas beamed. ''Course he's going to let you do what you want. I just can't picture it, that's all.'

'And he'd rather you didn't.'

Silas drifted off again, looking at the wardrobe and nodding silently to himself.

The bawdy exchange had lifted his spirits somewhat, but James was unable to identify his problem, except to see that it was still needling him.

'What about you?' he asked, fishing for a match. 'I know I shouldn't ask, but…'

'Ah, no, you're alright.' Silas turned back, cheerful again. 'We have the same arrangement as you. We talk like this alone, but never in public. He's in charge, and that's fine by me, in fact, I learn faster 'cos I want to please him, but I don't criticise him in public. No need. When it comes to…' He pointed to the bed. 'I'm what you'd call a bottom, and he's the one telling me to tighten my arse. Bloody cheek. Like I don't know what I'm doing.' He was being playful.

'Does it hurt?' James ventured. If he didn't ask now, he'd never know. 'I'm not… built like Thomas down there. It's not going to be easy to squeeze him in, if you get me.'

'No, mate, doesn't have to hurt. Didn't even hurt me the first time 'cos Fe…' Silas sighed and swallowed, remembering an incident from his past. 'Well, it was me first time, but he was gentle. If you want to do it, and Tommy wants to, and you take it slow, then no trouble. I love it, being honest. But you should be asking Tommy about this, not me.'

'Yeah, I should,' James agreed, stung by a sharp pang of guilt. He struck a match and held it to the grate. 'Did you ask what you wanted to ask?'

'About what?'

'The reason you brought me up here,' James reminded him. 'Are you alright?'

Another sigh, this time more resigned. 'I am for now, mate. There's something I'm not sure of, and I want to ask Archer about it, but it concerns him, so it's difficult. That's all.'

'I get it.' The kindling had caught, but James watched it closely. 'Well then, as you've been good enough to ask for my advice and share some secrets with me, I'll tell you what I think.'

'Go on?'

James considered Silas as he put his words in order. The conversation had been brief, but exciting. He was aroused and hoped it had nothing to do with being alone with the man talking about sex. Silas was younger, but so much more experienced. He was pretty, for want of a better word, smooth and boyish, shining with innocence one moment and dark with knowing the next. He was alluring, and any man would be proud, not to say aroused, to have him as their lover.

Realising his stare might give the wrong impression, he attended to the fire-irons. 'I think,' he said, 'that it depends. If what you want to tell His Lordship is related to his work, then that's fair game. If it's personal, you have to find the right time and judge his mood.'

'I'll do that, mate, no question. But it's just struck me that I don't know how he'll react, because I don't know who he is. Not really.'

'Me neither,' James admitted. 'But we will. His Lordship's a book that wants to be read one page at a time. Whatever you've got to tell him, he'll thank you for being honest.'

'Yeah.' Silas nodded in agreement and with finality. 'Right, thanks again, Jimmy. Sorry to be so soft.'

Inside James, something had altered, and it was thanks to the conversation. It had lifted him from the rank of servant to the status of friend, and even if they had to play roles beyond the bedroom door, they would only be a temporary disguise. The true nature of their relationship would always lie beneath; that they were new friends bonded by similar circumstances.

James was about to thank Silas for his trust when a piano sounded from below. He felt it through the floorboards as a dull vibration of muffled notes. A tune floated up followed by a voice, clear, loud and high-pitched.

'Is that a man? Roxton?' James was incredulous. He mimed the man's height and broad chest, muscled arms and manliness.

Holding in a laugh, Silas waved his hand for silence. They listened carefully, but James could only make out vague words.

'What's he saying?' he mouthed, shrugging.

'"When I am laid in earth".'

'Cheerful.'

Silas released the laugh. 'Yeah. I better go and join the fun.'

James put the guard across the fire and stood. 'Very good, Sir. Will you require me later?'

Silas rolled his eyes and huffed a laugh. 'Sounds like you've got better things to work on,' he said looking at the ceiling. 'Don't worry about me, Jimmy.'

'Very good, Sir.' James crossed to the door, straightening an occasional table as he passed.

'Before you go.'

'Sir?'

'Can you tell me, and this is right out of nowhere, did you know many other messengers when you were at the post office? Any others like you, I mean. Like us.'

'Yes,' James admitted. 'Not intimately if you know what I mean, but some of the lads were up for it, so I was told.'

'Up for it?'

'Making money on the side.'

'I get you. You didn't, by any chance, know one by the name of Edward Lovemount, did you?'

The name gave life to a cascade of snatched, unpleasant images: Tall, lanky, a bully, an enormous cock, inviting James to sell his body, standing at a urinal, the smell of piss.

'You don't want anything to do with him,' he said. 'Why?'

74

'Doesn't matter.' Silas crossed to the door.

'Did you know him in the East End?'

'Like I said, it doesn't matter. Thanks, yeah?'

Silas was gone, leaving James intrigued and concerned.

Eight

The evening was deemed a success by Lady Marshall who called it to an end promptly at ten-thirty. Silas followed the guests from the drawing room where Thomas and James waited to help them into their coats. Miss Arnold, still in awe of the star, practically ran to help Roxton with his. Nudging James out of her way in her haste, she dropped the garment. The footman, unfazed, helped her gather it, but she fumbled it away from him and won the prize; a salacious, 'Thank you, Angel,' from the singer, which caused Markland to clear his throat pointedly.

Lady Marshall led her nephew from the house, steadying him against the effects of too much alcohol. Archer was swaying similarly, but managed to give his farewells to the others without incident before he joined Silas waiting at the bottom of the stairs.

'Ready to go up?' he asked as Archer approached.

'Oh my God!' Archer exclaimed, turning a circle with his arms spread. 'It was so good. Everything is in place for Saturday. Seeing Cadwell again. Finding him so amenable to our cause. I knew he would be. He's incredible.' He focused on Silas, but even that didn't prevent him from tacking unevenly towards the banister.

Silas was glad to see him so happy, but the niggling doubts about Archer's friend didn't allow him to share so much enthusiasm.

'You didn't tell me you played the piano,' he said, catching Archer's arm.

'I used to. Hardly touch the thing now.'

'Away with you! It was perfect.'

'You weren't there!' Archer held Silas around the waist as he was led upwards.

'Yes, I was.' Silas laughed, even though the words hurt. 'I sat at the back so I didn't put you off. He's got a good voice.'

'The best. Don't you think so?'

Silas didn't. It was high and affected as if he was impersonating a woman. He preferred a real man's voice, deep and bawdy, preferably singing a folk tale about shipwrecks and maidens, not tragedy and death. 'I do,' he said. There was no point discussing anything with Archer when he was in this mood, and yet he had something to tell him that, unless he spoke of it soon, would keep him awake through the night.

'No, I mean, don't you think so? Really?' Archer persisted.

'I said yes.'

'Everyone's going to be there to hear him.'

'And hear what he has to say about your Cheap Street Mission,' Silas reminded him.

'It will cause discussion in the newspapers,' Archer grinned. 'His performance and the subject of the speech. Our mission will be talked about openly, and we will benefit from so much publicity.'

The idea that a famous singer would speak before a performance was, according to Lady Marshall, a new thing, at least for those who attended the opera. Silas was doubtful that Archer's charitable work would be looked on charitably simply because of a speech, but he said nothing as he helped his lover to his room. Thomas had laid out his night clothes and attended the fire. Archer sat heavily on the bed, and Silas fetched him a glass of water from the bathroom.

'Are you very drunk?' he asked, as he put it beside the bed.

'I'm not drunk,' Archer protested, and, as if to show it, grabbed Silas around the waist and pulled him backwards.

Silas fell on him in a heap, doing his best to laugh through his annoyance. He rolled off, but taking advantage of Archer's now prone position, immediately leapt on him, wrapping their legs together and leaning over.

Archer tried to kiss him, but Silas pulled away wagging a finger playfully.

'How much have you had?' he asked.

'I don't know. What does it matter? Everything is perfect, and I've got you in my bed.'

'It matters 'cos I've got something on my mind.'

Archer struggled to lie on his side. Facing Silas, he said, 'He's just a friend. I love you. I know I am giddy, but it's the excitement of seeing him and hearing him sing. Isn't it the best voice?'

'Yes, I told you.'

'But isn't it though? The best?'

'Yes, Archie, it's the fecking best, now shut up and listen.'

'You're angry.'

'I'm not.' He wasn't; he was frustrated.

'Sorry.' Archer pulled a baby face and nuzzled his head.

'Yeah, alright,' Silas pushed him away. 'But honest, Archie, listen. You listening?'

Archer nodded, his forehead resting on Silas' chest.

'He has got a good voice, but I think I've heard it before.'

'Then you're lucky.'

'It's where I might have heard it that's the problem.'

Archer grunted.

'Here…' Silas rolled him onto his back and leant on one elbow as Archer tried to focus on the ceiling. 'He said he was married, right?'

'Yes. I've not met the girl. He says she's very ill. Poor man.'

Poor man? What about her? Silas let it go. 'Are you sure he's meant to be married and he's not like us?'

It took a few seconds for the words to travel from Archer's ear to his brain, but when the connection was made, he jerked his head in surprise. 'Why do you say that?'

'You're sure?'

'Well, I've never done anything with him, if that's what you're insinuating.'

'I wasn't.'

'You're jealous.'

'I'm not.' It was true. Silas didn't feel threatened by Roxton despite Archer's over-enthusiasm for the man. 'I'm not, Archie. Honest,' he said. How could he be? Archer was the most handsome, caring man in the world, and the most trustworthy. 'But I'm worried.'

'What about?'

'You might not like it.'

Archer fumbled, ploughing one arm beneath Silas and dragging him closer with the other.

'I like this,' he giggled, and gripped Silas' arse.

'Listen.' Silas stroked his face hoping it would help him concentrate. 'What if I said I might have seen him in a molly house?'

Archer blinked several times. 'I'd say you were mad. Why? Have you?'

'I'm not sure.'

'Then I am. No, you wouldn't have seen Cadwell in such a place.'

'Will you ask him?'

'No I will not!' Archer slapped his arse, agape with mock outrage. 'Anyway, so what if he has? Oh!' Outrage turned to shock. 'Have you…? I mean, you think you've…? With him?'

'No.' Silas shuddered at the thought, although in the blacked-out alleys and doorways of his past, who could tell?

'Then there's nothing to discuss.'

Not even the fact that Silas was concerned?

Archer's voice changed and became salacious. 'Undress me.'

'Not yet. Look, what if he has used a molly house? What if he's got a past?'

'For heaven's sake, man,' Archer derided. 'We all have a past. Look at mine these last two months. Look at yours.'

'You're not getting it,' Silas complained. 'What if one of them hacks snouts around and finds out he's a secret queer?'

'He'd deny it, and that would be the end of it.'

'What if he couldn't? And there he is, standing on the stage, singing your praises and encouraging the gents to hand over their cash while banging on about boys who have to turn to vice to survive, or whatever he's going to say.'

'Then good for him.'

'No, Archie.' Frustration boiled into anger. 'No good for no-one. Can't you see it in the papers? "Viscount Clearwater's raising money to keep boy-whores healthy so his friends have clean arses to fuck"? Jesus!'

'No newspaper would create such a headline.'

'You know what I mean. Can't you see it?'

Archer grinned. 'I can only see you.'

'Oh, fuck off, Archie. This is serious.'

Silas had never told him to fuck off and meant it.

'Rather fuck you,' Archer sniggered.

He wasn't taking this seriously.

'You'll end up in a scandal. I'm thinking of you, Archie.'

'And I've got dirty thoughts about you.' He tried to kiss Silas.

Silas struggled free. 'It would be in all the newspapers. You'd be ruined.'

'No-one reads those things.' Archer dismissed it, his lips still reaching. 'Only the lower classes, and what does that matter?'

Silas rolled away and stood. Archer groped for him, but his arms fell under their own weight. 'Where are you going?' he asked, his voice small and pathetic.

'Bed,' Silas said. 'If you won't do anything about it, I'll have to.'

'Come to me.'

They were the last words Silas heard from him as he left the room. They were plaintive and childlike. Archer was drunk and wouldn't remember anything in the morning. Silas could forgive him. He shouldn't have brought up the subject when he was in that state.

His own bedroom was warm and softly lit. James had been in and turned back his bed, the fire was stoked, and clean clothes were set out for the morning.

Silas rested against the door, ripped off his collar and sighed slowly, ejecting his anger and settling his thoughts. He had been right to speak with James. Archer had Thomas to confide in, Silas had Jimmy. It was too late to find him now, but they would speak in the morning. James might know a way of contacting Lovemount. He had been there the night Silas might have seen Roxton, and if he didn't remember anything, he might know the whereabouts of the boy with the scars on his back. He, more than anyone, would be able to identify the man who had marked him. If nothing else, Lovemount could tell him where the molly-house was, and he could go straight to Danvers.

His plan made, he undressed, washed and climbed naked into bed. Come the morning, his concerns would be forgotten, and he wouldn't mention them again.

At least, not to Archer.

Nine

The Times, Friday, December 2nd, 1888

Clearwater's Gala Raises Eyebrows

*T*he Clearwater Foundation has caused a stirring of feathers among society. The charity aims to assist impoverished men. Men are the breadwinners and should be encouraged to find and fulfil employment, and some have said that a charity to assist only men will strip them of their natural masculine urge to hunt and gather, procreate and provide.

The Times has now discovered the exact nature of the men the Foundation will assist, and procreation is not on their agenda.

There is, as we know, a thriving under-class in our East End. Men and boys are forced to survive by following in the footsteps of female members of the oldest profession. Whatever our thoughts on such matters, the gala is for their benefit and has already drawn a surprising amount of support from a number of wealthy donors, earning it the nickname of The Clearwater Fundation.

Whether we consider it serious or frivolous, it is, without doubt, a bold and controversial move by Lord Clearwater, and yet one that has attracted the interest and unlikely support from many an unexpected patron. Chairman of the board of trustees is Lord Clearwater's godmother, The Viscountess Delamere, a personal friend of Her Majesty and aunt of Cadwell Roxton. Lord Ribble, Earl Romney and other liberal peers, plus members of Parliament are also members of the board.

Why so much interest in such a provocative endeavour? It can only be due to the recent attention brought to those in the East End who seek the career of the 'renter' either by choice or necessity. These are the victims of The Ripper still in the headlines of today. Or at least, of two months ago as no further Ripper murders have been recorded since the 'double event' of October last. The murders may have abated, but the controversy, however, shows no signs of lessening.

But, is the timing of this gala profiteering on the part of the Foundation? It is, in our belief, not. Now is the time for the plight of the unfortunates to be made more publicly known, and we have the Ripper to thank for that if we as decent human beings can thank such a monster for anything. Viscount Clearwater, it seems, has found a way.

It has only this day been made public that the cost of admittance to seating above stalls and first circles will be paid by Lord Clearwater himself as his contribution to the Foundation's coffers. It is said that this act of generosity towards the unfortunates is itself a ploy, one engineered to prompt those in the better seats who can afford their ticket to pay more than the asking price. All profits, of course, to be donated to the cause. Whatever the strategy, it appears to have worked, and the Foundation has already raised sufficient funds to cover the performance twice over.

This is something which has caused consternation among others who seek to promote charitable endeavours. The East End Mission of the Hospital of Saint Mary, for example, has expressed concern that lines beyond the bounds of Christian charity have been crossed. 'If we are to extend our Christian goodwill to men who indulge in such unspeakables,' the Reverend Arthur McQuinn stated in a public letter, 'are we not sending a message that such behaviour is acceptable? Are we not, in effect, treating a diseased dog which should otherwise be put down?'

The Times sought an opinion from the Commissioner of Police, whose job it is to protect society from the evils of men, and a reply was furnished by Inspector Adelaide, of late swamped by the Ripper murders of course, but also a man charged with 'cleaning house' in the city's East End. Readers may be surprised to learn that the Foundation has communicated with the police throughout the refurbishment of the property, and Inspector Adelaide is himself in favour of the mission. 'When word gets around that there are safe places for these men,' he has said, 'then more will come to it and find, through the good works of the mission, that they have alternatives. I am hopeful that some of the less salubrious and organised houses [of male ill-repute] will take notice and see that their days are numbered.'

Whichever side of the thorny fence one sits, there is no denying the gala will attract a full house. The evening is to be attended by lords and ladies taking the stalls, boxes and grand tier, but the Foundation has reserved the balcony for the general public, and the gallery and 'gods' for ordinary working men and women whose home is Greychurch. As we reported last week, it is to be a night "For all people", although it is unlikely Her Majesty or the Royal Family will attend, due to the nature of the piece, and the Royal Box will stand empty.

Another intriguing aspect of the event is the announcement to be made by Mr Roxton before the performance. We cannot help but wonder if this break in tradition is another reminder from Lord Clearwater that the status quo is perhaps in need of what our American cousins call, "A shake up." A polite stirring of conscience, we British might say. We will have to wait until the speech is made before taking an opinion on its value, because the subject on which Mr Roxton will speak is a closely guarded secret.

Whatever the outcome of this most unusual spectacle, The Times shall be reporting the gala with interest.

The King Visits the Capital

King Wilhelm III, King of the Netherlands and Grand Duke of Luxembourg, will be visiting our shores from tomorrow. His Majesty, known for his eccentric behaviour, will be accompanied by the Queen Consort, but not their eight-year-old daughter Wilhelmina, and will be staying with Her Majesty here in the city.

Ten

Each time Silas woke during the night, the first thing that came to mind was his suspicion. He lay in the darkness listening to the clock ticking monotonously until sleep triumphed over his unease, only to wake a short time later, because the clamouring annoyances refused to let him rest.

He was awake when James knocked and entered, bringing a recently laundered shirt.

'Good morning, Mr Hawkins,' he said, turning up the gas before crossing the room to pull back the curtains. 'We're rain-free today, but there's a chill wind.'

James always arrived with a weather report and a friendly expression. He appeared even more cheerful than usual, and Silas flashed back to their conversation.

'Morning, Jimmy,' he said. 'Good night?'

'It was relaxing, Sir,' the footman replied.

Silas decided to take that the way it was intended. 'Good for you,' he said, smirking.

He dragged himself upright expecting to feel tired, but now he had company, his mind was suddenly less cluttered, and he was surprisingly alert. James' presence had lifted his mood and, in doing so, allowed a decision to drop into place. It had been hanging over him through the night, he realised, and now it had landed, it did so with a pump of adrenaline that fed a positive mood.

'How's things with you?'

'All good, thank you, Sir.'

The curtains open, James hung the shirt in the wardrobe before handing Silas his dressing gown.

'Would you like me to ring for coffee?'

'No, I'm alright thanks.' Silas threw back the warm sheets and was hit by cold air. He slipped into the gown as he stood.

'Are your thoughts any clearer this morning?' James asked, passing through to the adjoining bathroom to prepare the shaving table.

'Not exactly,' Silas admitted. 'But I know what I want to do next. What are you doing today?'

He joined James in the bathroom where the footman, now in the habit of acting as valet, was running warm water into a bowl. He set it on the stand beside a brush and a tub of foam and laid a towel over his arm.

'Just my usual duties,' he said. 'It's not a calling day, we're not expecting visitors.'

Silas was slowly adjusting to the routine of the house. On some days, visitors could arrive between certain hours with no appointment and no invitation. Archer was expected to be at home to receive them, a task that in most houses fell to the mistress. At Clearwater, with only one man in residence, all duties fell to Archer, and he was often absent when visitors came. The only person Silas had seen arrive unannounced was Lady Marshall. On days when Archer was not at the House of Lords, or meeting with his business manager or solicitor, he preferred to spend his days in his study, or when the weather permitted, in the park riding with Fecker and exercising the horses.

'Your plans, Sir?' James asked. He stood beside Silas with the shaving bowl in one hand, offering the brush with the other.

Silas took it and lathered his face. 'I want to talk to His Lordship first,' he said. 'But will you be free to come out with me?'

'If Mr Payne will allow it.'

'He will if I tell him. I'll let you know later.'

'Very good, Sir.'

'Are you still in touch with your old work colleagues?' Silas asked, dipping the brush and wiping off the excess foam.

'I've seen a couple of them at The White Hart on my nights off,' James admitted. 'But not often.'

'What about Lovemount?'

'He drinks at The Crown and Anchor, but I stay away these days so as to avoid Mr Tripp. You need to be careful of Lovemount.' James passed him the razor.

'Why?'

Silas regarded him in the mirror. James' ruddy-cheeked expression of healthy, boyish fun faded as he gazed back and was replaced by concern.

'I never trusted him,' he said. 'Like me, he was over the age where messengers get promoted to postmen, but unlike me, he had the chance to better himself. He never went for it, as if he didn't need the income and preferred to hang around the dispatch room with the younger lads. I think he made more money out of them than he would have done up at Mount Pleasant. I found him shifty.'

'I only met him once, and I got the same feeling,' Silas said. 'Hey, don't worry about me.'

'I can't help it.'

'Thanks, Jimmy.' Silas was warmed by his concern and winked at his reflection.

James blushed and looked away.

'Anything else, Sir?'

'No, you're alright.'

'Then I shall draw your bath and leave you to it.'

James left the shaving bowl on the stand and ran the taps before he left Silas to bathe.

Silas held the razor to his cheek. He always experienced a tingle of nervousness when he shaved. It had been a rare pleasure to find a decent blade and soap when in the East End. His shaving routine then, which he maintained daily no matter his condition, had consisted of cold water and Fecker's knife. His face was often left burning from the scrapes, but with his new life came scented soap, a warm bowl and a cut-throat that James kept sharp on a strop. He still caught the occasional nick, but this morning, the razor glided smoothly, and shaving was a joy. It also helped him put on a different persona as he washed away the night and prepared for another day as Lord Clearwater's private secretary.

'It's all just acting,' he said, as he slipped into the hot water, where he lay considering his chosen course and adding in the details.

Silas was apprehensive when he joined Archer at breakfast. There was no way of knowing what the viscount might remember of the previous evening, or how he might act. It was the first time Silas had turned him down.

He had no cause for concern. Archer behaved as if no crossed words had been said and greeted Silas as warmly as ever. Although he gave no indication that anything was wrong, Silas wanted to test the waters.

'How's your head?' he asked.

Archer glanced at James standing attentively at the end of the sideboard and turned his back.

'Was I terrible?' he asked, under his breath.

'What do you remember?'

'Playing Bruch badly as Cadwell sang, saying goodbye to Marks' dreadful wife as politely as I could, and waking up clothed on my bed. How did I get there?'

Although Silas was annoyed that he hadn't remembered the seriousness of his warning, he was also relieved. While in the bath, he had decided the time was, after all, not yet right to involve Archer, and it would be better if he knew none of Silas' intentions. Archer had other things on his mind, and Silas needed to be sure of his accusations.

Archer was waiting for an answer.

'Ah, I helped you up,' Silas said as if it was nothing. 'You were drunk, but didn't do anything to upset anyone.' It was partly true. He had behaved well with his guests, and the only person he had hurt had been Silas.

'I was over-excited…'

'To see Roxton. Yes, that was obvious.'

He changed the subject and asked about Archer's day. He was to be busy with patrons and would be out for most of the time, leaving Silas free to pursue his own business.

'I need to go out too,' he said, as they sat opposite each other to eat. 'I'll take James with me if that's alright.'

'Of course. Let Thomas know, would you, James?'

'Yes, Sir.'

The conversation continued as it did most days with general talk of the morning news. Archer liked to read the paper as he ate, but Silas preferred to watch him in silence. He loved the way Archer read, concentrating on each line, making faces when he read something he didn't approve of and occasionally laughing. The shifting of his smooth features was entertaining. He was lost in his reading, engrossed in the activities of the outside world, but he looked up to smile from time to time or to impart some piece of news.

'No more murders,' he said, turning a page. 'The Ripper is down to sheet seven.'

'Nothing about Quill?'

Archer shook his head. 'Still not been seen since he boarded that train,' he said. 'Definitely gone to Davey Jones.'

The train wreck had been mentioned in the London papers only once. Quill's name had not been attached to it, the only bodies found at the scene being the engine driver and the fireman. There had been a sighting of "Men on horseback riding the moors under darkness, as mysterious as smugglers", and the idea that the wreck had been sabotage or retribution by known criminals had taken hold. The northern papers ran the story for a week, and the last Silas heard, the police were still investigating, but there had been no repercussions. Quill had not shown up at the sanitorium in Holland and had not returned to the city. Archer might be right, and Quill had been killed in the crash, or he might have escaped justice again. Either way, there had been no more Ripper murders, and that was what mattered.

That and the hypocrite Cadwell Roxton and his sordid past. *Possibly* sordid, he reminded himself. Nothing yet was proved.

Thomas arrived to announce the morning post which Archer took with interest.

'Morning, Tommy,' Silas greeted him like a friend as he always did. It was naughty, but he enjoyed seeing Thomas' face twitch uncomfortably when he used his Christian name above stairs.

'Good morning, Mr Hawkins,' the butler replied. 'You have a letter.'

'Excellent!' Silas grabbed it from the silver tray. He had written one personal letter since moving to Clearwater, and this could only be the long-awaited reply.

He used his knife to slit the envelope and removed the thin paper contained within. Turning it towards the weak sunlight filtering through the lace curtains, he squinted to decipher the scrawled writing.

'It is what you were hoping for?' Archer asked.

'Yeah.' Silas was unable to keep the smile from his face. 'They're not dead, and Father Patrick's given me the exact place to send to.'

'You might have trouble with that,' Archer advised. He had flicked through his correspondence, but found nothing that couldn't wait until later and was paying more attention to his devilled kidneys.

'How?'

'Sending money. I assume they don't have a bank account.'

'Leave it out, Archie,' Silas laughed. ''Course they don't. They've only just got an address.'

'Are they well?'

'They're so-so. Bad chests.'

'Canter Wharf?'

'Yeah, but Mam's cousin says there's no work. I send them cash.'

'What, by post?'

'How else?'

Since moving to the city, Silas sent his twin sisters money when he could, but until now, had only managed a few pounds sent via the parish priest. He told Archer he'd also promised to buy a headstone for his mother's grave.

'Leave it with me,' Archer said. 'I have someone who does business in Westerpool. I'll arrange for them to deal with it. Just let me know how much you want to send.'

'Would you? That'd be great. I'll pay you back.'

'If you must.'

Archer had set Silas up with a bank account not long after he moved to Clearwater and paid him the standard amount for the time he put in as an assistant. After hours was, of course, unpaid, and the wages were for his secretarial duties. Although they were few and far between, he was well paid, as were all of Archer's staff.

'I'll have Culver deliver it to the girls by hand,' Archer added. 'To make sure they alone receive it and it doesn't get commandeered by anyone else.'

That was the man Silas had fallen in love with. Not the childish drunk of last night, but the warm-hearted man who did favours without being asked and thought nothing of it.

Archer returned to the newspaper, sipping coffee, and Silas reread the letter.

His sisters were suffering from breathing problems, a common complaint in the wharf-side tenements, caused and spread by the cramped and overcrowded conditions. They were unable to work and needed medicines. The last time Silas had seen them they were twelve, standing hand in hand and waving through tears as he climbed onto the roof of the stagecoach; big brother leaving to establish a better life for the family. His eyes pricked with tears now as they had done then, and he sniffed back more when he saw they had added their names to the letter within a love heart.

He put it away for later and called Thomas to the table.

'Tommy,' he said. 'I'm borrowing James for an hour this morning.'

'Of course, Sir,' Thomas replied. 'May I ask for what?'

'I'm going out in the trap when Archer's done with it.'

'I'm not going far, I'll walk,' Archer said, without looking up.

'You will need your carriage livery,' Thomas informed the footman and James nodded.

'It's only me, Tommy,' Silas said. 'No need to posh up.'

'None would disagree, Mr Hawkins,' Thomas said as if he'd won a point. 'But you are His Lordship's secretary and James, his footman. You are both his representatives.'

'We can represent without wearing all the garb,' Silas tutted, and leant over for the coffee pot.

'James?' Thomas reached the pot first and poured, forcing Silas to sit back and wait. 'It may need pressing.'

'Alright, Tommy,' Silas sighed. 'Whatever keeps you happy.'

'Just doing what's necessary, Sir.'

'You wouldn't know necessary if it sat on your face.'

'Boys,' Archer warned, smirking behind his newspaper. 'Be nice.'

James, trying hard not to laugh, pursed his lips at Silas and turned to attend to the serving dishes before Thomas noticed.

Luckily, Archer didn't ask the purpose of Silas' trip, and with the arrangements in place, Silas was able to put his mind to the questions he had for Eddie Lovemount.

Eleven

Despite the cold weather, James enjoyed riding in the trap sitting on the driving seat with Fecker, a cloak wrapped around his shoulders. Beneath it, his tails gave some protection against the biting breeze, but his nose soon began to hurt and his eyes watered. They trotted the half-mile to the postal depot in South Riverside and the closer they came, the more his excitement mounted. He didn't relish meeting Lovemount again, but he was friendly with several other messengers and hoped they were there so he could show off his new position.

He directed Fecker, who replied to instructions with shrugs, and they arrived at the back yard after an easy and pleasant ride. The air was unusually clear, the sky one shade of pale blue. It was good to be away from silver polish, washing up and the hall broom for a while, even though James was still unsure of Mr Hawkins' purpose.

Fecker drew the horse to a halt and jumped down from the bench, the trap rocking under the shift in weight. He opened the door for Silas while leaving James to fend for himself, and they stood beside the yard gate sheltering from the breeze.

'Right, Jimmy,' Silas said, rubbing his gloved hands together for warmth. 'Can you go in and see if he's there?'

'As you wish, Sir. You want me to bring him outside?'

'Yeah, it would be easier. And try not to call me Sir would you?'

'I'll try not to, but it's becoming a habit.'

'Fecks and I'll wait here.'

James crossed the empty yard, and when he entered the back office, there was no sign of any messengers, just the dispatcher.

'Bloody hell,' the man said, looking up from his desk. The sound of rhythmic clicking came from the wire room where telegrams were being received and sent. 'What's happened to you, Wright?'

'Hello, Langton.' James pulled off his gloves. 'How's tricks?'

'Same as,' the old man said. He wore a full beard that although skilfully kept, was long enough to cover his tie. His yellowing eyes were made comic by the thick glass of his round spectacles, and hunched behind his pile of envelopes and papers, he resembled a furry, burrowing creature.

There was no-one to see apart from Langton, but James parted his cloak to show off his livery.

'My new job,' he said, enjoying what he could see of the old man's surprise. 'Is Lovemount here?'

'No,' Langton said, admiring the uniform. 'Sent him out…' He glanced to the wall clock. '…half an hour ago. Should, be back soon, why?'

'Just wanted a word.' James was not prepared to tell him the exact nature of Mr Hawkins' business. He couldn't. All he knew was that Silas wanted to speak with Eddie, and that was all he needed to know. 'I'll wait outside,' he said.

When he returned to the trap, he found Silas and Fecker huddled beside it, and they climbed aboard, preferring to wait in the back beneath the hood. Fecker sat up front, buried in his greatcoat. As far as James knew, he was the only coachman to dress in that fashion. Most he had seen wore top hats and trimly-fitting, three-quarter coats. Fecker had all that, but preferred a military-style peaked cap, and always looked like he was driving into battle.

'I should tell you what we're doing,' Silas said, when they were pressed together on the seat.

'Only if you want to.'

'Yeah, I do. It's nothing bad, I hope, but I reckon I've met Lovemount before. He took me to a house back in August, and I want to ask him about someone I saw there.'

James was not uneducated, and he was observant. Apart from having to rescue one of His Lordship's crystal glasses from Silas' clutch at dinner last night, the man's behaviour through the rest of the evening had been strained, and their later conversation unorthodox, suggesting there was more on his mind than just the forthcoming gala.

'You told me to be wary of him,' Silas said. 'Why did you say that?'

There was a long history between James and Lovemount that he was not prepared to talk about. Instead, James related the story in one simple sentence. 'He tried to recruit me to work as a molly boy.'

Silas wasn't surprised. 'But you didn't?'

'Hell, no.'

'But a lot of post-boys get into that.'

Silas, if anyone, should know how the underworld of male prostitution worked. James knew his history, and when he had been told, thought no less highly of him for it. If anything, the horror stories Silas had related during the past weeks only endeared him further. How anyone could survive in the conditions he described, was a mystery to a man brought up in the semi-respectable cottages of South Riverside where the only poverty experienced was that of the ordinary working-class man. The hardships of living on the breadline were nothing compared to men like Silas who had lived below it.

'Many must,' James said. 'Delivering telegrams doesn't pay that well, and around here commissions are few and far between.'

'But you've never done it?' Silas asked again.

The idea of having sex for money made James' feel ill, but he remembered who he was sat next to and didn't make his disgust obvious.

'No, Sir. Thankfully I have never had to.'

'Ever wanted to?'

'No.'

'Good for you, mate.' Silas nudged him. 'It's not all it's cracked up to be.' He laughed, but James didn't understand why.

They sat in silence watching messengers returning from their deliveries, but Lovemount was not among them.

'How's things with Tommy after our chat?' Silas asked. 'Did you talk to him?'

James felt his cheeks redden. 'I did,' he said quietly, although there was no-one to hear.

Admitting his love of men inside Clearwater House had taken time to get used to, despite the way such things were discussed openly and without judgement, at least by the men of Archer's close circle, but talking about it in the open, he felt unprotected. With the hefty Ukrainian guarding them like a stone lion, and with Silas, street-clever beside him, there was no necessity to to worry.

He was protected and any unease was of his own making.

'And?' Silas encouraged.

'One step at a time,' he said, repeating Thomas' words when he had broached the subject of more intimate sex.

'You mean one finger at a time?'

'Oh, please!' James protested the vulgarity, but couldn't help sniggering. 'Something like that.'

'That's a start, mate,' Silas said. 'There's plenty else you can get up to, and it's not the be all and end all.'

'It?' James knew perfectly well what he meant, but Silas was the only person he could discuss the subject with, and as he couldn't bring up the conversation himself, he took his chance to learn more whenever he could.

Silas was describing some eye-opening experiences of his own when a movement at the gates caught James' eye.

'There he is,' he said, only half-glad to end the discussion of man-with-man sex. 'Wait here.'

He climbed from the trap, put his fingers in his mouth and whistled to catch Lovemount's attention. When the messenger noticed him, his scraggy face broke into a taunting smile.

'Blimey!' he exclaimed. 'Look who it ain't.'

'Yeah, well look who it is and all.' James approached. 'Got a minute?'

'Got a shilling?'

'Get over here.'

Lovemount saw the trap, and his head jolted in shock at the sight of Fecker towering above. He leant his bicycle against the wall.

'What you up to?' he asked nervously as he joined James by the horse.

'Got a new job, ain't I?' James flicked one fall of his cloak over his shoulder to show the livery beneath. 'But that ain't why I'm here.' He had slipped into his natural voice without realising. Lovemount's presence angered him. There was a history between them, incidents which James preferred to forget.

Lovemount was surprised to see his old colleague elevated in station, but he was confused when Silas stepped down from the trap.

'Here,' he said. 'I know you, don't I?'

'Mr Hawkins requires a word,' James said. 'Shall I leave you alone, Sir?'

'No, James,' Silas replied. 'We'll all talk right here.' He stood directly beneath Fecker as if he needed his bodyguard close.

'Mr Lovemount.' Silas offered his hand, and Lovemount took it, his face set in a quizzical twist. 'You remember me?'

'Your face rings a bell.'

'A bell, *Sir*,' James corrected.

'Ah, Jimmy, if me memory's right, this ain't no Sir. What you doing all togged up, Irish?'

James bristled and was impressed that Silas kept a calm head.

'I want to ask you something delicate.' Silas ignored the jibe. 'Mr Wright tells me you are a man who can be trusted.' That wasn't true, but Silas knew what he was doing. 'He also tells me you are a man with knowledge of a certain house and its customers.'

'We calls them occupiers in residence,' Lovemount said grandly.

'I don't mean where you deliver telegrams,' Silas clarified. 'A house you took me to one night last August.'

'I don't remember that.' Lovemount was immediately defensive, proving to James that he knew exactly what was being discussed.

'I'm not here to judge you.' Silas sounded like the viscount. 'I am here for information of a delicate nature, and I will reward you for your honesty. I shan't keep you long.'

His well-spoken accent and flowing words didn't impress the messenger. He became suspicious.

'Depends on what information you're talking about,' he said. 'I can't tell you nothing about me deliveries.'

'I don't see why not,' Silas countered. 'I was one such delivery.'

'Don't know what you mean.'

'Surely your memory is not that short?'

'Nothing short about him,' James put in. Lovemount was never going to open up if Silas treated him like an idiot, and his tone implied that he thought of him as one. 'That's how he makes his bit on the side. Ain't it, Eddie?'

Silas understood, and changed his tone.

'Yeah, Eddie,' he said. 'We're pretty much the same you and me. Now, for the sake of old times back in Greychurch, what d'you remember about that night.'

'Nothing.'

Silas took a wallet from his pocket and thumbed through banknotes. Lovemount's eyes widened to the size of saucers, and his attitude changed immediately.

'What night was it, Sir?'

'It was August,' Silas said. 'The hot week. We met in The Ten Bells, and you took me to a house run by a man called Danvers. Remember that?'

Lovemount's eyes shifted from Silas to James who moved his own to look at Fecker. Lovemount followed and when he saw the coachman glaring down at him and tapping his whip in the palm of a hand, swallowed and turned his nervous attention to Silas.

'I might know that place,' he said. 'But you ain't to tell no-one.'

'We won't, Eddie,' James reassured him. The man was firmly caught between greed and cowardice, he just needed a little more persuading. 'Mr Hawkins is a good man. Remember when you met him? Look at him now. You can trust him.'

'Do you, Jimmy?'

'Totally, mate. Go on. You'll get a tip.'

Lovemount looked at his watch before taking a ready-rolled cigarette from his pocket and lighting it.

'Got to say first off,' he said. 'I don't know what you're talking about, and I was never here. I got caught up on a delivery. That's why I'm late back.' He looked knowingly at James.

'If Langton ever says anything, I'll tell him I called by to catch up on the backchat,' James said. 'Blame me for your being late, he knows I'm here.'

Lovemount's eyes smothered James with doubt before they narrowed, and he took a long drag of his cigarette.

'You ain't working for Adelaide, are you?' he asked, transferring his mistrust to Silas.

'I reckon you know that ain't never going to happen, Eddie,' Silas laughed. He dropped his impersonation of a gentleman, presumably to put Lovemount at his ease.

'Only, I heard that now the Ripper's gone quiet, he's onto Danvers. Different case, of course, and behind the scenes.'

'Why? Has something happened at this house?'

'All kinds of strange things happen in houses,' Lovemount said.

'Not saying I know nothing about them, but that place ain't one I care to talk about much. Not right now.'

Silas ran coins noisily through his fingers.

'You've already incriminated yourself, Eddie.' James was unable to hide a smirk. 'Besides, I know what you get up to in the restroom with the new lads. I could do with a few shillings for my silence, but information will do as payment.'

Silas grinned and said, 'Reckon Jimmy knows quite a bit about you, Eddie. And don't worry about Adelaide. He calls at our house sometimes. I'll keep an eye on him.'

The statement, although as far as James knew not truthful, suggested Silas was offering protection or a threat, and it was up to the messenger which he chose.

Lovemount understood the seriousness of both. 'What can I tell you, Irish?' he asked, shuffling his feet and lowering his head.

'The night I was there.' Silas put away his wallet. 'There was another boy. He came in naked and had scars on his back.'

Lovemount waited for a question, but when none came, shrugged. 'And?'

'You know who I'm talking about. What was his name?'

'Stella.'

'That was it!' Silas clicked his fingers as if he had been trying to remember the name all night. 'Poor sod. Well, he was told he had a gentleman come to see him, and this geezer called for him by name. I was leaving at the time, didn't see his face, but he went upstairs to wait for Stella. Remember? He had a black coat with a red collar.'

Lovemount was thinking, and it didn't look like a pretence. His cratered face scrunched, and his eyebrows met.

'He was popular,' he said. 'Might have been anyone.'

'Was popular?' Silas queried.

'I ain't been to that house for weeks now,' Lovemount continued. 'Last time was around the second of third Ripper murder, see? Everyone was talking how the molly-houses would be next, and they wasn't safe. So I stayed away.'

'You didn't go back?'

'I did, once. I was hard-up for cash, and we'd got some new boys in.' He thumbed towards the post office. 'No need to go trawling

The Ten Bells when there's fresh faces here after making a few shillings.'

'And was Stella still there?'

'No, don't think so. Least, I didn't see her.'

'Her?'

'They call the boys by girl's names, Jimmy,' Silas explained.

'Well, that ain't right.' James shuddered.

'Nothing about it is right,' Silas said. 'Go on, Eddie.'

Lovemount smiled. Among messengers, it was seen as a mark of respect for a customer to use a Christian name. James and his friends had kept a scoresheet in their lockers. Each time a customer asked for a messenger by name, they gained a point. A Christian name, two, and the points were doubled if the customer was gentry.

'Things were different when I went back,' he said. 'The rozzers had been sniffing around 'cos...' He jerked his head, drawing his audience closer and whispered. 'Word was, some of the classier gents were drawing too much attention to the place.' He stepped back. 'I didn't want to get investigated, so stayed clear. Don't remember Stella being there.'

Silas was deep in thought, silent until James nudged him.

'Yeah,' he said, looking up. 'Cheers, Eddie. But you don't remember who Stella's man was that night?'

'She probably had a few,' Eddie said. 'Wouldn't be unusual.'

'Jimmy,' Silas said taking his arm. 'I need to ask him something, and you might be shocked. If you want to stand away, I understand.'

'No need,' James said. 'It's about last night's guest of honour, right?'

Silas nodded.

'Allow me.' James turned to Lovemount. 'Did Cadwell Roxton ever use the house?'

Impressed, Silas grinned, but the messenger's face remained expressionless.

'Dunno,' he said. 'Who's he?'

'An opera singer.'

'They get all sorts. Might have done. I don't know.'

'Are you sure?'

'Yes, Sir.' Lovemount sucked on his cigarette with a hiss, pinching the end between thumb and forefinger. He released the smoke

98

slowly. 'But I remember Stella weren't there last time I went 'cos she'd got a better job.'

'Better job?' James was aghast. 'You call it a job?'

'Jimmy', Silas sighed. 'It's a wage. Go on, Eddie. What about Stella? Where was she?'

'Dunno,' the man replied and took another drag. 'Ask Danvers, he'll know.'

'He's my next port of call.' Silas handed the man half a crown. 'Where is he?'

'At work, I should think,' Lovemount said, inspecting the coin with his teeth. 'Like I should be. Anything else?'

'Yeah.' Silas dangled another half-crown. 'What's the address?'

Lovemount snatched the money. 'Cleaver Street,' he said. 'Number nineteen, and you didn't get it from me.'

'Okay, here's what we'll do,' Silas said, once Lovemount had wheeled his bicycle into the yard. 'We'll drop you back at the house, then Fecks and I'll go and have a look at Cleaver Street.'

'I'm happy to come with you,' James volunteered. Apart from the intrigue, he was enjoying being away from his chores.

'Better not,' Silas replied. 'If that place is getting a reputation, we don't want his Lordship's livery seen in the area.'

It was a valid point. 'I'll get changed.'

'Thomas wouldn't allow it.' Silas was climbing back into the trap.

'His Lordship is out for lunch, I won't be needed.'

'Look, Jimmy,' Silas smiled. 'I'm touched you want to help, but this ain't a game, and it don't need all of us.'

'Do you know where Cleaver Street is?' James asked. Perhaps he was being too eager. If so, it was only because he wanted to help.

'Now that's a good question,' Silas said. 'No. And Fecks won't either. Can you draw a map?'

Disappointed that Silas hadn't taken the hint, James joined Fecker on the front seat.

Silas had already given away too much to the footman. James was trustworthy, but it wasn't Silas' place to take him away from his work and put him in danger. What he had in mind was something he and Fecks could see to alone; it was safer that way. He watched

James take up his place and noticed he sat with his shoulders slumped lower than before. He was only trying to be of use, and he was. He was a sensible voice in Silas' ear, here to keep his head level and lend an open mind when needed. He was Archer's footman and Thomas' junior, and much as Silas was uncomfortable having one, he was his servant. As a gentleman, Silas had a responsibility to consider his well-being, Archer had hammered that message home many a time. It confused Silas to consider himself as a gentleman, but that was what he now was, albeit one plotting to go behind another's back. Behind his lover's back at that. It was not what Archer would call sportsmanlike behaviour, but Silas hoped he would never find out. He was probably mistaken, and Danvers would confirm that Roxton was unknown at the brothel. That would put an end to his suspicions, and he could give Archer his full attention.

The trap moved off with a jolt that brought his thoughts into focus.

Even if Danvers let him in and agreed to talk, Silas couldn't trust a man who dressed like an old hag and sold boys for sex. He couldn't turn up at the house and state his true purpose or his position. Archer's name must not be mentioned or even suspected. It was risky enough to mention Roxton's, considering the publicity the gala had already attracted. Someone like Danvers wouldn't think twice about blackmail, and if the police were interested in the house, someone poking around asking about a specific punter was going to make the man clam up tighter than a prison door. Maybe driving straight there and confronting him wasn't the best thing to do.

Silas spent the rest of the journey working through other scenarios, and by the time they pulled into Clearwater Mews, he had only one viable option.

'Thanks, James,' he said, once they were out of the trap and heading for the back door.

'Are you not going straight out again?'

'No. I've thought of another way. You've been a help, though.'

'You know,' James said, giving the back of the house the once over to make sure no-one was watching. 'If you want to discuss it with me, I'm all ears. Just say.'

'Cheers, but I'll be fine.'

'Oh, alright.' Disappointment was written across that footman's face. 'Very good, Sir. Shall I bring you anything?'

'I'm sorry, mate,' Silas gripped his shoulder. 'Chatting in my room is one thing, but what I have in mind… It's best you don't know. And not a word to Archer, right?'

'If he asks, we went to send a telegram,' James suggested.

'Oh, bugger. I meant to do that.' His concern for Archer had driven his sisters' money from his mind. 'Maybe you could post a letter for me later.'

'Whatever you need, Sir.'

It was correctly spoken, but the more Silas heard himself called Sir, the more he disliked it.

'Whether it's Sir or Silas, you've got me.' James fixed him with a look of concern. 'Agreed?'

Silas considered the offer. His new plan was a simple one. To go to Cleaver Street after dark on the pretence that he had changed his mind and now wanted to work for Danvers. The madam had seen his potential in August and apparently liked what he saw. If he was still interested and engaged Silas in conversation, he might give away details about the clientele. If he was not interested, Silas would drop Stella's name and see how Danvers reacted. That way, he might find out where he was living and take his investigation there. James wouldn't need to enter the house, but after what Lovemount had said about the police keeping the place under observation, it might be useful to have a lookout. Fecks would have to park out of sight and stay with the trap. If Danvers saw Silas arrive in a private vehicle, he wouldn't believe his story, and whether he needed James' help or not, the man's calm and assured manner would help temper Silas' anger.

He relented. 'You win, Jimmy,' he said, and enjoyed the pride that spread across James' face. 'Right now, though, I reckon I need coffee in my sitting room.'

'Right away, Sir.'

'But…' Silas held him back. 'Bring a tray for two. If you're serious about helping me, Jimmy, we need to put our heads together.'

Twelve

The afternoon warmed beneath dense cloud that rolled across the city trapping factory fumes and coal-fire smoke. It clung to the buildings, each year bringing another layer that blackened the stone. Intricate detailing crafted decades before had gradually become lost beneath layers of filthy air that disguised the beauty of the stonework on private houses, banks and churches alike, as if hiding the grandeur behind a widow's veil.

Greed was the cause of the growing imperfection. As if unable to stand the beauty of the past, the factory owners and capitalists relished the pumping pollution. They held the regularly falling smog in high regard, uncaring of its long-term effects on the work of their artisan ancestors. The city's degeneration was a reminder of their success.

The peasouper thickened imperceptibly in the still night air, wrapping itself around streetlights and dulling the light until the roads became little more than a progression of softly flickering torches either side of the wide thoroughfares of Fitzrovia. People moved carefully from the cafés to carriages, feeling their way along iron railings, scarves and shawls wrapped round their faces, their irritated eyes squinting against the fog. The sound of coughing was as muffled as the cautious clatter of hooves, all sounds subdued and distorted in the thickening air.

Fecker drove the trap slowly, following directions given by James beside him, while Silas sat in the back running through his plan and looking for pitfalls. They passed grand houses, curtains drawn, gas lights burning ineffectually in the smog they contributed to, and encountered little traffic until they took the wider, fashionable Cambridge Street towards the West End. Here, carriages moved at a crawl giving passers by the opportunity to gawp at gentry on their way to the theatre, but the nosey were rewarded not with the wrappings of finery, jewels and expensive gowns, but with smudged faces and steamed windows.

As Fecker pulled left into Cleaver Street, James turned to Silas in the back, only his eyes visible beneath his scarf.

'Be coming up on the right in a minute,' he said, his words muffled.

'Go past slowly,' Silas instructed, and, sitting up, raised his collar.

He pulled down his cap more tightly, the peak shielding his eyes, and paid attention to the row of identical house fronts they passed. The street was quiet, but well-lit behind the haze, and there was enough lamplight for him to be recognised, not that he could think of anyone who would know him in this part of the city. They had brought the trap, because unlike the carriage, there was no crest on its doors. It was anonymous, but still obvious as the vehicle of a wealthy man.

James turned again, and holding his arm low, pointed to the right. Silas followed the finger and shifted to the end of the seat for a better view.

He had been to this house before and not that long ago, but he had no recollection of its frontage. Even if he had, it would be barely recognisable through the peasouper. The house was the same as the others around it, one in a terrace of respectable but ordinary four-storey buildings. Steps led to an arched porch, two windows of a reception room to one side, three symmetrical windows above, the same on the next floor and above them, barely visible, two garret windows in the sloping roof. It was a decent sized house, the kind of place a well-to-do businessman or popular writer might live, someone with enough money to run a house that would, Silas guessed, take at least four staff. It was not the kind of squalid brothel he had seen in the East End, and, from the outside, there was nothing out of the ordinary about the building.

They drove by, and Fecker took them right at the next turning before making another right to enter the alley behind the terrace. It had been six houses from number nineteen to the end of the row, and Silas asked Fecks to stop. There were no other carriages or people in the ginnel, but he didn't want to be too close to the house, just near enough that he didn't have far to run if things turned sour. He had spent the afternoon plotting with James, and together they had come up with a simple course of action. 'A quick in and out,' Silas had called it.

They had been full of bravado and daring ideas as if they had no thought for their own safety, or being discovered and shamed. Silas didn't expect trouble, and if it did come his way, he would fight it off, and Fecks would be nearby. Now they had arrived, however, the first tremors of nervousness unsettled his gut.

'It'll be easy,' he told himself as he stood. Standing behind his companions, he supported himself with one arm around Fecker and the other resting on James' shoulder, leaning in between the two. 'Wait here Fecks, I won't be long.'

'I come with you.'

'No, mate. Stick to the plan. You alright, Jimmy?'

'Yeah, fine.'

'I go, Banyak,' Fecker insisted.

'Yeah, well, if I don't get the information I need, you might get a chance to bull-in and bang about a bit, but I'd rather not resort to violence.'

Fecker shrugged.

'If there's any trouble, the signal's whistle, yeah?' Silas double checked the arrangements and his companions agreed, Fecker more reluctantly than James.

He slipped from the carriage, disturbing the thicker, lower mist at his feet and took off his coat. He passed it up to James and attended to his disguise. The scarf would come away from his face once he reached the house, it was one of James' and had smelt as old as it looked. Now it was greasy with smog, as were his bare hands which he had dirtied-up before leaving Clearwater. His clothes were the oldest and shabbiest they could find. He didn't exactly resemble the wasted street-rat who had been brought here two months ago, but it was as close as he could manage.

James jumped down from the trap. Dressed in a long overcoat, a newsboy cap and a scarf around his face, all that could be seen of him was a dark shape with two eyes.

'Ready?'

Silas nodded, and, with a last wave at Fecker, they headed back the way they had come. They paused on the corner of Cleaver Street to see how many people were about, but the pavements were quiet.

The immediate vicinity was murky beneath the struggling glow of nearby lamps, the shadows a darker shade of gaslight yellow than the road which glinted where it could, damp from the moist air.

'It's six houses down,' Silas whispered. 'You can just see it from here. Don't come closer, though. Just watch to see if anyone comes to the door after me.'

James faced him, his back to the row of houses opposite number nineteen. 'How about over there?' he asked, nudging his head backwards towards a shop. 'Deep doorway, better view.'

Silas looked. His friend was right. He could hide in the shadows and not be seen.

'Okay,' he said. 'Go now while there's no-one watching.'

'Hang on.' James held his arm. 'Your ring?'

'Oh, shit. Thanks, mate.' Silas slipped off the ring Archer had given him on his birthday. It was best not to present himself as a pauper wearing personalised jewellery. He handed it to James knowing it would safe.

'Good luck,' James said, and put it in his inside pocket.

Silas didn't need luck, just his wits, but it was good to know someone was watching out for him. They had rehearsed signals. One long whistle from James meant that someone was approaching, two meant danger. He would hear James' piercing signal probably even from beyond the door, assuming he gained entry.

He waited while James crossed the road unseen and slipped into the shop's recess, becoming one with the shadows. There was nothing out of the ordinary here, nothing to suggest the police were watching, or even close by. In fact, Silas had not seen any bobbies since leaving Riverside. All the same, Silas already had the distinct feeling that he was being watched. Remembering his last visit caused his unease to deepen.

With James in place, Silas drew in a deep breath, wished he hadn't, coughed and focused.

It was a short, eerie walk. Alone, guilt nagged at his concentration; Archer had no idea what he was doing.

The viscount was dining out with Roxton, oblivious to Silas' concerns, which he wouldn't have entertained even if Silas had been able to discuss them. When Archer found out, he would most likely be angry, or accuse Silas of mistrust. He might hate him for trying to shame Roxton, but that that wasn't his intention. His aim was to protect them both, and if he ever had to explain himself to Archer, he hoped the viscount would understand.

The thoughts were not helping, and he told himself he was not alone. James was watching, Fecks was on hand, and this was all for Archer's good.

He checked the time; ten-thirty. Archer and Roxton would have finished their dinner, but he was not expecting Archer home until well after midnight. With plenty of time, he mounted the steps to number nineteen.

A painted, wooden front door, a letter box, a bell-pull and a boot scraper. Nothing remarkable. The curtained window to his right was framed by the warm glow of lamps, and above the front door, more light welcomed callers through a semicircle of glass. Silas steadied himself and pulled the bell.

For a while, nothing happened, and he wasn't sure if the bell had worked. Perhaps there was a code? He tried to remember how he had arrived that night in August, but it had been different then. The air had been clear, the smog not yet settled, and the night had been warm. He thought the door had been green but now it was blue, and he'd probably remembered incorrectly. He checked the number; it was the right house.

There was no time to think further. Footsteps approached, and he messed up his fringe, wishing he hadn't washed his hair that morning.

The handle rattled before the door was opened by a smartly-dressed, middle-aged man wearing a smoking jacket and a round, tassel-cap on his head in the bohemian style. It was not the broad-set Danvers, but Silas was unable to see past him into the hall.

'Yes?' the man said, holding the door open only halfway.

'Evening, Sir.' Silas put on the voice of an affable Irishmen. 'I was told I might find some gentlemen here.'

'Who are you?'

'Name's Billy O'Hara.' He offered a grubby hand. 'Sorry I don't have an appointment, but Mrs Danvers knows me.'

He studied the man's reaction at the mention of the name. His grey eyebrows rose briefly, but his pale expression remained distrustful, and he didn't accept the handshake.

'I think you have the wrong address, lad,' he said.

Silas might have believed him had he not looked up and down the street as if nervous that they would be seen.

'Number nineteen?'

'What do you want?'

'To see Danvers.'

'No-one here by that name.'

Silas was worried that Lovemount had given a false address, but there was a way to test that.

'Eddie sent me.'

Another twitch of bushy grey brows suggested he had hit a nerve, but the man shook his head and started to close the door.

'Eddie Lovemount.'

The closure was halted, and half a face peeked out. The eye, tired and sagging, painted Silas with suspicion. He winked when it returned to his face.

The door opened fully, and the man stepped aside.

Silas recognised the place immediately. The same heavy drapes across the passage leading to the back, the two armchairs by a small table and a closed door behind a beaded curtain to his right. It was no doubt the same as any other entranceway to a house in this street, but the atmosphere was unmistakable. A heightened sense of anticipation in the lighting, the softness of the rug and the staircase running up one side to a dimly lit landing, the darkness beyond suggesting anonymity and temptation, it was all sickeningly familiar.

'What was your name?'

'Billy. Danvers knows me as Marjorie.' Both lies.

'We're all Marjories, dear.' The man closed the door and threw his hand to one of the chairs. 'Wait there,' he said, and when Silas was seated, ducked through the heavy curtains.

Silas held down anger as he pictured the bored faces of boys waiting silently in the salon, Stella's naked, scarred body trudging the stairs, and his own climb to the room with a bath. There had been muffled sounds from behind closed doors, fumbling and grunting, the slap of flesh, and he walked through them knowing what each one represented. They came back to him in snatched fragments of a cloudy memory. He was among the ghosts of past misdemeanours waiting for the only connection between them and his current suspicions; a man built like a blacksmith who dressed like a duchess.

He only had to wait a short while before the drapes parted and the host appeared. Or should he say, hostess? The man's face was plastered with makeup and sat too small atop a large crinoline dress of black and midnight blue. It shimmered in the lamplight and rustled as he appeared, straightening a badly-fitting wig. He stopped when he saw Silas, who stood, cap in hand, doing his best to appear lost.

Danvers stayed within the safety of the arch, the curtain held to the side by a hairy hand with painted nails. In the other, he clutched a pair of opera gloves. He drew his head back as if he didn't want to be too close to anyone less than a lord, and sneered at Silas' appearance. 'Who or what are you?'

Behind him, the passage to the salon was a tunnel of whispers Silas was unable to decipher.

'I was told you might have work for me,' he said, in the voice he had used when renting. 'Some of me mates already help you out.'

Danvers dropped the curtain but remained static. 'Don't I know you?'

'I've been here before.'

'When?'

'August. Eddie brought me.'

Danver's face, naturally crooked, skewed further as he tried to remember. He shook his head.

'You have the wrong place,' he said, a direct repeat of what Silas had been told, as if he was working from the same script.

'Not what Stella said, Ma'am.'

The change in Danver's expression proved Silas correct. This was the right house and the name Stella meant something.

'You know her?' Danvers asked.

'In a way.'

'From when?'

'A while back.'

If they were going to play a game, Silas wanted to make sure he had the upper hand. In this case, being vague was the safest strategy.

'She told you to come?'

Silas moved his head, noncommittal, letting Danvers make up the rest of the story for himself.

'Where is she?' Danvers asked.

'Was hoping you'd tell me,' Silas replied. 'She said she would bring me here, but I ain't seen her since. I need money, Mister, and I know what I'm doing.'

Danvers was not convinced. 'I don't invite just anyone to my parties,' he said, studying Silas in detail. 'You look too old for my friends, and I expect those I invite to be properly dressed.'

'I weren't the last time I came, and you was good enough to borrow me some clothes, Ma'am,' Silas said. 'I smarten up nice. Oh!' He fumbled for some change. 'Promised I'd pay you back for the garb, and this is all I got. Sorry.' He offered the money.

Danvers considered it, it was only a few shillings, but a priceless gesture.

'Keep it,' he said, warming. 'And come closer.'

Silas stood before him still wringing his cap in his best impression of a down-and-out renter in need of protection, and kept his eyes on Danver's feet which poked from beneath a beaded hem. He wore pink silk shoes and jewellery, but stank of smoke and alcohol.

'Age?'

'Younger than I look.'

'Age?'

'Eighteen, Ma'am, but I knows what I want.'

'And what's that?'

'You know. Same as the other boys.'

'A nice little scar.' Danvers touched his cheek with the back of a finger.

A large, uninvited hand cupped Silas' balls but he didn't flinch even when guilt stabbed. He blocked Archer's face from his thoughts and reminded himself he was doing this for the viscount.

'Not very big,' Danvers complained, and turned Silas around to fondle his arse. 'Firm enough I suppose. Had a cock in it?'

Despite the nausea rising from his stomach, Silas said, 'Not yet.' It was an evening of falsehoods.

'Really?' Danvers was doubtful. 'They all say that.'

Silas pulled away and turned. 'Yeah, well, I heard gents pay well for a tight arse, whether it's been used before or not. Stella told me what to expect. Ain't she here?'

'Let me see you without these.' Danvers flicked his gloves towards Silas' trousers. 'I do insist on seeing the goods before tasting them.' His tone became salacious, excited that he would be the first to examine, and probably bed, the potential recruit.

Silas had no intention of undressing.

'I want to see Stella first.'

'She's not here. I told you. She left a couple of months ago.'

'She said she'd be here tonight.'

'Then she lied. Drop your trousers.' Danvers was fiddling with the buttons.

Silas stepped away. 'Sorry, Ma'am,' he said. 'But no. Not without seeing Stella. For all I know, I might be in the wrong place.'

Danvers laughed. 'Look at me,' he said, and raising his hands in an affected manner, turned a circle. 'Does this look like the wrong place?'

'Still need to see her.'

The madam's expression changed in an instant. Fierce this time, he grabbed Silas' lapels and forcefully dragged him closer.

'She ain't here, Irish,' he spat. 'But you are. If you want to work, you've got to do as you're told. Drop your kegs and show me your young, Irish cock.' His hands were grappling more desperately. 'My gents like young and untouched. Got to make sure you ain't diseased. You ain't even getting hard.'

Nervousness blossomed into anger, and Silas pushed him away.

'No,' he said. 'Not 'less I see Stella.'

A stinging slap from nowhere jolted his head, and he bit his tongue, staggering to the side. Danvers was on him, yanking their faces together. 'How many more times I got-a tell you?' he growled, spittle and powder spraying Silas' raw cheek. 'Piss off and stop wasting my time.'

He was hurled towards the door where he stumbled, reaching out to stop himself falling.

Silas had one card left to play, and forced tears to his eyes.

'Stella said he'd be here belts and all,' he whimpered, a cowering puppy. 'He said the gentleman would pay good for me 'cos I ain't been fucked before, and I ain't a sissy.'

'Who would want you?'

Silas sheltered his face with his arms, but left enough of a gap to see clearly.

'I'm meant to meet Mr Roxton.'

Danvers was taken by surprise, and his eyes flicked to the ceiling. It was a blink, but it sent a pump of horror to Silas' heart.

'I don't know who you're talking about.' The madam made a decent job of covering his mistake, but he'd been too slow. 'Get out and don't come back.'

Silas had seen enough. It was obvious that the boy known as Stella was not at the house, but Danvers knew where she was. It was also clear that the name Roxton had wrong-footed the madam. That was enough to convince him he was right. Archer's friend was a punter.

'Alright,' he said, reaching for the door handle. 'No need to go mental on me.' A movement at the curtains stopped him.

A lad appeared, topless, his thin, pale chest glinting with sweat. He ignored Danvers as he brushed past but lifted his face to Silas. It wasn't Stella, but the boy was young and just as pallid. His breeches were undone, he wore nothing on his feet, and he carried a leather barber's strop. His shoulders hung limply as he mounted the stairs in silence.

'Out,' Danvers barked. 'I'm busy.'

'Is that Mister Roxton's new boy?'

Silas was thrown against the door, banging his head. His immediate reaction was to fight back, but he kept in character and snivelled pathetically.

'Please, Mister,' he said, shielding his face. 'I'm going. I only wanted to earn a bob or two.'

He threw open the door and fought his way free. Danvers slammed it against his back as he hurried through and Silas was sent tumbling into the street. As soon as he heard the door close, he straightened.

'Fucking eejit,' he mumbled.

Instantly composed, he pulled on his cap and cleared his throat.

He was alone except for the dim figure of James who emerged from hiding to join him as he walked towards the corner, angry but in control.

His friend followed a few paces behind until they turned into the alley.

'Are you alright?' he asked, catching up and putting an arm around Silas' shoulder.

Silas wanted to shrug it off, but it was kindly meant. 'Yeah,' he panted. 'Give us a minute.'

James helped him into the back of the trap.

'They hurt you?'

'No, Fecks. Don't worry.'

The trap swayed as Fecker stood.

'No, Fecks, honest.' Silas pulled him down. 'Leave it. We don't need to make a scene.'

'What happened?'

Silas told James what he had seen, what had taken place and how he was convinced the madam knew both Stella and Roxton. 'What's more,' he added. 'That strop looked familiar.'

'You think he's there?'

'I reckon so,' Silas said, remembering the glance to the upper floor. 'Just got the feeling. Roxton should have been with Archer, but…' He looked across to the house. 'He's been here before for sure.'

'That's enough, isn't it?' James asked.

'I don't know.'

There had been something about the leather the boy had taken upstairs, the whispering from the salon, the atmosphere. It was as if he had walked into a room where people had, until that moment, been talking about him. Blank faces radiating guilt because they had been caught… Doing what?

Running an illegal house.

That made sense of the secretive atmosphere, but what niggled him was Danver's nervous twitch and the leather strap with its brass buckles at either end. He had seen similar things in St Mary's hospital when he was taken there after the warehouse fire. In fact, the more he recalled it, the more convinced he became that it wasn't a strop, it was a restraint.

He stood to peer at the rear of the house in time to see a light extinguished at a first-floor window. The others were dark and probably closed; it was hard to tell at that distance. As far as he could see, an iron downpipe rose from the ground to the guttering four stories above, there was an area and a lean-to on one side.

'You didn't see either of them?' James whispered.

'No,' Silas said. 'Not yet. But that doesn't mean they ain't there. Fecks, lend us your horse-knife, mate, and if I'm not back in thirty minutes, Jimmy… Do whatever you think is best.'

Thirteen

Scaling the back wall was easy, as was scurrying across the yard and pressing himself against the brickwork of the house. The climb, however, was not going to be so simple. He looked down into the area where weak light spilt from the basement window, shifting in tone as someone moved about the room. There was no way in through the back door. Looking up into the milky, jaundiced gloom, he made out the uncurtained window of the first-floor landing, those either side of it dead and dark. Now he was closer, he could see that the lean-to, although offering a leg-up, was constructed from wood and tin. It would likely creak and rattle if he tried to climb it, and that left him only one option.

He gripped the downpipe with both hands and gave a hefty tug, expecting it to fall away from the bricks, but it held firm. He examined the bracket holding it in place and reassured himself that the screws were new, and nothing had rusted. Pulling his cap down tightly, he gripped the pipe, his fingers laced in the gap behind, and put one foot flat against the wall. A helpful shove from Fecker wouldn't have gone amiss, but Fecks was on guard back at the trap with James, watching from a distance and ready to whistle.

Silas doubted they could see him, but he thought it only to reassure himself. If anyone came into the yard or even the one next door and brought a light, he was a sitting duck. With no time to think about it, he leant back, hanging all his weight from the pipe, and jumped. Both feet connected with the bricks and the pipe held him. Sliding his hands to the first bracket, he climbed with his toes, shuffling his legs higher. His foot slipped, and his knee smacked painfully against the wall, but his handhold was firm. He remembered climbing down the rope at the Limehouse crane that night with Thomas. 'Hand under fist and don't look down,' he'd said. It was good advice when on a knotted rope, but it had been the sound of Tommy's voice that gave him strength, not his technique. He imaged James' voice now, encouraging him, telling him he was doing the right thing. Behind him, there was Thomas, calm and methodical, and again, telling him to go hand under fist.

Imitating the way he had descended the rope that horrible night, he crammed his toes between the pipe and the wall, twisting his legs to the correct but painful angle, and reached beyond the bracket with one hand, letting go the other and grabbing again quickly. He found a rhythm and ascended.

Making it safely to the first floor, he climbed level with the window and hung on by one hand and two wedged feet as he reached across for the recess. His fingers clutched at the corner, giving him leverage and he was able to stretch his leg to meet the sill. After that, it was a case of stepping gingerly onto the ledge and holding the casement for balance. Praying that there was no-one on the other side, he crouched to peer in. A corridor ran ahead to the top of the stairs just as he had imagined. The staircase turned and ran up another flight, and down, directly into the hall. There was no movement and pressing his ear to the glass, heard nothing.

Taking Fecker's knife from his pocket, he unfolded the blade and slipped it between the windows, sliding it along until it met with the catch. It shifted with a scratch of metal on metal as the blade pushed it into its housing. The knife back in his pocket, Silas stood, one hand pressed against the inside of the alcove for stability, the other on the glass where he drew the window open. It only needed to move an inch before he was able to slide his fingers beneath and lift it. The casement weights did most of the work, and it opened silently. Checking inside and finding no obstacle, he crouched and ducked his way through, taking up a similar stance on the inside sill before lowering himself to the floor one leg at a time.

There, he paused to listen.

The house smelt of sweet pipe smoke mixed with the acid tang of opium. The night mist found its way inside, and the hall light filtered up through a faint veil that looked like dust as if the place had not been used for years.

It was in use now. Overhead, Silas heard the muffled rumble of voices, and a floorboard complained. He drew the window down silently, leaving a gap to aid his escape, and crept to the nearest door.

His ear against it, he heard nothing, nor behind the next. There was another towards the front at the top of the stairs where anyone coming up would easily see him. As he cautiously approached the stairwell, he heard men's laughter from below. Someone was singing quietly, a plaintive, lone voice that was drowned by rough guffaws and sliced by shrieks of camp laughter. He imagined the salon crowded with punters and drugged young men, youthful legs draped over the thighs of married gentry, and boys' fingers stroking greying beards.

Stella could well be downstairs with the rest, but there was no way to tell. He would have to wait and watch. He was listening at the third door when the sounds from below increased in volume and a second later, a hand appeared on the bannister below.

'Go right up, Your Honour. He's waiting.' It was Danvers using a high, effeminate voice.

Silas opened the nearest door and slipped inside.

He was in a cupboard large enough to stand in but pitch black. He groped the walls and felt sheets resting in piles on shelves. Outside, footsteps stopped at the top of the stairs with a resounding creak, and Silas ducked, cramming himself beneath the bottom shelf and the floor. The footsteps passed him, and he relaxed but stiffened again when the wall vibrated as a door closed. He pressed his ear to the plaster and heard the dull thud of feet crossing a room.

A muffled grunt. Indistinct voices, one low, one higher, neither angry or scared, just as if an everyday conversation was taking place. An older man was talking to one younger, he concluded, and he didn't recognise either, the sound was too distorted. He waited for the sounds to fall silent when he imagined that the two were engaged in some sensual act, and unwound himself from beneath the shelf. He gave his circulation a moment flow naturally before feeling for the handle.

A bell rang somewhere, and a faint cheer went up from the salon. Opening the door a fraction, he was able to squint down to the hall in time to see the doorkeeper arrive and admit a visitor. He was only able to make out that it was a man, his head was hidden by the lay of the floor, and he spoke too quietly for Silas to hear his words.

The guilt he had been suffering in spasms hit him in one mighty blow. What if this was Roxton? What if he did use the place and

116

Silas saw him? He'd have to tell Archer he had broken into a molly-house to spy on a man Archer loved, and Silas didn't trust. Not only that, if it ever came out, it wouldn't be Billy O'Hara, street-rat and renter who was called up before the law, it would be Viscount Clearwater's secretary. He'd told James to stay in disguise and clear of the place, not wanting his livery recognised, and now here he was with a lot more to explain if he was caught.

When he heard the doorkeeper say, 'Go straight up, My Lord,' he thought his heart had stopped.

What if this wasn't Roxton? What if it was Archer?

'How long?' Fecker asked.

'Only ten minutes.'

'Too long.'

'Does he know what he's doing?'

Fecker nodded. His back was to James, his eyes set on the window where they had last seen Silas. James wasn't sure whether to be impressed, scared or outraged that the man had so blatantly broken into a private house. He said nothing. That afternoon, in the warm comfort of Mr Hawkins' private sitting room, he had promised to do whatever Silas asked of him. He had said it was out of gratitude for the kindness shown him by the viscount and his staff, but underneath it was from genuine concern for Silas, a man he liked and admired more each day.

'I get him,' Fecks grunted and turned back. 'Stay here.'

'No, Andrej.' James dared place a hand on the man's arm. 'He said to wait. There's no sign of trouble.'

Fecker was uneasy and his disquiet transferred to the horse. It snorted and pulled against its bridle. He lent over the rail and patted it, instantly calming the animal. When he sat back, he said, 'Ten minutes, I go. Watch clock.'

From the snatched glimpse Silas had, he knew the man was not Archer, but the possibility left him hollow. He hadn't stopped to think how he would feel if his lover had been there, the idea hadn't even entered his mind, and he berated himself for allowing it to infect him. Of course Archer wouldn't be involved in a place like this, and if Roxton was, the viscount would be outraged. He would also be devastated, and his gala night and possibly his reputation and charity would be in ruins.

He heard the floorboards creak as the man passed, taking the stairs to the next floor. Now was Silas' chance. This whole idea was a mad one, and he needed to leave. He waited until the punter was out of sight, gave him another minute to reach a room and shut himself in, and sidled out onto the landing. He was at the back window ready to lift it when the door handle beside him clattered. With no time to escape, he let himself into the opposite room, closing that door as the other one opened.

He wasn't alone.

The bedroom was bathed in a dull red light thrown through draped shawls that disguised two oil lamps either side of a large bed, itself swathed in material like a tent in the desert. Beneath one lamp, an opium pipe lay by an ice bucket. The sheets were askew, and crumpled further among them lay a naked man. He was face down, his features lost to the shadows, but his dark legs were long and hairy, and his broad back crisscrossed with red welts. He appeared to be sleeping, his head on one side. He lay prostrate with his wrists and ankles tied to the bed.

Silas felt sick. Sicker when voices in the corridor alerted him to another visitor. He fumbled for the lock. There was no key.

'Where the fuck have you been? Ah, don't bother. He's in the Arabian room.' Danvers' called, clear and camp from somewhere near the stairs. 'Take as long as you need, but I want all the details after.'

The clink of glasses against a bottle, and approaching feet drove Silas into action. There was no wardrobe and not enough space beneath the bed. A clothes rail was the only camouflage and he darted to it, stepping between the dresses and furs to press himself against the wall behind.

The garments had only just fallen back into place when someone came in and closed the door. The footsteps were light and accompanied the clanking glass until a gentle thud suggested they had been put down. Clothes rustled on the far side of the room and Silas heard the slip of a belt through hoops.

'Are you awake, darling?' It was a boy's voice or at least a younger man, and feminine with a rolling west country accent. 'My lover...?'

118

The creak of bedsprings. 'Are you awake?' It was subtle and caring and met by a deep murmur. 'That's the way to wake up now isn't it?' Another murmur, indistinguishable as words. 'More to smoke?' A girlish chuckle. 'But how can you reach your pipe with your hands bound so?'

Knowing what the boy was talking about made his compassion unsettling.

'Naughty, naughty, naughty,' the voice chided. 'Oh, such a strong back. Such a handsome man.'

It was an excruciating, amateur disapply of seduction and accompanied by the sucking of air and, after that, a long exhale of satisfaction.

'My lover? Are you awake?'

The springs complained again, and this time the man's voice was stronger. He growled.

'Aw, who left you trussed up like this?'

'Huh?'

The boy laughed. 'Hello.'

Silas imagined the man waking up not knowing where he was.

'No, don't struggle,' the voice said. 'I'll look after you.'

The man complained more loudly, and Silas realised he was gagged. All he could manage were grunts in rising degrees of surprise. The bed springs were being given a hard time.

It was either part of the man's deviant games, or someone had drugged him well enough to tie him up when he was passed out.

The scene became apparent when the boy spoke again.

'Got you where I want you,' he said, and gone were the false feminine wiles and the seduction, replaced by a tone as spiteful as the Ripper's knife. 'Struggle all you want, you're not getting out of here 'till we know you're going to do it.' The accent had changed too, and so seamlessly that Silas wondered if the boy had an older accomplice.

Demonstrations from the punter, now a victim, went unheeded as the bed began to rock.

'Don't get nasty,' the boy mocked but the victim struggled harder. 'Oh! You want nasty? You're going to get it.'

A stinging slap of leather on flesh and a gagged yell were followed by a cackle.

'Like that? Like how it feels?' Another whip, another yell. 'Get used to it.' A third and then a fourth brought the man to sobs.

Silas' heart was in his throat. His face was screwed taut against the sounds as he tried to block his imagination.

'That's better.' The demure girl was back. 'See how worthless it makes you, Lover?'

The bed creaked gently, and the man mumbled.

'What do I want? Is that what you're saying, my lover?' A laugh, high and mocking was strangely familiar. 'What was that?'

Another undefined murmur was followed by a sniff and a louder word that sounded like 'Please.'

'Oh, we'll stop, Sir,' the boy mocked. 'When you do as we say.'

The bed shook briefly. The man had agreed.

'You will?' That laugh again. 'I know you will. What would you do to stop me? Hmm, darling? What will you offer me to make me stop?'

'Anything.' The word was more distinct as if the gag had been loosened.

'That's a good answer.'

A second of silence was interrupted by a gasp of agony from the victim.

'So, mate,' the rough, East End growl was back. 'This is what's going to happen, and I'm only going to say it once. You've already got your instructions, and you'll follow them right down to the letter, got it?'

An agonised squeal muffled by a hand, perhaps the gag being stuffed back into the mouth.

'To the letter, mate.' The voice left no room for debate. 'You'll only get one chance. You do what you're told, and everyone'll be safe. What's that?' The man had spoken, but Silas was still unable to make out his voice. 'No, we don't want money.' The lad laughed, deep and scornful. 'I ain't after taking your money,' he said, almost pleasantly. 'I want your fucking reputation mate. I'm going to take you down and them others the same way you take us down, but it'll be worse for the likes of you. I'm going to hurt you where it matters, and that ain't in your wallet.'

A savage lash of the belt and the room filled with a scream that should have brought people running. Another lash came straight after, but this lad had no need to fear interruption. Danvers knew what was going on, and it chilled Silas' blood further to realise this kind of exploitation probably happened all the time. That was fair, wasn't it? The men used the boys knowing the boys could turn against them, but the risk was part of the allure. It was also part of an unspoken agreement, the trust between client and renter. "I'll be good to you, but you have to repay the respect and keep your mouth shut." Silas had heard similar words on many occasions in his past, but there was no sign of that kind of honour system at Cleaver Street. Whoever this man was, he was being threatened with more than a beating.

The victim's groans had quietened, and over soft sobbing, Silas heard two distant whistles sharp enough for him to recognise the signal.

'Just remember this,' the boy said. By the sound of it, he was climbing off the bed. 'You do what you've been instructed to do, or little Stella ain't going to be happy.'

Silas' caught his breath. This was the boy he was looking for exacting his revenge on one of his abusers. He prepared to reveal himself and had his hands ready to part the clothes when the house vibrated with a dull thud and banging from below.

'Shit!'

The next few seconds happened in a blur of sound. The bedroom door opened to admit the sound of footsteps pounding the stairs and from the front of the house, the shout of 'Police!' yelled through the letterbox. A scream upstairs, panicked hurrying, the opening and slamming of windows, and a long wail of helplessness from the victim on the bed.

Silas was out from behind the rack in a heartbeat. The man was struggling against his bindings, his back now an angry zigzag of swelling red. The belt still lay over it, dropped there in haste, but Stella had escaped into the mayhem of urgent voices, slamming doors, whispered messages, and more loud thumping on the front door.

Sensing Silas in the room, the man turned his head into the light and pleaded. Their eyes met, and Silas swore.

'Been too long,' Fecks said. 'I go.'

'Fecker, no.' James was stern despite his fear.

From what he knew of Fecker, if he got anywhere near that house he'd carve up the place. That was not going to endear anyone to their cause, and he couldn't allow it to happen.

Fecker was half out of his seat, gripping his whip. 'I go.'

'No! You can't. You'll hurt Silas.'

The notion hit home, and Fecker faltered.

'You'll cause a scene, and they might call the police.'

'Don't care.'

'You do. Look…' James tugged him back into his seat. 'I know he's your best mate. I know how you two are…' Fecker was already losing patience. James got straight to the point. 'You love him, yeah? Well, I like him a lot, and if we charge in there'll be a fight, and we'll all get done. None of that would be good for His Lordship, right?'

Fecker considered, his nose twitching in annoyance. 'No good for Geroy?'

'No, no good at all.'

Unhappy, but resigned, Fecker's shoulders slumped. He gave James a sideways look, still not convinced.

'Hey,' James said, an idea sparking. 'You remember how you saved me on that train? You rode past and shoved me back on.'

'You were idiot.'

'Yeah, probably. Well, thing is, you did it 'cos it was the right thing to do, right? Well, I want to help you the same way by telling you to stay here and let me do what I think's right. Yeah?'

'What you do?'

'Don't worry about that,' James said, and smiled. Whether Fecker could see it or not didn't matter. 'Agreed?'

'Da.'

He had Fecker's silent blessing, and James had never felt so honoured.

'Stay here, watch the back, have the horse ready.'

Fecks nodded.

'If Silas comes out that way, get him and clear off. Don't worry about me, I'll meet you back on Cambridge Street. Look for me there.'

'Where you go?'

'Taking a stroll, mate. You watch the house and count to sixty.'

122

'In English?'

'It doesn't matter, Fecker! When you get to sixty, whistle twice, loudly.'

'Da, understand.'

James jumped from the trap and set off towards the front of the house. The closer he came to Cleaver Street the more concerned he became. His idea was a simple one, perhaps too simple, but it was all he had. Fecker was right to be anxious. Silas had been away too long, and the house was becoming busier. More lights had been lit in higher windows and Silas would soon be discovered if they didn't do something.

He rounded the corner into Cleaver Street giving each direction a quick scan. As far as the fog would allow, he saw no-one else. Visibility was at ten yards, he estimated. He could run that in a few seconds and be lost to the gloom as soon as someone approached the door.

Stopping outside the house and, under the pretence of tying a shoelace, he confirmed he was still unobserved before confidently climbing the steps. He cleared his throat, crouched to the letterbox and lifted the flap. There was no-one in the hall, but he could smell cigars and hear voices. He took a deep breath and balled his fists.

'Open up!' he hollered, hammering the door. 'Police!' Silence. Another breath. 'Oi! Police.'

He waited until he heard movement inside, hammered again and scarpered.

One by one, lamps lit the bedrooms of disturbed neighbours. Some opened their windows to lean out but saw no-one, only the swirl of fog. Others, on hearing no more commotion, dimmed their lamps and returned to sleep.

In the shop, directly above where James had stood, the apartment had been in darkness all night. Had the lamp been lit, Tripp would not so easily have seen the young men coming and going from number nineteen. What was more interesting and of much more use was seeing Hawkins leaving. He had noted a man with his gait arrive at the house, and his suspicion had been aroused when, at the same time, another masked youth took up a watch in the doorway below. He'd not been able to see their faces, but he was the same boy who had just cried wolf through the door.

Clearwater, or his staff at least, clearly had an interest in the place, and he silently thanked Lovemount for his loyalty.

Tempting though it was to alert the authorities, Tripp knew he would not be taken seriously. He needed more than one sighting of the viscount's boy, he needed a scandal involving the man himself. It would be a slow process, months probably, and he was prepared to wait and bide his time. "There's no point letting the gun go off half-cocked," the late viscount would have said. The sodomite Clearwater had called Tripp the tortoise, behind his back of course, but worse, among the servants. Tortoises lived long, gradual lives where every step was for a purpose and Tripp admired the animals. They always got there in the end.

His goal could not have been clearer, and now he had the first proof of a connection between Clearwater House and the Cleaver Street brothel, all he needed was the patience of a saint.

Fourteen

James ran until he reached the junction with Cambridge Street where he slowed his pace. There were more people on the wider road, a few private carriages and some Hansoms trundling cautiously through the fog. His scarf was around his face, and he was sweating beneath it, but he wasn't out of breath as he walked briskly, staying close to the pavement's edge so that Fecker would see him when he passed. Silas had told him to do whatever he thought was right, and it had been the first thing that came to mind. He would have panicked the men inside the house, giving Silas a diversion. After that, he was on his own.

He had walked half a mile when a whistle attracted his attention, and Fecker drew the trap alongside. He clambered onto the front bench and investigated the back. Silas sat beside a hunched man who had his face in his hands. From what James could see, he wore only an overcoat. His legs were bare.

'You alright?' he asked.

'I am,' Silas said. 'Not so sure about him.'

'Who is it?'

As soon as the man raised his head, James recognised his receding hairline.

'Mr Roxton?'

Roxton groaned and dropped his gaze.

Fecker had the horse trotting steadily, making it easy for James to climb over the bench and into the back. He squeezed in beside Silas and handed him his ring.

'What happened?'

Putting his ring back on, Silas explained how he had found the singer tied to the bed and left there when the warning went up. At first, he thought it was a real raid, but he had faintly heard the whistles and took a gamble. The whole affair had been a gamble,

James thought, but Silas waved that away.

'I cut the binding,' he said, and James noticed Roxton was unknotting lengths of material from his wrists.

'How did you get out?' James had seen Silas climb the gutter but couldn't imagine Roxton shinning down it.

'I was ready to throw him out of the window,' Silas said, trying to control his anger. 'Let him break a leg if necessary. Would have served the fecker right, but by the time I'd got him up, the house had gone quiet. I recognised your voice the second time, Jimmy. So, I knew there were no bobbies. Got him into the corridor, and everyone else had disappeared. Don't know if they ran from the back or what.'

'Da,' Fecker said, speaking over his shoulder. 'Rats from fire.' He laughed.

'I took him out the front door as if nothing had happened,' Silas continued. 'Had to be quick, but no-one saw me.'

'You were lucky.'

'Yeah, we both were, but now we've got a bigger problem.'

Roxton sat back and filled his lungs. His face was streaked with tears and his eyes puffy. He fell against the seat and gasped.

'He's got an injury,' Silas explained. 'A deserved one.'

'What do we do with him?'

'Now, there's the question, Jimmy. I ain't had a chance to get any sense out of him yet. He was drugged, he said. Thing is… Hang on.'

Silas manoeuvred himself to the other side of Roxton where he could lean against the door and face both James and the singer.

'Thing is,' he said. 'We need to find out what's going on before we decide what to do.'

'Take me home.' Roxton's voice was brittle. He was shaking and not just from the cold.

James took off his cape and placed it over the man's knees.

'Drugged?'

'Yeah. He was meant to be with Archer.'

James looked at Silas sharply, and the Irishman knew what he was thinking.

'No,' he said. 'He wasn't there.' He poked Roxton. 'Was he?'

The man shrugged and buried his head as he cried. The sight unnerved James.

'Shock,' Silas explained before turning his attention to Roxton. 'Oi, you ready to tell me what you were doing?'

Roxton wiped his eyes. Any attractiveness he had about him melted into red and sagging features. He was unshaven, and the passing rise and fall of ineffectual streetlamps turned his skin from grey to yellow, hiding the pallor beneath.

'Take me home,' he repeated, this time adding, 'Immediately.'

'I reckon we need to take you to Archer,' Silas said.

Roxton groaned, his head fell, and he closed his eyes. 'It wasn't my fault.'

Silas was thinking, biting the cuticle of a nail, his mouth taut. His head moved from side to side as he decided his next course of action. It was one James didn't expect.

'You eejit!' He exploded, grabbing Roxton's lapels and yanking him forward. 'What the feck were you thinking? If that had been the police, you'd have fucked everything, you half-wit shitten-prick.'

'Silas.' James tried to separate them.

'Some fecking friend you are.' Silas shoved Roxton back into his seat, and he yelped in pain. 'Yeah, well you fecking earned that. It was you I saw before wasn't it? How long you been going to that house? How long you been slapping boys for sport?'

'Silas, please.' James reached over the sobbing man and gripped Silas' arm. The touch distracted him. 'Remember who you are.'

Silas glared, his anger boosted by the interruption, but James spoke calmly.

'You're not going to help His Lordship like this.'

Silas growled, knowing James was right. He sniffed and ran the back of his hand across his nose before spitting into the street.

James turned his attention to Roxton. 'Where are you staying?'

'Chuck him out and let him walk,' Silas grumbled.

'Where are you staying?'

Roxton was comforted by James' tone and, after looking nervously at Silas, said, 'With my aunt.'

'Oh, well that's easy.' James told Fecker to take them directly to Bucks Avenue. 'And it gives us some time to talk *calmly.*' He emphasised the last word, fixing Silas with narrow eyes. 'Okay with you?'

'Do what you want,' Silas grunted in disgruntled agreement.

'Let me get this right.' James spoke directly to Roxton using what he thought was a consolatory tone. 'You were drugged, yes?'

'Yes.'

'Where?'

'How would I know? Who are you people?' Roxton was recovering and had stopped crying.

'That's charming,' Silas said. 'I only had dinner with you last night and he…'

'Yeah, alright, Silas. Easy, mate.'

Silas swallowed as if ridding his mouth of an unsavoury lump of gristle. Still angry, he turned his head to watch the poorly lit shopfronts.

'What do you remember,' James persisted. 'The last thing?'

Shivering, Roxton pulled the coat tighter by the lapels. 'I was due to meet Clearwater at eight,' he said, his voice barely a whisper. 'The Garrick Club. I left rehearsal at six… Went to The Golden Lion for a drink.'

'Dean Street?'

The West End pub was known for its discreet, higher-class renters. Foppish boys who dressed well, behaved appropriately, and to everyone else, appeared to be well-off customers like the rest. James had never been, but other messengers had spoken of it in the past.

'Then what?'

'I took wine and sat at the window while I waited.'

'You were going to meet Archer there?' Silas' outrage was back, and James held up a hand to contain it.

'No,' Roxton said. 'We were meeting at the club directly he finished his meetings.'

'The Garrick Club is a short walk,' James explained, still doubtful. 'But the two places have nothing to do with each other.'

'You sure of that?' Silas was dubious.

'As far as I know.'

'Yes.' Roxton was finding his confidence. 'Clearwater would never use The Golden Lion. I only stopped because it was convenient.'

James knew full well that Roxton would have crossed Garrick Street to reach Dean Street from the opera house, and there were any number of respectable pubs closer to the club. He didn't want to inflame Silas with the information and kept it to himself for Roxton's sake.

'Yeah, convenient for picking up boys and giving them a flogging…'

'Silas!' His anger was wearing off on James. 'Just hold it, yeah?'

Maybe it was his city accent, perhaps it was the direct way he spoke, but Silas took the hint. He folded his arms and sulked. It might take him hours to come around, but at least he was quiet for now.

'Did you speak with anyone?' James continued to question Roxton, aware that they had left Cambridge Street and had only another couple of miles to travel.

'I spoke to one man,' Roxton admitted. 'Didn't know him, but he was legitimate.'

'What does that mean?'

'Means he didn't smell like rent and had nice manners,' Silas mumbled. 'Same shit, different wrapping.'

James ignored him. 'What did he look like?'

'Why does that matter?'

'Did you recognise him?'

'No.'

'A name?'

'No.'

'Anything?'

'No!' Roxton burst into tears again, embarrassing James and making Silas laugh with derision.

'So, the last thing you remember is talking to this stranger. And then what?'

'Then I'm tied to a bed,' Roxton moaned. 'And some tart is whipping me.'

'And asking you how you like it, you gobshite maggot.'

'Yeah, alright, Silas. Point made.' James said. 'Did you see who it was?'

'No,' Silas admitted grudgingly. 'Heard his voice is all. Voices. Girl one minute, boy the next, stupid-sweet then nasty. A real pro, ask me.'

'Get a name?'

'Stella. The one I was looking for.'

'Why?' Roxton moaned. 'What were you doing there?'

'Proving myself right, you fecking nob.'

'Silas, mate.' James held back his annoyance. 'Why don't you sit up front with Fecker?'

'No chance. I'm not turning my back on this thick hoor.'

'Insulting His Lordship's friend is not going to help.'

Silas returned to his sulk, his way of showing acceptance, and James was left to continue his questioning.

'Why?' James asked, but Roxton didn't understand. 'Why would anyone want to knock you out, take you there and do that to you? And I'm asking Mr Roxton, Silas.'

Silas huffed and buried himself in his coat.

'I don't know. Where are we?'

'We're taking you home,' James said. 'Before we get there, I want to know who might have something against you. You say you've not been to Cleaver Street before?'

Roxton shook his head vehemently. 'Is that where I was? Certainly not.'

'But you've used The Golden Lion?'

'They have a good port.'

'Do you remember leaving the pub?'

'No.'

'Did you recognise anyone at the house?'

'I didn't see anyone apart from this foul-mouthed…'

'Yeah, alright. Don't make it worse.' James had never spoken to a gentleman this way, but these were unusual circumstances, and his directness was producing results. 'So, you were drugged, kidnapped, held against your will and beaten, all for no reason.'

'Yes! Now shut up and get me home.'

It was too much for Silas. He twisted in his seat and drew back his fist in one shocking flash of anger.

'You don't give a shite what'll happen to Archer when this gets out,' he shouted. 'You lying, toe-rag of a…'

The trap lurched to a sudden stop, sending Silas staggering backwards. His arms flailed, and he let go of Roxton who was shunted to his knees in the well. Before James could react, Fecker had Silas around his chest and hauled him, legs kicking, onto the front seat. He manhandled him to face front, trapped him beneath one arm and rooted him there. He calmly clicked his tongue, and the trap moved on.

'Jesus Christ,' Roxton swore as he fumbled back to his seat. 'What the hell is this?'

'That's what we need to find out,' James said. 'And you've got to be honest with us.'

'I have been.'

'You have no idea why those people would want to harm you?'

'How many times do I have to say it?'

'Instructions,' Silas yelled. 'Ask him about his instructions.'

Fecker hugged him more tightly.

'Go on.' James prompted when Roxton said nothing.

'There was something…'

To James, it looked like he was genuinely trying to remember, and unlike Silas, he was prepared to give the man the benefit of the doubt.

'He said something about instructions. Said I had them.'

'What instructions?'

Roxton shrugged.

'Was that it?'

'"You've already got your instructions, and you'll follow them right down to the letter",' Silas quoted, apparently calming in Fecker's grip. 'That's what he told you, word for word.'

'You remember anything else?'

'Yeah, Jimmy, I do.' Silas twisted in his seat. James wasn't certain but it looked like he too had been crying. 'He threatened to destroy his reputation unless he did what they tell him. Him and "Them others" the same. You can guess who she meant. It's blackmail. Simple and deserved.'

'Except with the gala coming up, and his speech, His Lordship's charity, their association?'

'Now you see why I'm so bloody angry.'

James understood completely, but where Silas was furious, he was intrigued.

'Why pick a random sexual deviant and drug him…'

'I am not a like that!' Roxton protested louder at the accusation than he had at his rough treatment. 'I'm married.'

'And so are half the men who fu… fumble with messenger boys,' James said, unimpressed. 'But it doesn't matter. If they think you are, and they're prepared to say it publicly, you're the one in the dock, Mr Roxton.'

'I shall fight it.'

'Of course. But you've got to ask yourself, why you? It doesn't matter if you're queer or not, you were at that house.'

'If they expose me, they will expose themselves.'

'They're clever enough to find a way not to,' James reasoned. 'I mean, they're clever enough to kidnap you in plain sight.'

Roxton moaned. 'I'm ruined.'

'Not yet you aren't. Not if we help you.'

Silas shrugged off Fecker's arm, but not his watchful gaze and turned, glaring.

James wanted him to be sure where his loyalties lay, and they were not with the snivelling, indignant opera singer trembling beside him. 'Not for him,' he explained. 'For His Lordship.'

Silas understood and faced front.

The immediate problem was how to get Roxton home without attracting the attention of Lady Marshall or her servants. Her nephew couldn't very well turn up naked apart from his overcoat.

'Fecker,' he said, tapping the man on the back. 'Take us to Clearwater Mews.'

Fecker nodded.

'Why?' The suggestion had added to Roxton's nervousness. 'I can't face Archer. I can't face anyone. How am I going to sing?'

'Last of your worries, mate.' Silas laughed.

'We'll find you something to wear.' James took hold of Roxton's arm.

He was confused, upset and above all, terrified. He might not be Silas' favourite person, but he was a man in need of help. James had heard the Good Samaritan story so many times it had soaked into his psyche. Each time his mother read it aloud, she explained it wasn't the influence of some higher power that changed lives, it was the influence of ordinary people lucky enough to be in a position to help those less fortunate. James firmly believed that, and this was his chance to put her preaching into practice.

'We'll find clothes,' he repeated. 'You can go home without

arousing suspicion. I suggest you go straight to bed, say nothing and lay low until the performance.'

'I have rehearsal with the maestro.'

'Then go if you are up to it, but don't stop off at any dodgy pubs in Soho.'

Roxton shook his head like an admonished schoolboy. 'But then what?'

'Leave us to think about that,' James said, squeezing his arm to show support. 'We'll work something out.'

He could think no further than reaching Clearwater House, being rid of the man and having a drink. He also had Thomas to consider, and then there was the viscount.

Roxton regarded him with empty eyes, hollowed and black-ringed. 'Who are you?' he whispered.

'Just a footman, Sir. Here to serve the best interests of my master.'

Under instructions from Silas, Fecker drew the trap to a stop outside Clearwater Mews and waited while James checked there was no-one in the yard. Finding it empty, he beckoned to Silas but kept one eye on the back door, looking out for Thomas. The coast clear, they smuggled Roxton into the coach house where Fecker and James tended to the horse.

Mr Roxton was still shivering and wretched, and Silas' anger still simmering.

'Right, Roxton,' he said. 'I expect you need a good sleep. Fecks will come home with you, by the back door. He can explain to the Russian man, what's his name?'

'Oleg,' James said.

'Explain what?'

'To keep his mouth shut,' Silas said. 'Go up the backstairs, straight to your room, and say nothing about this.'

'What if someone sees me?'

'I'll cut throat.'

Roxton blanched visibly as Fecker handed him a pair of trousers and some shoes.

'He's joking, Roxton. Look...' Silas sat the opera singer on a stool and crouched to him. 'I'm being as nice as I can to you at the moment, but I'm still not convinced that was your first time at that house. So, you're going to have to prove it to me.'

'Who are you to make threats?' Roxton bristled as he dressed. 'My father is…'

'Yeah, I'm sure he is, mate, but he ain't going to help you here. I am, though I don't know why I should.'

A hand on his shoulder and a gentle pat from James tempered his annoyance.

'I shall go now.' Roxton made sure his coat was buttoned. 'You will, of course, not say anything about this to anyone.'

'Can't help you there,' Silas said. 'Archer needs to know, and before you say anything, he'll know what to do. You go home and think what these instructions are that you already have. If you come up with anything, tell us in the morning.'

'Us?' Roxton questioned.

'Yeah, all of us.' Silas indicated James, Fecker and the house. 'You're lucky I didn't trust you, Mr Roxton, and that I have the luck of my Irish mother. Otherwise, you might be a lot worse off than you are now.'

'You don't trust me?'

'Huh. I might accept that you didn't know anything about it, 'cos that was how you sounded, so what we've got to do now is work out what the hell that lot at Cleaver Street are playing at, why you, and what next. The person to do that is Archer.' He turned to Fecker. 'Fecks, mate, will you walk him home? You can translate if Oleg or the others ask him anything.'

'We'll finish with Emma,' James said, patting the horse.

'Please, Mr Hawkins.' Roxton was suddenly contrite. 'I implore you not to do or say anything. I am putting this incident down to mistaken identity, and intend to ignore it. Thank you for your assistance, all of you, but here is where the matter ends.'

'I can't allow that.' Silas stood his ground. 'It could affect Archer and his Foundation. He has to know.'

'In which case…' Roxton's tone changed again and he became haughty. 'I suggest you consider the laws of slander and how easy it is for a leading light of the opera to withdraw from an unpaid performance at any moment.'

The threat was obvious, but Silas paid it no attention.

'Good night,' he said and nodded to Fecker.

Once Fecker had led Roxton away, Silas helped James unbridle the horse. He hadn't done it before and was forced to forget his anger and concentrate on instructions. Strangely, the manual task helped him think more clearly.

'What did you tell Thomas?' he asked.

'Said you wanted me with you on a visit, that's all. He won't ask me anything else. We don't talk about your business when we're alone.'

'Not worried about that,' Silas said. 'Just making sure you're not going to get in trouble.'

'I won't, but what about you?' James turned the horse to its trough, and Silas gave the animal a wide berth.

'I've got to tell Archer,' he said. 'It'll be fine.'

'What do you reckon it's all about?'

'That's a hard one, mate.' He closed the bottom half of the stable door leaning on it and using it as a barrier between him and the horse. 'I can only think it's 'cos Roxton's been in the papers lately, and with this gala coming up, he's a good target for blackmail.'

'But you said he'd been at that house before?'

'Yeah, maybe.'

Silas tried to picture the man he had seen in August. He had been a similar height to Roxton, and well dressed, neither of which were specific enough to make a positive match. He couldn't remember the voice too clearly, but it had been well-spoken, like so many other men in the city, although croaky as if the man had tonsillitis. There was, however, a similarity in the presence, the way both men stood and carried themselves. 'If it was him,' he said, thinking aloud. 'Then there'd be a reason Stella wants to get his own back. You know, give him some of the same treatment, the flogging. She said something like that.'

'That makes sense,' James agreed. 'And people who run brothels probably know criminals they can pay to drug and kidnap a man. Might as well try blackmail while you're about it.'

'Yeah, but blackmail how? Roxton's got to do as they say or they'll… What? Tell the newspapers he's queer and into flogging boys who dress as girls in their own shag-shop?'

'The papers would love that.'

'But he was right. They'd land themselves in it along with him.'

'Which the news sheets would lap up even more.'

'Right, so that doesn't make sense.'

'If not expose him to the press, then what?' James asked, freshening the horse's feed and water.

'That's the thing.' Silas stood back to let him work. 'He said something about exposing Roxton and his kind, or the rest, or something as if there were more people they wanted revenge on.'

The horse seen to, James closed the stable doors and hung his lantern on a hook to light Fecker's way home. 'Maybe things will seem clearer in the morning,' he said.

'I can't make sense out of this, but Archer will.' Silas sighed. 'Only thing I'm not so sure about is how to tell him why I was spying in the first place.'

James threw an arm around his shoulder and gave him a brief hug. Silas instinctively returned the gesture and was reassured. They walked to the back door, and it wasn't until they reached it that they realised they were still holding each other.

The footman coughed and stepped away. 'You're tired, Sir,' he said. 'Shall I go up and prepare your room?'

The switch was instant and prompted Silas to change his attitude.

'No, don't worry,' he said. 'And thanks for your help.'

'At your service, Sir.'

Silas smiled, though he doubted James could see it in the dim light. 'Come on, mate,' he said. 'Let's get back to our menfolk.'

Fifteen

Silas found Archer in his study, reading by the dying fire, at least that's what he first thought. He hung back at the doors watching, and it took Archer a time to notice. He was frowning, considering some matter in the distance and not the printed page, but when he realised he wasn't alone, his face brightened.

'Thank God,' he said. 'I was worried. Had a good time?' He put the book aside.

'I need to speak to you.' Silas thought it best to get it over with.

Archer stood, his concern deepening. 'What's happened? I can see it on your face. Are you alright?'

Silas went to him, and they kissed. 'I missed you,' he said. 'How was your dinner?'

'It didn't happen. Here…'

Archer led him to the couch where they sat. He wanted Silas to lie in his arms, suggesting they watch the fire die before going to bed, but Silas sat beside him holding his hand.

'I know,' he said.

'Know what?'

'That Roxton didn't turn up for your dinner.'

'How do you know that?'

'Archie,' Silas said, 'I want you to listen and not say anything until I'm done. You might not like what I have to tell you.'

Archer was quizzical. 'Go on,' he said, his brow furrowing. 'What's happened?'

Silas told him the story, beginning with, 'I owe you an apology,' and ending with Fecker taking Roxton home. Archer listened, his face unmoving until the story was finished.

It was hard to tell his lover that he didn't trust his friend and had gone behind Archer's back to discover the truth. He said he hadn't gone to spy, but wanted to put his mind at rest, and Roxton had been lucky that he had. Silas' heart was thumping, but the viscount was interested more than outraged, and showed no signs of anger.

'Good Lord,' he said as if had received a report of bad weather. 'And you did all this without talking to me first?'

'That was the part I was bothered about,' Silas admitted. 'I didn't want to worry you, but I didn't what to lie to you either. I did go out in the trap, and James came with me, so that part was true. I just didn't tell you where I was going. I expected to be back before you, having learnt nothing. I would have told you either way.'

Archer's smile was sad, and he nodded. 'I know you would,' he said. 'And I'm not angry with you. How can I be?' He smoothed Silas' hair, and Silas nuzzled his face into the hand.

'You mean it?' he asked.

'Yes. I'm concerned, but because you are unhappy.'

'I should have spoken to you first.'

'I would have told you that you were imagining things,' Archer said, pulling Silas to him. 'But I probably would have told you to go and then worried about it all night, so you spared me that.'

He was calm, and Silas didn't detect any resentment or anger.

'He said he was drugged?' Archer clarified.

'Yeah, and I have to admit, he did sound it when he woke up.'

'Explains why he didn't show at the club.' Archer turned Silas to rest against him, put his arm around him, and kissed his head. 'I can't be angry with you,' he said. 'And I'm not. But I might be angry with Cadwell if this is true.'

'It's true. I saw him there, and the lad said they had given him instructions. He said he didn't know why they took him or what they were talking about.'

'And who are they?'

'Don't know. Danvers and the men who use the house, I suppose.'

'Why would they randomly kidnap anyone?'

'Blackmail.'

'Blackmail?' Archer considered that for a moment while he stroked Silas' arm. 'He's only an opera singer, not a politician or a peer.'

'James reckons it's because of the gala.'

'Did James see him there?'

'No. Well…' Silas paused to put his thoughts in order. Archer's reaction had taken him by surprise. Where he expected anger, he received passive understanding, and, if it was needed, forgiveness. The list of things to love about the viscount grew every day, and although his ability to instantly forgive was already there, Silas mentally underlined it and shifted it to the top. 'James caused the diversion,' he went on. 'He thought I was in trouble. I wasn't, but he was just in time. Roxton would probably have been beaten more otherwise. We picked him up on the way back, so no-one saw him at the door.'

'And no-one saw you?'

'There was nobody about, and I kept my head down. And Roxton's.'

Archer's grip tightened, and his hand slipped to Silas' hip. 'How do you feel?' he asked.

'Me? I'm alright. How about you?'

'Confused. I need to sleep on this news and come back to it in the morning.'

'Have I disappointed you?'

'Not at all,' Archer said. 'Roxton has, possibly. If he's innocent, then it's a different matter, but either way, he's still in trouble whether it's of his own making or not. As his friend, I need to help him. We'll talk about it tomorrow.'

'Sorry.'

'For what?'

'I'm not jealous.'

'I didn't think it for a moment.'

Archer shifted his weight so that Silas could lie with his head in his lap. He lay looking up at Archer, feeling the heat of his groin and the press of his crotch against his head. Archer played with his hair with one hand while the other idled on Silas' stomach.

'You are beautiful,' Silas whispered.

The viscount's gaze was far away. He was still lost in contemplation, but as his fingers circled gently over Silas' shirt, they travelled down until his hand was flat against the front of his trousers. Beneath him, Silas felt Archer's cock stiffen, and his instantly did the same.

'Everything will become clear in time,' Archer said.

He looked at Silas, his brown eyes misty, and his mouth held in the same sad smile. Silas stroked his face, Archer's stubble rubbing against his palm. As his fingers passed his lips, the viscount caught one and held it in his mouth. Around it, his smile grew into a leer.

'Is that all you can think about?' Silas smirked.

'It's your fault for being so damn gorgeous.'

'Even though I went behind your back?'

Archer's grip strengthened around Silas' cock, now pressing urgently inside his trousers. 'You didn't,' he said. 'You did what was best, and you've told me. That's an end to that matter, but not an end to this mystery.' He bent to kiss Silas on the forehead.

'I love you, Archie.'

Suddenly, the viscount's mood changed. He lifted Silas into a sitting position, stood, laid him down and knelt by the couch.

'So, now my man is a cat burglar,' he grinned. 'A master of disguise. A rescuer of men in distress. You're a slippery customer, aren't you?'

Silas pulled an apologetic face. 'Oops.'

Archer's lips were on his in a flash, pressing hard, his tongue demanding entry. Silas welcomed it, wrapping his arms around Archer's back to hold him tighter. Archer didn't let him. Instead, he pressed him against the couch, and still kissing passionately, unbuttoned his fly. Silas tried to reach for Archer's, but again was denied. He held Archer's head, his fingers lost in his dark hair as he breathed in the man's scent.

The viscount's hand explored his underwear, his palm running up and down Silas' shaft as his fingernails scratched teasingly at the mound of his balls. When he felt Archer's skin on his, Silas moaned gently, and when the cool air of the room touched his exposed cock, he tried again to return the pleasure, but again was deprived. It was as if Archer only wanted to give not receive.

Silas felt his shirt unbuttoned, and Archer's mouth moved. He kissed Silas' chin, gave a salacious wink and his soft lips parted as he licked them.

Lower, his kissed Silas' chest, damping the vague line of soft hair before creeping closer to his nipples. They screamed for the heat of his lover's mouth, and Silas' body jerked when Archer touched them. He pressed his head harder to Silas' chest, and the viscount bit gently. His fist wrapped around Silas' cock, covering it all, apart from the tip which was covered and uncovered as the fist slowly stroked. He moved to the other jealous and craving nipple, and Silas bucked again.

The kisses descended. He put one hand on Silas' face where he slipped a finger into his mouth for Silas to suck as his lips attended to his stomach. Archer's tongue investigated his belly button and then gradually approached the tuft of hair beneath. He kissed there, his chin casually touching Silas' inflamed cock head as his hand continued its rhythm unbroken. When Archer pulled Silas' hood back and licked the bead of juice from the tip, Silas wanted to push his head down all the way and hard, but Archer eked out the agony, swallowing Silas' length a fraction at a time. His finger delved into Silas' mouth, mirroring the depth until his face was pressed to Silas' crotch, and his throat closed around the raging cock.

'Oh, fuck, Archie,' Silas whispered, before grabbing at the finger with his mouth, sucking it eagerly.

The heat on his shaft and the vice of Archer's lips increased when he cupped and massaged Silas' balls. His head rose and fell steadily, his fingers delved below, and one circled Silas' arse, probing it, entering, and sending thrilling shots of ecstasy to clash with the tingling in his balls and the swelling of his shaft. Archer didn't let up and continued to draw him closer to a climax until Silas was jerking his hips and groaning, clenching Archer's finger and gripping his neck.

There was no way to hold back, and Archer didn't want him to. He sucked harder. More fingers slid deeper and faster until Silas was alive inside and out. His head spun. Unable to control himself, his gasps came with laughs of disbelief. How could anyone give him so much pleasure?

'Archie,' he gasped. 'Archie...'

What had he done to deserve this much joy?

Archer grunted as Silas exploded deep in his throat, but he still didn't let up. He drew his lips back to the tip, and they fell again firmly as Silas spurted and thrust until there was nothing more to give.

He jerked, wanting his over-sensitive flesh free from its ecstatic torture. The pleasure was unbearable, and he had to take a firm grip of Archer's head and pull him away.

'Stop,' he said, a half-laugh a half-plea, sitting up to release himself. 'Stop, you've had it all.'

Archer grinned up at him, his lips swollen and glistening.

'Will you sleep in my bed tonight?' he asked adding, 'Please,' as if he was a boy pleading for his parents to let him go out to play.

'I'll be there,' Silas panted. 'But I can't promise I'll do much sleeping.'

Sixteen

The City Arts Review, Saturday, December 3rd, 1888

Aeneas and Dido

*A*eneas and Dido is a re-imagining of the classic myth of Dido and Aeneas in which the tragic heroine, Dido, takes her own life on the sword of the man who spurned her. In Bruch's retelling (with a libretto by Giulio Cesare), it is Aeneas who takes the role of the spurned lover suffering all the dramatic consequences of lost love. The opera has received nothing but praise on the continent, but it remains to be seen how our own public will take to the story. As was recently mooted in this journal, such a daring presentation for a debut performance and in aid of such a new and controversial charity, could either be the success of the season and the making of Mr Roxton as Aeneas, or the undoing of everyone involved.

Johann Bruch, a contemporary of Wagner, was born in Korneuburg, outside Vienna, in 1823 to impoverished parents. Poverty didn't prevent them from recognising his talents, and, after completing his basic schooling, an endowment from a benefactor enabled him to attend St Thomas' School.

He was in good company, although not at the same time. The establishment's notable alumni include sons of JS Bach, and Richard Wagner himself. Indeed, Bruch was tutored in counterpoint and harmony by Weinlig, as was Wagner, and one can detect similarities in Bruch's early works. Following his schooling, Bruch was mentored by Holzer, then kapellmeister at Saint Stephen's Cathedral, who was also responsible for his appointment as Director of Music at Die Josefstadt Theatre.

There, Bruch was able to develop his talent for theatrical music (his first opera, 'Die Liebenden' had been performed at his school *when he was twelve), studying opera under Muller while composing incidental music for theatrical productions.*

At twenty-five, he met and married actress and singer, Julianna Volti, daughter of Italian composer, Volti. His father-in-law is now more widely known as the man who "found" Bruch, more so than he is for composing sixteen operas. Volti's influence, however, can be heard in Bruch's earlier staged works, although by the time "Aeneas and Dido" was composed, the style is unmistakeably Bruch alone.

His fame spread when, in 1853, Bruch was awarded a commission by the King of the Netherlands, Wilhelm III, then in the fourth year of his reign. His Majesty is due to arrive in the city today, but his itinerary is unknown, and it is unlikely that he will attend the Clearwater Foundation performance of "Dido", despite it being, "A work of unnatural beauty", the King's words, and composed by his former friend.

Johann Bruch died in August 1887, after suffering a long illness. He left behind no children, giving rise to the rumour that although he was a maestro at the composition table and podium, he was also a devotee of the beastliness now more politely referred to as aestheticism; a euphemism in anyone's book.

"Aeneas and Dido" will be performed by the Opera House chorus and orchestra, with the title roles sung by Mr Cadwell Roxton and Signora Campanelli. Mr Arthur McDurling, a favourite with City audiences, will take the comprimario role as Aeneas' confidant-come-messenger who delivers the method of suicide to the hero before the classic aria, "When I am Laid in Earth".

"Aeneas and Dido" was Bruch's last completed work and has never been performed in this country before.

The City Arts Review will be present, and our opinion of the gala will appear in next week's edition.

Seventeen

Silas woke at some point during the night to find the bed empty. He was in Archer's room, the fire had died to a few faint embers, and the sheet beside him was still warm. The scent of sweat and sex remained in the air, and he spread himself to Archer's side to breathe more of the heady memories.

There was no sound from the house at first, and he assumed that Archer was in the bathroom, but then he heard a door close and a floorboard creak overhead. Probably Thomas rising early, he thought and drifted back to sleep.

When he awoke next, Archer was back in bed, and Silas was spooning him, their warm bodies pressed firmly together, with Silas holding him as if he couldn't bear to let him go. Archer's solid chest beneath his hand and his steady in-out breathing were as reassuring as they were welcome. Archer hadn't flown off the handle last night as Silas had first feared, he'd listened calmly, and the fact that Silas had gone behind his back hadn't disturbed him. If he was angry, Archer hadn't shown it and had forgiven immediately. Silas was grateful for the way Archer believed his story without question. The problem now was what were they to do.

He wrapped himself more tightly, and Archer mumbled something in his sleep. Daylight was creeping around the edge of the curtains and the embers he had seen during the night were gone; the fire was now only ash, and the room was cold.

A light, rhythmic knock on the door alerted him to Thomas' arrival, but there was no need to hide or flee.

The door opened, and the butler entered, stately and quiet as always. He placed a tray beside the bed and caught Silas' eye.

'Good morning,' he mouthed silently, and Silas replied with a gentle finger wave.

Thomas was used to finding the viscount in bed with his

secretary and thought nothing of it. He glided to the curtains and parted them quietly, hooking them back with their tasselled ties and peering through the nets at the morning.

'Another grey one,' he announced with a little more volume. 'Ah, good morning, My Lord.' He turned his attention to the dressing room.

'Morning, Tom,' Archer mumbled, pulling Silas's arm and drawing him closer. He kissed his hand by way of greeting, and Silas hugged him. 'How did you get on?'

Silas didn't understand the question, but it wasn't aimed at him.

'A success, My Lord,' Thomas said. 'You are expected at nine.'

'It was too early in the morning for Silas to wonder what he meant, and reluctantly letting Archer go, he rolled onto his back and covered his eyes. Beside him, the bed dipped and when he looked, Archer was standing over him, his hair all over the place as it usually was, and his smile fixed and ready.

'Meet me in the study at ten,' he said, before kissing Silas and throwing back the covers.

The chill air hit him, and he was about to pull the blankets over and go back to sleep when Thomas announced the time.

Archer was already walking naked into the bathroom, as unbothered by the butler's presence as Thomas was unconcerned about his master's nudity. It was strangely erotic to know that his lover was attended to by his best friend, and that when dressing and bathing, Thomas saw as much of the man's arousing physique as Silas. Thomas was as discreet as James when he assisted Silas in the mornings; there was no discussion of nudity. It was expected for a valet to know his master intimately, and yet nothing was ever said. It never bothered Silas, he had no problems showing off his body. Although it was nowhere near as fit and strong as Archer's, he had caught James watching him on many occasions; not leering as Silas might have done had he seen James naked, but just watching out of interest, as if the sight of a naked man was something new.

Thinking of James spurred him into action. It was eight o'clock, and the footman would be on his way to prepare him for the day. Not that James was a valet, or Silas needed help dressing, but he enjoyed the alone time and wanted to talk through the events of last night.

146

Mumbled voices discussed shirts and collar studs, as Silas swung his feet to the carpet. He collected his discarded clothes from the floor, and, putting on his trousers in case Lucy was about, returned to his own room.

James didn't attend him that morning, and he remembered he had told him not to. He found him in the breakfast room by which time, Archer had already eaten and left.

'Good morning, Sir,' James greeted him, placing the newly arrived newspaper on the table. 'His Lordship ate early, but left instructions for you to join him in the study at ten if you would.'

'He told me. Morning, Jimmy. You alright?'

'I am, thank you, Sir.' James attended to the array of dishes on the sideboard. 'Shall I serve your usual?'

Silas played by the rules and allowed James to wait on him. Every time it happened, it felt more awkward, because every day he felt closer to James and saw him as a friend rather than staff.

'Did you get any trouble from Thomas last night?' he asked, as James poured his coffee.

'Not at all, Sir.'

'That's good. Where's the viscount gone?'

'He had an early visit,' James explained. 'I don't know where. He will be back shortly.' Leaning in to add sugar to Silas' cup, he whispered, 'Did you tell him?'

'I did, Jimmy, and there's no need to whisper. He took it well and was interested rather than angry.'

'That's good.'

'What do you make of it? Have you had time to think about what happened?'

'Not a lot of time, Sir,' James replied, putting down a rack of toast. 'Eggs?'

More used to existing off a crust of bread and the occasional pie, Silas fell on his breakfast like a starving man. He still ate as though every meal would be his last.

'I believe...' James went on, '... that His Lordship has already started on a course of action.'

'Really?' Archer had said nothing to Silas, but then there hadn't been time.

'Ten o'clock in the study. I am to be there too.' James, now standing opposite, was concerned.

'Don't worry about it,' Silas said, offering a comforting smile. 'If he's angry, it's my fault, not yours.'

Archer wasn't angry, but he was late for the ten o'clock meeting. Silas arrived at the study to find hot coffee in a pot and James lighting the fire. Outside, the sky was a mass of grey drizzle, and the wind blew the rain against the windows in short, sudden squalls. It was a day for being by the hearth, cosy and warm. On similar days in the East End, he would have hung about Molly's rope-house for as long as she would allow before finding shelter at the bathhouse if he could afford it, or a church mission where at least he would be fed and could stay dry. Today, he could easily stay in the study, or his private sitting room upstairs, and do nothing but read the newspaper, or lie in Archer's arms. If Fecks wasn't so busy grooming the horses for the evening's carriage, he would have spent the morning with him in the coach house.

He had taken up a seat in the armchair nearest the fireplace when Thomas entered, bringing a tray of coffee.

'Unlike His Lordship to be late,' he said, examining the mantle clock and comparing it to his pocket watch.

'Do you know what this is about, Mr Payne?' James asked, rising from the fire and watching it take.

'I do not, James,' Thomas replied. 'But we are instructed to take a seat and wait.'

It was strange to hear the two speak so formally to each other, particularly as Silas knew the closeness of their relationship. The game had to be played, but at least they had learnt to bend the rules. They sat beside each other on the couch in silence, something which, according to Thomas, would never be seen in any other house.

Archer didn't keep them waiting long. They heard his approach through the drawing room and stood before he entered.

'Good, you're all here,' he said. 'Shall we sit at the table?'

His men did as instructed and sat one on each side. Archer collected the tray from the sideboard. 'Anyone else?' he offered as if they were a group of same-status individuals meeting for a game of cards.

'Allow me.' Thomas was on his feet in a second, but Archer told him to sit as he brought the coffee to the table so everyone could help themselves.

He put a folded newspaper in the centre with a notebook and a pen.

'Fecker and Lucy are out seeing to groceries or some such,' he said. 'We shan't be disturbed. From now on, until this meeting is concluded, we are a team and come together for the sake of an old friend.'

'Sounds official.' Silas helped himself from the tray.

'It's baffling,' Archer said. 'But, following on from what Silas told me last night, I have done some thinking. Now, we can't stay still for too long, things will have to move fast, and I have people to see later today, appointments that I must keep. But, for now, I suggest we start at the beginning because I am not sure what Thomas knows, if anything. We will bring him up to date and pool our thoughts.'

Thomas poured coffee for James opposite and slid it across. The footman glanced at the viscount for permission, but Archer waved it away.

'As you want, Jimmy,' he said, using the name to show the roles of footman and viscount were to be dropped.

His eyes twinkled as if they had met to plan an evening's entertainment. He had washed his hair and shaved, he wore a high collar, a green cravat and had donned an intricately patterned smoking jacket. He fingered his fringe away from his face, sweeping his thick hair back over his high forehead before cracking his knuckles.

'Right! The way forward,' he said, as if everyone knew what he was talking about, 'is to go back.'

'You're going to have to explain what you're getting at,' Silas said, furrowing his brow.

'Yes, quite,' Archer agreed. 'Tom, can you write while I speak? We have questions to answer. Everyone chip in. Perhaps you should start, Silas.'

Archer gave him one of his raised eyebrow looks. It was his way of delivering an order without actually giving one.

'Oh, right.' Silas sat straight. 'Everything?'

'Facts you know to be true,' Archer clarified. 'But also anything you might think important. Start with why you went to Cleaver Street. If you hadn't happened to have been there, we wouldn't know about this letter.'

'Luck of the Irish,' Silas joked, but it fell flat. He had been extremely lucky, but only because he didn't trust Roxton. 'I went, because I've seen him at that house before.'

'You think you have,' Archer corrected.

'You wanted known facts and suspicions,' James said, coming to Silas' aid. 'Shouldn't we write down everything?'

'Quite right, Jimmy.' Archer nodded. He smiled at Silas to make him feel better, and it helped. 'So, you had a suspicion that Cadwell uses, or used, Cleaver Street, and you went to ask them?'

'Yeah, kind of.'

'Why were you so sure?'

'It was the overcoat he wore to dinner.' As soon as the words were out of his mouth, he knew someone would shoot them down, and continued quickly. 'I saw the same kind of coat on a man at that house in August.'

'There are plenty of them about,' Archer said, as expected. He took a sip of coffee and made an appreciative noise before continuing. 'Friends,' he said. 'On the face of it, there is a simple question. Why would anyone want to blackmail Cadwell Roxton?'

'Because he's got a nasty secret.'

Archer smiled to show he was not offended by Silas' mistrust of his friend. 'Maybe he does,' he said. 'Equally, maybe he told you the truth last night when he said he had no idea why he was drugged and taken to Cleaver Street.'

'If he was drugged.'

'Indeed, Jimmy. But whether we believe him or not, the fact remains that he was there. Either of his own volition — which I doubt — or because he was kidnapped. We can only work with known facts, and the details, Silas, are?'

Silas repeated his story for Thomas' benefit. He explained how he had learned the address of the brothel, visited in disguise, and was even more convinced that Roxton used the place to meet a boy called Stella. 'He likes to meet and beat,' he said, but no-one found it amusing.

Thomas wrote, grimacing, and it was only when he learned that

James had also gone to the house that he looked up sharply.

'James was following my orders,' Silas said, before the footman suffered any trouble. 'It wasn't his fault, Tommy, and he was excellent in the back of the trap. If Jimmy hadn't been there, I'd probably have murdered Roxton.'

'No, it's not that,' Thomas said. 'It's the fact that the place is now tied to here.'

Archer asked him to explain.

'It's obvious to me,' Thomas began. 'That whether Silas is right or not, this still has a bearing on you. I don't mean the blackmail, as that's what it clearly is, I mean Mr Roxton's involvement. If it's a general hatred of men like us, then we must ask why? These people make a living out of men paying for… whatever goes on, but why draw attention to their own illegal brothel? It only makes sense to me if either they want to bring bad publicity to you and the Foundation via Mr Roxton, or he *has* used the place before, Silas is right, and it's personal revenge.'

'Yes, I see all that,' Archer said. 'And if it is to do with me, then it's been made worse by three of my men visiting the place.' His boyish enthusiasm turned briefly to annoyance, but he was able to smooth it over. 'And by being there, may have saved my friend's life, so you don't need to look so worried, Jimmy. Whether Cadwell has used the whorehouse before, he was there last night and that's bad enough. Worse, is that he was there so close to our highly publicised gala, and even worse, is this threat against him.'

'Maybe now is the time to consider the details?' Thomas suggested. 'Mr Roxton was found at Cleaver Street, naked and tied to the bed.'

'Silas rescued him.'

'We both did, Jimmy.'

'He denied knowing why he was taken?' Thomas asked.

Silas nodded. 'And how he got there.'

'But he was definitely at the house,' Archer underlined. 'As to how? I take his word for it. Yes…' He interrupted Silas before he had a chance to speak. 'I know you don't, but that's fine too, and I don't mind. We need to consider all angles, and anything you say about my old friend will have no bearing on what I think of you. Any of you.'

'You want my opinion?' Silas said, leaving no room for an answer. 'His past caught up with him. He has used the place before, done some nasty things to some of the boys, they've turned against him and are getting their own back.'

'Perhaps they were looking for a man in a public position who would respond better to blackmail.' Thomas thought aloud. 'He's not a politician, and I dare say many of them use such places, but he is a man in the news and has a reputation he would, presumably, pay to keep.'

'Or it could have been random bullying,' James said, gazing into the middle distance, his face clouded.

'Too many theories.' Archer drummed his fingers. 'Let's turn to what you overheard.'

Everyone looked at Silas.

'I didn't hear much,' he admitted. 'Only that they were beating him…'

'Sounds like a warning to me,' James put in. 'I mean, a way of reinforcing their threat.'

'Which was to do what?'

'To expose him,' Silas said. 'I can't remember all the words, but the meaning was clear.'

'What do you recall?' Thomas asked, checking his notes. 'Bit by bit.'

'That someone arrived after I was there, and Danvers said "He" was in the Arabian room.'

'So, Danvers was expecting Stella?'

'Yeah, Tom, looks that way,' Silas nodded. 'It was the boy they call Stella 'cos I heard him talking about himself. He was a bloke one minute and a woman the next. Pretty good act, I suppose. But then he said something about "You're not getting away until we get what we want", or similar.'

'Did you recognise his voice, Silas?' Archer asked.

Silas thought carefully. It had been dark. He'd not seen the man's features, but had been able to concentrate on the voice. There had been something familiar about it, but probably only the accent.

'It was East End,' he said. 'English not immigrant. Least it was when he spoke as a man. After that, it was a girl's voice with something country about it. Can't imitate it accurately enough, but

152

I did think I'd heard the voice before.'

'When you went to the house in August with… Who was it?'

'Eddie Lovemount,' James said, and Silas agreed.

'Ridiculous name,' Thomas mumbled as he wrote.

'Yes, well, never mind what this Stella sounds like,' Archer said. 'It wouldn't help much anyway. So, we have Roxton on the bed, and Stella beating him, threatening him to do as they say or…?'

What came next? Silas wished he had written things down as soon as he returned home. A night with Archer, which didn't stop at sex on the couch, had left him full of erotic thoughts rather than ugly facts.

'Next,' he said, closing his eyes to remember. 'He said that Roxton had his instructions and he was to follow them down to the letter. Only one chance… They don't want money… "I want your fucking reputation, mate", were the exact words.' He said it in Stella's accent.

'Could still be a random victim,' Thomas offered, but Archer countered.

'Not if he already had instructions.'

'Yeah, but there was other stuff,' Silas was sticking up for his theory. 'Stella said things about how being lashed made you feel worthless like it had been done to him and this was revenge for it. And he said something about taking Roxton down the same way as "them others" like others had taken him to a room all posh and sexy, but then turned violent. Sorry, not totally accurate, but that was the gist. You see? Revenge for ill-treatment. He said again that Roxton had to do what he was instructed, or Stella wasn't going to be happy, as if he was talking about someone else, his other character.'

'But both voices, both characters, were definitely the same man?'

'Yes, Archie. To be sure.'

'Right,' Archer clapped his hands. 'If that's all you can recall, Silas, what else do we have?'

'In the trap after,' James said. 'Silas was a bit miffed, so Fecker sat him upfront…'

'Yeah, well no need to show me up,' Silas muttered.

'Sorry, Mr Hawkins, but you were very angry.'

'Still am,' Silas huffed. 'And there's no need for Mr Hawkins.' He winked at James, his usual signal that he was not offended.

'What about the trap?' Archer asked.

'We were bringing him back when he gave us the story about being drugged,' James continued. 'Seemed genuine to me. He also denied knowing what they meant about instructions.'

'They'd only left him his coat, is that right?' Thomas pointed his pen at Silas, ready to add details to his list.

'It was all I could find in the rush. I wasn't hanging about, but 'cos he was naked, couldn't let him leave with nothing on. He took ages trying to find his clothes, but they weren't there. I had to drag him away in the end.'

Thomas made another note, and Archer's face twisted in thought.

'One thing's clear,' he said and waited while the others tried to work out what he meant. 'He spoke of "us" and "we", as if he wasn't acting alone.'

'He wasn't,' Silas agreed. 'Danvers was expecting Stella, and by the sound of it, Stella hadn't been the one to drug Roxton, if that's what happened.'

'Then it's a conspiracy,' Archer said. 'I told him as much.'

Silas was surprised. 'You've spoken to him?'

'That's why I was a little late,' Archer explained. 'I caught him at breakfast, alone luckily, and told him I knew everything you had seen.'

'Bet he was angry we were there.'

'He denied it at first, Jimmy. I came up with a cover story as to why Silas was hiding in the room, but he wasn't interested. Just told me he didn't know what happened but assumed it was mistaken identity.'

'You offered to help him?' Thomas asked.

'Yes, but he doesn't want our help. I tried for an eternity to extract information, but he would only talk about his performance and how that was the only thing on his mind. He was insistent that I never speak of last night again. Now that I think of it, he didn't even apologise for missing our dinner.'

'Well, then we let him stew in his own juice.'

'No, Silas.' Archer was firm on that, even a little annoyed. 'He is her Ladyship's nephew and an old friend who may have landed himself in hot water. I offered to help, but he told me it was nothing and that I had more important things to concern myself with today.

He was not concerned, and, to be frank, I tend to agree with him. However, I side with Tom on this one. We should at least consider the situation. Perhaps it is something we can worry about after the gala.'

Typically, Archer had no thought for himself, only for his friends. It was admirable, but what Archer couldn't see, or what he didn't want to consider, was the knock-on effect Roxton's exposure would have on himself.

'There is more at stake than friendship,' Thomas said, seemingly picking up on Silas' thoughts. 'But the friendship is important.'

'Explain?' Archer sat back and folded his arms.

Thomas referred to his notes. 'They intend to bring down more than Mr Roxton,' he said. 'They have an agenda, though we don't know what it is, but the timing is important. The gala is this evening. It's your night, Archer, yours, Lady Marshall's and the Foundation's, of course. If this was simply personal, Silas, why wait until now?'

'I don't know, maybe Stella's taken this long to plot his revenge on his torturer.'

Archer, his eyes still on Thomas, pushed the newspaper to Silas and pointed out a column of print while he spoke to Thomas. 'I have to ask you why? What is their purpose?'

'Shut up.' Silas was so suddenly angry it surprised even himself. He held up his hand, and the others waited, open-mouthed as he read aloud sections from the newspaper.

'"Cadwell Roxton…"' he began. '"Successful season at the Paris opera… Blah, blah. Returned to our shores last week until when he had been touring France, Germany and Italy since April last." Fuck.'

'You see?' Archer's good humour was back. 'He was out of the country in August. He can't have been the man you saw.'

'Well, his laugh's the same.' Knowing he had been wrong, Silas slumped in a sulk.

Archer reached over and squeezed his hand. 'Sorry.'

'We're still left with why,' James said. 'Do you have anything else, Tom?'

'Yes, quite a bit, but one thing at a time. First, I would ask, what are these instructions?'

Archer let Silas go, and they exchanged a glance. He would never understand how Archer did it, but in one brief exchange, he knew that there was no bitterness, only love.

'He didn't appear to know of these instructions,' James said, and Silas returned to the conversation.

'Which is a thought that occurred to me at about five this morning,' Archer said. 'Sorry to drag you out of bed so early, Tom. How did you get on?'

Silas remembered the creaking floorboards.

'I found this,' Thomas answered, and drew an envelope from his pocket.

Archer explained. 'I woke Thomas and asked him to go next door,' he said. 'I remembered that Roxton had nothing but an overcoat, and wondered if perhaps they had put instructions there without him knowing. As in, "You have your instructions" meaning, "I've just given them to you."' He nodded to Thomas.

'I called on her Ladyship's butler.' He continued the story, speaking to James and Silas as if Archer already knew what he was going to say. 'I told him His Lordship was keen to launder Mr Roxton's overcoat, because it had been soiled on the way back from the club. Mr Saunders was under the impression that the evening had gone according to plan and they'd dined together, so there was no suspicion. It doesn't need cleaning, it's in my pantry, but I found this in the pocket.'

He put the envelope in the centre of the table for everyone to see.

'May I?'

'You're the postal expert, Jimmy,' Archer grinned.

James examined it.

'You going to tell us it was made from pulped oak trees and pressed by the feet of Scottish nuns?' Silas joked, remembering the last time they examined an envelope. Another thought struck. 'Hey, Archie, you don't think this is Quill do you?'

Archer shook his head. 'Not his style, I'd say, but we can't rule out anything. Go on, Jimmy.'

'Sorry, Silas,' James said. 'It's just a standard post office issue envelope, unremarkable and not stamped. It wasn't posted, there's no address. In fact, it says nothing but the man's name.'

'No clues there,' Thomas noted.

'Inside…?' James extracted a folded letter. Before opening it, he held it to the light. 'Watermarked… W H Smith, nothing fancy, no pattern.' He unfolded it on the table. 'What the fu…? Sorry, My Lord.'

'Not at all,' Archer said. 'I had a similar reaction. Gentlemen, being honest, I am inclined to take this as an amateurish attempt to blacken someone's good name, but not a threat that has any great weight. However, Silas is concerned, and so you are welcome to give it the attention which today, I can ill afford.'

'That's up to you, Archie,' Silas said, hiding his disappointment. 'But I reckon we should take it seriously.'

'I'd agree with you,' James said, passing him the letter. 'Read it, but remember we have less than nine hours before the curtain goes up.'

Eighteen

The letter

*C*adwell Roxton,
    Go on stage before the opera and say this:
    Clearwater is opening a house for sodomites. It is not a hostel, it will be a brothel for sexual deviants like yourselves. Tell them what you do behind closed doors, and tell them the truth.

And, if you do not make this speech before your performance, we will kill you.

Death will come da capo, suddenly silent, and you will not hear your final applause.

Fail us and you die.

'That's it,' Silas said and passed the letter to Thomas.

'Er, police?' James asked.

'Cadwell was adamant it was a sick joke and did not want me to inform the authorities,' Archer said.

'It's sick alright.'

'It is, Jimmy,' the viscount nodded. 'But it's all we have, and because of what Silas witnessed, we can assume it's not a joke. I am meeting with trustees and others this afternoon at the opera house, and I will ask Bursnall about security arrangements. He's a very open-minded man, but I shan't tell him the reason for my enquiry. If I am not satisfied, I shall consider reporting the matter vaguely but urgently to the police. I think that is all we can do.'

'The bastards behind this will be counting on Roxton to be too scared to go to the rozzers,' was Silas' thought on the subject.

'The first part of this is very clear,' Thomas said, passing him the letter. 'As is the last line. But the one before last?'

Silas read the note, written in ink and block capitals. '"Death will come da capo, suddenly silent, and you will not hear your final applause". He passed it on to James. 'Is that the part you mean, Tommy?'

'Yes. Suddenly and silent make sense, though I am not sure how it's possible to kill someone silently during a performance of an opera.'

'Or halfway through a speech,' James added. When Thomas looked at him quizzically, he explained. 'As soon as it becomes apparent that he's not saying what they want him to say...' He left it hanging, but when no-one finished the thought for him, he sighed and said, 'No point waiting until the end of the show. Might as well kill him at the end of the speech when, I assume, there will also be applause.'

'Good point,' Thomas said, gazing at the bookshelves.

'And if he doesn't make this speech?' Silas said. 'They'd do away with him anyway?'

'Yes,' Thomas nodded. 'A death during the performance will cause a scandal for the Foundation, not to mention the opera house.'

'From what Jake showed me yesterday,' Silas said. 'There are plenty of ways you could kill someone in a theatre. Whole thing's a death trap.'

Thomas rose and, after asking permission, took a book from the shelf. Opening it and finding a page, he read, "'Da capo, an Italian musical term meaning *from the beginning*, literally *from the head*. Often abbreviated to D.C., it can instruct the player or singer to return to the beginning of a work or section." That's from Grove's, and he knows what he is talking about.'

'A sudden death from the head...?' James glanced from one to the other. 'A gunshot?'

'Hardly silent,' Silas observed.

'But possible for a marksman hiding in the auditorium.'

Thomas closed the book with a loud snap, as if illustrating his point.

The sound jolted James. 'It still doesn't give us any clues,' he said. 'Except that if he doesn't do as he's told, he's going to be killed, presumably at some time before the end of the speech or performance.'

Thomas replaced the book and began pacing the room, moving

from the fireplace to the writing table, his hands behind his head, his fingers laced.

'The man's an idiot,' Silas said, helplessly. 'He can't just ignore this, and neither can we.'

'So what do we do?' James was also at a loss.

'For a start, we don't go anywhere near Cleaver Street,' Archer complained.

He moved to his captain's chair and rested his elbows on the desk, his knuckles pressed against his forehead.

Silas went to him. Thomas could sit there making notes, being logical and aloof, but Archer needed someone to show him he was not alone. He didn't need this extra pressure, and as, like Roxton, he had chosen to ignore it, the best thing for Silas to do was humour him and offer reassurance while silently trying to figure it out. He stood behind him and massaged his shoulders.

'Here's an idea,' he said. 'I'll come with you to the theatre this afternoon. While you have your meeting, I'll get Jake to show me around some more, and while he's doing it, I'll check the place out. See if I can find out from Jake who's going to be backstage during the show.'

'What good will that do?' Thomas asked, and Silas wasn't sure if he was being methodical or critical.

'Put in extra security just in case.'

The viscount leant back in his chair and held Silas' hands, pulling them down so their heads rested beside side by side. The gesture, made without thinking, reassured Silas that he was still number one in Archer's eyes.

'That still leaves the auditorium,' James said. 'And I'd say that's the most likely place for someone to fire a gun. There will be, what? Two-thousand people in there, many of them in the upper balconies, people from the East End, people the theatre is not used to dealing with. Anyone could bring in a concealed weapon, shoot it and scarper.'

'They'd be seen.' Thomas offered, and James countered with, 'Depends where they were.'

They debated possibilities for another minute until Archer, pale and sighing, said, 'I've decided,' and the discussion was ended. 'I believe you are worrying unnecessarily. If that letter was meant to do anything, it was to distract Cadwell from his performance in the way that it is distracting us from our day.'

Archer sounded tired. It was hardly surprising. He had been building his Foundation since before Silas met him, and apart from Quill's interference, it had been the driving force of his life. He had worked tirelessly to make the gala happen while overseeing the conversions at the property in Greychurch, fighting the media and his peers while keeping all the threads of his life untangled. That was on top of the pressure he, and every man in the room, suffered when keeping their private lives concealed from the public. Where Quill had twice now sought Archer's death and failed, a threat like this could lead to a much longer-lasting end. Prison, a massacre of his reputation, and potentially the loss of his fortune. Silas doubted that Archer had concerns for those consequences. What meant most to him was the Foundation and the young men he aimed to help.

'Leave it to us, Archie,' he whispered. 'Remember what you said at that graveside? Every moment of your life is dedicated to us? Well, it works both ways.' He righted himself and addressed the others. 'While I'm backstage, Tom, can you check out the part where the crowd sit.'

'The auditorium,' Thomas corrected.

'If you say so.' Silas winked, and it almost brought a grin to Thomas' stern face. 'When the toffs... Sorry, Archie, when the posh lot come to watch, they'll bring their butlers right?'

'If they're in a box, they might,' Archer yawned. 'Why?'

'Well, as butler to Lord Clearwater, Tommy's got a reason to be there early snooping around the facilities on behalf of all the others. Your mate Bursnall won't be suspicious.'

'But His Lordship and guests are only using the one box.' Thomas wasn't so sure. 'What reason do I have if I am found in the grand circle or the gods? Apart from that, what am I looking for?'

Silas hadn't thought his idea through, he never did, but, making it up as he went along, his ideas came out in a sensible order. 'You're getting the lie of the land, so His Lordship is assured his important guests will have everything on hand they need,' he improvised.

Thomas' silence showed that he had considered the idea and was not against it.

'On the subject of guests,' Archer said, rising and stretching his back. 'My important guests will be the men and women from Greychurch, not the toffs in the stalls. But my most important personal guests will be with me, or wherever they can be.'

'Who's that then?' Silas asked, returning to the couch.

'You,' Archer said. He smiled faintly, but it was soon lost behind his concern. 'All of you. Thomas will attend me in my box with Lady Marshall, Markland and his friend. Oh, and Mr and Mrs Marks. James? You will be there with Tom as Silas' man. They have drop-down seats at the back of the box if you want to watch.'

'You mean it?' James' eyes lit up like a recently cleaned gas lamp. 'Me in the opera house?'

His reaction brought a laugh to Archer's throat which Silas was pleased to hear.

'Of course,' the viscount said. 'And in the correct uniform.' He addressed Thomas. 'It's not a royal performance, so no need for that particular monstrosity.'

'We've not yet ordered a new royal livery,' Thomas reminded him. 'Her Ladyship has not designed one, and I doubt I would fit into Tripp's old thing.'

'Well, it's not needed, but Fecker will have to wear his carriage livery, and we will ride with him.'

Thomas noted the request on a separate piece of paper as Archer continued.

'Mrs Flintwich and her husband, with Fecker and Lucy have seats at the front of the amphitheatre.'

'Better not put them in the back row,' Silas joked.

'There are opera glasses,' Archer said. 'You'll be able to see him.'

He'd missed Silas' point — that Fecks and the maid were growing closer every day and took every chance they could to be alone together — but he let it go.

Archer decreed that apart from passing the incriminating letter to the police should they be desperate, there was nothing else to do but ponder the clue, if that was what it was while forearming themselves with knowledge, in this case, the layout of the theatre.

Silas suggested they gather again later that afternoon to discuss what they might find, and Thomas, keeping an eye on the time, decided they should take a quick and early lunch.

'Shall I lay the dining room, Mr Payne?' James asked, as he stood and straightened his jacket.

'Don't worry, Jimmy,' Archer cut in. 'There's only us today, and I don't feel much like eating. Tom? Tell Mrs Flintwich we shan't need dinner as there's a reception after the performance. She and Lucy can take the rest of the day off, but we'll have a light supper before we leave, and they will need to be ready to depart at six-thirty.'

'She will be happy about that, Sir,' Thomas said, as he opened the doors. 'She needs to have her hair done.'

'Oh Lord,' Archer grinned. 'She's only got eight hours until curtain up. But joking aside, friends...' He became serious. 'I can't imagine what would have happened had Silas not gone out last night, but at least we are forewarned. We shall hopefully return from the opera house forearmed and possibly rid of this annoyance. Either way, we shall dress and meet together at six. That doesn't give us much time. James, would you and Fecker arrange the transport?'

'Certainly, My Lord.'

James' switch from Jimmy to first footman was impressive. Tonight, Silas would have to shift from lover to secretary, but before then, he had to play the part of investigator, and there was still the matter of Roxton's innocence to prove, or, more likely, disprove.

As they left the study, he pulled James to one side and waited for Archer and Thomas to leave the drawing room.

'I've got a job for you,' he said, when they were alone.

'Yes, Sir?' The midday sun was battling its way through an overhang of grey, and the light from the netted windows lit James in a mottled shaft of silver as he waited eagerly to hear what Silas had to say.

'You've got to be careful,' Silas began. 'And don't tell anyone what you're doing, but when we've gone, I want you to look into something.'

'Of course, Sir.'

'Dump the "Sir" shit, Jimmy,' Silas sighed. 'This is out of uniform, right?'

'Okay,' James nodded, fascinated.

'There'll only be you and Lucy in the house, but still, watch your back.'

'Lucy seems alright.'

'Yeah, probably, but if she says anything to Thomas, it's going to cause problems.'

'Why? What do you want me to do?'

'The both of us, Jimmy,' Silas said. 'Archer might not take this seriously, but I do.' He glanced to the hall, but the sounds of leather shoes on tiles had long faded. 'We've got to ignore the first rule of Clearwater and go behind his back.'

Nineteen

James set to work on Silas' request as soon as the others left Clearwater House. His livery covered by an overcoat, he hurried to the back of Delamere, Lady Marshall's adjoining property and rang the back doorbell. The hall boy who greeted him passed his message to the second footman, he to the first, and from there it was taken by Mr Saunders, the butler, to Her Ladyship in her private salon.

With the sky clouding over and threatening rain, James was glad to accept the offer to wait in the servants' hall. It was identical to Clearwater in design but reversed and busier. Lady Marshall favoured male servants, it seemed. Everyone James saw, from the cook to the hall boy, was a man, apart from one maid and the housekeeper, who, the boy told him, was married to the cook. Delamere had twice as many staff as Clearwater, and James assumed her Ladyship did more entertaining than the viscount. She also had a liking for foreigners, judging by the many languages spoken by the staff. The hall boy, Peter, was from South Riverside, the same as James, and was, he said, the only local apart from Mr Saunders. Interesting though the conversation was, James was keen to hear her Ladyship's reply, and it finally came back down the chain as a note. Written on a scented card, the message was exactly what he wanted to hear.

They will be with you in half an hour, dear boy. Intrigued. FFN.

'What's the FFN for?' he asked, as Peter showed him out.

'Her Ladyship writes that on everything,' the lad told him. 'It stands for Farewell For Now. Her Ladyship says we should never take one second for granted, because every second could be our last. So, she always says farewell in letters just in case they take longer to arrive than she has left to live.'

James returned to Clearwater thinking her Ladyship's habit apt considering her nephew might well have his final moment that evening. Although the task Silas had given him was not directly involved with Mr Roxton's safety, it was part of the story, and according to Silas, vital for him to know and Lord Clearwater not to discover. James was more than happy to assist, not only because he loved his job and Clearwater House, but because in Silas, he had found a kindred spirit. He was not alone in his new world, Silas too was an amateur in his station, and his presence gave James confidence.

He took it with him into the library. Having lit an oil lamp, because the curtains and shutters were closed, he set about clearing a large table. That done, and having made sure Lucy was below stairs, he entered the viscount's study and took away his copy of Bradshaw's Continental Railway Guide. Silas had told him he would need it and that he would have to betray Archer's trust by entering his study without permission, but he had also said that he would take full responsibility if the need arose. Once he explained to James what he was about, James was more than happy to join in with the scheme and didn't care that it might lead to trouble. They were looking out for the viscount, and Silas needed help. They were the only two things that mattered.

He was back in the library, arranging paper, pens and the large atlas when he heard Lucy crossing the hall. Lady Marshall was as good as her word. Better, in fact, because Oleg was ten minutes early. He carried a large pile of newspapers and refused James' help to heave the burden to the library. He placed them on the table as if they were weightless and stood erect. He was almost as tall and wide as Fecker and had a similar accent.

'From Her Ladyship,' he said, the words dripping from his lips like honey. 'She does not need them returned, but she is looking forward to an explanation.'

James thanked him, had Lucy show him out, and then shut himself in the room. Her Ladyship would be given one of two explanations depending on what he found. It was either going to be an inconsequential invention — that James wanted to brush up on previous court circulars and society news, or it would be something far more unpalatable. He hoped, for Silas' sake, it would be the latter, not because he wished trouble on Mr Roxton, but because he didn't want to lie to Lady Marshall, nor to anyone.

Examining the first few copies of The Times, he realised that they were stacked in date order, working backwards. That made his task a lot simpler, and he discarded October and September's publications immediately. Working through the August editions, he looked for headlines that mentioned the weather. The newspaper was a wall of small print in long columns and very dull, unlike The Illustrated Police News which he used to read at The Crown and Anchor, but each section was divided by a heading which was easy to spot, and he soon learnt where the meteorological reports were listed. He found what he was looking for in the August 17th edition, "The Impossible Heat", a summary of the then current wave of unusually hot weather. Looking at the paper printed seven days before, and following through from that date, he was able to find the editions printed during the hottest week of the month; the hottest on record, according to The Times.

He had found the period when Silas saw Roxton at Cleaver Street.

Putting that week's editions in order, he turned to the arts pages, running his finger down each column and muttering as he scanned the print looking for any mention of Roxton.

Nothing.

He checked the Society pages.

'Lady Somerset is giving a ball… The Earl of Broxton is planning a hunt… Sir John Sebastian Bach Stopford is…' He reread the name, 'That's got to be a joke,' and carried on, searching every appropriate section for the full seven days.

He found nothing, and time was moving on.

Checking the mantle clock, he was shocked to see the hour hand approaching the three. The others were due back at five, and in Thomas' absence, it was up to James to lay out and inspect the viscount's naval dress uniform. He gave himself one more hour, then he would have to throw away the papers, tidy up, see to the uniform and his own evening livery, and be ready for duty.

He looked at the stash of publications still to read; it would take him hours even at his scanning speed. There had to be a more logical approach. Thomas would have thought of one, and he missed his presence. Tom was always so calm and gentle, serene almost as if he floated through life on a never-fading cloud of contentment. He was the same in everything. Whether he was serving a vintage port or stroking James' hair, his long fingers were always assured, his voice soft.

'What are you doing?' He caught his mind wandering.

He considered the newspapers, now in four piles.

'What am I looking for?' He knew full well what it was, but he did what Thomas would have done, "The three S's on entering a room", he called it: Stop, take Stock, and Start again.

'I'm looking for someone who isn't there,' he said, an idea forming. 'He's not going to be in the society pages, because he wasn't in the country. If he had been, Archer would have known. Archer thinks he was on tour in…' He conferred with the notes Thomas had made in his perfectly neat handwriting. 'Paris for three appearances between the seventeenth and twenty-third. Before that, he was in Italy and Germany.'

The answer lay between those dates, and he reviewed his information.

The hottest period of August had run between 17th and 24th, coinciding with Roxton's appearances in Paris, and Silas' sighting of him at Cleaver Street. He drew a rough diary on his paper.

'You have your timeframe,' he whispered, tapping the pen against his teeth. 'What are you looking for now?'

The answer was simple. He was still trying to find reports of a man who wasn't there.

'Not wasn't there. Wasn't here!' The thought hit him out of the blue and with it came an image of Thomas grinning in that way he did when they'd just had sex. He looked like a hunting dog that had brought back a pheasant; huge eyes, panting hard, looking for a reward.

'Concentrate! He wasn't here…' He clicked his fingers. He almost had it. 'Because he was… Overseas.'

He knew where to look, and he had a good idea when.

'The best possible dates to slip away would have been between performances,' he reasoned, double checking the dates. 'But that's only one day off in between. There's no time to get from Paris to the city and back in twenty-four hours. He arrived in Paris on the seventeenth…' He was flicking through newspapers for the August twenty-fourth edition. It was after the hot week, but news travelled slowly from France, and events that happened on one day were rarely reported in the city papers until a few days later.

'Overseas Arts,' he read. 'Now we're getting somewhere.' A headline caught his eye.

The Times, Wednesday 24th August, 1888

A Fearful Time for Bruch

Had he been living, Austro-German born composer, Johann Bruch, might have wondered what fate would befall the revival of his acclaimed opera, "Aeneas and Dido". He would have been interested to be among the audience at the Opéra Populaire for the appearance of famed countertenor, Mr Cadwell Roxton, a performance that did not go completely to plan.

Bruch, a contemporary of Wagner, studied counterpoint and harmony under Weinlig at St Thomas' School, Leipzig, and his scores are praised for their use of compassionate…

James skipped ahead a paragraph.

How unsettling then it must have been for the company to learn of Mr Roxton's illness. Although the performance went ahead, his tone was noticeably underplayed and his projection not quite of the expected standard. Our correspondent tells us that the critics and commentators were benevolent, concerned for Mr Roxton's voice rather than critical of his performance. "I would suggest no vocal work for at least four days," Maestro Lamoureux, conducting, said.

There was no more, but after glancing at his diary, James searched the newspapers for August 26th, opened that day's edition to the same page and quickly found what he was looking for.

He slapped the air in triumph but wasted no time. He tore the page from the paper and piled the rest onto a bottom bookshelf partially hidden by the piano. He would dispose of them later, for now, he needed the viscount's railway guide.

Back at the table, he arranged the atlas to its double-page spread of northern Europe to one side, his paper in the centre and the railway guide to the other. The Times had reported, days after the event, that Cadwell Roxton had taken his composer's advice and bowed out of his second performance. He had been replaced by his understudy (who had done a remarkable job, apparently, but who had choked when drinking from the chalice, whatever that meant). Roxton had plenty of time between his first and third appearances, four days apart, to travel from Paris to the city and back. Silas had mentioned the man's voice had sounded croaky; that made sense. What didn't add up was why he should travel all that way just to find a boy. Surely Paris was overrun with corruption and whores. That's what the popular press said.

'Not important', he told himself. 'Give him the benefit of the doubt. Maybe he has a doctor here and came to see him. He really was ill, came to see the quack, gave a boy a slap and slipped back before curtain up four days later… Ah.'

He had located the Paris section of the guidebook and from there the railway timetables. There was no way of telling if this was how Roxton had travelled, but it made sense that he took the fastest route. Somewhere, there would be a record of him making the channel crossing, but there was no time to find that. He had the newspaper report of his cancelled appearance and the proof that the journey was not only possible but now, thanks to his illness, probable, particularly if that illness was to do with his instrument, his voice.

It would be good enough for Silas. What the viscount would make of it was another matter.

'All I need to prove is that it was possible.' James reassured himself as he drew his pen down the list of train departures.

There were more than Roxton would have needed. He could have left directly after the first show and reached Cleaver Street with a day and a night to spare before heading back. Or, he could have left on the Thursday morning and still returned in good time for the following Tuesday.

There was no doubt. Roxton could quite easily have been the man Silas saw at Cleaver Street.

That didn't mean it was him, but it was all James had. They were blackmailing Roxton to see him fall, and the person behind it was without a doubt Stella, the boy he had repeatedly flogged. The rest of the people involved in the brothel must have feared him to let him so dangerously risk bringing their operation to light, and James decided he never wanted to meet the man.

He understood how someone so used and discarded might want to take revenge. He had contemplated all manner of ways to get his own back on the workmates who bullied and beat him in his youth, but why bring down a benevolent man such as Archer and a Foundation as worthy as his? If it was for money, there were far richer public figures than an opera singer. What was the point?

His heart was beating too fast. He had allowed anger to seep in, and if he let it take control, he would do something rash. Taking deep breaths, he reminded himself that he was working for Silas, and concentrated on collecting facts. That done, and his pulse running less urgently, he folded his evidence into his pocket with the blackmail letter, tidied the library table and returned the railway guide to the study.

By the time the others returned, no further forward on the possible murder attempt, the uniforms were brushed and laid out, the fires lit in both suites, and his own, more formal dinner livery, ready for inspection.

He had just hung it when he heard the trap sweep into the yard, and looking from his garret window, saw only Fecker. Descending to the basement, he met Thomas coming from above stairs, his face a map of frowns and creases.

'Anything?' he asked, helping Tom off with his coat.

'No,' was the worried reply. 'Silas' friend says it's hard to keep a check on who's backstage during a staging, no matter how many staff there are to see to security. There's a chorus of over fifty, the principals have their entourages, Signora Campanelli alone has thirteen in her party, the carpenters are often still at work, the list goes on. Meanwhile, out front, there are so many curtains and doors, lanterns and seats to hide behind that the only time anyone would be aware of a firearm was when it was fired.'

That was the long, purging answer, and once Thomas had vented his frustration, James was about to ask Mr Hawkins' whereabouts, when Silas appeared on the stairs one floor above.

'James?' he called. 'Can I borrow you up here?'

'Right away, Sir,' James called up. 'Mr Payne,' he said, adopting his footman's voice. 'His Lordship's uniform is ready, but I would appreciate it if you have time to check it, as it's my first time. Mr Hawkins' clothes are also prepared. The fires are lit, and my uniform is hanging for when you want to inspect it.'

'Well done, James,' Thomas said, still distracted. 'We've decided to eat at six. When you've seen to Mr Hawkins, you can lay the breakfast room. It's informal.'

'Of course, Mr Payne.'

He left Thomas heading for his pantry and was in Silas' suite a minute later.

Silas was shirtless at the washstand. 'No time for a bath,' he explained. 'How did you get on?'

'You were right,' James said, as soon as he had closed the door. 'At least, it's possible.'

He explained what he had found, and showed Silas the newspaper articles. The first described Roxton's difficult appearance, and the later one his disappearance. He had also found a third that confirmed Roxton was in his role for the last of the three performances.

'Possible, probable and definitely happened,' Silas said, as James passed a towel.

'Will you tell His Lordship?'

'Ah, Jimmy,' Silas gave him a smile and patted his cheek. 'Now there's the dilemma, eh? Do we tell Archer his old friend has lied to him and everyone else, and that he *was* using Cleaver Street, and that's Stella's motive? Or do we say nothing and let him dream on?'

'I'm guessing,' James said, as he followed Silas across the room. 'That you're in favour of saying nothing.'

'I am, Jimmy,' Silas replied with a sigh. He removed his trousers and James looked away, as Thomas had told him to do. 'There's no point him knowing now, it would only spoil his night. Either way, we're in the shit if we can't figure out how and when the man's going be killed. If Roxton finds out we know, maybe he'll do as they want to save his life. He might do that anyway. Once he gets on that stage, he's got the audience in the palm of his greasy little hand. There'll be nothing we can do.'

'There's something we can do before that, though.' James turned

172

to Silas and found him completely naked. Mr Hawkins was unbothered, even when James stumbled in his role and ogled for too long.

'It's not a lot, Jimmy,' Silas laughed at his expression. 'But it's got me this far.' He began searching for clean underwear.

'Sorry,' James stammered. 'Just wasn't expecting that.'

'Get away with you, man.' Silas maintained his cheerful attitude unbothered. 'Tell me what you were going to say. What can we do?'

James swallowed and took a deep breath hoping it would take the heat from his cheeks.

'We can stop him from making any kind of speech at all.'

Silas, bending to pull on his long johns, inadvertently presented James with his bare backside. He hopped on one leg, turning and pulling up his drawers.

'Brilliant,' he said, beaming.

'The question is, how?'

'And the answer is easy.' Silas tucked in his cock which had popped through the fly. 'We need Roxton to go back in time.'

'No-one can go back in time. It's impossible.' James didn't understand.

'It'll be tricky,' Silas grinned. 'But luckily I know someone with just the right name.'

Twenty

Bucks Avenue was alight with lanterns. Outside Delamere and Clearwater House, burning torches fought the drizzle and won. Their flames danced elegantly against the backdrop of the fallen night and were supplemented by the warm glow of gaslight through netted windows. Across the street, drapes were drawn back to allow residents to see the fine display of warmth, and those neighbours not invited to the gala gathered to watch the arrival and departure of carriages.

Inside Clearwater, Silas descended the stairs to find the hall dazzling beneath the chandelier. He stopped to admire himself in one of the mirrors and blinked in disbelief. What would his sisters think of him now? His hair was washed, brushed and lightly coated with Macassar oil to keep it in place. The style was shorter, better kept and more fashionable than he had ever managed before, but it was heavy, as if he was wearing a cap. James had dressed him in a black, tailed dinner suit with satin lapels, tailored to contrast his shoulders against his slim hips. Beneath it, he wore a low-cut white waistcoat and a bow tie and a high collar. James, remembering how Silas detested the rigours of a starched collar, had gone easy, and the material was soft enough not to trouble him. With his suit trousers fitting perfectly and a new pair of polished, black dress boots, he felt like a waiter, but looked like a city gent. A far cry from his trousers held up with string and his buttonless coat of two months ago. The only relic of his previous life was in his pocket. The single pebble that Fecker had given him as a friendship token and which Thomas had saved from his rags when Silas was brought, exhausted to Clearwater last October. He had travelled a long way since leaving Westerpool on the mail coach, and his mam would have been proud.

A moment of sadness passed over him. She would never know

what her son had achieved. What Archer had let him achieve, he corrected. Without the viscount, he would be scratching gutters for coins and chatting up Molly at the rope-house to get the best bench for the damp night ahead. Now, he was dressed like a toff and about to sit in a box at the City Opera House. It was all thanks to Archer.

Another wave of sadness washed over him. The scene would have been perfect were it not for what he knew about Roxton. The moment passed when he turned his attention to what he had to do. It was not going to be easy. He had to lie to Archer to protect him while finding some way of saving Roxton's life without drawing attention. Not only that, he and James still had to work out how the murder was to happen and when.

It was six o'clock. Cadwell Roxton was due on stage in ninety minutes where he was expected to sing the praises of the Clearwater Foundation to the glitterati of City society. Or, he was to announce his crimes and implicate Archer. Whatever the man might or might not say, Silas had to stop him from stepping foot on the boards until after the overture, and even then, he had a duty to protect him, not because he cared for the man, he didn't, but because he cared for Archer.

It was not going to be easy, but when he saw James enter the hall behind him, he knew he had an ally.

'Look at you like a polished sovereign,' Silas said, turning.

'It's one of Lady Marshall's designs,' James said. He was smiling as he approached, but on seeing they were alone, the smile faded and was replaced by a less comfortable expression. 'To be honest, Mr Hawkins, I feel like I'm in the pantomime.'

'That'll be the breeches,' Silas grinned back.

He examined James from his feet to his face. Highly polished black shoes, tight white stockings to his knees where garters joined them to breeches the colour of autumn leaves that shaped his thighs. He wore a collar and large bowtie, but that was all that could be seen of his shirt, the rest was encased in a brocade waistcoat of rich green and gold, but it was the tailcoat that shone most. To his calves and with wide cuffs, it was tailored in emerald green, intricately patterned with gold thread and its buttons did, indeed, look like gold sovereigns.

'I'm glad I don't have to wear a wig,' James said. 'Apparently, that's only for when I have to go with His Lordship to the palace.'

'I wouldn't know, mate,' Silas whispered and drew him to one side. James was pale. 'Are you alright?'

'I suppose so. Are you?'

'We've got a lot to do,' Silas said. 'And no idea how to do it, apart from this…'

He ran through their strategy once more. They had discussed the situation while dressing, but their plan was limited.

'It's going to be difficult with Archer sitting with us,' he said. '… but I'll find a way to lose him before the show starts. Your job is to think, Jimmy. When and how.'

The baize door opened with a brush of carpet.

'I understand, Sir,' James said, straightening as Thomas appeared. 'The breakfast room is prepared.'

'Ah, Mr Hawkins,' Thomas said. 'May I say you look resplendent?'

'You may, Payne, thank you,' Silas replied with a grin. 'And may I say that you do and all, assuming what you said means you look like a million guineas.'

Thomas bowed his head gracefully. Where James' livery was dazzling, Thomas' was one notch up. Similar colours and design, but, if it was possible, with more opulence. Silas was worried that he might outshine his master, but when they entered the breakfast room, he knew that was not possible.

Silas had seen Archer smartly dressed before, but nothing compared to the sight that met his eyes. His heart missed several skips as he gazed on the man. *His* man. The man he had fallen in love with and adored more each day. Archer wore his clothes well, unencumbered by them and used to the confines of starched collars and tight breeches, but tonight he was a vision in naval blue and gold. His double-breasted jacket was adorned with tasselled epaulettes and cuffs wider than James', both stitched with two brocade stripes. The coatee had tails lined with white satin, and his trousers were belted with an ornate gold buckle.

'Will I do?' Archer asked, as Silas gawped. 'There's a hat somewhere, but it's hideous.'

'I don't have the words, Archie,' Silas said.

'Flatterer,' Archer grinned. 'But, for tonight, I think it's best if you call me Your Lordship and all that. People will expect it.'

176

'Very good, Sir,' Silas said, unable to disguise a smirk.

People would know he was the viscount's secretary, but it was more thrilling to realise that they would have no idea of the intimacy of their relationship. As amusing as that was, keeping the secret was a serious business. Silas was a good actor, but tonight he had to keep his private life in the dark while also hiding his intentions from Archer. Deceit was a sickening thought.

'We should eat,' Archer said, swirling to the sideboard. 'Payne, James? Have you eaten?'

'The staff have, indeed, Your Lordship,' Thomas said. 'Shall we attend?'

'I'd rather you went and found the others,' Archer said. 'I'm not that hungry, but we ought to get some of this gone before Mrs Flintwich comes up. Silas?'

While Thomas returned below stairs to hurry the cook and Lucy, Silas and Archer helped themselves to the spread, enough for six people, Silas thought.

'What do you do with what's left over?' he asked as they sat to eat.

Archer paused with a fork halfway to his mouth, caught by surprise. 'Do you know,' he said, putting down his cutlery. 'I've never considered it. I assume the servants have what they want, and the rest goes into... Well, into...'

'Thin air?' Silas regarded the remains of the spread. 'There's enough there to feed a destitute family for a few days.'

Archer ran his eyes over the cloches and trays, the bowls and dishes, with James, fine and silent beside them. He pushed away his plate.

'Oh, my god,' he said. 'How right you are. I'll speak to Markland, see if we can devise a way to have leftovers delivered to the hostel if they will be of use.'

'Or you could ask Mrs F to make less,' Silas suggested. 'You're already giving enough to your cause.'

'One can never give enough,' Archer said. 'I will think about what's best.'

'You are.'

'I am what?'

'The best.'

Archer gripped his hand briefly and laughed, embarrassed.

'You know I love you, don't you?' Silas asked, catching his hand before it was withdrawn.

'I do.'

'I'd do anything for you and not out of gratitude. Not just out of gratitude.'

'As you have told me on several occasions.'

Butterflies entered Silas' stomach along with cold ham and potatoes. He was aware of James staring over their heads to the curtains. 'But sometimes, to show someone you love them, you have to do things they don't like.'

Archer didn't understand.

'Not to worry.' Silas let him go. 'A bit nervous about tonight. Not sure how to behave.'

'You will be admirable, I have no doubt,' Archer reassured him. 'Were I asked for my opinion, I would say you will be the best actor in the house.'

Silas knew he would have to be.

Thomas reappeared as the hall clock struck the half-hour.

'Mr and Mrs Flintwich,' he announced, and Archer, dabbing his lips with a napkin, rose to greet them.

Where his cook was narrow and serious, her husband was wider and demure. He clutched a bowler hat and looked at his feet while Mrs Flintwich curtseyed.

'Good evening, and how splendid you look.'

Archer greeted the couple warmly, but Silas could tell from her nervous glances and twitching that the cook was not as comfortable above stairs as the other servants. Hands were shaken as if no-one knew each other, the offer of a quick glass of sherry was at first refused, but Archer pressed, and the couple accepted anxiously.

'You are not to be nervous, Mrs Flintwich,' he said. 'The evening is for you to enjoy.'

'Yes, Your Lordship,' she replied meekly, the sherry glass trembling in her hand.

'It's the uniform,' Archer whispered to lighten her mood. 'It's still Archer Riddington beneath it, the little boy you made cream-puff fancies for when he was ten. Just remember that.'

The cook relaxed after that, and Silas thought it such a generous

178

gesture on Archer's part he could have kissed him right there.

'The hansom is here,' James announced from the door.

Silas hadn't seen him slip away, despite the elaborate outfit that caught every glint from the chandelier.

'Thank you, James.' Archer examined his pocket watch. 'Yes, we should be moving along. Is everything secure, Payne?'

'It is, Sir. Her Ladyship's second footman is downstairs and will come and clear once we have left.'

'Then lead on.'

Silas wondered if his jovial mood was a cover for his own nervousness. He had everything riding on the evening and the performance, the speech and reception, and it was a huge burden to bear. Then again, he reasoned, Archer was used to large society occasions, knew how to behave, and what Silas was really doing was projecting his own qualms and apprehension onto his lover. His boss, he reminded himself. He had to get out of that way of thinking if he was to pass off successfully as a secretary, not a jumped-up renter with no experience of society.

Thomas showed the Flintwich couple to the front door where Lucy waited, smartly though not elegantly dressed. She had paid attention to her hair, one of her specialities, and it was braided and tied back from her round face. Her dress and overcoat were simple, and a welcome contrast to the spectacle of the men.

Silas watched from the porch as the party stepped into the cab and Thomas gave Mr Flintwich the fare on Archer's behalf. Along the street, Lady Marshall's house was a similar spectacle as those of her staff who wanted to attend the gala were collected by cabs and driven away. Her carriage, as ornate and fashionable as the lady herself, waited for her. Oleg was poised to assist her into it before taking his place beside the liveried coachman. Her Ladyship appeared beneath flaming torches, a blurred miasma of silver and glitter. She waved a slender arm to Archer, before allowing Oleg to help her into the carriage. When it drove past, following the cabs, she dropped the window.

'Your finest hour, Clearwater,' she called unbothered by her unladylike behaviour. 'Your mother will be proud when I tell her. See you in the bar, boys!'

Silas was trying not to laugh a release of tension, but was

distracted when Archer's carriage approached and drew up beneath the lanterns.

The coach was what Archer called a glass carriage, being more windows than wood. It was maroon with black trim, had a bowled underside and a flat roof, its back wheels larger than the front. It was pulled by Emma and Shanks, Archer's city horses, both groomed, their manes decorated, and with ostrich plumes rising from their bridal headpieces, their ears covered. Like everything else so far that evening, they were impressive, sumptuous even, but the most spectacular sight was Fecker.

Silas had no idea how Archer, Thomas or Mrs Baker had arranged it, but his best friend had been transformed. He wore a top hat, with his yellow hair pouring from beneath in a neatly ribboned ponytail (he suspected Lucy's hand at work there), and he held his crop with authority, drawing the horses to a gentle stop in exactly the right place for James to open the carriage door and drop the steps. Fecker's coat was black, but edged with silver, and his buttons stood out like stars. His top hat added to his height, but he wore it regally. He looked down at Silas and gave the tiniest hint of wide-eyed amazement as he handed a riding cloak to James. Both were majestic, poised and professional, and the sight brought a tear of pride to Silas' eye.

He sniffed it away when Thomas said, 'Sir?' and, having closed the front door, led him down the steps to the carriage.

It smelt of leather polish, the seat was soft, and unlike the trap, there was plenty of room. Archer climbed in beside him, and the coach dipped again as James mounted the steps to sit beside Fecker.

'Do you have everything, My Lord?' Thomas asked and, on being told that everything was in order, joined them and knocked on the ceiling.

The carriage set off. Its springs had been oiled, and Silas felt no shock or vibration as the horses picked up a rhythm, as Fecker led then towards the West End. The journey was mainly conducted in silence, Archer's mind, no doubt, on his duties. Meeting and greeting, he had called it. Thanking and wanking was another expression he had used when returning from their unsuccessful visit to the theatre. 'Wanking as in, giving them what they want, so we get their money', he had whispered wickedly, making Silas laugh. The expression had also given them ideas, but there had been no time for fun, and there was none now. They followed the procession through the lamplit streets, their lights blurred by the damp air, and Archer opened the window a fraction when it began to condensate.

'Must see who's there,' he explained. 'So I know who to greet first when I get out. Toffs…' he dug Silas in the ribs playfully, 'can be so tight about etiquette. If I greet Lord Dover before I greet Earl Davenport, there will be a scandal. This kind of display of wealth and status means so much to these people.'

'Aren't you one of these people?' Silas asked.

'I was never meant to be,' Archer replied. 'Yes, alright, I am, but if I had my way, I wouldn't be. At least… I'd do things differently.'

'I know,' Silas said, and patted his hand, causing Thomas to raise an eyebrow in warning.

He moved his hand away. Now more than ever he wanted to hold Archer and thank him for all he had done, not only for himself, but for Fecker.

'Oh, by the way,' Archer said, as they approached the opera house some fifteen minutes later. 'I heard from my contact in Westerpool.'

It took Silas a moment to remember his sisters. They were always on his mind, but with the visit to Cleaver Street, the blackmail letter and threats, they had slipped from his thoughts.

'The money you want to send,' Archer said, 'has arrived with my associate. You can pay me back as I suggested. Culver will deliver it personally to the girls in the morning.'

'You mean it?'

'I do. He is unable to go this evening, but has made contact with the cousin. The girls are in better health, he said, but the older woman was not so good. I telegraphed a reply and asked if he wouldn't mind taking a doctor to see to her when he delivers the cash in the morning. Add it to the bill.'

For the second time that night Silas' eyes welled with tears. Despite Thomas' glare, he gripped Archer's hand and kissed it. It was all he was able to do, if he had spoken, he would have burst into tears, and Archer understood.

The relief, knowing his sisters would finally be able to benefit from his good fortune, overwhelmed him, and the knowledge made him more determined to see that Archer's gala went off without a hitch.

How he and James were to achieve that, if they were, was something yet to be discovered, but he would do anything in his power to ensure the safety of Cadwell Roxton and the Clearwater Foundation, even if that meant acting against Archer's wishes, as he had already done. Archer would understand, he was sure of it, and, if it went wrong and a scandal rather than a triumph was announced, he would be there to help his lover pick up the pieces.

A knock on the roof from above alerted the passengers of their approach to the opera house, and the passengers sat straight and attended to their costume. The carriage slowed, but Silas' heart beat faster. He pushed his nervousness aside, concentrating instead on his voice, recalling words he needed to use, polite words and not his usual lazy way of speaking. He was private secretary to the mastermind behind the gala, people would be asking him questions when he had far too many of his own.

'No need to worry,' Archer said, as if reading his mind. 'The people we will meet are all friends or colleagues. Answer their questions simply, or refer them to me. You know how it works. Think of this as a family event, just a small gathering of acquaintances. Thomas knows what to do.'

Thomas nodded and was about to offer Archer his bicorn hat to complete his military uniform when the carriage jolted to an unexpected stop.

'Sorry,' Fecker's voice boomed from above.

Thomas and Archer shared a troubled glance, and Thomas pulled down the window. He leant out, looked back and said, 'Wait here, My Lord,' before alighting.

Alone with Archer and not knowing the reason for the delay, Silas was desperate to explain what James had discovered that afternoon. To tell him now would only add distress to Archer's load, and hard though it was, he kept his thoughts to himself.

'We only have half an hour before curtain up,' Archer said. 'It won't be too long a trial. If you want, you can go straight to the box, and I will join you there.'

'I might,' Silas said. 'If that's alright. It's not that I won't be any good, but I don't want to say the wrong thing.' He would also have the opportunity to slip away and put his plan into action. It involved Jake the runner, James the footman, and Silas Hawkins the East End rent boy turned gentleman. If Silas was inclined to write dramas, he couldn't have come up with a more convoluted and, he had to admit, feeble plot, but circumstances were the leading characters in his story. They had taken over, and he needed to find some way of regaining control.

Thomas returned, his face speckled with droplets of water.

'There's been a complication,' he said, glancing back along the line of waiting carriages.

Archer was on alert immediately. 'What? Is Cadwell unwell? Miss Campanelli playing up? What?'

'No, nothing like that,' Thomas said. 'But you are going to have to change your itinerary a little.'

He climbed in as Archer asked him to explain, craning his head from the other window to see.

'Who are all those people?' he asked. 'That's more onlookers than I would have expected.'

Silas pressed his face to the glass to see a large crowd lining the other side of the street, some in evening gowns and suits, others dressed in work clothes; a mix of classes sharing the same interest in the spectacle. They were not the audience of lords and ladies, nor the queue of public who had been given free tickets to the upper balconies; those people were waiting patiently outside the theatre or were filing into the door marked "Balcony".

'Surely not even an appearance by Lady Marshall warrants such a crowd,' Archer joked weakly, looking to Thomas for an explanation.

Thomas was drying off his livery with a handkerchief and wiping his worried face.

'They have not come to see her,' he said. 'Your gala has attracted an unexpected guest.'

'Oh?' Archer leant further but was unable to see. 'Who?'

'Oh dear.' Thomas lost his usual unruffled composure. 'I am not dressed.'

'You look perfect, Tom,' Archer gripped his knee, either to calm his butler or himself. 'Who is it?'

Thomas regarded him, white-faced and worried. 'It's the King of the Netherlands,' he said.

'Oh?' Contrary to what Silas expected, Archer was amused. 'Well, that's good of him.'

'But I don't have my royal livery.'

'Is that such a bad thing?' Silas asked.

Apparently, it was, for the King of The Netherlands, at least. Elderly and eccentric, his demand for what was proper now far exceeded his grasp of all other reality.

'The problem with His Majesty,' Archer explained, 'is that he's lowering himself to support a humble viscount and in a controversial venture. If I don't show him enough respect, he will likely walk out and that would reflect poorly on the Foundation. He's that demented these days he might well demand I be stripped of my title.' He bit on a knuckle, thinking before glancing at Thomas. 'Don't listen, Tom.'

'To what?'

'This.' Archer thumped the seat. 'Fuck! There's no time to head back.'

He stared at Thomas, and their faces distorted in panicked thought.

Silas, on the other hand, always saw a threat as an opportunity. 'How long until you have to meet him do you reckon?' he asked, plotting quickly.

'Oh, a little while,' Archer said. 'Twenty minutes? He's arrived before me, and my absence is acceptable because he has sprung the visit. But, I shall be expected to sit with him in the Royal Box with Thomas behind me, and glamorous though he looks, that is not suitable livery.'

'Okay, Your Lordship,' Silas said. 'Hold your horses. Tom…?' He wasn't listening. 'Thomas… Mr Payne!' He snapped his fingers in the butler's face to drag him away from his horror. 'Do you trust me, Tommy?'

'What?'

Silas tutted. 'Do you trust me?'

Thomas looked at Archer for support.

'Of course. We both do,' Archer replied on his behalf. 'Why?'

'Right then, Archie, you get out and slip in with Lady Marshall. When you meet the king, you'll appear with her butler, so if anyone's underdressed it will be Mr Saunders. Meanwhile, your own man will be waiting in the Royal Box before you get there.'

'Yes, so?'

'Out, Archie. Leave this to me.'

Another brief exchange between the viscount and his butler and Thomas leapt from the coach, helped the viscount down, passed him his hat and jumped back in.

'You better know what you're about,' he growled.

'I reckon I do, Mr Payne,' Silas winked. He leant from the door, standing to call up. 'Fecks?' he said. 'Stage door, mate. And fast.'

Twenty-One

Fecker turned the carriage in the street, giving Silas a chance to see towards the front of the theatre and the throng of well-wishers gathered there. He heard the cheers and saw that due to the numbers, several carriages were waiting in line to drop off their passengers. He couldn't imagine how an incorrectly dressed butler could cause such a problem, but the viscount and Thomas knew far more than he did, except they didn't know where he could find the necessary uniform so quickly.

They pulled up at the stage door a minute later, and Silas was the first man out.

'You better come with me, Jimmy,' he said. 'Fecks, you see to the horses and then meet Lucy and the others.'

'Da.'

'You have your ticket?'

Another short, affirmative answer came down to him along with James. Thomas stepped from the coach, and Fecker drove off as soon as the door was slammed.

'What are you doing?' Thomas hissed, as he followed Silas to the stage door.

'Just leave the talking to me,' Silas said, ushering them in.

He was surprised to find the lobby empty apart from Mr Keys at his counter. He expected backstage to be alive with runners and singers, musicians and everyone else needed to stage a large production, but it was silent.

'Hello again, Mr Keys,' he said as the old man looked up. 'Bet you didn't think you'd be seeing me again so soon.'

'Mr Hawkins,' he replied, and his eyes immediately flashed to Thomas and James. 'Can I help you?'

'You can,' Silas beamed and leant on the counter. 'I need to speak with Jake, and it's urgent. Where is he?'

'He'll be prompt side running the calls,' the doorkeeper said. He was still eying the others suspiciously. 'You should sign in.'

Silas knew the routine. 'You remember what I told you this afternoon about security?' he asked as he scribbled. 'Well, Mr Payne is the viscount's butler, and James is his first footman. You probably know that the King of… um…' He passed the pen to James and cocked his head. James understood and signed the book. 'He's here now, and His Lordship wanted me to bring the staff this way so they would already be in the theatre when he accompanies His Majesty to the box.'

James passed the pen to Thomas, and by the time Silas had waffled through an excuse, all three were signed in and heading towards the stairs.

'You've not seen anyone suspicious have you, Mr Keys?' he asked as he swept by, hoping the man would make no objection.

'No, Sir. No-one's come through here who's not listed, apart from you… Do you know where you're going?'

'Yes, thank you.' Silas was already at the first turn of the stairs. 'Much obliged, Mr Keys. All above board.'

'What exactly are you doing?' Thomas demanded with no etiquette as they reached the entrance to backstage.

'Trust me, Tommy, and you'll see.' His hand was on the door as he looked them up and down. 'Just wanted to say, you make a stunning couple.'

'Get a move on!' Thomas was not in the mood for pleasantries.

The first time Silas had passed through this door, he had entered a kind of heaven. A huge towering place of peace and intrigue. This time, it was like entering hell. The tower still rose a hundred feet above, and the walls were still lined with ropes and levers, but now, the floor space was crowded with men rushing here and there, musicians edging through singers with their instrument cases, and men in shirtsleeves, sweating over floor-plans. Despite the mayhem, it was strangely peaceful. Most people were silent, but those who spoke did so in calm, controlled voices, whispering and saying only what needed to be said, as if everyone concerned was fearful of waking the set that slept in dimly lit anticipation. An occasional whistle echoed from above followed by the rumble of pullies and the creak of ropes.

Silas led his friends forward to the stage manager's desk, passing the props table. This time, the labelled trays were in use. His eyes flicked over a scroll, a golden chalice and other necessary items neatly placed, and at the end, Aeneas' sword. He stopped, checked he was not being watched and picked it up.

'Da capo?' James queried.

'It's wooden,' Silas said. 'As blunt as my tongue.'

'Da capo?'

'From the head, Tommy,' Silas reminded him. 'It doesn't have to be a gunshot.'

'Oi! What d'you…? Oh, very sorry, Mr Hawkins.'

They had arrived at the stage manager's corner, but there was no sign of Jake. Silas checked his watch and kept a cool head.

'Good of you to remember me, Sir,' he smiled at a man whose name he couldn't remember. 'Lord Clearwater has a problem, and I believe Jake can help. But we are pressed for time…'

The stage manager interrupted him with a wave, his other hand flying to his mouth where he whistled a shrill, distinctive note.

'Tricky will be here in a second, Sir. Is there anything we need to know?'

'Actually…'

Silas was desperate to remember his name, but it escaped him. To cover it, he coughed and put a finger to his lips. The man's bushy eyebrows came together, and he leant closer.

'I need to let you know one small thing,' Silas whispered. 'It's his Lordship's wishes, and to be made known only when necessary.'

His words, contained between his cupped hand and the older man's ear, were lost in the general hubbub, and when he had finished, the man removed his cap and wiped his forehead.

'If you are sure, Sir.'

'I am, my friend.'

'Well, you're His Lordship's secretary, and he's paying us Sunday wages on a Saturday night. Does front of house know?'

Silas wasn't sure what he meant, but said, 'Yes.'

'Hm. Very well.'

Jake came to a skidding stop at Silas' feet.

'Hello, Mr Silas,' he chirped. 'Didn't expect to see you back here.'

'Jake, I need your help. Actually, I need this butler at the Royal

Box in the right livery in fifteen minutes. Can you do it?'

He stepped back to show the lad Thomas dancing anxiously from one foot to the other, and James beside him, gawping up at the fly tower.

'And Jimmy there needs to get out front.'

'They don't call me Tricky for nothing,' Jake beamed. 'Follow me.'

Jake spun on his heels and was off in a shot, leaving Silas to drag James away and encourage Thomas, once again, to trust him. They caught up with the runner at the base of the downstage spiral staircase.

'Through there, Sir,' the lad said, pointing James towards a door. It was black and painted into a black wall, a brass fingerplate the only clue to its presence.

'Jimmy, I won't be long.' Silas held his arm as he passed. 'If you get the chance, tell his Lordship everything will be fine.'

'Are you sure, Sir?' James was concerned. It was the first time Silas had seen him worried.

'Yeah.'

'You know what you're going to say?'

'Not a clue, mate,' Silas laughed. 'I'm making this up as I go along. Remember, eyes open.'

James nodded and hurried to the door. Silas didn't see him leave; he and Thomas were running to keep up with Jake. It was easy to see why they called him Tricky. He was as slippery as an eel, and just as hard to catch.

'You're not putting me in a costume,' Thomas gasped, the realisation finally dawning on him.

'Certainly am, Tommy,' Silas replied. He was already short of breath, and they were only on the first landing.

'What did James mean?' Thomas asked showing no signs of fatigue.

'About what?'

'What you are going to say.'

'Ah, don't worry about that, Tommy.'

'At present, I am worried about everything,' Thomas muttered. 'Good God!' He ducked just in time to avoid an overhead beam. 'Are we safe?'

'As long as you stay with me,' Jake said. 'Keep up, Mr Butler.'

They followed him along the gantry dodging stagehands to another staircase where he bounded upwards.

'Who do you want to be tonight, Tommy?' Silas puffed. 'Think of it. You've got the entire costume department of the City Opera House. What do you reckon, Sweeny Todd?'

'This is not a joking matter.'

'What about Quill the Ripper?'

'That is completely inappropriate.'

'Bill Sykes?'

'Stop it.'

Silas laughed. No matter the situation, it was always fun to wind Thomas the wrong way.

'In here, Sirs.'

Unfortunately, there was no time for games. Jake had led them off the stairs and into a passage lined with doors. The sound of background bustle was replaced with the sounds of machines spinning and irons hissing. The air was scented with powder underscored by a faint tang of sweat.

Jake stopped at an open door and hurried Silas closer as he knocked. They stepped into a workshop. The walls were lined with wardrobes and chests, racks of clothes hung in rows and a line of workbenches to one side was a forest of wigs. In the centre, a grand, well-dressed woman stood beside a rail of outlandish costumes while around her, maids stitched and ironed. The woman held the end of a hanging skirt in one hand and a needle in the other, scrutinising a seam over half-moon glasses. She looked up.

'Oui?'

'Sorry to bother you, Madame LaRache, but Viscount Clearwater's man needs assistance, and I need the Figaro rack. May I?'

'Vou certainly may not!' the woman exclaimed, as horrified as if Jake had asked to eat her firstborn. 'Who are zeez people?'

Silas, who had been checking his watch, dropped it with improvised horror.

'I may ask you the same thing, Madam,' he blustered, seemingly outraged. 'You clearly do not recognise a gentleman's man when you see one, but I can assure you, we are both.'

He wasn't quite sure if what he said made sense, he had borrowed the tone from Mrs Marks, but the woman was clearly not used to being spoken to in such a manner.

'Vot are you insinuating?' she retorted, her French accent thickening. 'Zat I do not know…?'

Thomas interrupted her with a string of words in a language Silas assumed was French, and his mouth dropped open. Madame LaRoche was similarly shocked. She crossed herself, removed her glasses, and by the time Thomas had finished saying whatever it was he was saying, she had thrown her arm wide, and was ushering Jake towards a wardrobe.

'What the hell was that?' Silas whispered as they followed. He nodded graciously to the costumier as he passed, there was no point in making enemies.

'Flattery,' Thomas replied.

'You speak French?'

'Not at all,' Thomas chuckled. 'It was from a song. Something about the charms of fair ladies and fields of poppies, I think. "Maiden fair I am sore distressed, my master has me thus undressed," is the English translation,' he explained, pleased with himself. 'Or it might have been something about getting naked behind a hayrick.' He looked back nervously.

Jake threw the wardrobe doors wide and presented them with a row of costumes.

'The house production is set in modern times,' he explained, sorting through red and gold tailcoats. 'There are wigs upstairs.'

'Not necessary,' Thomas said, elbowing Silas aside and raking through the jackets. He paused, dropped his head and turned to Silas. 'Thank you.'

Silas saw he meant it. 'You've got ten minutes, Tom,' he encouraged. 'Jake?'

He took the younger man to one side out of earshot of the maids, and without thinking, put his arm around his shoulder.

'Jake, man,' he said. 'I need you to do something for me, and you're going to want to say no.'

Jake pulled away with a worried glare.

'No, nothing like that,' Silas tutted. 'You're a nice lad and all, but, no… Not that.'

Jake relaxed, and Silas didn't know whether to be insulted or impressed. The runner had read him as well as Silas was able to read any man, but there had been no intention, only force of habit.

'Listen,' he continued. 'I need you to change the calls.'

'Do what?'

'I've spoken to the stage manager, Mr What's-his-name, and he knows the score. I assume he'll tell everyone who needs to know, but the only person who is *not* to know is Cadwell Roxton.'

'Know what?' Jake was keeping an eye on the time. 'You got to be quick.'

'What's the next call?'

'It'll be the fifteen, and soon.'

'Then give everyone fifteen, but give Roxton twenty. Can you do that?'

'No, Sir.'

'Can you do it for Viscount Clearwater?'

'I shouldn't.'

'Can you do it for me?'

Jake regarded him with uncertainty. Beside them, Thomas was exchanging his tailcoat for another.

'Why, Mr Silas?' Jake asked. 'I might if I know why. Only, I could lose my job and granddad's too probably.'

'The viscount takes full responsibility,' Silas said, knowing it to be untrue. 'You see, the King of the Nether Regions has turned up, and they need to delay everything for five… Why are you laughing?'

'Netherlands,' Jake smirked. 'Not… Never mind. You sure Mr Butterworth knows?'

'Is that his name? Yes, he does. Honest Jake, it's a very urgent matter. Keep Roxton away from the stage until after I've made his speech.'

'What did you say?'

Thomas was caught half into a pair of breeches. He stared at Silas, his mouth open, trying to keep his balance on one leg.

Jake slipped to his side and caught his elbow. 'Let me, Sir,' he said, and the call boy turned instantly into a dresser.

'What do you mean, make his speech?' Thomas was so aghast he didn't object to Jake's assistance.

'If he goes on and says anything, they'll kill him,' Silas clarified. 'Even if he carries out their instructions this Stella character is going to do away with him.'

'There's extra security out front,' Jake said, overhearing. 'If there's any trouble brewing, His Majesty has guards. Granddad's been special cautious like you asked, Mr Silas, and front of house are wide awake 'cos they're not used to having rough folks up in the gods.'

'Thanks, Jake, very good to know,' Silas smiled. 'But it's not going to help. Tom, if he makes the speech he is supposed to, they're going to do it, that's what the threat's all about. But if he doesn't make any kind of speech at all, we will have longer to look for whoever might be planning it. You get me?'

'Not entirely,' Thomas admitted. He was buttoning his fly as Jake tugged the breeches to align the hems below his knees.

'Trust me,' Silas said.

'You ask that too easily and too often.'

'Hey, Tom.' Silas approached and straightened the waistcoat Jake was slipping him into. 'You've got your duties, I've got mine. You keep an eye on His Lordship and Lady Marshall. Doctor Markland and his bird are part of Archer's party, so watch them too…' Thomas glared and threw his head towards Jake, now preparing the tailcoat.

'It's alright, Tommy,' Silas said, hooking the buttons while Thomas pulled on white gloves. 'Your job is to support Archer. I know he doesn't look it, but he's a wreck inside.'

'You don't have to tell me.'

'You're right, I don't.' Silas brushed his epaulettes. 'You're his best mate, and I'm not here to replace you. I'm here to protect him and all of us. Tell His Lordship not to be alarmed. I'm going to watch you from our box. If you suspect anything or anyone, give me a signal, yeah? Do this.' He ran his hand across his hair as if flicking it back. 'And I'll do the same. If I see you do that, me or Jimmy will be there like a shot, yeah?' Thomas nodded. 'You look outrageously handsome, by the way.'

'Give over.'

'Gents, I've got to run,' Jake said. 'You know the way back?'

'Yeah, go. And thanks, Jake. Remember, five minutes late for Mr Roxton, right?'

'Whatever you say, Mr Silas.'

'And, Jake? You haven't heard any of this.'

'Any of what, Sir?'

'Good man.'

The runner doffed a cap he wasn't wearing and scurried away, calling 'Fifteen minutes, ladies.'

'Fifteen minutes!' Thomas paled. 'And we have no idea what lies ahead.'

'You're telling me.'

Silas draped Thomas' discarded livery over one arm, bowed cheekily to Madame LaRache who was too busy licking her lips at Thomas to notice, and hustled him from the workroom.

'Who am I looking out for?' Thomas asked as they took the passage. 'What does this Stella look like?'

'I don't know,' Silas admitted. 'I've never seen his face, not properly. But you can bet he'll be doing something he shouldn't be doing. There's not a lot you can do now, but keep your eyes open and check in with me from time to time.'

They reached the spiral stairs and carried on down.

'I hope you know what you're doing,' Thomas muttered, leaping nimbly from the bottom step. Stopping at the house entrance, he turned to Silas. 'Look,' he said. 'I don't want you to be jealous of my friendship with Archer.'

'What?' Of all the things Silas had on his mind, that was the last. 'I don't get jealous.'

'Well, actually, you do. I noticed it yesterday. Only in small ways and not so that Archer would see, but I feel it. Please. Like you, I only want what's best for the man I… I am lifelong friends with.'

'The man you love, I know,' Silas said. He winked, but Thomas could see it was tainted with sadness. 'Happy to share his love, Tommy. As long as you're not coming from the same direction as me, I'm not stepping in the way. Now, shift your arse, and put on your poshest buttle, or whatever it is you do. You got a few minutes to get 'round the other side. Oh, one last thing. Don't blame Jimmy for any of this. It's all down to me.'

'What is?' Thomas asked, placing his hand on the finger plate.

'Whatever comes next.'

'And what's that?'

'Tommy, mate,' Silas sighed. 'That's what I've got ten minutes to work out.'

Twenty-Two

James had been left with his head spinning and his pulse racing. The backstage door led to a lobby hidden from the auditorium by a weighty, black curtain, and once through that, he found himself at the end of a curved passage with more drapes masking the boxes to one side. He easily found the box reserved for the viscount's original party as it was the one closest to the stage, and there, he stepped into a small room and a huge, new world. If he had been amazed by what he had seen backstage, he was mesmerised by what he saw in the auditorium.

Four dazzling horseshoes curved above the stalls, ablaze with lamps and gradually filling as the audience arrived. Above them all, the ceiling appeared to be made of daylight as if he was looking through the roof directly into the sun that shone on a world of red and gold. Ladies in fine clothes, furs and jewels, inched their way along rows clutching programmes, and James noticed there was one on each of the six chairs in his box.

He collected one as he stood at the balcony and looked down over the heads of the orchestra, their chairs and music stands spread beneath the stage and out of sight. Musicians tuned their instruments as an oboe played a single consistent note. Over their heads hung the biggest pair of curtains James had seen, and he realised with a shock, that Silas was soon going to stand there, unannounced and alone in his attempt to foil Stella's plan.

It was the first time he had felt nervous all day, and he took a deep breath to settle himself.

'That's only a delay tactic', he said, scanning the audience. 'Let's them know we're onto them, gets them off guard, but there's still the how and when.' He recalled what Archer had suspected was a clue, *Death will come da capo, suddenly silent, and you will not hear your final applause.*

It made little sense apart from when 'Da capo' was translated. The word 'Suddenly' was logical if the assassin was planning to use a gun, but in that case, the word 'Silently' didn't add up. James knew how loud a gunshot was, and anyone drawing a pistol would also draw attention.

He looked to the top tier where the seats sloped sharply to the roof. It wouldn't be possible for a shot from so far back to its a target accurately, if at all. Coming down the levels, he reasoned that the only sure way to shoot someone in the head was from close proximity. A box, one like his, close to the singers. Such a place would allow cover and, as he'd seen, an easy escape backstage.

'Then again,' he said, facing the stage. 'A shot from the wings would do it.' He looked into the orchestra pit. There was no way anyone down there could see the stage well enough except the conductor, a highly unlikely suspect.

People were arriving at other boxes, and he heard voices in the corridor.

'What if it's not a gun?' he asked himself, and considered how someone might be killed 'from the head' suddenly, and silently. Strangulation was slow, slitting a throat was too intimate, clubbing the victim's skull was possible. There were many ways, and the killing didn't have to happen on the stage.

'No, it does,' he said, picking up a small pair of binoculars. 'The whole point is to blame and shame. No point in Roxton snuffing it in his dressing room.' The theatre would cover it up, and Archer would get more sympathy than hatred.

He scanned the balconies and saw Mrs Flintwich taking her seat. Her husband and Lucy were with her among other smartly dressed servants from Delamere, but Fecker had not yet arrived.

Movement lower down and opposite drew his attention. The drapes at the Royal Box were being drawn back and tied. He noticed that the ones at the back of the box were open, and thinking he should do the same, had just tied them when a man in a red and gold costume hurried from backstage.

James was about to ignore him when he saw it was Thomas.

'Blimey,' he said. 'You look smart.'

'Do I? Will it do?' Thomas was gasping for breath and sweating.

'Tom, calm down.' James pulled him into the box by his

shoulders. 'Take a deep breath. Take two. Three S's remember? Stop, take Stock...'

Thomas nodded, and his shoulders relaxed. 'Thanks,' he said with a sigh. 'Do you know what to do?'

'Just stand here and wait for the Marks comedy duo. Do you?'

'I hope so.'

'Look, Tom.' James made sure there was no-one near but was aware that people were approaching. 'If it helps,' he whispered. 'I'm mentally hugging and kissing you right now. You're only over there. I can see you plain, better with the glasses, don't worry about me. But look, can you tell His Lordship that... Well, Silas is going to make Roxton's speech.'

He expected outrage, but Thomas already knew. 'And he explained his reason,' he added. 'I honestly can't think of anything else we can do.'

'You make sure Archer's alright,' James said. 'Leave the rest to us.' He gave Thomas a lingering look of admiration. 'You're beautiful,' he said. 'In every way. Now, get to work.'

Thomas tapped his heart twice, and James knew what he meant. His body filled with warmth as his confidence came flooding back.

Becoming the butler, Thomas left sedately and with a smile, leaving James to stand to attention as the Marks couple advanced.

Mrs Marks, looking as dowdy as before, but with a string of pearls to lessen the blow, was taking her time. Stopping at every other guest, she bowed her upper body as if showing them her cleavage, clutched her pearls to draw attention to them, and threw back her head, laughing. Her husband walked a pace behind his mechanical wife, admiring every inch of the wallpaper in an attempt to distance himself. As they drew nearer, James was able to hear her stark voice.

'Buona sera, buona sera,' she yapped, and as she rustled into the box, smiled sympathetically at him and said, 'That's Italian to you,' as if she'd just won an honorary degree in the language. 'To match this theatre's design.'

Italian? The word seemed important.

'Good evening, young James,' Mr Marks was more congenial and less condescending than his wife and having reached the safety of the private enclosure, relaxed. 'A glass of something?'

'Certainly, Sir,' James replied, bowing.

The viscount had ordered champagne, and two bottles stood on ice at the back of the box. It was after he had served the couple and there was nothing more to do but wait that the word Italian dropped back into his head.

'Da capo!'

'What's that, son?'

He hadn't realised he had said it aloud.

'My apologies, Sir. I said, da capo.'

'It's a musical term,' Mrs Marks preened, fanning herself with the programme. 'Do you read music?'

'No, Ma'am,' James admitted.

'Yes, I would have been surprised if you did.'

James wanted to slap her, but replied politely, 'There were no decent teachers in South Riverside, Ma'am.'

'Quite understandable,' she said, mistaking his sarcasm for truth. 'But I thought you might have read it on the score.'

She peered through the opera glasses and leant over the balustrade to examine the orchestra. James hoped she might tumble and be impaled on a double bass.

He controlled his imagination. 'The score, Ma'am?'

'Yes, on the music.' She waved grandly at someone.

'Get down, woman,' Marks complained and tugged her into her chair. 'We're in these seats so everyone gets a good look at us. We're representing Clearwater, so act like it.'

Opposite, Thomas had arrived at the Royal Box and was talking to another butler, similarly dressed. He couldn't hear their words, there was too much distance and hubbub as the final rows filled, but whatever they said, their conversation ended with an agreement, and they shook hands. They took their places either side of the entrance, hands behind backs, looking directly ahead. James could see why Thomas had wanted to change his livery. Both men matched the colour scheme of the box's furniture and the decor of the auditorium. Had Tom been wearing the uniform designed by Lady Marshall he would have stood out like a Christmas cracker.

'Take a chair if you want, lad,' Mr Marks offered.

'Husband, really?' His wife slapped his arm with her fan. 'It's bad enough we are unable to sit with Archer, but... must you?'

198

'Never mind her,' Marks said, rolling his eyes. 'Have a decent seat if you want, I'm sure Mr Hawkins won't mind.'

'Thank you, Sir,' James replied, not sure of the etiquette. 'Perhaps when the performance starts.'

'Won't be long. Where is Hawkins anyhow?'

'I believe he had some business behind the scenes, Sir,' James said, as vaguely as possible. 'I'm sure he will be with us shortly.'

Marks nodded and returned to his programme.

As the audience swelled, so the temperature rose, and the air became heavy with the scent of perfumes and smoke. Behind that was the smell of the gas lamps, intensifying as the humidity climbed. James was wondering if Mr Marks' generosity extended to allowing him to strip shirtless and drink from the ice bucket when a fanfare brought the audience to silence and to their feet. The Marks couple stood, and not sure what to do, James remained motionless.

Thomas and his colleague snapped to attention, and the gas lamps began to dim as the fanfare continued. A white-haired man entered the Royal Box with a younger woman on his arm. He wore a military uniform, weighted with medals, and a swathe of a blue sash, while his companion, like many below her, shimmered in silver and jewels. Just behind them came Lord Clearwater, his bicorn hat under one perfectly crooked arm, Lady Marshall on his other, and behind them Doctor Markland and his partner, confident and upright as if they did this kind of thing every day. James was impressed, particularly with Markland's girlfriend. At the dinner, she hadn't struck him as a woman used to being among society, let alone royalty. She had said little at the party, but gawped endlessly at Roxton during the meal as if she had never seen an actor before. He was relieved that she knew how to behave; it would make things easier for the viscount.

His Majesty came to the edge of the box with Lord Clearwater. They waved, and the audience applauded politely. Some in the gallery whistled inappropriately, but that was the only sign of rowdiness, and the Dutch King seemed to approve. They were joined by their female companions, and the orchestra played the National Anthem.

When it was over, more applause was followed by the further

dimming of the lights and the sound of two-thousand people arranging themselves in their seats.

'Such a stirring tune,' Mrs Marks said, fanning herself. 'It quite takes…'

She was interrupted by the orchestra and the sound of two thousand people standing.

The orchestra played the Dutch anthem. It dragged on, and when it finally ended, Mrs Marks drained her glass and retook her seat with a loud sigh.

'Thank the lord that's over,' she mumbled, arranging her copious skirt.

The simmering hubbub returned, and James watched Thomas and his accomplice bending gracefully to the guests and, presumably, offering Champagne. Where James' box had been supplied with fluted glasses and very fine ones at that, the royal party were offered wine from silver goblets.

It was the dimming of the lights which brought home the reality of the danger. Anyone with a pistol could easily hide it in the darkness. Even with some lights left glowing in the boxes, there were so many shadows offering cover to an assassin.

He scouted the crowd as silence fell, but saw no unusual movement. The killer had the whole opera before Roxton's final applause, it was unlikely he would strike right away. If he was aligning his sights now, expecting to see the singer, he was about to be disappointed.

'Ah,' Mrs Marks whispered, leaning back to show off to James. 'The audience is subito tacet.'

'I'm sorry, Ma'am?' James crouched to her, aware that he was being watched. He had seen Archer staring at him intently just before she spoke.

'More Italian for your elucidation,' she said. 'The audience is suddenly silent.'

'And so should you be. Hush, woman,' her husband scolded. 'Mr Roxton's coming on.'

Footlights cast a stark glow onto the curtains, and from places around the balconies, large lanterns were swung to aim at the centre of the forestage. The house waited in keen anticipation, a few people cleared their throats and rustled programmes, and then even those sounds evaporated as the curtains shivered.

James' throat was dry, his heart was pounding again, and the viscount's stare was eating into him. It wasn't the only cause of his unease; Mrs Marks' words had triggered a thought.

It was as if he was in the process of firing a gun. He imagined the hammer hitting the bullet *subito,* suddenly, and expected a loud retort, but none came. The bullet was his thought, an intangible, vital idea that he needed to eject, but it was travelling in painfully slow motion. An answer had been struck, but it refused to be shot from the barrel. Not yet. It wouldn't come, but it had something to do with the letter, the clue, the only way out.

He was reaching into his pocket for the letter when the audience let out a collective gasp, and Mr Marks said, 'What the flippin' blazes...?'

Twenty-Three

Silas hadn't been this nervous since the day he pulled his first trick. It had been a cold evening in Greychurch where Fecker had taken him to show him the safest places and the best hunting ground.

'You be safe here, Banyak,' he had said, pointing to a deserted yard. 'I stand over street.'

Fecker had kept watch, turning down two possible punters of his own to keep vigil, and Silas didn't have to wait long. He looked his sixteen years in those days, and his was a fresh face on a well-worn path. A pair of merchant ships had docked that day, and after several months at sea, many of its crew were ashore and hungry for company. He was approached by a man he put in his late twenties, dressed in civilian clothes but with a kitbag slung from his shoulder. Silas was fearful, not being sure what he might have to do, or whether he could do it, and a mix of emotions tangled his thoughts and knotted his stomach. He knew he was about to have sex with a man he didn't know, and he knew that was what he wanted. That was not the problem. His nervousness stemmed from what lay beyond the badly chained gate: shadows, darkness, a stranger inviting him to intimacy, he would be vulnerable. It was only Fecker's presence, size and strength that saw him through what turned out to be more pleasure than pain, and he came away with a generous two shillings.

His legs then were as weak as they were now as he stood by the props table looking between the flats at the stage. A commotion was taking place on the opposite side where the striking figure of Signora Campanelli had arrived with her entourage. Trying to focus, he used the time to look at the tower where men at their posts leant on the catwalk rails and stared down. On his side of the stage, actors were taking seats, but there was no sign of Roxton.

Jake appeared. He had spent the last ten minutes running here and there and had given his final call.

'Do you know what you're doing, Mr Silas?' he asked, not even out of breath.

'To be honest, mate. No. How's Mr Roxton?'

'Oblivious,' Jake said. 'I told him there was a delay out front and he was happy with that. He likes his own space and silence before going on, he said. He was reading this, though.' He handed Silas a sheet of paper. 'Asked me to leave it prompt side for when I call him.'

Silas took the speech. Knowing Marks and Archer had approved it, he read it quickly, but each sentence brought him closer to the moment when he would have to walk through those curtains and face the rich and famous, the public and the viscount.

He suffered doubt as his flesh crept and his hands shook. His idea to prevent Roxton's speech was intended purely to confuse Stella, or whoever the Cleaver Street men had hired for the job, and he now wondered if he was only going to make things worse. What if he said the wrong thing? He could read the script, but could he make his voice heard?

There was also the possibility that the killer, frustrated at being tricked, might take a shot at him instead.

The orchestra had tuned their instruments. The cast and hands whispered, glancing at Silas as the message was passed along that this youth, the unknown secretary to Lord Clearwater was to take Roxton's place. Behind that was the sound of a thousand voices beyond the curtains.

Silas swallowed hard. 'I could do with some of your wise words, Jake,' he said trying to understand the longer sentences on the page.

'There ain't nothing to worry about, Sir,' the lad said. 'When you get out there, you won't be able to see much. Don't look straight at the lights, especially the new spots, they'll blind you. Speak a bit louder than normal, but you don't have to shout.'

'Where do I look?'

'If I were you, I'd bow to the royals first, then look straight ahead into the dark. You better start with "Your Majesty, my lords, ladies and gentlemen", that's what they usually do. After that, you'll have enough light to read by.'

It wasn't the kind of reassurance Silas was looking for, and across the way, Signora Campanelli was now staring daggers and causing a fuss.

'Two minutes, Sir,' Jake said. 'I'll call Mr Roxton soon as the maestro takes the podium.'

'I don't think I can do this.' Silas was horrified that his voice cracked when he spoke.

Jake passed him the chalice from the props table.

'Drink this,' he said. 'It's only lemon water. I'll refill it after.'

Silas held the goblet and wondered how much stranger the evening could be. The prop was real gold, heavy and encrusted with rubies. The water was bitter, but it helped take away the taste of bile. It struck him that this simple prop summed up his life. Here he was, an immigrant street-rat, holding a solid gold goblet and about to appear at the grandest theatre in the country, in front of a king who was sitting with his lover. He wished he'd never turned into that alcove on Cutpurse Lane to take a leak and bumped into Fecker. If he'd used another doorway, he might not have ended up renting, but then he would never have met Archer. He might well have been dead from starvation, but at that moment, it was preferable to what he was about to do.

'Not long now,' Jake said.

'I can't do it.'

The scrawny youth patted his back. 'You'll be right, Mr Silas. It's all fake.'

'What?'

The stage was slipping in and out of focus, and Silas could no longer feel his feet. He was floating.

'It's all fake,' Jake repeated. 'That set is made of wood and canvas. The sky is painted. The Diva is wearing her own gems, for sure, but her crown's made out of tin, and her words are written on the back of props. Out front, it's gold paint, some gilding maybe, but no-one cares. Even your audience is playing a role. They've come here to support your master, not to hear some old soprano wail about lost love, nor a poncy countertenor trill away on a high F for two hours — no offence to your master's mate. They're here to be seen helping men like you.'

The words jolted Silas, and the stage settled.

'Men like me?'

'His Lordship's cause,' Jake said. 'We know all about it back here. Actors are a funny lot, they'll support anyone. The hands are a bit tight-lipped about it, but no-one cares, 'cos His Lordship's paying us double wages. Me point is, no matter who reads them words, they're going to be kind to you. You'll be fine.'

Applause crackled through the drapes, and Silas was unable to breathe. Slipping a hand into his pocket, he felt for Fecker's pebble and clutched it in his fist. He stared at the speech, but it made no sense. It talked about good deeds and the need for change. It thanked the patrons for their support and went on to tell an invented tale of a boy the Foundation had already saved. The only use Silas could see for it was as a reminder to greet the King first. Someone had scribbled in the correct address as an afterthought.

This wasn't what he wanted to say. He wanted to tell the truth, to explain why he was talking and not the star they had come to see. If he could tell them about the danger, he might avert Roxton's death, but if he did that, he would have to admit the reason. Cleaver Street. The boy with the scarred back, the man in the black and red coat. Opium. Blackmail. Betrayal.

His thoughts were no longer making sense. He didn't know what he was meant to say. How could he have been so stupid? With his mind so scrambled inside his weak and trembling body, he was going to say the wrong thing. He was going to tell the world Archer's secret by mistake and do Stella's work for him.

Music played, and Silas thought he would be sick.

'Just the anthems,' Jake said. 'The leader will play both, the lights'll go down, and you'll go on.'

Silas was aware of the muffled orchestra, but hardly heard it. Jake's words repeated in his head, and he imagined this was what it felt like to be led to the gallows. A calm and sympathetic gaoler was guiding him towards the noose, reassuring him that it wouldn't take long, he wouldn't feel much, and the hangman knew what he was doing. The analogy didn't help, but there was nothing he could do. The disaster was unstoppable, he couldn't fight the momentum he had created and it was too late to turn back.

'You should go and wait out there,' Jake whispered to the disapproval of the stage manager who, like everyone else, had stood silently to attention. 'Mr Bellows over there will pull the curtain back for you, and hold it open when you're done so you don't get tangled.'

'I can't do it. Go and get Mr Roxton.'

'What? Are you sure, Sir?'

'Yes. No.'

Silas glared at the paper again, but the words were scooting around and changing their order. His sweaty palms were blurring the ink.

Suddenly there were two hands on his face, and they weren't his. Jake turned him, and eye to eye forced him to look.

'You're doing this to help those boys who ain't been as lucky as you, Sir,' he said. 'Just tell them what it's like.'

In the beat of a fast-pumping heart, Silas understood. The prepared speech was not going to work, but his plan was. He was one step ahead of Stella and, with any luck, he would stay there until the final curtain, and see Archer's friend safely home.

'Here you go,' Jake said, nudging him forward. 'We're right behind you.'

The curtains were crimson velvet. They weighed three tons. Silas walked just over seven yards to the centre of the stage — it felt like a mile. Below him, there was room for ninety players in the orchestra pit, and they were now bringing the anthems to a crashing climax. The curtain trimmings were made of gold. Jake's wealth of useless information flooded through his mind, blocking out any thought of what he might say, and with it came Jake's voice.

'*Life's not a rehearsal.*' He had said it only the other day. '*You got to make the most of it.*'

The words fought the inane facts and won. Silas remembered them so clearly, the lad might have been standing beside him. '*Find something you love, work hard, enjoy it, don't hurt no-one else and you'll sail through.*'

Sail through. That's all Silas had done with his life so far; it's what he could do now.

He took a deep breath and growled it out through his nose. The music finished, and the stagehand gripped the curtain, waiting for Silas to give the signal.

He closed his eyes, raised his head and nodded.

'One pace forward only, Sir,' the stagehand said. 'I'll open when you're done. No need to touch the curtain.'

The darkness behind Silas' eye lightened as he was hit by a wall of warmth. When he opened them again, he had taken a step, but hadn't felt his feet move. A shocked gasp rolled across the glare of the footlights, and above them, curved rows of flickering lamps sparkled among glinting diamonds. He was still holding the chalice.

From somewhere in the void came his name.

'Banyak!'

Fecker's joyous yell was followed by a lone handclap and muttering, but the clapping wouldn't be stopped and was soon joined by more until Silas was deafened by sound. He blinked, trying to see Fecker, but there was nothing out there except a sea of blurred faces stacked behind the footlights.

The applause died as he turned to face the Royal Box. It was still illuminated, giving the audience the entire performance to gaze at royalty, but all Silas could see were shapes, one of which he knew was Archer. He was probably as confused as everyone else, but he would also be terrified. His world hung on what was about to come out of Silas' mouth, but all Silas could think of to say was, 'Your Majesty, my lords, ladies and gentlemen...'

He bowed to give himself time to think, and righting himself, saw one of the faint blurs in the Royal Box come into focus. Through the haze of dust and shafts of spotlights, he saw Archer. From that distance, his eyes were two black dots, but Silas knew every fleck and shade in them. He knew the feel of the man's stubble, the ridge of his battle scars and the power in his muscles. He was given strength by them, but they were not the real Archer. There was more to him than a body that lit Silas' passion.

Suddenly, he knew what to say and remembered to raise his voice.

'I'm not who you were expecting,' he said. 'Sorry about that.'

A ripple of laughter from above trickled down to him bringing confidence.

'Don't worry, I'm not going to sing.'

The laughter was repeated, fuller this time.

'Mr Roxton asked me to do this,' he said, and realised that he had just lied to a crowned head of Europe, his friends and his lover in front of two thousand witnesses. 'He is a supporter of the Clearwater Foundation,' he continued. 'As is everyone here, but do you know what he said to me?'

Not even Silas knew what Roxton was supposed to have said to him, it was as if someone else was in his body. Luckily, that someone knew what it was doing.

'He said he had a speech that had been approved by the Foundation and was all very technical. It's about doing good deeds too, of course, but he didn't think it was real enough. He thought that you good ladies and gents didn't need to be reminded of your own generosity, because you are already good people.'

Archer's head moved and, glancing, Silas saw him whisper to the king, possibly explaining who this man was, possibly apologising for the disaster, but whatever he said, His Majesty nodded solemnly, interested not angry.

'No,' Silas said. 'He said everyone here was clever enough to know all that. What you may not know is exactly who your generosity is helping.' There was some uncomfortable shuffling from the front few rows, but he ignored it. 'Men who are lost,' he explained, and the rustling gave way to murmurs. 'That's who you're helping by supporting His Lordship.' He cleared his throat. 'Let me tell you a story. I'll be quick. About four and a bit years ago, there was this young lad from Westerpool. He had twin sisters, even younger, see? And their mam had died. I don't want to upset anyone, so I'll spare you the details, but if you can imagine twelve people sharing a room, half of them sick with coughing, the other half bandaging their fingers after twelve hours on the looms, and only one of them over fifteen, then you're on the right path to getting where I'm coming from.'

He was speaking to the darkness, but the image before his eyes was far removed from the opera house.

'Rather, where I came from when I was sixteen,' he said. 'Left my sisters behind in the hope I could send them money. Streets were paved with gold, you see, only they weren't. But, I'm not here to give you a sob story. I became a renter...'

A loud gasp was accompanied by some obvious tutting, and someone close by said, 'I say!'

Silas sailed on through.

'Well,' he said, imagining he was talking to Archer. 'You can't be here to support a cause and be shocked by who that charity is for. Out there...' He pointed the gold cup towards the wings. 'Not that far away, there's a hundred lads like me, some younger. Young as fourteen, and they're starving. They've got families. They come from someone, and they've got friends they care about, same as you all. They've also got no choice but to do what they have to do. That's why some ended up under the Ripper's knife...' There were louder gasps at that. 'Sorry, but truth hurts. It hurts as much as frozen fingers and an empty stomach. But, because of you, out there right now there's a building where my mates can go and find help. You, by putting on your best clothes and walking proudly into this theatre, you, standing up to be counted as people who care, you've saved me from starving.'

Sounds of discontent faded, to be replaced by what he hoped was sympathetic silence. James wasn't far away, and Silas' confidence was further boosted by catching sight of him discreetly holding up his thumb for support.

'You've saved another young man,' he continued. 'Let's call him Edward. He's fourteen, and you've given him a safe place to sleep. There's this other one, Martin, fifteen, and then Micky, a year older. Micky-Nick they call him. You've helped him recover from an illness, find assistance, have a hot meal. Well...' He raised the cup to the Royal Box. 'Men like Doctor Markland have. Like he helped a lad called Alex, like you've all done by supporting the genius behind all this.' He bowed, not knowing if it was the right thing to do, but not caring. 'Your Lordship,' he said, and to his total surprise, the audience erupted into applause.

He was doing something right. He took a moment to look back to James, smiling behind a large mound of black that could only have been Mrs Marks. Her husband was leaning on the plush balustrade, his chin on his hands. He was studying every word, and when Silas caught his eye, he nodded approval.

Boosted, Silas waited for the applause to fade.

'Except,' he said, and left a pause. 'I'm sorry to say you didn't help those other lads. Oh, you're helping men *like* them right now, but Martin, Micky-Nick, Alex? They were the victims of...' He stopped himself repeating the name. '...a killer. You know who. I could have been one of them, but I was saved. That's why Mr Roxton thought I should do this, and I'm happy to do it. I just wanted you to know that right now, there are desperate men who would do anything to get what they want.' He was aware that he was sending a direct message to the Cleaver Street hitman wherever he was. 'We're not going to let that happen. All these good people here are not going to let that happen.'

That was enough of that message. He had explained his meaning.

'You see, all those young menfolk want is a warm room to sleep in, a wash and a chance. I was given that and now look at me. Two months ago… Well, it doesn't bear thinking about, but now look. You've done that, My Lord, Your Ladyship, Doctor, Mr Marks, all of you here tonight.' He took Fecker's stone from his pocket and held it high. 'Especially you up there.'

A rowdy cheer erupted from the gallery, and through it Silas heard Fecker roaring approval.

'Yeah, alright,' Silas said, forgetting where he was. 'Don't fall over the edge.'

He pocketed the stone as he waited for the laughter to subside. He had said enough. 'I'm sorry if I spoke out of place,' he said. 'And I'm going to go now. I just wanted you to hear from one of us from the gutter before these talented people take you on a journey to the stars.' He directed his voice to the King. 'Those gutters are real, Your Majesty. I know because I came from them. On behalf of every boy or man who's still in them, thank you. All of you.' He raised the goblet. 'Sláinte!'

He flinched at a sudden crack of sound, expecting a bullet to thwack into his head, but it was only applause. His Majesty stood to clap, and the audience hastily followed.

Silas had got away with it. He'd removed the reason for Stella to kill, but not the threat. He had let her know that he knew what was going on, and he'd suggested that he was not alone. He hoped he had also done right by Archer.

Thomas was also applauding, and on the other side of the theatre, Mr Marks was beaming approval while his wife bowed to the audience as if the reception was for her. At the back, James was beckoning urgently.

Twenty-Four

Jake was waiting at the side of the stage, where Silas was suddenly the centre of attention from the backstage crew. Many were watching him, whispering between themselves, a couple gave him a thumbs up, and one of the chorus men hissed, 'Are you still working?' when he passed. Silas ignored him, handed the prop goblet to Jake and thanked him for his help.

'What's going on?' Jake asked, accompanying Silas towards the auditorium.

'Last minute change of plan,' Silas said. His legs were weak, and sweat had gathered uncomfortably at the back of his neck. 'Fuck, that was weird.'

'I meant who were you warning?'

Silas stopped dead. 'What do you mean?' He feigned ignorance, but Jake was as intuitive as he was wiry.

'Murder victims?' Jake said, wide-eyed. 'Desperate men determined to get what they want, and you're not going to let them?'

'I was talking generally,' Silas said. 'I have to get back.'

The auditorium exploded into applause as the conductor took the podium.

'Yeah, and I better go and get Mr Roxton,' Jake said. 'Look, Mr Silas.' He took his arm. 'If you need any more help, just ask, yeah?'

He said it was a natural twinkle in his eye. Unlike the man from the chorus, there was no hidden meaning.

'I will, Jake,' he said. 'I'm in the first box. If you see anyone back here who shouldn't be here, come and get me. See you later.'

The applause had faded to silence, and he closed the connecting door carefully behind him before poking his head through the curtains. The boxes were now all closed, their drapes untied and hanging. James was waiting for him.

Silas opened his mouth to speak when an unexpected crash of cymbals, a deep drum and trumpets shook the floor, and he jumped. The crash of music was followed by a second or two of silence during which he and James exchanged shocked glances. A quieter, calmer theme began on strings and woodwind, and Silas recognised it as the tune Roxton had sung after the dinner party.

'Bloody hell,' James said, sidling up to him and whispering. 'How did you do that?'

'No idea, mate,' Silas replied. As soon as he'd finished the speech, he'd switched from abject fear to elation, but the moment was fleeting. 'I reckon I've put the bastard on guard.'

'Mr Marks approved,' James said. 'Not so sure about His Lordship.'

Silas peeked through the drapes and looked over the audience to Archer. Despite the overture playing, he and the King were still talking, Thomas and the King's steward were serving Miss Arnold and Markland, and by the look of it, Lady Marshall was discussing the stitching of her glittering dress with the King's wife. Either they were all putting on an act, or no-one had been upset by Silas' speech.

'Yeah, well, I've done it now,' he said, letting the curtain fall. 'The question is, what do we do next?'

'His Lordship did say if we ran out of options we should inform the police,' James suggested.

Silas considered this for a moment. 'Well, His Majesty has his bodyguards,' he reasoned. 'Apparently, there's already plenty of security in the auditorium. If Stella was planning to take a pot shot, I reckon he's changed his mind.'

'You think?'

'Only because it would be suicide to be caught firing a gun when there's royalty close by. He is related to the Queen.'

'I see your point,' James agreed. 'But I don't think he means to shoot anyone.'

'Why not?'

James held up the threat letter. 'Da capo is a musical term,' he said. 'Mrs Marks explained that although it literally means "from the head", in music, it's taken to mean "back to the beginning", or similar. Back to the beginning, sudden and silent. Subito tacet.'

'Oh, right.' This was news to Silas. 'Maybe it doesn't mean

anything. I need to sit down. Any drink left?'

'There's a whole bottle. Mrs Marks has polished off the first, but her husband won't let her have any more until the interval.'

James held the drapes and Silas, having straightened his suit and wiped sweat from his brow, entered the box and sat in a spare front seat. Marks, beside him, leant close.

'What was all that about, lad?'

'Sudden change of plan,' he said, his eyes on Archer.

'You did it well. Bravo.'

Marks retreated and examined his programme as the overture played.

Across the way, Archer and His Majesty finished whatever conversation they were having and also settled back into their seats.

Silas stared at Archer, hoping he would catch his eye. He needed to know that he approved of his actions and his words. They had sprung from a deep well of honesty and, once he had accepted that he was standing in front of all those people, he had found the task less daunting than he thought. Imagining he was talking to Archer, it had been easy to say what he felt, and he had let it flow while another part of his mind worked on how to deal with the death threat.

As the curtains parted, Archer became fixated on the stage, and Silas' eyes wandered to other parts of the house. Using the opera glasses, he identified Fecker on the top tier front row with Lucy beside him, and Mrs Flintwich choosing to ignore the fact they were holding hands. That was kind of her, he thought. They were at the front of a swathe of faces sweeping towards the ceiling. Many of the working class audience were more interested in the architecture, chandelier and toffs below than the story about to unfold on stage.

Silas looked for anything suspicious, but saw nothing.

'Your Champagne, Sir.' James offered the glass.

Silas patted the seat next to his, but James shook his head. He threw a glance towards Thomas, staring, his eyes wide.

Silas understood, raised his glass to Tom, who remained expressionless, and slid from his seat to join James in the corridor where they could whisper without being seen.

'Mr Roxton isn't on until later,' James said, showing Silas the libretto printed at the back of the programme. 'It's when he's on stage that we have to be alert. Maybe you should be back there?'

'I've got Jake looking out for strangers,' Silas said. 'Mr Keys is guarding the stage door, and there's no other way in other than from the front of house and across the stage.'

'What if Stella's in the chorus?'

'You think that's likely, Jimmy?'

'I don't know what to think.'

James was agitated, and Silas wasn't sure if it was because he was nervous or itching to be of more use. He too was frustrated that they had come so far, but didn't know where to go next.

'But that's what you've got to do, Jimmy. Think. I need to be seen watching at least part of this… Jesus!'

Signora Campanelli had made her appearance, or at least, her voice had. A high, sustained note rang out, piercing his ears, and beneath it, the orchestra swelled to a deafening climax as she entered at full tilt. The audience burst into applause.

'Sit, watch and think,' Silas mouthed over the din, and they took up chairs, this time behind the Marks couple.

The next forty minutes passed in a blur of panic. Roxton made his appearance in battle dress, marching onto the set crowded by a following of rowdy soldiers celebrating a victory, and Signora Campanelli swooned. Warbling handmaidens attended her, and someone sang a long, boring song about love, or so James said as he followed the translation in the programme. When Roxton came to sing, the audience listened in reverent silence, and Silas found himself unexpectedly mesmerised by the voice.

Roxton was a big man. He had the kind of physique suited to a rower or a boxer, and yet the sound that came from his mouth was that of a woman. His voice was high, unlike anything Silas had heard, higher than the other men, and clearer. Each held note hung on the air, cutting through it, but without disturbing it, and, in sections, climbed to unimaginable heights.

Silas couldn't help but be impressed, and on more than one occasion found himself so engrossed, he forgot about the imminent threat on the man's life. He was reminded of it when another soldier appeared, throwing threats of his own and brandishing a sword. Silas knew them to be wooden props and harmless.

When the chorus was on, he watched each man and woman

closely to see if any bore a resemblance to the Cleaver Street boy's stature. None did, and he doubted that a boy-whore would have found himself as a member of this production. He would have to be an excellent artist, and although Silas had heard him change his voice, that was hardly enough to get him a place on this stage.

The more he watched, the more convinced he became that the business with the letter was a hoax, and put there to teach the man a lesson rather than extort a confession. It was a comforting theory, but no matter how hard he tried, he couldn't make his peace with it. A nagging voice in his head fought against the trilling chorus, Roxton's passionate vocalisations and even the soprano's protestations of love. It would have itself heard, and after a while, Silas gave in to it.

"He's here." The words came from somewhere deep in the orchestra pit, a repetitive motif that seeped up from the low strings to tangle itself among other instruments before finding itself beaten out by drums. "He's here. He's here. He's here." Over and continuous like a heartbeat, a constant reminder that somewhere in the building, a man was planning to kill.

The pulse altered its words and "He's here" became "His head. His head. His head," until the two mixed and all he could think was, "He's dead. He's dead. He's dead."

The sweat at his neck trickled to his back, soaking his shirt while his mouth ran dry.

From where he sat, he could see into the wings as high as the proscenium arch would allow. If he stood, he could see over the balustrade to off-stage at floor level and down into part of the orchestra pit. There was nothing to suggest anything was amiss and, as the performance rattled into a long and complicated vocal firework display from Campanelli and a similar display from Roxton, he battled the warning voice and convinced himself that the combination of the King's entourage and his speech had deterred Stella from her plan.

The opera was well into the first act when James nudged him. 'I think I've found something,' he whispered. 'Out here.'

Silas followed him back into the corridor.

'What?'

'I think we're alright until the end,' James said.

'What do you mean?'

'The letter mentions his final applause.' He showed it to Silas. 'It's not definite, because he could be struck down now and still not hear his final ovation, but why mention the word "final" unless to worry him.'

'I don't get it.' Silas winced against another barrage of Campanelli's coloratura stabbing through the velvet drapes.

'It's torture,' James said.

'You're telling me.' Silas stuck a finger in his ear. 'Given me a headache.'

'Not her.' James suppressed a laugh. 'Stella. Look, you said that Roxton liked to take a belt to the boy. Punishment? Torture of some sort?'

'It's how some men get off,' Silas said. 'Not my kind of thing, but it goes on a lot.'

'Okay, but I bet it's painful.'

'Probably, what's your point?'

Roxton was now matching the soprano's technical challenge, in a softer tone, though just as high.

'What would be more torturous for Roxton than being made to think he's going to be killed, but not telling him when? Only that it's likely to be right at the end. He's got to go through the whole performance thinking he's going to die, but he can't not go on.'

Silas looked at him. 'While we're drowning men clutching at flotsam,' he said. 'We may as well cling to that. Still doesn't help us with the how.'

'He, I mean his character, dies at the very end of the story.' James showed him the programme notes. 'Perfect cover, don't you think?'

'Yeah, but it's a blunt sword. I've handled it.'

'Read that.'

Silas took the programme and slouched against the wall. A footman standing to attention outside another box gave him a look of annoyance, but Silas turned his back and read.

Perhaps the most dignified death in opera, in the closing scene Aeneas gives us the famous lament, "When I am laid in earth". Aeneas, the proud king of Troy is mortally offended when his visitor and betrothed, Dido from Carthage reveals she must leave him to

216

return to her homeland at the behest of the gods. When she offers to stay, he rejects her, considering the mere thought of abandoning him an unforgivable betrayal. She has left it too late for the proud man to accept her protestations of love as sincere. Thus spurned and alone, Aeneas arrives at a decision: "Death will come when she is gone." Aeneas' tearful manservant, Belindo, can only look on as the king succumbs to death, a "welcome guest." He throws himself on his sword** against a final, sorrowful, off-stage chorus, "With drooping wings." Cupids appear in the clouds and scatter roses like drops of blood on Aeneas' waiting tomb. The curtain falls.

He handed the programme to James, unconvinced. 'You think it's going to be then? How?'

'I can only think of the sword,' James admitted. 'Could it be swapped?'

'I suppose so, but he'd know. It's wood, light, what he's used to. Swap it for a metal one, and it'd be obvious. Anyway, he wouldn't actually fall on it, and if he knew it was real, he'd definitely be careful.'

'True.' James frowned. 'I've looked through the whole libretto, and he's on stage for just about all of the second half. The ending is the only time he's in danger from anything.'

'Except her bloody voice.' The soprano was bringing act one to a startling conclusion.

'Ah, but he, the character, does actually die before the audience's eyes.' James left a pause so Silas could pick up his thread. 'Nice and dramatic to engineer some way that the two become one and he commits suicide.'

It was too vague, and Silas was unable to compute the ideas. He understood James' point about torturing Roxton with a threat on his life, forcing him to perform the entire piece with death hanging over his head, but still, it was too haphazard, too farfetched, and, more ridiculously, it depended on Roxton taking his own life. Archer had said the man had shrugged the whole thing off as a hoax and was ignoring it. Why then change his mind and gut himself with a prop?

'Final applause.' Silas thought aloud before fixing James with a blank stare.

James was concentrating as hard as he was and his determination to help and his loyalty were heart-warming. Silas respected his ideas, but they weren't bringing clarification.

'Just torturing him with the possibility of being killed is too silent,' he reasoned. 'It's too hidden, isn't it?'

'Yeah,' James agreed. 'Sorry, I'm thinking as hard as I can.'

'I know, Jimmy, and I appreciate it.' Silas encouraged him with a hand on his shoulder as applause rang out. 'And you've given me an idea. Sounds like we've got half an hour off from that racket. I need to see Roxton. He might not listen to Archer, but he's going to have to listen to me.'

Along the passage, curtains were being lifted as the well-to-do emerged to stretch their legs.

'Go and see to the Marks duo,' Silas said. 'Everything as normal. I'm going to look around backstage and do battle with Roxton.'

'Mr Roxton is in a foul mood and not receiving visitors,' the stage manager informed Silas a minute later. He was poring over a large book of music, distracted. 'And, if I may, Mr Hawkins, your persistent presence back here is not helpful.'

'Yeah, well, sorry about that, Mr...' He still couldn't remember the man's name. 'But I have been asked to keep an eye on his well-being.'

He was rescued by the sight of Jake beetling along the catwalk above and waved him down.

'I'll get out of your way.' He touched his forelock to the stage manager, and noticing the book, asked him what it was.

The book was bigger than Archer's atlas. Music was printed on one page, and lines led across the spine to the facing page linking specific places in the score to handwritten notes.

'It's my bible,' the man said. 'Now, if you wouldn't mind.'

Silas caught a fleeting glimpse of the music as he walked away. The words were written in a language he couldn't read, and he assumed it was Italian. Why a story about a Trojan hero should be written in Italian, by a German, for the English was beyond Silas, but then so was most of what was taking place. Whistles from the men in the tower, sweaty stagehands carrying pieces of a temple and replacing them with the decks of a ship, and women scurrying about with powder puffs; Silas hadn't seen this much activity since the Greychurch riots.

'Yes, Sir?' Jake was at his side.

Silas marvelled at the lad's habit of speedy and silent arrival. 'I need to see Mr Roxton.'

Jake passed an uneasy glance to the stage manager, but he had turned his back and was ticking items off a list.

'It's alright,' Silas said. 'It's His Lordship's business.'

'You're the boss.'

Silas took the opportunity to touch the sword on the props table as he passed. It was still made of wood and, better, this time he saw the tip was rounded.

Jake led him to the back of the stage, onto the brick stairs and up one floor. Here, he trotted along a carpeted corridor to a dressing room labelled with Roxton's name. A man stood outside dabbing his forehead.

'Mr Roxton is not receiving guests,' he snapped as they approached. 'He won't even see me.'

'And who are you?'

'His dresser, of course,' the man replied, shocked to have been asked. 'Who are you?'

'Lord Clearwater's private secretary, out of the way.'

'I can't allow that…'

'It's His Lordship's business, Arthur,' Jake said.

The dresser looked Silas up and down in a way that Silas had seen a thousand times before, his handkerchief hanging from one, limp hand, a smile spreading.

'Sorry, mate,' Silas said. 'But I ain't in that business anymore.'

'Ha!' The man was scornful. 'I haven't been to sea for years, and they still call me a sailor.' He flicked his wrist. 'Do what you want, love, I'm beyond caring.'

Growling, Silas sent Jake away and let himself in to the dressing room unannounced. He knew what he had to say, and was prepared for Roxton's anger.

What he wasn't expecting was the sight of the man, collapsed on his couch, weeping.

'Get out!' Roxton yelled, on hearing the door.

Silas slammed it to draw his attention and to relieve some of the instant anger the dresser had instilled. Stepping deeper into the room, he flicked his eyes over mirrors, costumes, chairs, cards, flowers and baskets, and made sure they were alone.

'You're in trouble,' he said, ignoring the man's pathetic state.

Roxton's head snapped up. His face glowed pink through the makeup, his eyes were puffy, and his eyeliner smudged.

'Is it Clearwater?' he said, and leapt to his feet. 'What's happened.'

Silas was taken aback. He hadn't anticipated the man's first thought to be for the viscount.

'Nothing,' he said. 'Yes, he's fine. You're the one in trouble.'

'Me? What about you? Cancelling my speech, robbing me of the limelight…'

'Get over it,' Silas snapped. 'I was trying to save your life.'

'Rubbish.' Roxton threw himself back on the couch. 'I've been so stupid. Are you going to do it now?'

'What?' Confusion replaced anger. 'What d'you mean?'

'I can't talk about it,' Roxton wailed. 'Go away or do it now. I don't care. I am resigned.'

'You ain't dead yet.'

Maybe it was his choice of words, maybe it was because Silas reverted to his natural accent, but Roxton was shocked. He sniffed, and dragged his head to stare Silas in the eye. They held each other's gaze until Roxton gave in.

'When are you going to kill me?' he asked, weak and wretched.

'Me? I ain't going to do nothing, not to you.'

Roxton stared helplessly. 'You work with them,' he said. 'I saw you there.'

'I pulled you out of the place,' Silas reminded him.

'No, before.' Roxton was beginning to calm. 'It was hot. I came back to see my throat doctor… It was you.'

'Ah, yeah,' Silas admitted. 'I was there that night, and I saw you.' Judging it safe, he lowered himself onto the couch beside the snivelling man. 'I recognised your coat when you came to dinner. I was at Cleaver Street the other night to find out for sure.'

'They drugged me.'

'I know. But they didn't before, did they? When you called to find yourself a renter you could… do whatever you do with. You went 'cos you wanted to, and from what I heard, you went there regular. They even looked after your personal belts.'

'Yes, yes,' Roxton complained. 'You've made your point, Hawkins.'

'How's your back?'

It was more of a taunt than a question, and Roxton wasn't in the mood for answers. 'What do you want?'

'Why didn't you listen to Archer?' Silas asked. 'Why didn't you let him help you?'

'It's ridiculous.' Seeing that Silas meant him no harm, the singer reached for a towel. Drying his eyes, he said, 'I considered it a joke at first. Some kind of elaborate jest as we used to play on each other at school.'

'You thought it was Archer?

'Yes, of course. The letter wasn't in my pocket when I arrived at Clearwater. I'd just had the coat cleaned. The first I knew of it was when Archer waved it at me. I told him to grow up. We had a bit of a row, but, well… I thought it bad taste, and told him to go away.'

He brushed his hand forlornly towards a water jug and Silas, considering sympathy might produce answers, poured him a glass.

'Then,' Roxton went on. 'I started to think that perhaps it was serious. Someone had drugged me, and that was too much even for one of Clearwater's pranks. I thought, maybe the boy had the wherewithal to mean it, but then I thought, how could he get away with it? It wasn't possible, didn't make sense.' He threw the towel across the room and pulled off his wig. Beneath, his hair was flattened by a net, and with that and his makeup, he looked like a worthless puppet, discarded and no longer loved. 'Then,' he continued. 'Yesterday, it began preying on my mind. Of course it wasn't Archer. I remembered what the letter said, and I knew what they planned, and when. It was all in there. I had to make a choice, Hawkins.' He regarded Silas as if he could smell his scepticism. 'It's not easy to be noble when one's life is in danger, you know. I could cancel the performance and dent Archer's good name. Or I could carry on as if I didn't care. As if I didn't know. Despite what you might think, I am a decent actor, and it was easy to pretend I had never seen the threat.'

'As easy as it was to pretend you never went to Cleaver Street and smacked the lads around.'

'Please, it's not like that.'

Silas laughed scornfully.

'It was consensual.'

'You mean a teenage opium addict asked you to scar his flesh?'

'Don't judge me so, Hawkins. That "boy" is no boy. Stella, or whatever his name is, is a professional con man well into his thirties and has spent half his life aboard ship. Don't ask me how someone with such feminine looks and ability got away without being keelhauled, but that man is as masculine as you or I. The world is full of duplicity masquerading as actors.'

Silas had to admit Roxton was also an excellent actor. He was aware of the threat against him, but covered his concern and chose to take a risk rather than discredit Archer. He couldn't bring himself to admire the man's devotion to the viscount, but the news made Silas' job easier.

'Have you seen Stella here tonight?' he asked. Roxton shook his head. 'But you knew what was going to happen to you and you still went ahead?'

'Yes, Hawkins,' he sighed. 'I made my choice, because contrary to what you might think of me, I love my friend.'

'And you agreed to help his Foundation 'cos it made your guilt easier.'

'What?'

'If anyone found out you used Stella as your personal whipping boy you could say, "Look at me! I support the Clearwater Foundation, how could I be a man who does that?"'

'You're sick.'

Silas laughed. He could tell from the shame behind the makeup that he was right. He felt no satisfaction in being proved correct; the performance was still in jeopardy.

'Okay,' he said, putting his personal feelings aside. 'Tell me what you know, and I'll find a way out of this mess.'

Roxton regarded him dubiously. 'Why would you do that?'

It was an easy question to answer, but time was against him. 'I'm not doing it for you,' Silas said. 'Tell me what the message meant to you.'

Roxton shook his head, his eyes closing briefly, and shuddered. 'If someone is going to kill me, they are going to do it on my final note. That's why I am sitting here blubbing like a baby. Not because

I know I'm going to die, but because of the stress. I am trying to give Archer the performance of his and my life while holding at bay the knowledge that it will be my last. I would rather be shot in the head than stand there admitting my sins and bringing his good name, and the name of this opera house, into disrepute.'

Silas had misjudged the man, but he wasn't about to apologise. 'What do you mean about being shot?'

'Da capo,' Roxton sniffed. He cleared his throat and looked at a watch. 'Not long now.'

'And why will they do it on your last note? Because it says you won't hear your final applause?'

'That's part of it,' Roxton admitted. His hands were shaking as he picked up a book and dropped it on the couch between them. 'Last page.'

Silas opened the cover. Unlike the stage manager's score, music was printed on every page. He turned to the last one, but as before, nothing made sense.

'What am I looking at?'

'That stave.' Roxton pointed to a line of music buried among black dots, some with tails, some massed together, others far apart. It was like reading code. 'That string of notes is my last sustain. After it...'

He tapped some words written where the note ended, and Silas read them aloud. 'D. C. All Fine?' he queried. It sounded oddly reassuring.

Annoyed, Roxton slapped his finger on an empty section of music. 'Da capo, al Fine,' he corrected in Italian. 'To the beginning and repeat to the end. The direction sends the orchestra around in a circle. It's a musical joke by the composer. He did it, he said, to give the players some humour after the hero's death. Complete tosh.'

'I still don't get it.'

'There is no music.' Roxton explained, indicating an empty bar. 'All that direction does is send the reader back to the beginning of that bar of nothing. It's pointless.'

'So what's the joke?'

'The joke, Hawkins, is that after the final notes, everyone is already subito tacet.'

'Which means suddenly silent.'

'Exactly. Pointless humour from a genius, but used by my assassin as a message. This is when he, or she, intends to strike.' He balled his fists, infuriated that Silas had still not understood. 'The empty bar repeats ad infinitum because Aeneas enters everlasting peace. Death is endless. Only, in this case, it is me who will be locked in an endless loop of sudden silence. For real.'

'If you'd listened to Archer… If I'd known this before…' Silas' swallowed his anger. Frustration was not going to help his cause. 'Never mind. What we've got to do now, Mr Roxton is make sure it doesn't happen.'

'No,' Roxton said, taking away the score. 'Let it happen. I deserve it.'

'Oh, please,' Silas dismissed his self-pity. 'I probably agree with you, and I wouldn't be much bothered, to be honest, but Archer would be. Why didn't you report this to the police?'

'Hell, you're thick. Because there would be a scandal. They would want to know why. Stella would tell them about the house, I would have to explain…'

'Yeah, I get it. Blimey. Calm down, mate.' Silas was fed up with sympathy, and there wasn't time to challenge him for calling him thick. He let it go, but Roxton's behaviour fired so many emotions, he didn't know what to think of the man. 'If what you say is right, we've got the second half to watch, think, and stop it happening. James doesn't think you'll get shot. There's too much security guarding the King, and my speech robbed old Stella of her chance to do the public a favour.'

'I beg your pardon?'

'Stella could have claimed that he killed you to prevent embarrassment to Archer,' Silas reasoned. 'Or the ladies present. You get me?' Roxton didn't, so Silas put on an imitation of Stella's soft, West Country voice. '"You see, Your Honour, he was talking about sodomites in front of decent ladies and gentlemen. I had to do something out of common decency."'

He imitated her so well, Roxton moved away.

'Sorry,' Silas said in his own voice. 'But you see what I'm getting at?'

'Yes. I suppose I should thank you for what you did.'

'Later.' Silas stood. 'At least we know the timing,' he said. 'Just got to think of a way to stop your murder without knowing how it's going to be done.'

'Mr Hawkins.' The singer rose and, slightly more composed, offered his hand. 'Please do nothing that disrupts the evening. Archer is a beloved friend. I won't do anything to harm his good work.'

'Yeah, well, it's a bit late for that.' Silas ignored his hand. 'Good luck.' He turned and was at the door when Roxton stopped him.

'My life is in your hands, Sir,' he said, as calmly as a greeting. 'But I am prepared to die.'

'Hm,' Silas huffed. 'And I reckon I'm inclined to let you.'

He slammed the door as he left.

Twenty-Five

Ignoring the dresser now nipping from a hipflask, Silas ran to the end of the corridor and turned onto the stairs. Down one level, he hurried to the stage entrance and burst through the door to find himself face to face with the King of the Netherlands. Archer was beside him, and they were examining his tourmaline ring. Surrounded by an entourage of the viscount's guests, royal bodyguards and members of theatre staff, the party was enjoying a backstage tour, directed by Mr Bursnall.

Silas skidded to a halt, clocked Archer's look of horror and, behind him, Thomas, equally shocked. On seeing him, Thomas snapped to attention, indicating that Silas should do the same. He also mouthed the word, 'Bow', showed Silas what to do and held a finger to his mouth for silence.

'Ah,' Archer said as if he was expecting the interruption. 'Sir, may I introduce my private secretary, Mr Hawkins.'

Having bowed, shaking all other thoughts from his cluttered head and leaving only mild panic, Silas stood with his hands behind his back. Thomas' finger remained at his lips.

'Hoe gaat het met u?'

His Majesty's language was unintelligible, but Silas got the gist. The King offered a handshake, Thomas nodded, and Archer's eyes stretched wide. He surreptitiously showed his ring finger, watching in horror as Silas lifted his hand and accepted the greeting.

Silas had already removed his ring. Identical to Archer's, it would have drawn the King's interest, and not taken him long to realise it was a love token. He shook the King's hand once and firmly, saying, 'Your Majesty.'

Thomas approved, and Archer relaxed.

The King was supported by his younger companion, a lady Silas put in her thirties. His Majesty was at least seventy, had trouble standing, and held a faraway look in his eyes as if he didn't know where he was. Despite that imperfection, he was not only surrounded by uniformed staff, but by an aura of grandeur that demanded respect.

'It was Mr Hawkins who made the speech,' the viscount said directly into the King's ear.

'Ah!' His Majesty focused on Silas. He squinted, and his bushy moustache turned down in a serious frown. 'Je hebt goed gesproken,' he said.

Thomas mouthed, 'Thank you, Sir.'

'Thank you, Sir.'

'Er... Vell done.'

Thomas tipped his head graciously, and Silas copied.

'Gefeliciteerd.'

Thomas was helpless with that one, and Silas bowed to cover a nervous laugh.

'If Your Majesty would like to progress this way...'

Luckily, Mr Bursnall was keen to move the party along. The scenery was being flown in, and backstage was not a safe place to loiter. He directed them across the stage behind the backcloth, and His Majesty, with his young wife's assistance, progressed. Archer threw a look of intense bewilderment as he passed, but there was no time for explanations. Lady Marshall and Miss Arnold followed the party, both engrossed in the flymen and stagehands, and Doctor Markland came last.

'Bloody well done, Silas,' he whispered, slapping his shoulder before hurrying on.

It was only a small thing, but it was reassuring. The mystery was unravelling, and Silas was sure he almost had the answer. He stopped Thomas and pulled him to one side.

'It's going to happen right at the end,' he said. 'Keep watch from your side. You can see off stage, yeah?'

'Some. How do you...?'

'Shush. If you can, tell Archer it's under control, everything's fine. We don't want to worry him. But if you see anything strange, you... you...'

'Exactly!' Thomas whispered his eyes on the royal party. 'What *can* I do?'

'You can either scream murder or let Roxton get killed,' Silas said. 'Don't feel under pressure, Tommy.'

He slapped him on his gilded shoulder and, slipping the ring back on his finger, left him to his duties.

Silas' duty now was to protect Archer. If he failed to prevent the murder, the least he could do was prevent it causing outrage on the stage. He remembered the programme notes, that when Aeneas dies, someone came down from the roof, dropping roses before the curtain fell. If he could bring the curtain down before Roxton pretended to stab himself, he could spare the audience the sight of a real and possibly bloody death, or even thwart the assassin. He couldn't end the performance any earlier without arousing suspicion, but he did at least have a window of opportunity.

The stage manager was not pleased to see him, and by the time Silas had told him what he wanted, the man was outraged.

'Don't be ridiculous!' he roared. 'I can't do that.'

'It's on His Lordship's authority,' Silas lied.

'I don't care. There is only one man I take orders from, and that is Herr Director. God orders me to follow the script. Go away.'

'It is of vital importance.'

'I shall have you removed.'

'Look… Whatever your name is, you have no idea what's going on here…'

'Mr Cookson? Fetch Mr Keys and have this man removed.' The stage manager snapped his fingers and turned his back.

'Don't trouble yourself, mate,' Silas called. 'It's going to come down on your head, not mine.'

He glanced into the tower where a hundred and one things could easily come down on someone's head, Roxton's included and continued to the auditorium.

James was alone in the box, straightening chairs.

'Well?' he asked as Silas entered.

'I can see how you got your surname,' Silas said, confusing his friend. 'You were right, Mr Wright. It's going to happen at the end.'

He explained what Roxton knew and said, included his encounter with the royal party, and outlined his plan to end the show prematurely.

'I agree we're trapped, and it's the only thing we can try,' James said, when he'd finished. 'We can't inform anyone, we can't put guards in the tower or behind the scenes, and we don't know how he's going to do it.'

'That's about the sum of it, Jimmy.'

'But we can cover the tower ourselves if we're careful.'

'You mean sneak back there and watch?'

'Yes,' James said. 'One side each.'

'I can, but I'm not sure about you.' He indicated James' livery. 'I just need to take off my jacket and tie, and I'm a stagehand. You…? A bit more tricky. But yeah, I was planning to be back there later. Meanwhile, if we can figure out how Stella's going to do it, we might have a better idea of where he'll be.'

'How can we do that?'

The audience were taking their seats, and the curtains of the Royal Box were pulled back as the first of the party returned from their tour.

'I don't know,' Silas admitted. 'We sit and think.'

They were interrupted as Mrs Marks appeared, much assisted by the wall. James helped her to her seat where she dropped her fan, giggled and fell asleep. Her husband blustered in a moment later, rolled his eyes at no-one in particular, and sat heavily on the chair beside her. He arranged her hands in her lap with the fan, and her head so that it pointed to the stage. That done, he calmly read his programme until the lights dimmed, the conductor returned and the second act began.

For Silas, the next half an hour passed like a lifetime. There was no point being backstage until nearer the end, and James was trying to judge the timing from the libretto. By listening to the singing, he was able to make out the words, if not the meaning.

It was just after Aeneas had sent the wretched Dido away — a dismissal which Silas thought took far too long and was incredibly noisy — that James leant to him and whispered, 'We are approaching the last two pages of the story.'

Silas nodded to show he understood and felt his legs weaken. Taking deep breaths, he looked across to Thomas to see him scanning the auditorium in a wide arc. The royal party were intent on the drama taking place on stage, and Silas was drinking in Archer's look of rapture when something caught his eye. He moved the opera glasses a fraction and saw Miss Arnold admiring the audience through hers. She pointed them directly at him and waved her fingers.

'She must be bored,' he said.

He was about to wave back when James elbowed him urgently, showing him the programme with his thumb marking a line of text.

'What's that?' Silas asked, putting down the opera glasses. It was the same passage as before where the opera's basic story was written in summary. 'I've read it.'

'Not all of it.'

James was indicating the end of the paragraph, two symbols in particular. *He throws himself on his sword** against a final…*

'What do they mean?'

James turned to the last page in the booklet.

** Addendum

In the 1888 tour of 'Aeneas and Dido', Herr Muller, in his direction, has preferred and borrowed from the Giulio Cesare interpretation of the libretto and has Aeneas drinking the poisoned waters of the river Styx.

The meaning was only starting to sink in when James slapped his back and pointed to the stage. Roxton was in the centre, singing passionately to the goblet Silas drank from earlier in the evening. It stood on a pedestal, left there a second before by his servant, Belindo, now exiting.

'Jesus!' Silas said and earned a disapproving 'Shush!' from Marks.

'That's got to be it.' James pulled Silas from his seat. 'Think about it,' he hissed when they were out of earshot. 'It is silent, probably sudden, and you take it by mouth, da capo. From the head.'

'It's not right.'

'None of this is right.'

'No, not that.' Silas pulled away from his grip and inched towards the balustrade. There, he trained the opera glasses onto the goblet and knew he was right. He sidled back to James.

'It's silver,' he said. 'The prop is gold. Real fucking gold. I held it.

That one out there is silver.'

James leant across him, saw he was correct and swore. 'She's not there,' he said.

Marks gave him an aggressive glare.

Silas didn't understand. He was too busy thinking how he could swap the stage goblet with something else. 'Who's not where?'

'Look.'

James turned him and pointed to the Royal Box. His Majesty was drinking from a goblet, and those used by the rest of the party stood on tables beside the cushioned chairs. They were all silver, apart from one.

'That's it!'

Silas had to hold himself back from shouting. The golden chalice that should have been on the stage containing lemon water was now standing on a side table, and the silver one that had been there was now centre stage and, presumably, contained poison.

When he realised who was now using the golden cup, the pieces fell into place like a sandbag falling from the fly tower.

Twenty-Six

His lapels were the nearest thing to grab, and Silas used them to drag James into the corridor. They stumbled through the curtains and staggered to a stop beneath the supercilious glare of a nearby footman. Silas ignored him and tugged James to the far wall where they huddled, whispering.

'It's got to be,' he said, thinking fast.

'Who?'

'Stella. She… *He* is Miss Arnold.'

'Don't be ridiculous. She's with Doctor Markland.'

'Who doesn't know who she really is. He's not been… intimate with her.' Silas remembered Markland's endless declarations of love. 'Least that's what he told me. Either way, it wouldn't bother the doctor, he goes for both.'

Markland was smitten with the 'woman', too smitten to see clearly. Miss Arnold wore a high collar — to cover his Adam's apple. Her flat chest, her manly appearance that Roxton commented on saying something about her playing a character who dressed as a man and a woman. She was a good actress.

No, *he* was a vicious whore intent on murder.

'The letter.' James waved it. 'She could have put it in Roxton's pocket at the dinner. After it. Remember? She was in a hurry to help him with his coat?'

Silas remembered. The more he thought about it, the more sense it made. He'd not seen Stella's face in August, only a part of it, the rest had been covered by the man's long hair. He'd recognised a laugh from that night, it could have been Stella or Roxton, but either way, they had both been at Cleaver Street.

'She wouldn't take her eyes off Roxton all night,' Silas said. 'He must have seduced Markland hoping he would get close to Roxton. He was using the doctor to get into our box.'

'For a good shot?'

'Ours is in the perfect position,' Silas agreed.

'But the King showed up…'

'So she had to change her plan…'

They were talking over each other in tumbling realisation.

'The goblet?'

'She was backstage with the others in the interval.' Silas slapped himself on the forehead 'She switched them. Had a plan B.'

'Poison?'

'I'm guessing, Jimmy, but she knows we're onto her.'

He took a pace away, his hands pressing down on his head as he thought. James peeked through the drapes and reported that Miss Arnold was still in the box.

'She's not going to leave until it's done,' Silas reasoned. 'Better for her to be seen leaving with the rest of the royal party. Less suspicious. Perfect alibi.'

'Good point. But what can we do?'

'I'm working on it, mate.'

'Listen!'

James clamped his hand over Silas' mouth and lifted a finger. The music had changed. Before, it had been heavy and full of deep strings and brass, but now it was lighter. A flute played a melody Silas recognised.

'It's the last aria,' James said. '"When I am laid in Earth." It's a direct copy of the lyric from Purcell's "Dido and Aeneas." The words of this aria were written by Nahum Tate in the seventeenth century, not by Giulio Cesare in this one.'

'Jimmy,' Silas said pulling a face. 'You read too much. Come on, we've got to work fast.'

'I reckon we have about six minutes,' James said, heading towards the backstage entrance.

'How d'you know that?'

'Because that's how long it took Roxton to sing this song with Archer playing the piano.' He held back the drapes.

'Really? Felt like two hours to me,' Silas muttered as he slipped through.

Beyond the connecting door, he kept his back to the wall, staying out of sight of the stage manager.

'What are we doing?' James was also pressed flat and static, but his eyes were darting like fireflies.

'I'm looking for Jake,' Silas explained. 'He should be near that desk.'

The stage manager was hunched over his book and didn't look up from it even when he raised a hand to give a signal. A second later, a light dimmed. From where they stood, the music was distorted, the sound coming partially from beneath the floorboards and partially from the orchestra pit. Silas made his way cautiously around the desk, creeping deeper upstage with James following, and the music became quieter still. They caught snatches of Roxton's voice, but only when the singer faced them. Otherwise, all other sound was magically projected outwards, over the heads of the audience. Silas stole carefully to the props table. Sure enough, the tray for the chalice was empty, but in the tray beside it lay the scroll. It gave him a brilliantly idiotic idea.

He felt the familiar tug on his arm as Jake appeared.

'What's up now?' he asked, barely audible.

Silas cupped his ear and whispered while James looked on apprehensively. Jake pulled away, shrugged and cocked his thumb at James.

The footman raised his palms questioningly.

Silas pointed to Jake, who was now pulling at James' jacket, trying to take it off.

Seeing that Silas was orchestrating the events, James allowed the lad to take his tails but insisted on removing his own waistcoat. Silas was busy writing on the scroll at the time, using a pencil he pulled from behind the ear of a surprised, but unquestioning stagehand. He didn't see the tussle when Jake tried to remove James' trousers, and by the time he turned back, Jimmy still wore them, but Jake had disappeared.

'What the fuck?' James mouthed urgently.

Silas kept him at bay with one hand while searching beneath the props table. He didn't find what he was looking for.

'Damn!' It was said through gritted teeth.

'What are you doing?' James mimed.

Jake was back carrying another frockcoat. He passed the garment to James, and the shock on the footman's face was comical.

234

'If I can do it, so can you,' Silas hissed. 'Put it on.'

'I'm not doing this,' James protested.

Silas took no notice. 'I need another gold cup,' he whispered urgently. 'A glass? Anything.'

The lad was off again, leaving Silas to help James trembling into the costume.

'I don't know what to do.' James had turned pale.

'Do what you were doing before.' Silas grinned and handed him the scroll.

The music was building to what Silas expected to be a chorus, but it suddenly changed. Aeneas apparently sang an even longer version of the aria than that provided by Archer's library. All the same, the end of the act was fast approaching, the chorus had started to gather at the back of the wings, and two youths were clambering up the gantries to the clouds suspended high above.

Jake was back, thrusting a champagne glass into James' hand.

'Do what you've been doing since you came to Clearwater, Jimmy.' The words were mouthed rather than spoken, and only the faintest breath escaped Silas' lips. 'You're a footman and a messenger. There's no-one better qualified.' Jake was about to fill the glass, but Silas stopped him.

'Mr Roxton wants lemon water,' Jake breathed.

'He's not going to get it. Empty is safer. How long until…?' He sliced a finger across his throat.

Jake held up five fingers.

'We better get a move on. Ready Jimmy?'

'No.'

'Wait!' Jake held James back and whispered, 'You'll put Mr Roxton off. Give him ten bars, and he'll be downstage. You can do it without him seeing.'

Thomas was confused and concerned. One moment Silas and James were in the opposite box apparently not interested in the opera, and the next they had vanished. Silas had been coming and going all evening and had even turned up backstage. There had been no time and no way to communicate, and he could only hope Silas knew what he was doing.

The viscount had been panicked by His Majesty's unannounced

visit and would have been on edge even without the threat against Roxton. Lady Marshall had calmed him and taken the lead until Archer was able to clear his head of everything apart from entertaining a royal. Thomas kept a close eye, discussed the King's preferred etiquette with his steward, and had done all he could to ensure the viscount didn't put a foot wrong.

It hadn't been easy, but Markland and Miss Arnold had been charming, the actress distracting His Majesty's young wife when the conversation turned to foreign affairs. Silas' appearance instead of Roxton had made Archer blanch, and Thomas caught him trembling. He gave him more Champagne to calm him, and Archer was grateful, but when the speech was over, His Lordship demanded something stronger.

That had been the first of a few surprises. The second came when the audience gave Silas' impromptu speech a loud ovation, and the third when Archer told Thomas he had no idea it was going to happen. The royal party were blissfully unaware of what was taking place backstage and finding Silas scurrying about behind the scenes had been the next shock. It was made more troublesome because it was apparent to Thomas, and probably to Archer that something was wrong. His frustration increased through the second act when, luckily, there were no more surprises, but the closer they came to the finale, with no sudden assassination, the tighter the knot of tension gripped.

He had just completed a scan of the auditorium and was turning his head imperceptibly to the wings when Lady Marshall sat bolt upright. Archer did the same a second later, but no-one else in the house made a movement, so intent were they on Aeneas' impending suicide.

Thomas glanced to the stage to see a messenger enter at the back. He was a fine figure of a man, dressed the same as Belindo, but he carried himself with more precision, balancing a tray on one palm like a waiter. Thomas thought he would make a fine butler.

Then he saw it was James and nearly fainted. The viscount turned his head accusingly, and all Thomas could do was shrug and gape.

He was distracted from his amazement when Miss Arnold rose to excuse herself and he held back the curtain.

When he turned back, Aeneas was downstage, singing powerfully to the audience about a welcome death and milking the scene for all it was worth. Thomas held his breath. James walked calmly to the pedestal and collected the poisoned chalice Mr Roxton was, at that moment, bewailing. Some of the audience exchanged whispered words, and a few hurried to confer with their programme notes, but by the time they looked up, James had exchanged the chalice for a wine glass, and a scroll had appeared on the pedestal, partly unrolled.

James took two steps back and turned away. Thomas assumed he would exit where he had entered, but he stopped mid-turn. His head spun to the opposite side of the stage and lifted as if he was watching something climb the wall beyond the flats. He changed his tack and walked sedately off stage towards it as Mr Roxton thrilled his audience with complicated vocals that ended with an impossibly high note.

Aeneas had accepted that his end was inevitable, but the composer had decided that the aria wasn't, and the verse began again. He turned and once again aimed his words at the chalice. To give him his credit, he didn't flinch when he noticed it had miraculously become a Champagne flute, and approached it, entreating it to bring him a swift end. He reached for it and lingered, presumably reading the note which curled away when he lifted the glass. Holding it for the world to see as if it was a beacon of hope for mankind, he launched into another section of music. It brought a few sniggers from below, and Thomas assumed he was singing the praise of godly gold and ancient jewels while holding something bought at Fortnum and Mason the previous week. Not only that, the goblet should have held the elixir of death from the river Styx, and the wine glass was blatantly empty.

Roxton wasn't perturbed. He sang with invigorated passion, joy almost, and real tears came to his eyes. He brought the glass to his lips, but Aeneas couldn't bring himself to drink from it, and crumpled to the floor, wailing that he was not brave enough to die. At least, that's what Thomas hoped he was saying, there was no other excuse for his outlandish behaviour.

The aria was starting to drag, and Thomas wondered how much suffering one man could endure. His feet were thumping, and his back was sore from standing to attention for over two hours.

He pulled his shoulders and heard them crack. It relieved some tension but didn't ease his confusion.

Roxton trilled on, now sounding more like a happy sparrow than a suicidal hero. Saving the best for last, his notes were high and true, his range incredible, and he employed excellent projection. He shook the dust from above, and waves of it floated down, catching in the lights, some of which shimmied as if the lanterns, high up and out of sight, were being blown in a breeze.

After what seemed like the longest death scene in theatrical history, the music finally gave an indication of the home straight. The pace increased, the timpani beat a heartbeat cross-rhythm against the swelling strings as death stalked nearer. The orchestra swelled, and more dust and debris fell as if the heavens were being rocked by grief. Aeneas gripped the glass with renewed determination, lifting himself from the floor with the resolve of a fatally wounded man about to throw himself back into the battle. His voice rose and pierced the humid air, bringing tears to the eyes of men and women alike. The lower-class audience cried the same as the upper-class below them. Dock workers passed greying rags to their wives while in the stalls, lords passed monogrammed pocket kerchiefs to theirs. Roxton's voice temporarily healed the class divide, and for a few emotional minutes, there were no barriers. Everyone knew his pain, understood the agony of his loss. They wept for his suffering as the poisoned glass came ever closer to his lips. Death was classless.

The lights darkened, and smoke crept through the stage floor. Hades was coming to take Aeneas; the fires had been lit. Parts of the stage descended, and the smoke billowed through, driven by inaudible machines and turning the scene into an ever-changing blur of colour and light with Aeneas in the centre accepting his tragedy.

Falling rose petals preceded descending cherubs, while from below, a tomb appeared beneath Roxton's feet. Aeneas was lifted with it as if he would escape to Heaven after all, the poison held at arm's length. The music swelled to an ear-splitting climax, and the singer hit his final sustain. He carried it effortlessly as smoke poured and petals rained. It swelled, a swansong, a pitiful cry of lost love, a farewell to all, until, with no warning, he broke off.

The music ended, the last strains soaked up by velvet and gold as the vibration settled into the woodwork.

The audience held its breath in the sudden silence. The conductor, watching closely, held the orchestra ready but at bay, and Aeneas drank the poison.

He dropped the glass. It shattered, and he collapsed onto his tomb. The music picked up where it had left off twice as loud, and the two massive curtains swept together as the lights blacked out.

The conductor appeared shocked, but led his men onwards until the last bar as the audience gave the performance a standing ovation. Thomas was pretty sure the curtains should have closed gracefully while the music reached its natural end, but he was less sure about what he had seen as the tabs closed, swished open a fraction on the rebound, and shuddered into place.

He couldn't say what, but something had fallen from the sky, passed in front Roxton and vanished into the smoke pit. Perhaps it was theatrical symbolism of some sort. If so, he couldn't for the life of him think what, but it had resembled a body.

Twenty-Seven

T here was no way Silas could be unimpressed. James made his entrance as if he had been an actor all his life. His back straight, his face dispassionate despite nearly throwing up as Jake led him towards the stage, he walked calmly down the rake to the pedestal and replaced the silver goblet with the Champagne flute. According to Silas' instructions, he left the scroll so that Roxton couldn't fail to read the reassuring words. Assuming Roxton wouldn't have time to read a fuller explanation, Silas had written, "We have him." Even if it was not quite true it would be understood. Silas had thwarted the killer for a second time, but had probably driven him to more desperate measures, and far from 'having' him, he had no idea where he was.

The runner was still by his side, agape at James' assured performance.

'Listen, Jake,' Silas said. 'As soon as Mr Roxton stops singing, those curtains have got to close.'

'I'm not allowed, Sir.'

'I know, but it must be done.'

'I'd lose my job.'

'You'll be saving the gala. It would be a huge favour to me.'

A movement in the opposite wings drew Silas' attention. It wasn't so much that the motion was unexpected, there was plenty of activity on that side, it was that it was frantic and unusual. Stella, or Miss Arnold as that was the character she was playing, was bounding up the spiral stairs heading into the fly tower.

James must have seen him from the corner of his eye because he stopped and, forgetting where he was, stared before he acted. He exited just as Roxton turned upstage by which time Stella was already at the first level and climbing. James emptied the poison into a fire bucket and dropped the chalice. Throwing off the costume and ripping away his bowtie, he gave chase. Above him, Stella scrambled onto the stage-right scaffold. He had kicked off his shoes, and by the time he reached the second gantry, Silas, stage left, was only at the first.

He stopped to look across and between the canvas flats, shielding his eyes from the glare of the wing-lights and trying to think one step ahead. Stella, her way blocked by flymen, searched for another route to ascend, and it wasn't until Silas saw him looking at the roof that he realised the killer's intentions. Stella swung out from the scaffold, narrowly avoiding a flyman's grasp as he tried to stop her, and scrambled upwards in a flash of silver satin. A stagehand pulled the flyman back to his ropes just as James appeared on their level. The men were too busy to do anything except glare at him as they hauled.

The music distorted and dulled as Silas climbed, his legs already beginning to tire and his chest heaving. He checked Stella's progress at each gantry. Thirty feet, forty, fifty, she swung back onto the ironwork and looked down to Roxton. He had collected the harmless glass and was singing for all he was worth. He had escaped the poison, but the opera was not yet over. Stella leant precariously from the ironwork and examined the ceiling.

Silas followed his gaze. Two levels down from the gridiron and suspended by wires hung the clouds that were about to descend as Aeneas died. They were reached by a narrow bridge that crossed the stage, and two cherubs were calmly stepping across the gap to strap themselves into fittings. It was a weird sight to say the least, but it wasn't what Stella had seen. The fake clouds, made of wood and metal, were counterbalanced by lead weights that fed through pullies on the gridiron and hung sixty feet above the stage floor. There were four of them, each one the size of a barrel and hovering directly above Roxton.

Stella knew Silas had seen the contraption and his face distorted into a manic sneer. He reached into his dress and pulled out a pistol, waving it teasingly, before leaning over the guard rail and taking aim at the man below. Silas would never reach the other side in time, and there was no way to warn Roxton.

A flash of white and a flap of silver. Stella hit the planks, with James on top of him. The pistol skidded from his hand and fell behind the ropes. Silas located the nearest catwalk, two levels above, and forced his trembling legs to take him higher. He reached the bridge in time to see James on his feet swinging punches. Stella was fighting back, giving as good as he received, and he had the advantage. He didn't care if he fell, his only intent was to disrupt the performance, and if that meant committing suicide, Silas had no doubt he would do it. He was forcing James to the upstage edge of the platform, and each time James ducked a punch, he took a step back towards a fall to certain death. He lashed out for something to hold and grabbed a lighting bar, rattling the lanterns and bringing men rushing to the levels below to see what was happening.

As Silas gripped the guardrail, the catwalk ahead of him, he flashed back to the Limedock warehouse. He had been here before; a narrow walkway with the flimsiest of handholds and a deadly drop on either side. The difference was the distance, and where there had been a river below him, there was now bare wood. Smoke began to billow, and dark openings appeared in the stage floor. Through them, he saw flames, but this was not the random burning of a wharf, men fanned the smoke, controlling machines that burned and blew, masking his view of Roxton, now ascending on a rising tomb.

Silas stepped onto the catwalk, shaking the dust from the metal, and glanced to James just in time to see Stella get the better of him. She laid him out with a punch to his jaw and, without looking back, grabbed a ladder and climbed.

He appeared at the far side of the bridge as Silas reached cloud level. The boys were throwing petals, facing front as the flymen lowered the scenery. As they descended, so the weights lifted, and Silas saw how the contraption worked. The leads hung on individual wires, but they were connected by a single line that threaded back to a fixed point to act as an anchor. The release pin had been installed beneath a beam above the centre of the catwalk, ten feet ahead of where Silas stood and four feet above. If the anchor was released without the flymen ready to stay its descent, half a ton of stage machinery would come down on Roxton's head. The pin was easily reachable from the beam above, but to free it from this level, Stella would have to jump.

Stella ran onto the walkway with no fear for his safety. The iron grille vibrated, and out of options, Silas sprinted towards him. They hurtled at each other while far below, drums beat the rhythm of a panicked heart, and Roxton built to his final cadence.

Stella leapt for the pin.

Silas' threw himself forwards, yelling as his feet left the metal. During the split second he was airborne, he pictured Archer's face in morning sunlight streaming through a bedroom window. His smile of intrigued confusion, that brief fluttering of an eyebrow as their lips met and the feel of the man's body against his, tender and loving…

The images shattered as his shoulder connected with Stella's chest. The impact winded him, and the lights flashed a savage red, but his impetus repelled the killer onto his back. Rebounding, Silas crashed to his feet, stumbling towards the edge and clawing for a handhold. Stella slithered to the side. Reaching for the rail and missing, his fingers dug into the gridded walkway as his legs swung over the drop. He slid, but his grip held him. Dangling with his legs kicking, he threw his free hand to catch anything that would prevent his fall.

Silas lurched for his wrist, his mind absurdly clear. Prevent the man from falling. The production would be over. No-one, apart from a few stagehands, would be any the wiser. He took Stella's arm with both hands. On his front, with his feet hooked over the back edge of the catwalk, he was forced to face the drop. Stella was terrified, his free hand flailing wildly, while beneath him the fires of hell flickered, and smoke engulfed the tragic Aeneas.

'Pull yourself up,' Silas shouted. He couldn't hold the weight for long. 'Reach, man.'

Stella's expression changed. The fear was wiped away by an insidious, taunting grin and for a second, Silas considered releasing him. If he let him die, no-one would blame him; he had done all he could.

Not quite all.

'Why are you doing this?'

He was so close, the last few bars of music were swelling, he just needed to cling on a few more seconds.

'Who's behind it?' Silas roared.

Stella's grin twisted into a laugh. As he released his fingers from the grille one by one until Silas bore all his weight. He tightened his grip, but Stella's opera glove was slipping from his flesh. Silas clawed with his toes, the metal edge cutting into his ankles. His breathing was restricted by his prone position and the man's weight flattening him against the iron. What air he could snatch was tainted with smoke. The lights blinded him. His muscles screamed.

'Who's doing this?'

The cherubs threw their petals of blood, Roxton sang his final sustain, and Silas' feet slipped from their anchor. Stella pulled him further towards the edge as he grappled in panic.

The curtain hadn't come down, but unless he let her fall, Silas was going to die with her.

Subito tacet.

No music, no voice, no heartbeat, just the realisation that there was nothing Silas could do but fall.

'He hasn't even started.'

They were the last words he heard as the glove came free, Stella fell, and Silas followed him over the edge.

For James, everything happened in a blur. He had done his best, but the man who was Stella was a more accomplished boxer and sent him sprawling to the decking. He was disorientated, the side of his head thumped, and he tasted blood. The shock passed as he shook himself and caught a glimpse of a silver evening gown slithering to a higher gantry like a winged insect.

The was the last clear vision he had until he found himself hovering sixty feet above the stage, a wire rail his only safety net, hurtling towards Silas who was flat on his front and sliding helplessly towards the drop.

He was only half aware of a whirring sound and the clank of chains rattling through an unexpected silence, and the next thing he knew, he had Silas' belt in his hand and was yanking him backwards. He was probably hurting the man, but the reaction came naturally, and he scrambled and tore, heaved and swore until Silas skidded back to safety. Beneath them, the silver body fell through a curtain of petals, material flapping, arms thrashing until Stella was swallowed by a pit of fake flame.

The lights blacked out. The curtains closed.

Twenty-Eight

Silas was on his back staring at the gridiron, his hands gripping the catwalk's edges and his chest heaving. Music played, muffled and quiet while beside him, two topless youths, adorned with gold wings, floated up to glare in wonder.

'What the fuck was that?' one asked as he hopped lightly from the cloud to the walkway with no thought for the chasm beneath. 'Did she jump?'

'What's going on?' the other asked as he leapt nimbly across. 'What you playing at?'

Silas felt arms beneath his back tucking in under his armpits as James dragged him to his feet.

'I ain't got no legs,' he mumbled. He could feel nothing below his waist, and he collapsed.

James caught him. Holding him from behind, he raised him again and allowed him to rest, while one of the youths directed Silas' trembling hands to the safety rail.

'You shouldn't be up here,' the lad said. 'Trying to stop her jumping was you? Good on you, Sirs.'

'I'm not moving until he's ready,' James said, dodging the question.

'It's the height,' the first youth advised. 'Let me, Sir, we're used to this.'

Silas was helped to the relative safety of the stage left gantry by James and a gold-painted cherub. The second youth followed, gazing below, unbothered by the altitude.

'There's something not right down there,' he said.

The lights brightened behind the curtain and Silas dared a brief glance. The smoke was clearing, and sections of the floor were rising into place. In the pit directly in front of where Roxton was being helped from his tomb, he made out lanterns and a small group of men gathered around a twist of silver and crimson; the broken body of the man called Stella. A plume of smoke escaped the funnels on which the torso was impaled. Silas looked away and, holding ropes for support, lowered himself to sit. He took deep breaths to prevent himself from retching and wondered if he would ever stop shaking.

'Lads? A quick word.'

James huddled with the young men out of Silas' earshot, but whatever he said to them, they left them alone with thanks.

'How are you doing?' James crouched, and Silas was aware that the music had stopped.

'Give me a minute.'

'Can you walk? Bloody hell, Silas. What were you thinking?'

Silas focused on James' face. 'You look rough,' he said, reaching and touching a bruise blossoming above his eye.

'Yeah, well, a bit embarrassing being slogged by a woman,' James attempted humour. 'I'd be grateful if you didn't say anything.'

Silas wasn't sure if James was impressed, or like him, stunned. Perhaps he was both. There was nothing impressive about letting a man fall to his death, not even a murderer. Archer would have found a way to save him.

'I saw it,' James said. 'She let go of you.' He placed a hand on Silas' shoulder and squeezed. 'You did the right thing.'

Light streamed up from below, and ropes creaked as flymen hauled open the curtains. The tower echoed with the sound of applause, whistles, the stamping of feet, and somewhere among it all, Silas was sure he heard Fecker's voice. He felt for the pebble in his pocket, and once reassured that it was still there, he took James' arm and struggled to his feet.

'Can you walk?' James asked, propping him up from behind.

'Not until I've done this.' Silas twisted into him, wrapped him in his arms and hugged. It wasn't so much a thank you — that would come later when he could think clearly — he did it because he needed to feel someone solid beside him. A tough body, a breathing body, something real to remind him that he was still alive.

'Hey, easy, Sir,' James laughed, returning the hug. 'Don't want people to talk.'

'Did you hear what he said?' Silas asked. Reluctant to let him go, he dropped his head onto James' sodden shirt. He smelt of sweat, but Silas still wanted to kiss him.

'I heard something,' James admitted. 'But I wasn't paying attention. In fact, I don't know what I did.'

'He hasn't even started.'

'What's that?'

Silas lifted his head. James was an inch away, his face turned, embarrassed.

'Sorry.' Silas reached for a rope and held it before letting go of James completely. He faced the wall and inched his way towards the stairs. 'He said, "He hasn't even started".'

'What does that mean?'

James walked beside him, a safety barrier between him and empty space, and Silas was grateful.

'I don't know,' he said. 'It's not making sense to me yet. What did you say to those two?'

The youths were way below them now, presumably hurrying to discover the juicy details and tell their version of events.

'I told them they were right,' James said. 'We were trying to stop the woman from killing herself. I made them swear they would say nothing, because you would be embarrassed. You didn't want praise, and would appreciate it if they remained silent.'

'And will they?'

'I added something about having their legs broken if not,' James said, with a wink.

'You would do that?'

'No,' James admitted. 'I was thinking of Fecker, but it's not going to be necessary. They were more interested in seeing the body than knowing how it got there. Will you be alright on the stairs?'

'Yeah, Jimmy. As long as I don't have to look down.'

'I'll go first,' James said, when they reached the staircase. 'Hold my collar if it helps.'

Not daring to look, Silas gripped the spiralling bannister with one hand and James with the other. His pulse was slowing, the bile in his throat had receded, and his legs remembered what they were meant to do. The lower they descended, the more his confidence returned. Their passage to safety was celebrated, it seemed, by the house as a standing ovation ensued and they arrived at stage level in time to see Signora Campanelli join Mr Roxton on the apron, the cast behind them.

Roxton bowed low, took his co-star's hand, and they stepped forward, the curtains swinging into place behind them.

Jake bounded up.

'Is he alright?'

'Yes, mate,' James said. 'Just need to get out of here.'

'There's a nasty mess in the engine room,' the runner enthused. 'Some posh bird's gone and thrown herself...'

'I heard,' James said. 'How strange.'

'Thanks.'

'What's that, Mr Silas?'

His feet were on solid ground, and he let go of James. He was able to stand unaided, and after a deep breath, was able to walk.

'I said thanks, Jake,' he repeated. 'Did you get in trouble?'

'Not yet, Sir, but it'll come.' He addressed James. 'Wait over there, I'll fetch your uniform. Watch out...'

Jake yanked him to one side as a stream of chorus filed from the stage. They were a good cover. Without them, Silas would have been spotted by the stage manager, currently tearing his hair out over the way the act had finished. The fewer people who saw them, the better. They headed for the auditorium door, straightening their clothes and brushing off the dust. A minute later, Jake arrived with James' uniform.

'Look, Jake,' Silas said, wrapping the lad beneath his arm. 'You know where I live, yeah?'

'Clearwater House?'

'That's it. If you get any trouble, you come and tell me.'

'It'll be alright.'

'No, you promise. You can't lose your job because of me.'

'Alright, Sir. I will.'

'And say nothing to no-one about this?'

'Well, that's going to be difficult.'

'Sorry,' James butted in. 'I need to need to get back to Mr Marks.' He had changed frockcoats and handed Jake the costume.

'Yeah, coming, Jimmy.' Silas turned Jake to face him. His likeness to Silas' sisters was uncanny, and he had an instant desire to help the lad just as he longed to help the twins. 'You don't know anything, right? Any trouble, find me. Whatever happens, the least you say the better.'

Jake tapped the side of his nose. 'I won't be able to answer any questions, Mr Silas,' he said. 'Saw a lot, saw nothing, you get me? The flymen might wonder what you were doing, but we've got a strike and set tonight, and they'll be busy with "Otello" until sunrise. That dead body's going to keep people guessing though, probably forever.'

Silas didn't want to think about it. The closer they came to the auditorium the more he had to pull himself together. He longed to be out of this place and with Archer. He kept telling himself, 'Tomorrow morning,' as he pictured sunlight on his lover's sleepy eyes, waking up in a world where his secret, his charity and his friends were safe.

'Thanks again,' he said. 'We've got it from here.'

'Right you are, mate.' Jake beamed at him, but winced when he heard his name being shouted. 'Better make myself scarce.' He slipped away.

'Are you sure you're alright?' James asked, his hand on the door.

James had risked his life the same as Silas, and without his bravery, Silas would be puffing smoke ten feet below the stage. Yet, he was only concerned for Silas, and despite the angry welt on his face, he now showed no signs of shock. Silas touched the bruise gently, holding James' eyes and hoping that his own were shining with admiration. He pulled his head closer and kissed him on the forehead.

'Thanks, Jimmy,' he said. It was inadequate, but it was all he had at that moment.

'That's what Mr Payne would call inappropriate,' James said, his eyes twinkling.

'Yeah, well fuck the lot of them.' Silas was back to his old self. 'Come on.'

Applause was still clattering around the auditorium as they entered the box to find Marks standing, and his wife gradually coming to.

'Ah, there you are Hawkins,' Marks said as Silas joined him by the balustrade. 'Wondered where you'd got to.'

'I went to watch from up there,' Silas said, waving his hand in the direction of the uppermost gallery.

Marks asked for no further explanation and continued applauding while Signora Campanelli collected roses, and Roxton stood rooted by disbelief. Across the theatre, His Majesty decided he had applauded long enough and sat sharply. The rest of his party followed suit, apart from Archer who continued to applaud until the stars had left the stage. He wasn't applauding Roxton, he was looking directly at Silas. He might not be so jubilant when he discovered the truth.

The chair beside Markland remained empty, and the doctor kept looking at it as if Miss Arnold would somehow materialise. He glanced to Thomas a couple of times, and the butler checked the passage for him but returned a negative response each time. Markland was crestfallen and confused until he was joined by Mr Bursnall who whispered in his ear and led him away.

The royal party left the box with Archer accompanying His Majesty and Lady Marshall engaging his wife in a deep discussion about something, probably the spectacular finale, while in his own box, James assisted Mrs Marks with her stole.

'Well, that's that, lad,' Marks said, surveying the departing audience. 'What did you think?'

'All very exciting, Mr Marks,' Silas replied. 'But to be honest, I'm not in a hurry to see it again.'

'Ha!' Marks huffed. 'I know what you mean. All that screeching. By the by, Hawkins,' he continued with one eye on his wife who had both of hers on the remaining Champagne. 'Can you let me have a copy of that speech you made? I should run through it in case you said anything controversial.'

'I'll see what I can do,' Silas said. He couldn't remember a word of it and hoped the solicitor would also soon forget. 'Perhaps we should find His Lordship? There is a reception, I believe.'

James assisted Marks with his overcoat.

'You banged your head, young man?' Marks asked as he threaded his arms through the sleeves.

'In the dark, Sir,' James replied. 'An unfortunate encounter with an unexpected obstacle.'

'You should get Markland to look at it,' the solicitor said, slapping his wife's hand away from the wine bottles.

'Shall I meet the King?' she slurred.

'I think not. James, tell His Lordship I'll be in touch. Sorry to miss the reception but it's probably safer for all...'

James understood and nodded sympathetically. Once the couple had left, he joined Silas at the balustrade, watching the public leave and squinting to the gallery. 'What's our story?' he asked.

'Been thinking about that,' Silas replied. He saw Fecker and waved. 'Best to tell Archer the truth. And Tommy. When we get home though, not here.'

A series of hand signals flashed from gallery to box and back as Fecker mimed driving the carriage, Silas made a circle in the air with a finger and held it up to indicate one hour, Fecker pointed to the front of the building, Silas held up a thumb, Fecker did the same and then mimed drinking. Again, Silas held up one finger. Fecker trudged up the steps to the back of the gallery where Lucy waited and tucked his arm through hers.

'That's sweet,' James said.

'Yeah,' Silas agreed. 'We should go. Not a word until we get home.'

They discussed their cover story as James ensured no-one had left anything in the box, paying attention to how James might have received what was now turning into a raging black eye. His eyelid was swelling, and Silas wrapped the remaining ice in the serving towel, holding it against the footman's face until James moved away complaining of the cold.

'What on earth?' Thomas appeared in the entrance. 'What's happened?'

The footman straightened his back and stood to attention. 'Terribly sorry, Mr Payne,' he said. 'I stupidly walked into an open door.'

Displeased, Thomas looked to Silas for a more believable answer.

'Tell you later, Tommy,' he said. 'Your clothes are over there. What do we do now? Is the King staying for the party?'

'It's a reception, and no, he's not,' Thomas said, as he changed out of his costume. 'And James won't be needed there.'

'Yes, Mr Payne.'

'Staff have use of the balcony bar. I suggest you wait there, use more ice and leave the alcohol alone.'

'He's not been drinking, Tommy,' Silas said, mildly annoyed. 'I can vouch for that, but I dare say we could both do with one.'

Thomas' suspicion increased. 'Are you going to tell me what was happening back there? I saw you in the wings on a couple of occasions.'

'When we get home,' Silas said. 'For now, though, your man's a hero.'

'He's a footman who left his post,' Thomas snapped. 'And in plain sight of His Majesty and the viscount.'

'Oh, get over yourself,' Silas tutted. Thomas was starting to anger him, and after what had just happened, if he didn't soften, Silas could see himself saying something he would regret.

'Mr Hawkins…'

'Mr Payne!' Silas stepped up to him. 'Do you remember that night in Greychurch when Fecks and I pulled you and Tripp from the mob? Eh? You and I ended up rolling around on the carriage floor, you know, close and all. You were embarrassed 'cos your dick…'

'You don't need to remind me.'

'Yeah, well I will. And I'll embarrass you again if you don't leave Jimmy alone. We're going to tell you everything but not until we're out of here. All you need to know for now is that your lover saved my life.'

'Silas, don't…'

'You refer to him as Mr Hawkins.' Thomas squared his shoulders, talking to James, but keeping his eyes on Silas. 'And do not use that word in public.'

The auditorium was empty.

'Let's go and find Archer.' Silas, on tip-toes, spat the words into Thomas' face. 'Who happens to be *my* lover.'

'Mr Hawkins, I hardly need remind you…'

'Tommy, you sound like Tripp. Lighten the attitude.'

'His Lordship will be waiting.' James was keen to separate them.

Thomas took a step back and looked from one to the other. 'Where did you go?' he demanded. 'You were not in your box for the final scene.'

'We were busy,' Silas said.

'Together?'

It suddenly struck Silas. Thomas was jealous. More than that, he was worried. Silas had felt the same thing at the dinner when Archer gushed over Roxton. Insecurity wasn't a pleasant feeling.

'Jimmy's my mate, Tom,' he sighed. 'And he's right. We should go, but I want to show you something first. Both of you.'

He was surprised how clearly his mind was working. Leaving the box, he made sure the passage was empty. It was, but voices spoke distantly, and he heard doors closing. He would have to be quick.

'Here,' he said, beckoning the pair to the backstage door.

'We don't have time for this,' Thomas complained. 'What?'

Silas drew the curtain and offered them the lobby.

'I suggest you keep one hand on the handle in case,' he said to James, winking. 'I reckon Tommy needs to know where he stands, though I've got no fecking idea why he's worried. Get in there.' He bundled them into the cramped space. 'Just kissing, Jimmy,' he whispered. 'And quick, before your face looks like a balloon.'

It felt like the right thing to do, to give the pair a moment alone and, once Thomas' grunts of protest had mellowed into murmurs of reassured delight, he knew the matter was ended. James was an easy man to lust after, but there was more to him than handsome masculinity. He needed space to show his true colours, and Thomas needed to relax, get out of the butler-footman divide and appreciate his lover's courage and sincerity. They were the heart of the man.

Life was too short for petty jealousies, Silas decided, although he couldn't help feeling a little envious. It was a ridiculous thing to admit. He had no passionate feelings towards Thomas, despite his good looks and fine physical form, and he had no passionate feelings towards James either. Except, maybe, there was something…

He pulled himself up short. No, that was never going to happen. 'Time's up.'

Clearing his throat pointedly, he walked away, turning after a few paces when Thomas and James came out of hiding, James adjusting the front of his livery.

'Do you get me, Mr Payne?' Silas asked, deciding the proper address showed respect.

'I do, Mr Hawkins,' Thomas said. 'And I think you're completely mad.'

'Yeah, maybe. But your Jimmy is completely…' He mouthed the words, 'in love with you' but vocalised, 'And don't you forget it.'

'I shall do my best, Sir,' Thomas replied, with a smirk that might have been patronising, but was hopefully good humour.

They walked the corridor towards the grand stairs with Silas between them. He put an arm around each one for support and to show that he cared. He wasn't offended when Thomas politely removed it and walked ahead.

'Oh, Tommy,' he laughed to himself and gripped James tighter.

'Actually, Mr Payne is correct, Sir,' James said, with an apologetic grimace.

Of course he was. Silas released him. He was being inappropriate. This wasn't Archer's study, and the sounds of clinking glasses and polite conversation were growing louder.

Thomas' reluctance to show friendship so publicly turned out to be timely as they rounded the back of the auditorium and arrived at the landing. The foyer was crowded with lords and ladies, and glittering with diamond tiaras and chandeliers. Theatre staff mingled with trays of Champagne, the air hummed with congratulatory conversation, and in the middle stood Archer and Lady Marshall, accepting praise and looking more than satisfied.

'The upstairs bar, James,' Thomas whispered. 'But return here in one hour. If I need you before, I will send for you.'

'Enjoy it,' Silas said. 'You deserve it. And tell Fecks to keep his hands off the maid.'

James sniggered as he left them, and Thomas shot Silas a horrified stare.

'You're right, Tommy,' Silas grinned. 'I know how to behave.'

'Good.' Thomas' tone was flat. 'Because we are here for His Lordship.'

'I always am, Tom. I always will be.'

Silas took a deep breath, cleared his throat and straightened his jacket before descending the stairs. This was the game he had chosen to play, and he relished every chance to practice. Adopting a refined gait and a pleasant smile, he approached the viscount. Archer stood proudly amid the sea of faces, unaffected by the undulating waves of fur and glitterati as his peers pressed him for a handshake. The titled toasted themselves for their daring generosity while servants stood in attendance, scrutinising their every move, prepared to do whatever was needed.

They weren't Silas' world; they couldn't have been further from it, and he briefly debated if he should stand with the attendants, or with the upper class. He would rather have been in the bar with Fecks and Jimmy, but this was Archer's time, and His Lordship should have his secretary on hand.

Sensing his arrival, Archer turned, and Silas' heart skipped when their eyes met. They were worlds apart and yet two halves of the same existence. They knew where they belonged.

'Mr Hawkins!' Archer exclaimed, as if he had forgotten Silas was in the theatre. 'We have missed you.'

'My apologies, My Lord, Your Ladyship,' Silas bowed as he greeted them. 'I was asked to assist with a technical matter. I am now all yours, Sir.'

'And he couldn't have asked for anyone better.' Lady Marshall took his arm and whisked him away. When they were at a safe distance from the viscount, her grip tightened, and she lowered her voice. 'What the hell was all that?' she hissed, guiding him away from the reception to a quiet spot beside the staircase.

'Your Ladyship?'

'Oh, come along, Silas,' she said, glancing over his head. 'Something dreadful has happened to Miss Arnold. Doctor Markland is beside himself, and I am intrigued.'

'What's happened, Ma'am?'

'I only know that Miss Arnold is no more,' she replied, pinning him with her grey eyes as if he was a butterfly in a frame.

'No more?'

'A terrible accident, and one which I am presently keeping from Clearwater. Bursnall gave me the news as we attended His Majesty's farewell. Having heard the details of Miss Arnold's departure, we decided it was best not to worry Archer, but somehow I suspect you know something about the business.'

'I don't see why I should,' Silas said. It was another lie. He had told enough of them that evening to last a lifetime. He had a lot of explaining to do, but not to Lady Marshall.

She smothered him with doubt before replacing it with adoration. Cupping his face in her hands, she said, 'You are a cherub,' which Silas thought was in bad taste considering where he had recently been. 'I can see why my godson is smitten, but...' She released him and once again checked they were alone. 'He has never cared for anyone as he cares for you.'

'You are very kind, Ma'am.'

'I am. And you are very naughty. But, you are also very discreet, and that's why I respect you.'

He bowed his head, not sure if she was being sarcastic or genuine. 'I am honoured, Your Ladyship. But I am only doing what my employer needs.'

'You know, Silas,' she said with a sigh. 'You're a damn fine actor. You should have been on that stage tonight.'

'Ma'am,' Silas smiled. 'I was very nearly all over it.'

Twenty-Nine

The last of the guests left the opera house at eleven-thirty, but Archer stayed behind to see if he could be of use to Doctor Markland. Mr Bursnall had done well to keep the tragedy from the guests, but someone from below stage had informed the Central News Agency, and he was forced to tell Viscount Clearwater. When Archer found him in the Champagne bar, he explained that the police were investigating, and wouldn't let reporters into the theatre, but eventually, word would leak out.

'And what is that word, Philip?' Archer asked, before giving Silas a sideways look.

'That Miss Arnold was an imposter,' the doctor replied. 'Duped me, you, everyone.' His eyes were ringed with red, and he clutched a sodden handkerchief.

'Not quite everyone,' Archer said. He patted the doctor's knee. 'You weren't to know she was a he,' he said, but it didn't help Markland's mood. 'And you weren't to know he was suicidal, not to mention over-dramatic. What a ridiculous way to end one's life, don't you think?'

Markland nodded. 'I can't comprehend it at this moment.' He sniffed. 'I've told the police all I know. Apparently, it's quite common.'

'Quite common?' Archer laughed. 'Forgive me.' He remembered himself. 'I am not making fun of your loss. It was easy to see how fond you were of… Well, of…'

'Of his disguise?' Silas offered.

'Exactly. But tell me, Philip, how can such a thing be common?'

'I don't know,' the Doctor huffed. 'One of the runners told me it happens a lot in other theatres. Said the papers wouldn't be that interested, and I shouldn't worry.'

Silas smiled. Jake was a canny bugger.

'I'm sure he is correct,' Archer said. 'Now, if they've finished with you, shall I drive you home?'

'I'm sorry for my behaviour, Sir,' Markland said. 'I shall resign as superintendent immediately.'

'You will do no such thing.' Archer was outraged. 'You will go home, drown your sorrows in a decent Scotch and go to bed.'

'But if my connection to him is made public…'

'We shall sort it out. I am not leaving my charity in anyone else's hands, Philip. You weren't to know. You're a gentleman. A great many men would have discovered her… his gender before an appropriate length of courtship had elapsed. You have done nothing wrong, and I won't hear another word.' He stood. 'Silas, will you inform Thomas we are leaving?'

It was approaching one o'clock when, having taken Markland to his home on the edge of Greychurch, Fecker drew up at Clearwater Mews. Archer insisted on helping him unshackle the horses, asking Thomas to lay out anything he could find from the pantry. He ordered James straight to bed, but the footman insisted on staying to help.

Silas had waited until they were home before explaining what had happened, by which time they were in the servants' hall.

'Maybe we should bring this up to you?' Thomas said, hovering behind his usual chair at the head of the table.

'I don't have the energy for that,' Archer said. 'If it doesn't upset you too much, Tom, we'll eat together and now.' He flashed Silas a devilish smile and took a seat at the table below Thomas. 'I can't wait to hear about black eyes and disappearing secretaries.'

When they were seated and helping themselves to the spread, Silas began his story. He explained every detail from his point of view. How he and James had unlocked the clue in the letter with the help of Mrs Mark's ostentatious display of limited Italian. How he had found Roxton in the interval where Archer's friend had identified the timing, and how, thanks to the King's arrival, Stella had been forced to change his plan.

'I'm sure he was going to shoot,' he said. 'He had a gun on him at one point, but when the King turned up, and your party had to sit with him, he knew he wasn't able to do that. I guess he saw the story in the programme about Any-Arse drinking from a…'

'Aeneas,' Archer corrected, half-smiling.

'Whoever. So, when Stella saw you were using those silver goblets in the royal box… It was a risk, and he nearly got away with it. Then, when he saw we were onto him, he did the only thing he could think of.'

'I am still reeling from the sight of my footman's debut appearance,' Archer said. 'Why on earth did you do that?'

'Mr Hawkins noticed the goblets had been swapped,' James explained. 'And Miss Arnold was backstage during the interval. It might have been harmless, and I can't tell you if he had poisoned the poisoned chalice or not, but Mr Hawkins didn't want to risk it. Neither did I.' He emphasised their working together to protect Silas rather than to steal his thunder. 'But by that time, it was already on the stage. The audience had seen Silas so he couldn't go out there.'

'Yes, I must speak to you about your speech,' Archer said, with narrow eyes.

'Like I said, spur of the moment thing.'

Silas shuffled uneasily. Of all the things he had done that evening, speaking without thinking was the most dangerous. He could easily have put one word in the wrong place and caused embarrassment.

'I thought it was brilliant,' Archer said. 'I don't know why we didn't think of it. Everyone was commenting on how correct it was.'

'Correct?'

'Yes. As in, correct of the Foundation to, as Lady Marshall said, put its mouth where its money is and have someone who knows…' He took Silas' hand. 'Someone who has witnessed that kind of hideous life first-hand, talk to those who had sponsored him. It showed the patrons and public that we are serious in our work, and that it can make a difference. You couldn't have said anything better, and I doubt Roxton could have either.'

Silas squeezed his hand. 'Meanwhile, back at the interval,' he said cheekily. 'Roxton knew what the letter meant all the time, but was determined to go through with the show no matter what. He was prepared to do it for you, Archie, because that's what you do for people.'

'I rather think I have a habit of putting them in danger.'

'I think Silas meant, that's because you inspire people,' Thomas suggested, and Silas nodded. 'I interrupted, I'm sorry.'

An apology from Thomas was something to savour, but it was late, and every muscle in Silas' body ached. He continued the story and explained about Jake dropping the final curtain early, at which point Archer backed him up completely and offered to write to Bursnall if there was any comeback on the boy.

'That Butterworth man is something of an ogre,' Archer said.

'Butterworth!' Silas slapped his forehead. 'That was his name. More like Lord Jobs-Worth.'

He went on to describe how he and James had chased Stella, explained about the lead weights, but when he reached the part where he was dangling an inch from death, the words refused to flow.

'He was trying to save him, Sir,' James explained. His face was a lively palette of colours, and he held a cold steak over one side, watching the conversation through one eye. 'Silas had both hands on his arm, and it was only his toes keeping him from being dragged over. He didn't let go.'

'I did, Jimmy.'

'Sorry, Mr Hawkins, but you did not. I took hold of your legs and pulled you. If anything, I was the cause of his fall, but from where I was standing — in a much less stressful situation than you — I clearly saw him withdraw his arm from the glove. He meant to fall.'

'By the sound of it, he was desperate,' Archer added.

'Desperate to the point of being suicidal, Sir,' James agreed. 'I mean, if he had gone with his original plan and fired from your box, he would have been at the very least arrested, if not hanged. It makes me think he was under huge pressure from someone to get the job done, but in the end, not prepared to be hanged for it.'

'Go on.'

James put the steak on a plate. 'I'm just thinking like Thomas,' he said, loading a slice of bread with two kinds of cheese and folding it in half. 'It reads to me as if he had instructions and he was motivated by more than personal revenge, as we suspected. He had his orders. Kill Roxton after or during the speech with the defence that what Roxton was saying was a public outrage. Silas put paid to that, and so did the unexpected royal visit. He had a backup plan, maybe

260

because he disagreed with his orders to shoot and wasn't prepared to hang. Perhaps he brought the poison with him, I don't know.' The bread was at his mouth, but he thought better of eating while speaking and put it down. The others were listening intently. 'His fallback, as you would call it, Sir, might have been to get backstage and shoot from the rigging, he certainly had a go at it. Or, learning of the backstage tour which you mentioned at dinner, and knowing the opera, he planned to use poison, thereby making sense of the words, "Your final applause." That way, he could carry out his orders with less fear of detection. When all that went bottoms-up, he panicked, tried to shoot him from the wings, lost the revolver, saw the scenery mechanism, and went for that instead. By the time Silas got to him, he knew he was caught, and the only way out was to use himself as the murder weapon by falling on Roxton. But that's only conjecture and it's daft, because if he was willing to die, then why not just shoot the man in the first place? Either way, Silas did his best to stop him falling. I reckon he was a cross-dressing madman. Stella, I mean, not Mr Hawkins.'

He continued eating until he noticed the open mouths and shocked stares.

Surprised at the silence, he put down his sandwich, and said, 'What?'

'Bloody hell, Jimmy.' Archer was impressed. 'You should be a detective.'

'It's easy to analyse things after they've happened,' James said, shrugging off the compliment. 'Only wish I'd come up with it before.'

'Well, you've come up with an explanation now, apart from one thing.'

'Sir?'

'Who would apply such pressure? Who was behind all this? The letter said "We", didn't it? It seems so random. They had nothing to gain from killing Cadwell apart from bad publicity for us, and if they were discovered, for themselves. Or himself if he was acting alone, but I don't think he was. The way you describe it, Jimmy, it sounded like a military operation.'

'I've been thinking about that,' James said. 'If I might?'

'Please do,' Archer enthused.

'I hadn't thought of a military connection. I may have misled you there. I used those expressions, because I learnt them from you when we went to Yorkshire.'

'You see?' Thomas said. 'You *are* an inspiration, Your Lordship.'

'And you are part of what inspires me, Tom,' Archer said. 'But His Lordship lives upstairs. Go on, Jimmy. Who does your analytical brain tell you was pulling the strings?'

'It's obvious. Whoever has a vested interest in the Cleaver Street brothel.'

'Why? Cadwell didn't go there of his own volition,' Archer countered. 'And if they simply wanted to disrupt the evening, why not choose any member of the male chorus or one of the other principals? I would have been quite grateful if they'd taken a pot shot at Mr McDurling. Quite the wrong casting in my opinion. Did you hear…?'

Silas coughed pointedly and nodded to James.

'Sorry,' Archer grimaced. 'Go on. Why Cadwell?'

'Because of what he did at Cleaver Street,' James repeated.

Silas leapt in. 'No, Jimmy.' He stared hard across the table. 'That was the *only* time he was at that house. I'm sure of it.'

James didn't understand. 'But you…'

'I know. I wasn't certain before, but I am now.'

Silas should have told James his intentions to keep Roxton's secret from the viscount, but there hadn't been time. James didn't understand why, but he understood he was not meant to discuss the matter further. Silas would explain when they were next alone.

He changed the subject. 'Anyway, Archie, now you can see why we weren't able to come to you. You were with the King of wherever and there wasn't time. I'm sorry I had to make up a few lies in your name. I could have dropped you in it.'

'Not at all,' Archer waved it away.

The list of things to love about the man increased. His acceptance of Silas' actions and his unwavering trust were enough reasons to keep Roxton's past a secret. If Archer knew his friend had been a regular at Cleaver Street he would be devastated.

'I think we can say tonight was a success,' Thomas said, lifting his glass.

'Thank you, Tom.' Archer repaid the toast. 'Thanks to all of you.'

262

'I did nothing.' Fecker had been so busy eating, Silas had forgotten he was there.

'You did, mate,' he said. 'I heard your voice over all the others, and it kept me going.'

Fecker huffed and tore the flesh from a chicken leg in one bite.

'But I still don't understand the Cleaver Street thing,' Archer was not going to let the matter rest.

'We'll talk about it in the morning,' Silas said, directly to James who nodded discreetly. 'It's late.'

'I suppose they will eventually find out who the man was,' Archer continued. 'Perhaps that will give us some clues.'

Silas and James exchanged uneasy glances, and Silas couldn't think of any way to move Archer's interest along.

'I have a theory about that too,' James said. This time, it was him fixing Silas with a stare, and asking to be trusted.

The man had pulled him back from a sixty-foot drop. Silas nodded for him to continue.

'It seems to me,' James said, picking his words carefully. 'That such an establishment has, by its definition, something illegal about it. From what I heard when I was a messenger, it makes its money from offering young men to paying guests. The boys receive a couple of shillings, but the owner gets a lot more. Now...' He held up his wine glass. 'Let's say this is Cleaver Street...' He moved a plate out of the way and placed the glass. 'It's there, on the edge of the West End, and this...' He placed a pickle pot. 'Is the opera house.'

'What's that?' Fecker asked, pointing.

'It's the salt, Fecks.' James moved it. 'But now, it's the Cheap Street hostel here in Greychurch.'

Fecker frowned. 'There?'

'Yes.'

'Nyet.' He moved the salt closer to the pickle. 'Is there.'

'Fair enough,' James conceded, with a smile. 'You're the driver. Anyway, my point or my suggestion rather, is that the men behind Cleaver Street are not happy that someone such as Your Lordship is making their business more difficult.'

'I don't see how,' Archer said. 'Our hostel is a plate of ham distant.'

Archer, like the others, was displaying signs of exhaustion and alcohol, a cocktail that allowed the men's tensions some escape in humour.

'How does it make it more difficult?' Thomas asked.

'Because the Foundation is publicly stating that the way to assist these young men is through charity, not exploitation. If Cleaver Street was discovered, they would be in all kinds of sh… trouble, while a couple of miles up the road, your foundation is saving the lads from having to resort to that kind of work.'

'I think I understand,' Archer said. 'And I can see your point. So…' He examined the vaulted ceiling as he thought. 'Yes, I see now. It's a good theory, Jimmy, and sets my mind at rest that the whole thing was an assault on my name via a man with an unsullied reputation. It was a random kidnapping.'

'Lucky timing for them,' James said, with a sideways glance at Silas. 'The gala was only made public a few weeks ago.'

'Which is maybe why Stella, or whoever he was, acted so rashly.'

'Yes, Sir. No time to plan anything foolproof, but the perfect opportunity to act.'

Archer seemed happy with that explanation, and Silas gave James a thankful smile.

'But…' Archer still wouldn't let it go. 'It still leaves the question of who these men are.'

'We can consider that in the morning,' Thomas suggested.

He stood and, as they had been trained, Fecker and James followed his example. There was no need for Silas to stand, but he did. This was Thomas' domain, and despite their differences, he was determined to stay on the right side of him.

'Oh, terribly sorry, Payne.' Archer scrambled to his feet.

'I shouldn't have stood up,' Thomas mumbled, waving the viscount back into his chair. Archer remained standing. 'It is late, as you say, Mr Hawkins. You have no visitors tomorrow, Sir, unless Mr Hawkins has any business for you?'

'I do, Tommy,' Silas said. 'But we ain't going to talk about that kind of thing here.'

Archer cleared his throat. 'On which note, it's a bath and bed for me. I'll see to it myself, Tom, after I've helped clear the table.'

'I don't think so, Sir.'

'Sorry, Payne, but His Lordship insists,' Archer said with a grin.

'And as you advise, tomorrow, we can put our minds to who this Stella might have been.'

The answer arrived in the morning with The Times. Perfectly ironed and open to a particular page, it waited on the breakfast table under James' worried gaze. He was pacing the room when Silas and Archer entered and caught him glaring at it with his one good eye.

'Good morning, My Lord.' James bowed his head and pulled out the viscount's chair.

'You look tired, Jimmy.' Silas also noticed that James walked more stiffly than usual, no doubt the aftereffects of their exertions above the stage.

'I didn't get much sleep,' the footman admitted. 'I was up most of the night.'

His gait was not the only thing stiff about James that morning. Silas glanced to his crotch, a habit he was unable to be rid of. James was in a state of semi-arousal, trying hard to hide it by positioning himself behind the chair. Silas put two and two together and raised an eyebrow to the footman who blushed so hard his cheeks matched the red at the edge of his bruising.

'Today's news may interest you,' James said. 'Although I don't think interest is the right word.' He pointed to a particular column on page four.

Archer read while James poured his coffee and Silas helped himself at the sideboard. By the time he had sat, Archer had pushed the newspaper over to his place.

'I suggest you eat first,' he said, his face grim, his coffee untouched.

The Times, December 4th 1888
Tragedy after Triumph

To say that the charity gala held last night at the Royal Opera House was a success would be to understate the incredible.

The performance of 'Aeneas and Dido' by Johann Bruch and starring Italian soprano, Signora Campanelli and English countertenor, Mr Cadwell Roxton, was one of the finest to grace the city stage this season. It was, however, also one of the most tragic.

At the very end of the opera, after some spectacular staging by Director Muller, and sublime musicality from the cast and orchestra, the curtain came down to thunderous applause. (A separate discussion of the Clearwater Foundation's marked triumph in front of His Majesty King Wilhelm III of the Netherlands and Grand Duke of Luxembourg is printed on page two.)

Unseen to all but a few, a man leapt from the fly tower, that bastion of theatricality above the stage area, and fell to his tragic end through a trap and onto the smoke machines. Had this happened in sight of the audience, they might have been forgiven for thinking it was an interpretation of the heroic Aeneas plummeting to Hades, but the unfortunate gentleman had no association with the production, the House, or the Foundation, other than he had, it is believed, manipulated his way to a ticket, and thus, easy access to the backstage realm. If this form of chosen suicide was not curious enough, the man was at first thought to be female due to his apparel.

The police authorities have little to say other than it was an act of suicide, but they have been able to identify the body as that of a Mr Sherman Quill, half-brother to the eminent (and still missing — see page 17) Doctor Benjamin Quill. No other information pertaining to Mr Quill (senior), of Harland's Park, is available.

'You're right,' Silas said, pushing the newspaper aside. 'I should have eaten first.'

'I'm sorry to speak out of turn, Sir,' James said. 'But... the connection?'

Archer chewed his bottom lip. 'Is pretty obvious, Jimmy,' he agreed. 'It explains why my gala and my Foundation, and thus why Cadwell Roxton, but I don't... That is... I never knew Quill had a half-brother.'

'Do you think he's not at the bottom of a river after all?' Silas asked. It was a worrying thought.

'I can't think about it,' Archer said. 'I have yet to recover from last night's business. In fact, I think I need a holiday.'

Thomas arrived with two telegrams on a silver tray and, greeting Silas, offered them to the viscount. He too looked as if he hadn't slept but he bore a more contented look than usual. Silas smiled inwardly; his suspicion was proved correct. 'Morning, Tommy,' he said, doing his best to appear cheerful. If Archer didn't want to think about this new development, that was fine by him. A holiday sounded like a perfect idea.

Archer took the telegrams. 'I hardly dare open them,' he said, threading a knife beneath the flap of the first. 'I have to say, Silas, there have been few dull moments since you came to Clearwater.'

'And I have to say,' Silas replied. 'It was Your Lordship who brought me here.'

'Touché.' Archer grinned as he slit the paper. He unfolded the message and held it away from his face to read.

'You need spectacles,' Silas said.

Archer read the words, and his grin became a broad smile. 'At last some good news,' he said. 'My mother will be spending Christmas abroad.' He handed the telegram to Thomas. 'Lord alone knows why. Bran is as cold as a witch's tit at this time of year.'

'What's Bran?' Silas asked, registering the concern on Thomas' face and the glee on Archer's.

'A freezing cold outcrop belonging to one of her Habsburg cousins, a relative as distant and impenetrable as the castle itself. Why so worried, Tom?'

'Larkspur, Sir,' he said. 'The men will be left in the hands of Robert and Mr Harrow.'

'The first footman and estate manager,' Archer explained to Silas. 'Which is why we need to ship Thomas up there as soon as possible. The estate has been suffering since my father's death, and there are problems with the staff. Mrs Baker shouldn't have to deal with them on her own.' Archer attended to the second message.

'Shall I make the arrangements, Your Lordship?'

'Yes, please, Tom. We'll all go, shall we?'

'That's up to you, Sir.' Thomas said.

'Hm?' The viscount was distracted. 'Oh, yes, of course it is. That's that then. We'll talk, Tom. Meanwhile...' He waved the second telegram to Silas. 'More good news. Your money has been safely delivered to your sisters, and Culver is happy to repeat the arrangement whenever it is required.'

Silas felt tears behind his eyes. 'Are they alright?' he asked.

'"Girls healthy",' Archer recited. 'Next time I will impose on Mr

Culver the question of the girls' employment. See if he has anything they can do.'

Silas was unable to contain himself. 'Don't look, Tommy,' he said to the confused butler.

He rose from his chair, walked around the table as calmly as he could, took Archer's head in his hands and kissed him. The kiss lasted until Thomas felt it necessary to remind them they were in the dining room.

Thirty

Charles Tripp was frustrated. He had kept watch on nineteen Cleaver Street for several days and nights from the apartment above the shop, but had seen little activity. The table under the window had on it the tools of his new-found fascination; a spyglass and a notebook. They and his dogged determination to catch Clearwater entering or leaving the house were all he needed. It could, he knew, take some time before he saw anything that incriminated the viscount, but he was prepared to stay for as long as necessary.

He quickly learnt that there were two active times of day at number nineteen, two periods when more than a usual number of visitors came and went. The hours between six and nine in the evening usually saw the arrival of one or two young men no more than fifteen or sixteen years old. Decently dressed, they could easily be mistaken for innocent visitors had they not also been seen arriving at the property through the earlier parts of the day in blue messenger uniforms. His spyglass allowed him to see their faces as they approached and left, and the faded, rather yellowing net curtain supplied by his landlord acted as cover for the implement. He was able to rest it on the bottom frame so that only an inch of curtain need be disturbed; something a viewer from the street below would easily overlook if they could see it at all.

The boys, the vile youths who used their innocent bodies for the depraved practices of the older men in heinous sexual acts, gave the outward appearance of respectability. Tripp believed their intentions were anything *but* acceptable.

He came to recognise them and gave them names. Lanky, a scrawny lad of six foot had called twice, one who was no more than seventeen had called four times and first been christened Angel on account of his looks. Tripp changed the name to Lucifer after his second appearance. Another youth, he simply called Vile Victor.

These men and others who called in the early evening stayed for several hours. He marked each one's number of visits against their name, the date and time of arrival and departure. Sometimes, the tally of those he counted in didn't match the number he recorded as having left during the second busy period, between midnight and two in the morning. He pondered this enigma for a few days until he decided that he must have been sleeping when the visits ended. From then on, he changed his sleeping pattern, staying awake through the night and only resting between the hours of ten in the morning and five in the afternoon. After a while, he found himself waking earlier until, in recent days, he slept for only two hours in every twenty-four. He became so convinced that if he turned away a boy would slip out unseen, that he broke his daily shaving ritual, ate as little as possible to minimise the times he had to leave the apartment, and brought a piss pot to the table rather than leave the window to use the bathroom.

The mystery of the non-departures was solved in two ways. By staying awake, Tripp was able to ascertain that some boys didn't leave the house until the very early hours, but one day, he witnessed a lad entering the house who had entered the day before, but apparently never left. Forcing himself from his eerie to buy supplies, he took a longer route than usual and passed the back of Cleaver Street, noticing that it was possible for someone to enter from the front and leave from the rear. It was an obvious solution, and he realised that he needed to think harder, concentrate more and take his work more seriously.

His desire for revenge became an obsession.

The street below was quietening as residents returned from their daily business to settle in for the evening. One boy had already called at number nineteen. Simple, he'd called him, on account of his gait. He noted the details in his book.

It was seven-ten, the sun had long set, and as it was a smogless night, the streetlight gave good illumination.

This was the time of evening when the youths arrived. When they did, the door was opened by a burly, unattractive man with a balding head. Later, when gentlemen took the steps to the front door, it was opened by a finely dressed woman who although

270

welcoming and feminine, was no less unattractive than the man.

When he realised they were the same person, he vomited into his piss pot.

He was distracted when two gentlemen arrived at nine-twenty-six. It was hard to tell who these men were; they arrived cloaked and wearing brimmed hats. It was only when guests left that he was able to see their faces. That was good enough, but often, he was unable to tell which departing gentlemen had arrived at what time. When these annoyances occurred, he channelled his frustration into practicality and wrote a question mark against the entry. Tripp was, and always had been, meticulous in both planning and execution.

The men were welcomed by the man-woman, the Beast as he now referred to the creature, and the front door was closed. His next call to action would come when an upstairs room was illuminated, and that didn't usually happen until much later.

It was the older men he scrutinised the most for any one of them could have been Clearwater. He was a sodomite, therefore he would use this cesspit for his vile pleasures. If his belief wasn't reason enough to pursue his task so avidly, the regular sight of Lord Somerset, and the prominent High Court judge, Lord Russel of Galloways, along with several other recognisable public faces proved Tripp was on the right track. It was only a question of time before Clearwater became somehow involved.

The chance sighting of his man Hawkins set him on the path he was now unable to leave.

It was Tripp's first evening in the apartment. He had acted quickly following his talk with Lovemount and taken the rooms sight-unseen that very day. Seeing Hawkins enter the house came as a shock. Tripp was never lucky, and he took the sighting as a sign that higher powers had called him to his vocation. The knowledge spurred his enthusiasm.

Hawkins had not stayed long, however, and Tripp was aware of his past. The boy might well have had an association with the house before he arrived at Clearwater and ended Tripp's career. He didn't only blame Clearwater for firing him and bringing him shame, the Hawkins boy was part of the problem, as was the nancy-boy, Payne.

No matter. Whatever Hawkins had been up to that night, he had been there, and he worked for Clearwater.

There was a connection between the house and Hawkins. Perhaps it was that which caused the inner workings of his mind to start churning like a windlass behind the scenes, slowly raising the curtain on a master plan. The idea was still in dim lighting, however, but would burn brightly if he left it alone.

His memory drifted through that foggy night as he recalled what he had seen. Hawkins had entered, soon to come hurrying out, laughing as he walked away. Later, Tripp witnessed a young man arriving at the house clutching a bag. The Beast hurried him inside, but before the door was closed, the younger man dropped his cloak and revealed a dress. He took from his bag a wig. Every detail was noted. (The hairpiece was short and blonde, the dress was full-length with bare arms, he wore opera gloves, and the door remained open for nine seconds.)

The next interesting thing to happen came forty-two minutes later. Various rooms had been used, the lights extinguished in-between times, and each event was recorded. It was the time of night when arrivals were rare, as if the gentlemen were invited to attend a function that began at a particular time and arriving uninvited was not the done thing. On this night, Tripp's attention was drawn to a man in an overcoat and bowler. Sensibly, he wore a scarf at his face against the smog, and he would have passed for any other lower-middle-class resident, had it not been for what he did. Marching to the front door of number nineteen, he banged on it and shouted through the letterbox. Tripp quickly tuned in and distinctly heard the second shout, 'Police!' The man then ran, and Tripp was convinced it was James Wright.

That was another name to add to his list of sodomites who needed to be punished. Wright was not to be trusted. He had taken money to supply information and then gone back on his word. Tripp had ascertained that he now worked for Clearwater, which made another connection. He underlined Wright's entry in his book in red ink, and the windlass wound harder, creaking the curtain open a notch and allowing the first beams of light to flicker at the corner of his idea. It was still too much in darkness to come into focus, but it was growing.

There had been surprisingly little activity after the false cry of

272

'Police!', and Tripp imagined the sodomites scurried from the back of the house like turds weaving down an open sewer. Two minutes later, however, Hawkins appeared at the front with another man bundled under his arm as if he was rescuing him from a fire. They too had run, leaving the front door open. It hadn't been closed until sixteen minutes later.

Thanks to Lovemount pointing out the name in the newspaper, Tripp suspected the rescued man was Cadwell Roxton. Another connection to Clearwater and a timely one, with the launch of his abominable foundation that weekend.

Unfortunately, Tripp hadn't yet thought of a way he could use the singer's visit as evidence of Clearwater's depravity, but today, he had discovered that some of the work had been done for him. At least, that was his theory.

He had read something in the newspaper… A story… A spotlight lit the metaphorical stage, but there was not yet any performer treading the boards for it to highlight. There was, however, certainty waiting in the wings.

Tripp had bought a copy of The Times every day since he became footman to the decent, recently deceased Lord Clearwater, and had arranged its regular delivery to his current rooms as soon as he had taken them. Today's edition carried praise for the current viscount's Foundation that poured from the pen of the so-called journalist like effluent from a dysentery victim. Tripp read no more than a few lines. Another article sang the praises of the singers and production, and having a fondness for the music of Bruch, he gave it a cursory glance. It was on page four where he found something of greater interest and potential.

The afternoon edition lay open beside him, and finding no activity across the way, but keeping his eye on number nineteen, he reread the article. The section described a death that occurred as the curtain fell, and Tripp was as fascinated by the story as any reader would be. What caught his attention, however, was the man's name; Sherman Quill. If he was looking for connections, then the half-brother of Clearwater's trusted friend and surgeon, Benjamin Quill was too good an opportunity to ignore. He had been pondering what he could do with this information all evening, and it wasn't until he reread the details that the answer presented itself.

Not only was the "suicidal maniac" a transgressor into the dangerous world of backstage, but he was also a "trans-dresser." The newspaper made great work of enjoying its own wordplay, and Tripp nearly stopped reading, but his intrigue was piqued. The later edition described the man in more detail and went as far as to define his apparel. The blonde wig found at the scene raised one of Tripp's hooded eyebrows, and the description of the dress raised the other. What was left of the man's facial features were described adequately enough for an identification to be made and a description written. (His head had roasted on a coal burner until a stagehand pulled it away to prevent a fire.)

As he glanced at the newspaper again, he realised with a heart-thumping shock that perhaps he didn't need a connection between Cleaver Street and Clearwater, not if he could employ clever men with criminal connections, as the Beast at number nineteen undoubtedly had. He would devise a scheme that could not fail to see Clearwater brought to justice, but cleverly, it would not directly involve the viscount. His shaming would come via one of his close group of catamites, not only bringing Clearwater to ruin, but robbing him of the youth he had so grotesquely fallen in love with.

The curtains flew apart, the spotlights glared, and a triumphant fanfare sounded.

He had a way forward.

Not being a man to rush, and having lived by his personal code of Stop, take Stock and Start again, he tempered his enthusiasm and let the idea germinate through the rest of that night and into the early hours. It was still at the forefront of his mind when he woke after an hour's sleep, and, shaving for the first time in days, prepared himself for what had to be done.

It was only a few feet, but the distance between number twenty to nineteen felt like crossing a chasm on a narrow plank. His collar was raised, and fighting his natural inclination to walk tall and proudly, his hands were in his pockets and his eyes on the ground. He was careful not to turn to the street as he waited for the bell to be answered, holding back bile that rose when he realised he was to come face to face with the Beast. The handle rattled, the door opened, and he looked directly into the eyes of Edward Lovemount.

'Bloody hell,' the youth said. 'What are you doing here?'

'The Beast, the man-woman,' Tripp muttered as he pushed his way past. 'Shut the door.'

'Excuse me, Sir,' Lovemount objected. 'You can't just scuttle in here like... Oi? What are you doing?'

'Where's the man in charge?' Tripp demanded. His voice was croaky; he hadn't spoken to anyone for days.

'What's this?' The man-woman appeared through garish drapes. He wore male clothing, but his face was painted, and although he had applied false eyelashes, for the moment, he was a man.

'You,' Tripp said, adrenaline pumping, his heart racing. 'You knew Sherman Quill.'

The Beast was taken by surprise. 'What of it?' he said.

'Clearwater.'

'You what?' Lovemount had closed the door, and on hearing the viscount's name, stepped into the discussion. 'What about him?'

'What was the man doing?' Tripp's mind was turning like the paddles of a steamer gathering speed and churning up possibilities.

'What business is that of yours?' the Beast demanded. 'Who are you?'

'He was butler to Lord Clearwater,' Lovemount said. 'His name's...'

Tripp swiped him across the face with the back of his hand. 'No names,' he growled. 'Keep silent.' His enthusiasm was bubbling into anger. These men were idiots. They didn't understand his cause, and they didn't have his determination. He was wasting his time.

Lovemount complained at being hit, but the Beast was happy about it and told him to stay quiet. His dark eyes narrowed as he stared at Tripp.

'Go on,' the man-woman said. 'I will hear what you have to say.'

Perhaps they weren't all idiots.

'The man wasn't a suicidal maniac.' Tripp stated, so sure was he of his theory.

The Beast gave nothing away.

'He was acting under your instructions, and something went wrong.'

'Who knows?'

'You do, Mr Danvers.' Tripp had done his research.

'That's not my name.'

Maybe it wasn't. What did it matter?

'I think you and Sherman Quill had an alliance,' Tripp said, holding the man's repulsive stare. 'You had a plan that involved Cadwell Roxton, because you have something against Clearwater. I am not here to find out what, but to tell you how we can work together.'

'And if I don't know what you're talking about?'

'If you pretend to not understand, then you are a fool. If you listen to what I have to say, you will benefit. The choice is yours.'

The Beast considered and looked at Lovemount.

'He's got money,' Lovemount said, with a grudging nod of approval.

'Go on.'

'I believe you and I share the same aim, Danvers.' If he was to work with the man, he would have to stop thinking of him as a beast. 'You realise, of course, that I have had this house under surveillance.'

Danvers blanched, and Lovemount scrambled to the front door.

'No!' Tripp caught his arm, and the lad was surprised at his strength. 'I don't intend to do anything with my information, although Inspector Adelaide and the police force would, no doubt, be grateful for it.' He let the monkey go and focused his attention on the organ grinder. 'And, I am prepared to hand it over, along with the names of those I recognise who have used this place.' He allowed his enthusiasm to return and simmer close to boiling point. 'With a little cooperation on your part, some investment from me and a pinch of cunning, you can assist me in bringing Clearwater to his knees and lower. Alternatively, I can find a way of doing it myself, and report my findings of your house to the authorities if you don't help me. I, of course, will have to trust you, Danvers. Even that.' He meant Lovemount.

Danvers considered him carefully, his eyes dragging from Lovemount to the wizened creature with the forceful grip. 'Go on,' he said, this time with more interest.

'I assume you are not averse to lying?' Tripp queried.

Danvers waved his hands before his face, displaying his makeup. 'This is the lie that tells the truth.'

'And it is all you need to find yourself in prison,' Tripp replied, unimpressed at the man's self-admiration. 'I, however, have much more. Where you have the valuable resource of no morality, I have information. Together we can ensure that Viscount Clearwater is stripped of his title and forfeits his fortune, while his catamite, Hawkins, is taken away in chains and left to rot in Newgate.'

'What do you need, Sir?' Danvers asked, his face breaking into a twisted grin as possibilities occurred.

'Do you, perchance, have any criminal contacts in Westerpool?'

Danvers considered this before replying. 'It can be arranged. For what purpose?'

'I witnessed Roxton being bundled from carriage to house and, later, from house to street,' Tripp said. 'I could give the police the exact time and date, or I could ask you to arrange a similar kidnapping elsewhere, for which, Sir, I would pay handsomely with my silence.'

Danvers indicated the curtained arch. 'Perhaps you would like to come into my parlour,' he offered.

'I wouldn't,' Tripp grimaced. 'But I must. We have people and dates to discuss, namely the street rat, Hawkins, and the sodomite, Clearwater.'

On the nod from Danvers, Lovemount parted the curtains. 'And what dates?' the lad asked.

'October the ninth and eleventh,' Tripp replied, removing his overcoat.

'October the ninth?' Danvers and Lovemount exchanged quizzical glances. 'That was the night of the Ripper's last murder, wasn't it?'

'It was, Mr Danvers.'

'And the eleventh? What happened that night?'

Tripp handed his coat to Lovemount. 'That, Sir is what we are about to fabricate.'

Watch out for Fallen Splendour
The Clearwater Mysteries book four

If you have enjoyed this story, here is a list of my other novels to date. With them, I've put my own heat rating according to how sexually graphic they are. They are all romantic in some way apart from the short stories.

References to sex (*) A little sex (**) A couple of times (***) Quite a bit, actually (****) Cold shower required (*****)

Older/younger MM romances
The Mentor of Wildhill Farm ****
Older writer mentors four young gay guys in more than just verbs and adjectives. Isolated setting. Teens coming out. Sex parties. And a twist.

The Mentor of Barrenmoor Ridge ***
It takes a brave man to climb a mountain, but it takes a braver lad to show him the way. Mountain rescue. Coming to terms with love, loss and sexuality.

The Mentor of Lonemarsh House ***
I love you enough to let you run, but too much to see you fall
Folk music. Hidden secrets. Family acceptance.

The Mentor of Lostwood Hall ***
A man with a future he can't accept and a lad with a past he can't escape. A castle. A road accident. Youth and desire.

MM romance thrillers
Other People's Dreams ***
Screenwriter seeks four gay youths to crew his yacht in the Greek islands. Certain strings attached.
Dreams come true. Coming of age. Youth friendships and love.

The Blake Inheritance **
Let us go then you and I to the place where the wild thyme grows
Family mystery. School crush. A treasure hunt romance.

The Stoker Connection ***

What if you could prove the greatest Gothic novel of all time was a true story? Literary conspiracy. Teen boy romance. First love. Mystery and adventure.

Curious Moonlight *

He's back. He's angry and I am fleeing for my life.
A haunted house. A mystery to solve. A slow-burn romance. Straight to gay.

The Clearwater Mysteries

Deviant Desire ***

Book 1. A mashup of mystery, romance and adventure, Deviant Desire is set in an imaginary London of 1888. The first in an on-going series in a world where homosexuality is a crime. Mystery/adventure.

Twisted Tracks **

Book 2. An intercepted telegram, a coded invitation and the threat of exposure. Viscount Clearwater must put his life on the line to protect his reputation. Mystery/adventure

Unspeakable Acts *

Book 3. A murder will take place unless Clearwater's sexuality is made public; can his lover stop the killing and save his reputation?

Fallen Splendour

Book 4. A poem, a kidnapping, a race against time for Archer and Fecker, but what if it's a diversion? And then, Silas is arrested and James is on his own...

All these can all be found on my Amazon Author page.
Please leave a review if you can. Thanks again for reading. If you keep reading, I'll keep writing.
Jackson

Printed in Great Britain
by Amazon

78723963R00160